Dear Reader,

I've been hearing [...] the Harlequin Duets stories and how they're finding our 2-in-1 format convenient. Keep your comments coming, so that we can keep publishing the kinds of stories you want.

BEST OF THE WEST features exactly that: three exciting, sexy cowboys tamed by the love of a good woman. Written by Cathie Linz, a nominee for a *Romantic Times* 1998 Reviewer's Choice Award, *The Rancher Gets Hitched* has a generous dose of humor and sex appeal. Look for the second title in January 2000.

Then we're pleased to welcome Marissa Hall to Harlequin. She pens a delightful tale of two driven workaholics with no time for love, but plans for a perfect affair. In *An Affair of Convenience* these plans, naturally, go awry.

Then we have two books about people on unusual journeys to love. A runaway bride pretending to have amnesia in Renee Roszel's *Bride on the Loose* finds herself trapped on an island overrun by eccentric characters, too many animals and one very sexy veterinarian. Then Colleen Collins returns with another quirky story about the most unlikely opposites who attract: a millionaire and a showgirl. Their dizzying courtship is captured in *Married After Breakfast*.

Keep those letters coming!

Malle Vallik

Malle Vallik
Senior Editor
Harlequin Duets
Harlequin Books
225 Duncan Mill Road
Don Mills, Ontario
M3B 3K9 Canada

Bride on the Loose

"*You're a* vet?"

Dana felt a creeping unease begin to envelop her. "I *hope* you mean you were in the army!"

Sam's blue eyes sparkled. "Sorry. No."

"You lied to me!" she accused, working at covering her nearly naked self. "You said you were a doctor!"

"I *am* a doctor."

"For animals!" Thwarted, humiliated and furious, she cast out a hand. "Give me your shirt!"

When he shrugged it off she slung it on. "You fondled me!"

"I did not fondle you. I examined you. You're not that different from a dog."

"Not that different...ooooh!" She might not be Miss America material, but she was no dog! Seething, she tried to stand, but her legs gave out.

"You'd better let me help you."

"Not if you were the last man on this entire island!"

"I'm the *only* man on this entire island."

For more, turn to page 9

Married After Breakfast

Here I go again. Fantasizing the impossible.

Belle inhaled slowly, trying to take her eyes away from the sleeping figure of Dirk.

She rubbed her fingers together, imagining the coarseness of his stubbled jaw. *I wouldn't let you shave on the weekend, either. I'd want you rugged and disheveled, the way you'd look after tumbling out of bed.*

She ran a tongue along her bottom lip, imagining that mouth against hers.

She closed her eyes, envisioning what it would be like to wake up next to Dirk and give him a wake-up kiss. A lingering, let's-stay-in-bed kiss.

She didn't know what he felt for her. After a full day on the road with her cat and her parakeet, he'd called her "one of the animals."

Her thoughts were cut off by a low growl. At first she thought her cat was having a bad dream. But when Dirk shifted and uttered another low growl, she had to curl her toes to keep from growling back.

Maybe they were *both* animals. A girl could only hope....

For more, turn to page 197

HARLEQUIN DUETS

ISBN 0-373-44076-6

BRIDE ON THE LOOSE
Copyright © 1999 by Renee Roszel Wilson

MARRIED AFTER BREAKFAST
Copyright © 1999 by Colleen Collins

RENEE ROSZEL

Bride On The Loose

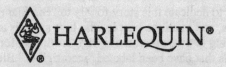

TORONTO • NEW YORK • LONDON
AMSTERDAM • PARIS • SYDNEY • HAMBURG
STOCKHOLM • ATHENS • TOKYO • MILAN • MADRID
PRAGUE • WARSAW • BUDAPEST • AUCKLAND

Dear Reader,

I am a cat person. I'm also a dog person. However, for purposes of this book, cats take priority. So I want to tell you a story about a cat.

Once upon a time a tornado whipped through Kansas. A lost Siamese was taken to a local veterinarian. This cat was big and mean and completely incorrigible, with nicks out of his ears from when he'd been in fights. Nobody came to claim this cat, so he sat in a cage at the vet's.

Little by little, the veterinarian drew this cat out. The animal slowly discovered that life needn't be a struggle. There were those he could trust. The veterinarian's office became his world. In emergencies, Siam gave blood, a painful process that he seemed to feel was worth the love he received in return. He spent his days lounging in the sunshine in the vet's plate glass window, but even on balmy days, when the door was propped open, he never ventured out. He knew he was home.

One day when I entered the office, Siam was sitting in the receptionist's chair, peering across the desk with a "May I help you or else" look in his eyes. I had to laugh. Just whose office was this now?

I want to dedicate this story fondly to "Big Siam" in Kansas, and to all the people who love animals and are unwilling to give up on those frightened, lost, forsaken animals that have been labeled "incorrigible." Bless the beasts and the children who care for them.

Renée Roszel

To my mother
Lenore Roszel
for asking the question "What if...?"

1

DANA CRAWLED OUT of the sea at dawn, grateful her stupidity hadn't turned her into shark *hors d'oeuvres.* Jumping off her fiancé's yacht in the dead of night might not be the dumbest thing that had ever been done in the history of the universe, but it was a close second.

The sand was white and as fine as talcum, making her hands and knees sink and slide with every attempt to move forward. Finally, *finally,* when she was sure her upper torso would be clear of sea water, she collapsed. "Don't crash now, you idiot," she muttered, one side of her face compacting damp sand. "You have to hide!"

"Hey, there!"

A man. Though instantly alert and on guard, she was too tired to lift her head. She opened her eyes and noticed a wooden dock around a distant curve of beach. A cabin cruiser was moored there. Unfortunately for her, a man had just leaped off the pier and was heading in her direction. She moaned. *Run away, idiot!* she told herself. *Tate probably has his people out looking for you by now! Run!*

She pushed up on one elbow. Her arm quivered. Spending heaven-knew-how-long paddling around in the ocean took a lot out of a person. As the stranger

jogged her way, she sagged down, her cheek once
again meeting cool sand. Squinting into the sunrise,
she couldn't tell much about his face, but he jogged
like a man who'd done it before—a lot. He had a
trim, strapping silhouette; purple and pink streaks of
early morning light underscored the sinewy power of
a great pair of long legs.

*Dana, stop ogling the man's thighs and make a
break for it!* she commanded herself. *You didn't risk
life and limb jumping off Tate's yacht just to be
caught like a beached whale.*

Dana felt herself being gently lifted and turned to
her side by a pair of strong hands. Her cheek no
longer rested on cool sand, but was snuggled against
a warm, very masculine chest. She fancied she could
even hear a heartbeat. A little rapid, but solid, giving
her a bizarre sense of protection even though he was
probably one of Tate's hired thugs!

"Are you okay?"

She blinked, lifting her gaze to bring his face into
focus. Even as exhausted as she was, her heart did a
high kick of appreciation. For a thug, his blue eyes
were appealing, and he was startlingly handsome. He
was the image of those to-die-for male models in the
TV ads where they do something particularly sensitive like mop a kitchen floor or diaper a baby. He had
the kind of face an eyeglass frame company would
hire to put on a pair of their glasses, knowing that
women all over the country would haunt frame shops
hoping he'll drop by.

If this guy was one of Tate's men, he wasn't one
she recognized. Those eyes, she'd remember. But
then, what did she really know about the conniving

jerk she'd almost made the mistake of marrying? She squinted, not sure what to say or do. "What?" Her voice was a croaking whisper. Maybe she'd swallowed a little too much salt water.

"I asked if you're okay." He looked concerned.

She eyed him, suspicious. *Yeah, he would want to know that. Tate couldn't pull off his little coup if I drowned.*

"How did you get all the way out here?"

"Out where?" What was he talking about? Hadn't she washed up on Miami Beach? A rather deserted part, true, but...

"This is a privately owned island."

She frowned, confused. When she'd jumped off Tate's yacht, she'd gotten a little turned around, yes, but the lights she'd seen, she'd thought...

"An island?"

He scanned her face, then the rest of her. His expression clouded and he returned his gaze almost guiltily to her face. She wondered why.

"What's your name?" he asked.

So what did she say? Even if he wasn't one of Tate's men, she still needed to hide. "Exactly where am I?"

"This is Haven Cay in the Berry Islands."

The Berry Islands? They were in the Bahamas! The yacht must have sailed farther off the coast of Miami than she'd realized during the big pre-wedding bash.

"Miss?" he said. "What's your name?"

She squinted at him, unsure what to say. She'd been abundantly dumb, leaving that note telling Tate she'd overheard his sleazy plan. If he got wind of where she was, he'd be Johnny-on-the-spot, slathering on the charm, telling her she was mistaken—had misunderstood. Not to mention her mother, so bent on this marriage she couldn't see the handwriting on the wall. She'd add to the brew, badgering relentlessly. There would be no escaping the marriage if anybody found out where she was.

Did she dare confide in this stud? Tate would offer a reward to know her whereabouts. Or was this man the one in ten thousand not motivated by greed? She smirked inwardly.

"You do know it, don't you?" he asked, drawing her back.

"What?"

"Your name." He shifted her, lifting her more into a sitting positing. She got a glimpse of the rest of herself and was shocked. Good Lord, she'd forgotten she'd shucked everything she'd had on but her bra and panties while she'd been in the water. And those lacy scraps were soaked, leaving nothing to the imagination but the brand name. Horrified, she flinched.

"Are you in pain?"

Dana shoved at his chest, dislodging herself from his arms. She fell back on the sand; her breath whooshed painfully from her lungs. For a minute the man hunched beside her had two blurry heads. She faced the fact she was more exhausted than she realized. She couldn't even sit up on her own.

With a moan, she drew a forearm over her eyes. It was as close to sticking her head in the sand as she could get.

"I'd better take a look at you." His fingers rested lightly on her head. She jerked away but only succeeded in throwing out her arms, making him visible again. He placed a hand on each side of her face and looked down at her, his jaw tensed. A swath of black wavy hair fell across his forehead, ruffled by a breeze. The lock shone like obsidian. "Don't be embarrassed, Miss," he said softly. His hands gently began to probe beneath her wet hair. "I'm a doctor."

"A—doctor?"

He nodded. A vague smile crooked his lips. She considered the smile as his hands moved tenderly, carefully, over her scalp. The expression wasn't sly or smarmy, but sympathetic. If he really was a doctor, he had a good bedside-manner smile.

Even so, she didn't dare tell him who she was. She needed a place to hide—and time. Two weeks, in fact, when she couldn't be found. By then the deadline for Tate's scheme would pass and their marriage would be worthless to him.

His hands slid down to her shoulders as he touched, probed, asked if she felt pain. She shook her head vaguely. No pain. But she felt something. His fingers grazed along her ribs, then below her navel, where he pressed gently. "Pain?"

She met his gaze. "No." Her flesh prickled at his touch and her breathing grew uneven and labored. She wondered if she should mention those symptoms, then decided they were best left unsaid—since they'd only developed after his hands had begun to explore her body.

Poor man. He couldn't help being good-looking, or that his routine checkup had a troubling seductive quality about it. She wondered if her reaction was typical of his female patients and if it caused him much trouble in the examining room. Of course, he probably had several muscular nurses at the ready to hold patients at bay when lust overcame them. Besides, he surely wore more than a pair of shorts and an unbuttoned cotton shirt during office hours.

His hands skimmed over her panties and she closed her eyes. She was afraid the groan she heard came from her throat.

"Something hurt?"

She shook her head, then decided she'd had enough. "Look, Doctor, I'm okay. Really." She dragged herself up on an elbow.

He sat back on his haunches. Whopping good haunches, if you were into men's haunches. She'd never thought she was, but being in such close proximity to really first-class haunches made her rethink. Irritated with herself, Dana pulled up to sit. "I—I'm just tired. Nothing's broken." *Except maybe my heart,* she added silently. *Tate and his shoddy, sneaky plans!*

The doctor moved to one knee, his smile reassuring. "My name's Sam. Sam Taylor."

That brief flash of teeth in the golden light held a burst of eroticism that was way over the top for your average bedside manner. She wondered if he had any idea how gorgeous he was early in the morning.

"Do you think you can stand?"

She shook her head, meaning she wasn't sure, but he took it as a no. Before she realized what was happening, he lifted her into his arms. "Well, then, I'd better carry you."

Dana swallowed hard. Why hadn't she thought of that! Well, as long as he had...

"You didn't tell me your name." He began to

carry her along the beach, away from the water and his boat.

"Where are we going?"

"My great-aunt Beena's place." He winked. "It's better for resting. And Beena will have food."

Her breath caught at the effect of the brief closing of that one eye. She had to make herself start the breathing process again. Breathe in, breathe out. Repeat. "Your aunt's place?"

He seemed to carry her effortlessly. Dana could detect no hint of breathlessness as he talked. "I told you this was a private island."

"Oh right. So it's your aunt's island. Must be nice." A private island? Dana had been so muddle-headed when he'd mentioned it before, it hadn't fully registered. What better hiding place could she hope for? Did she dare think she had a chance to stay here for two whole weeks without her whereabouts being discovered? "Is your aunt sick?"

That sexy, crooked grin reappeared. "No, but I'm not her doctor."

"Why? Aren't you any good?"

Though his skin was tanned, she saw a flush of darker color tint his cheeks. How charming. He was blushing. "I've never had any complaints."

Dana just bet he hadn't. He probably specialized in young women! "You're a gynecologist, right?" She blanched. Where had *that* question come from? She was aghast that only hours after discovering the man she'd promised to marry was a liar and a phony, she could even think such thoughts about a total stranger.

He cleared his throat. "In my practice I pretty much do it all."

She was surprised, but not quite so surprised as she was to find she'd lifted her arms and wrapped them around his neck. She noticed in passing that he had extravagantly broad shoulders and wondered how he carried all that breadth around and remained upright.

"Small town doctor?" she asked.

"No." He inclined his head, indicating something ahead. "There's my great-aunt's place."

Dana shifted around and caught her breath. The place looked like a Gothic castle that had managed to drag its gray granite bulk out of Transylvania and plop down in the middle of this tropical paradise. As the cardiovascularly fit doctor trudged over a sandy rise, she could see the whole amazing structure. "Wow!" She knew that sounded lame, but excused her brain-deadedness on bobbing around in the ocean for hours. An experience like that might even dumb-down Einstein.

"Mmm-hmm."

She stared at the doctor, confused. "Your aunt lives in a castle?"

He grinned. Shame on him! What if one of his young women patients had a bad heart? That smile would do her in. Since Dana wasn't in tip-top physical condition at the moment, either, in a self-defense move, she turned away to study the castle. Every gargoyle was fashioned in the shape of a cat, every spire held aloft by one. There were crouched cats, snoozing cats, leaping cats, snarling cats, running cats, prancing cats, cats in top hats, cats in ballet skirts, cats in boxing gloves.

"She likes cats?"

"How'd you guess?"

Dana faced him. He was grinning again. She sucked in an appreciative breath. "So, you live here with your aunt?"

"No, I come to visit every summer."

"You just got here?" She wondered how long he stayed, and decided to wangle the question into the conversation later.

"Just this morning."

"So, nobody's sick?"

"Not that I know of."

A shadow passed over them and Dana noticed that he'd carried her beneath a granite archway carved with frolicking cats. She looked around. They were within a stone wall that undulated with the landscape. The sand had given way to a lush lawn that led gradually upward toward the top of the low hill where the gray edifice loomed.

"Aren't you getting tired?" she asked. After all, they'd been heading gradually uphill for more than a quarter mile.

His brows pinched slightly in question. "No."

She inhaled, experiencing a charge of feminine admiration. She felt much better, all of a sudden. She could probably even walk, but didn't make the offer. He wasn't even sweating. Besides, riding in his arms was stimulating, somehow. She was surprised at how quickly her exhaustion was slipping away.

"How are you feeling?" he asked.

"Fine." She bit her lip. Stupid! Do you *want* to walk? "I—I mean, a little better."

"Good." He glanced toward the castle, then back at her. "So what was your name, again?"

It was her turn to frown. Cute doctor or no cute

doctor, Dana didn't dare tell him who she was. She
had to be cautious. She'd shown how stupidly naive
she could be, letting Tate sweep her off her feet the
way he had. If that experience taught her anything, it
was to not trust too quickly.

"You do have a name, don't you?" he asked.

She blinked, shooting him a cautious look.
"Uh—" She stalled. "I—of course I have a name.
Don't be silly." Her mind raced. What if she pretended to not remember it? What if she didn't have a
name—for two weeks? Would that help her cause? It
couldn't hurt, could it?

He came to a halt, his expression quizzical. "Okay,
let's hear it."

Unaccustomed to lying, she swallowed several
times. Fate hadn't led her straight to this private island for no reason. Surely she was meant to be here.
This private slice of ocean-going real estate was
meant to be her hiding place—she could feel it in her
bones.

Dana Lenore Vanover had no intention of flying in
the face of Madam Destiny's decrees. Steeling herself
with resolve, she made her decision. "I—I don't remember."

He studied her for a moment, looking dubious.
"You're not serious."

"I'm not?" She panicked, trying to think back.
Had she said something to give herself away? After
all, he was a doctor. He probably knew more about
amnesia than she did. He'd probably taken courses—
Amnesia 101 and Advanced Amnesia. She bit the inside of her cheek. What the heck did she know about

it, anyway? Something she'd seen on an episode of
"ER"?

"I don't like this."

She licked her lips, then made a face at the salty
taste. "You don't?" Don't panic! She told herself.
Be calm. "Why—I mean, you're a doctor. Surely—
surely it's not fatal—is it?" She wanted to shout,
*What don't you like? What do you know that I don't?
What am I doing to give myself away?*

"It's not that." His fascinating blue eyes, fringed
with lots of long, dark lashes, were narrowed in either
deep concern or high distrust. "It's just that I'm not
equipped for this sort of thing."

She exhaled a slow relieved breath. "Oh—well,
don't worry. I'm sure—I mean, don't most amnesia
victims regain their memory—in time?"

He shrugged. She detected the stretch and bunch
of muscle beneath her hands. "It's not exactly in my
domain, being a vet."

"Well, that's okay. I'm sure with plenty of rest and
quiet I'll be as good as..." Something about what
he'd said nagged at her brain, and she shifted to better
look at his face. "Being a what?"

The sunlight in his blue eyes sparkled like bits of
sapphire. She couldn't tell if they were twinkling with
amusement or if it was a trick of the light. "A vet,"
he said quietly.

She felt a creeping unease begin to envelope her.
"I *hope* you mean you were in the army."

His lips crooked into a wry grin. "Sorry. No."

With a rush of dismay, she cast her glance down
at herself. She was practically naked in this man's
arms *only* because she'd been given the impression

he was a man of medicine—as indifferent to examining the human body as a mechanic was to a carburetor.

Suddenly full of energy, she struggled from his arms, landing on her feet but quickly sagging to her knees. He reached for her, but she lifted a halting hand, while trying to cover as much of herself as she could with the other. "Don't—you—come—near—me—you—you—*veterinarian!*"

He straightened, looking a little put out. "Don't say it like it's dirty."

"You lied to me!" She worked at covering herself with both hands and arms, and one bent leg, as she dropped to the ground. "You said you were a doctor!"

"I am a doctor."

"For animals!" Thwarted, humiliated and furious, Dana cast out a hand. "Give me that shirt!"

He muttered something as he shrugged it off. She bet whatever it was didn't come close to the curses she was mentally flinging at him.

"Here." He held out the shirt, and it fluttered in the breeze.

She grabbed it and slung it on, pulling the front tight around her. At least it was big. She eyed him threateningly as she crouched in a mortified little ball. "You should be registered someplace—as the local pervert vet masquerading as a real doctor."

"I *am* a—"

"Do not say that again!" She fumbled with the buttons, but her hands shook so badly she couldn't get them to fasten. Drat men and their backward buttoning shirts, anyway! In frustration, she pulled the shirt close around her again and glared. "You fondled me!"

He crossed his arms over that great chest, and she gritted her teeth, hating the fact that she'd used the adjective "great" about this pervert.

"I did not fondle you. I examined you."

"Ha! That's *pervert* talk for fondle!"

"Look, you had just crawled out of the ocean, and you couldn't stand up. You needed a doctor." He exhaled heavily. "You're not that different from a dog."

"Not that different...*ooo-ooooh!*" Seething, she pushed up to stand. She might not be Miss America material, but she was no dog! Her determination to march to the castle was undermined when she fell on her butt.

She cringed and rubbed her backside, but refused to look at the pervert dog doctor.

"You'd better let me help you."

"Not if you were the last man on this entire island!"

"I'm the only man on this entire island."

She blinked, then turned to glower at him. "Huh?"

He watched her without humor. Apparently being called a pervert for being a veterinarian didn't appeal to him. But he deserved it, the rat. He'd purposely misled her!

"I said, I'm the only man on the island."

She rubbed her throbbing posterior absently. "Why?"

He let go with that wry, crooked flash of teeth again. It had an affect she didn't appreciate, coming from a pervert. "It cuts down on the raping and plundering," he said.

Dana squinted in confusion, wishing she could get up and stalk proudly away. She wondered how long it would take to get her strength back. Perhaps it had been naive of her—as a librarian—to think carrying around tons of heavy books built up lots of muscle. Evidently it didn't bulk you up as much as people might think—especially librarians. She sighed. "You mean, there are only women on this island?"

"There are around thirty male cats, and a couple of the iguanas are guys."

She turned away, pulling up her knees and resting her chin on them. "Good grief. They *need* a vet."

"Excuse me?"

She closed her eyes. "I said, you're a *pervert!*"

"That's it! You're through calling me a pervert."

Dana felt herself being lifted, and struggled to get free.

"*Quit* it," he said. "You have bigger problems than having a veterinarian see you in your drawers. If you'll recall, you have amnesia."

She glared at him, her jaw clamped. He was right! She must not forget that for a second. Clutching his shirt snugly around her, she stared away from him. "I hope," she decreed through gritted teeth, "when I remember my name, I *forget* yours."

"I think I know how you got into the ocean," he muttered.

She experienced a rush of anxiety. "You do?"

He nodded, his expression a striking blend of irritation and pity. "Somebody out there got fed up with the attitude."

2

SAM CARRIED HIS UNHAPPY burden up the flagstone steps toward the double doors of the castle. By now, he was starting to notice Miss No Name's weight. Not that she was heavy, but he wasn't a weight lifter by trade. He was—apparently—a pervert.

He gritted his teeth. He was *not* a pervert. He simply wasn't accustomed to examining beautiful, nearly nude women who washed up on beaches. Even a little pruny, the woman in his arms was one premium specimen of womanhood. With her fine blond hair spread out over the sand, she had looked like a mermaid who'd shed her tail in the process of becoming human. Her lacy underthings were all but transparent, seeming more a drizzle of frothy seafoam than anything resembling clothing.

Watching her lying there on the sand like a fantasy coming to life had been the most eerie thing he'd ever experienced. He'd definitely been affected by all that soft, pale skin. Damn it. Any normal, healthy man would have been.

He halted in front of the board-and-batten door, roughly the size of a billboard turned on end. "Would you mind knocking?" he asked. "My hands are full."

She gave him an uneasy look, her big green eyes sparking with some unfathomable emotion. Without a word, she turned away and rapped. His gaze roamed to her long, pale legs. He felt an unwelcome surge of lust and bit back a curse. *Samuel Taylor, you are a doctor. Behave like one! Think of her as a cat!* He'd taken care of lots of cats with eyes that color and twice that number of legs.

He could barely hear the tapping her knuckles made on the solid wood. "Use the knocker." He cleared an odd raspiness from his throat and indicated a thick iron ring near her knees.

She reached out and wagged a hand to show she couldn't reach it. "Move me closer."

He shifted so her face was practically inside the circular handgrip. She grabbed the heavy iron, but couldn't lift it. Using both hands, she managed to raise the knocker and slam it against an iron plate. After three bangs, she let go, breathing heavily. "Enough?"

"That should do it."

"You can put me down now," she said.

He noticed she didn't look at him when she said it. "Thanks for the offer." He did nothing even slightly resembling letting her down.

After a minute she peered at him. "Well?"

He shrugged. "My arms are cramped in this position. You'll have to leap out if you want to walk."

She frowned and opened her mouth to speak. A loud creaking filled the air and she jerked around. Sam couldn't hide a brief grin. He was sure she expected Lurch, the Addam's Family butler, to be standing there. Or possibly a headless ghost wielding a hatchet.

The fact that his little mermaid curled her arms around his neck and clutched as though her life depended on it, didn't escape him. He couldn't blame her. The woman who answered the door was one of the most formidable people he'd ever run across. At six and a half feet tall and built like a Buick, Eartha was intimidating, to say the least. She was two inches taller than Sam and had him outweighed by a hundred pounds. She might be standing there barefoot and wearing a kimono of purple silk, but Sam had seen her in her karate togs and black belt. He'd personally hired Eartha as Beena's security chief, and knew she could stomp any man like a bug. And being a man with no urgent desire to be stomped, Sam was glad Eartha was on his side.

"Hello, Doc," Eartha said, her voice higher pitched and breathier than one would anticipate from a Buick. "We've been expecting you." She took a soundless step backward on the mat of woven rushes. With the sweep of a husky arm she indicated that he come inside.

He stepped into the dimly lit foyer; the scent of beeswax candles and lavender incense hit him full force. Sam never walked into the place without experiencing a feeling of being wrenched backward through time. It wasn't a bad feeling, just a bizarre one.

"Eartha, you're looking lovely for so early in the morning."

The brawny woman blushed like a sixteen-year-old.

"I'm here bearing gifts." He indicated the leggy enigma in his arms.

"Would you like me to take it, Doc?" Eartha asked.

His female cargo shifted to frown at him. "First I'm a dog, now I'm an *it?*"

"For the record, I never called you a dog—or an *it*." He grinned at her. "I've never carried a woman over a threshold before, either. Is it a first for you, too?"

Sam sensed a slight, watchful hesitation spiced with sadness in his mermaid's expression. But when she blinked, the look was gone. "I'm bailing," she grumbled, pushing out of his arms. She landed in a crouch, then pushed up, veering sideways a step before gaining her balance. She eyed him like an anxious child who'd stumbled into something she wasn't sure she could handle. Very quickly, that expression, too, was gone. "Thanks for the lift," she murmured.

He inclined his head in a half nod. "My pleasure."

She didn't smile, her pinched expression a clear sign she doubted it. Or, if she believed him, she didn't appreciate the sort of pleasure he'd derived. *Pervert* that she thought he was.

He made himself turn to face the head of security. "Never mind her, Eartha. She's cranky. Almost drowning will do that to a person. Just point us to Aunt Beena."

The big woman swept her arm toward the rear of the sparsely furnished entry hall. On a trestle table to his left, Sam noticed a pure white cat curled atop a fat red cushion. He recognized Mr. Chan, the patriarch of Beena's feline community, oblivious to the goings-on.

"Miss Beena is having breakfast on the back patio, Doc."

"Thanks. Ask Cook to rustle up some waffles and..." He squeezed Miss No Name's shoulder to get her attention. "What would you like for breakfast?" For some reason, he chose not to remove his hand.

"I'd love—" She bit her lip. "I have no idea. But I'm awfully hungry."

Evidently her fatigue was affecting her fighting spirit. She seemed almost meek. Or was it wariness he sensed? He experienced a prick of compassion. Of course she'd be cautious. The woman couldn't even remember her name. She'd be unsettled, to say the least.

He grinned encouragingly, squeezing her shoulder again in a reassuring gesture. "Awfully hungry's a good sign." He returned his attention to Eartha. "Tell Cook we have a starving guest, and to keep food coming. If it's edible, we'll try it."

His mermaid gave him another look and slipped from beneath his touch. In the candlelight he thought he saw tears glimmering in her eyes. His grin faded. "Are you okay?"

She nodded, her expression glum. "Look, I'm sorry about snapping at you..." Her gaze trailed away, lifting to the vaulted, beamed ceiling, then to wrought-iron candle stands flanking the arched stone portal at the back of the chamber. Finally she faced him again. "If I hadn't seen your boat out there," she whispered, "I'd think I'd somehow swam backward in time."

He chuckled. "Tell me about it."

She smiled reticently. "By the way, thanks."

He experienced a stab of guilt. He hadn't been one hundred percent "detached doctor" out there on the beach. A few of the thoughts that had darted through his head might be frowned upon by the A.M.A. But, damn it, he was a veterinarian, and the problem of caring for nearly naked beauties wearing nothing but soggy lace, had never come up before. "Yeah—well, don't thank me." He cleared his throat. "Concentrate on getting your strength back."

Shoving those lewd thoughts aside, he took her elbow and steered her toward the rear entry through which Eartha had disappeared.

"Who was that woman?" she asked, her voice hushed.

"Eartha Peele. She and her twin sister Bertha are in charge of security."

"There's another one like her?"

He nodded. "Except instead of wearing her red hair back in a ponytail like Eartha, Bertha wears hers in a bun on top of her head." He couldn't help chuckling. "Looks a little like she has a dip of orange sherbet melting on her head."

Her lips twitched, and that made him feel good for some reason. "They break bricks with their foreheads, and do some pretty fancy needlepoint. Eartha and Bertha are a couple of Renaissance Buicks."

His little mermaid didn't react this time. She merely gaped as he led her along a serpentine route through lavender scented hallways. He could tell she felt disoriented. She'd not only lost her memory, but the castle, with off-white plaster walls hung with rich textiles, was an amazingly faithful medieval recreation. She had to be hoping she'd wake up and everything would be back to normal—including the century.

After a few silent minutes Sam tugged his reluctant companion out a door into bright morning sunshine. The flagstone patio where they stood was alive with cats. Some relaxed in shady spots, some groomed themselves, some cavorted, playing chase-and-tumble. A gurgling tiered fountain fed a stony waterfall that splashed and swirled into an Olympic-size pool below the patio.

This was Sam's great aunt's favorite spot, with its view of a golf-course green perfect lawn and extravagant plantings of blooming roses and myriad tropicals. More cats, large and small, frolicked on the vast grounds. Palm leaves high in gracefully curved trees stirred with the whisper of a warming breeze. Off in the distance the ocean was visible, gleaming like antique glass.

Sam was accustomed to the sights, scents and sounds, but he could tell Miss No Name was gaping, though her face was turned away from him. He grinned at her reaction as he pulled her toward the petite elderly woman sitting at a wrought-iron table in deep shade.

His great-aunt Beena looked the same as always, her short hair standing out like a radiant corona of wispy gray. A chunky diamond broach shaped like a cat sparkled from the breast of her cotton shirt.

A skinny orange cat leaped up on the table. Beena leaned forward so the cat could clamber onto her shoulder, becoming a limp and happy fur collar. Stroking the kitty's rump, Beena turned and waved, then stilled, squinting. She grabbed a pair of rhinestone studded glasses hanging from a chain around her neck, and slid them on. She went stock-still and stared. Sam didn't blame his aunt for her surprise. He had begun very few visits with bedraggled female casualties in tow—at least not human females.

"Well, well, Sammy, love." She shooed a black cat off her lap, picked up her napkin and patted her lips. "You've always had a soft heart for strays, but when did you start collecting the two-legged kind?"

He laughed at her quick recovery. "I've been fishing, Aunt Beena. When I caught this angelfish, I decided not to throw her back."

The blonde glanced his way. "This is Beena McQueen." He moved to the table and bent to kiss his great-aunt's cheek. "The woman I love most in the world."

Beena chortled. "And why not, Sammy?" She patted his cheek. "One comes by perfection so rarely." She kissed his cheek, then shoved at his chest. "Enough mush." Beena turned her attention to the blonde leaning heavily on the table. "Who's this pretty little stray?"

Sam's mermaid held out a hand. "Hello, I'm—" Her fledgling smile faded abruptly. She peered at Sam, then glanced back at his aunt. "I—mean..."

She shook her head and stuck her hand out further. "It's nice to meet you, Mrs. McQueen."

"It's Miss." She cocked her head to indicate her surroundings. "I'm the proverbial old maid. I have seventy-nine cats to satisfy the stereotype. And you are?"

"I think what she was trying to say a minute ago was, she doesn't remember that detail." Sam walked behind a chair and held it out. "Why don't you sit?"

His female charge nodded and sank into the offered seat. She crossed long, pale legs and Sam had to compel himself to drag his glance away. He took a chair between the two women, but was disheartened to see those attention-grabbing legs through the glass tabletop.

What was with him today? You'd think he'd been

marooned on a desert island for ten years with his *bada-bing-bada-boom* reaction to this woman. He'd been around female legs before, and they'd been around him. He cleared his throat at his unintentional risqué turn of phrase—and mind. He had a perfectly adequate girlfriend who had perfectly acceptable legs. *Get your mind in the game, Taylor, and off body parts.*

"You don't remember your name?" Beena gawked.

A small gray cat bounded into the mermaid's lap and she let out a gasp.

Sam chuckled at her goosey reaction. "There's a rule around here. No lap shall go unoccupied for more than—*oof!*" Gargantua, a twenty-pound calico, hit him in the gut. He gave the cat a jaundiced look as it settled on his thighs. "...Thirty seconds."

Sam's mermaid looked at the gray in her lap, then tentatively began to pat it. He watched her hand slide cautiously over the fur. He might not know much about her, but it was obvious she didn't have pets. She treated the cat as if it was a bomb that might go off any second. When she snagged Sam's gaze, he had the strangest feeling of being caught doing something wicked. "What's this one's name?" she asked.

"She's Gray Ghost," Beena said, turning to Sam. "She's on the list to be spayed. Bertha found her the last time she was on the mainland. The little sweetie-puss was really malnourished. But she's doing super now."

Sam reached over and patted the gray between the ears, being careful not to graze his mermaid's thigh. He didn't need her leaping up and screaming *pervert* in front of his aunt. "I guess we'd better make friends

now, little one," he said to the purring kitty, "since
you won't like me much for a few days."

"Sam?" Beena asked, "did you order yourself
some breakfast? And some for Angel here?"

"Angel?"

Sam peered at the young woman who'd asked the
question.

"Yes, Angel." Beena smiled. "You're Sam's Angelfish, aren't you?"

A frown formed between the young woman's
brows and she passed Sam a look. Apparently she
wasn't crazy about being called "his" anything. Considering she'd called him a pervert not ten minutes
ago, he could see why she might be hesitant. He gave
her a quick grin. "It's as good a name as any until
you remember yours. We have to call you something
besides 'hey you.'"

She seemed to consider that. "I suppose."

Her lips lifted slightly, almost slyly.

Slyly?

Sam shook off the absurd notion.

"Angel it is, then," she said.

DANA HAD EITHER accidentally stumbled into an episode of the "X-Files" or she'd found a perfect hiding place. All she had to do was keep anybody who
wasn't on the island from finding out she was there.
That meant she had to make sure no communications
about her were sent to the mainland, and the grinning
pervert with the great pecs didn't go blabbing it
around—wherever he was from.

Considering what she just heard, it sounded like
this Dr. Sam Whatever would be staying on the island
for at least a few days. Did she dare hope his stopover

would last two weeks? How long did it take to doctor seventy-nine cats?

Seventy-nine?

Looking at Beena McQueen, Dana had to wonder about the woman's mental stability. With a purring cat collar and enough diamonds in that broach to pay Dana's librarian salary for the next decade, she wasn't your run-of-the-mill maiden aunt.

Completely sane or not, Beena's island was perfect for Dana's needs. All she had to do was make sure nobody radioed the coast guard or anybody else in Miami. Tate would monitor radio reports about somebody found paddling around in the sea. She was positive he wouldn't contact the authorities about her jumping ship. He'd want to quietly find her through his own sources, so there wouldn't be any bad press about her sudden change of heart. Tate was sure to count on his oily charm to change it back.

Not to mention her mother's whiny harangue. Dana cringed at the thought. Her mother had never gotten over the loss of the family fortune, though it had been twenty years. Dana's marriage to Tate had seemed like the perfect vehicle to replenish the family coffers, pairing the Vanovers's venerable old-money name with the Tates's nouveau wealth. Dana's mother's need to have her affluence and social position restored would blind her to any damning allegations Dana might have about Tate. She had no proof, just the fact that she'd overheard—

"Are you in pain?"

She jerked to stare at the doctor, noting his blue eyes had narrowed. His close inspection flustered her and heat rushed up her cheeks. She had the craziest notion he was trying to see into her mind. "Uh—no..."

"Did you remember something?"

She swallowed hard. "No—"

"Don't badger the poor thing, Sammy." Beena took off her glasses and let them dangle. The orange cat curled around her neck began to toy with the chain. Beena lifted a woven straw bowl and peeled back a linen cloth decorated with kittens. "Have a granola muffin, Angel, dear. I'm sure Cook is dispatching steamy coffee and other yummies to us this very minute."

Dana took a muffin, noting Beena's fingernails—long, each painted with a tiny image. She guessed they were cats. Every nail sported a different background color, and each finger held at least one gold ring encrusted with diamonds, opals, emeralds and all manner of costly gems. Dana was amazed the tiny woman could lift her hands. When Beena offered a knife and the butter dish, Dana pulled her gaze from the woman's hands.

"Thank you," she said, slathering butter on the muffin. To heck with cholesterol today. She'd almost drowned, so a little butter didn't look all that lethal. "Who does your nails?" she asked, trying to decide how to get to the subject of *Where's your VHF radio and how long is Dr. Blue Eyes planning to stay?*

"Madam Rex, my personal cat astrologist, does my nail portraits." She held up a hand, fingernails forward so Dana could better see. "Each is a work of art. Naturally I wear false nails, so after I've worn them, I can keep them in my fingernail portrait collection."

"She has over a thousand at last count."

Dana flicked her glance to Sam. His lips twitched, threatening to become a full-fledged grin.

"Oh, pish tosh!" His aunt waved him off as though he were so much flotsam. "Sammy is always kidding me about Madam Rex. He sees no purpose for either her astrological reading for my babies or the fingernail portraits." She gave her nephew a loving swat. "He's a perfect example of why I am single today. *Most* men have no sense of whimsy!"

Dana didn't know what to say, so she took a bite of the muffin. She wasn't sure she had enough whimsy to think cats needed their own astrologist. The fingernail collection was a little on the eccentric side, too.

"Ah, here's the fresh coffee and food," Beena said.

Dana glanced up to see two women, dressed in floral muumuus, hefting silver trays heaping with delicacies. After a flurry of activity, she found herself face-to-face with more food than she could eat in a week, starving or not. Nevertheless, she had a feeling if she'd been in an eating contest with a two-man team of ravenous truck drivers, she'd have whipped their tails.

Halfway through a heaping plate of hash browns, Dana came to the conclusion she would explode if she ate the forkful she'd lifted to her lips. Lowering it, she pushed the plate away with a sigh. "Those were the best potatoes I've ever eaten." She reached for her napkin, but remembered a gray cat was sleeping on it. She wiped her hands on her shirtfront, giving the doctor a quick peek.

He lifted a brow as if to say, "Gotcha!"

She pulled from his gaze and concentrated on the

sleeping cat in her lap, stroking the soft fur between its ears. The act was somehow calming, a strange but pleasant encounter. Dana's mother was highly allergic to animals, so she'd never had pets. She smiled at the feline, thinking that since she had her own little house now, she might go to a shelter and pick out—

"How do you know?"

She shifted toward the doctor, confused. "How do I know what?"

He leaned forward, resting his forearms on the table. With the move muscle flexed in his chest. "That those are the best potatoes you've ever eaten?"

The question jarred her. Had she actually said that? Good grief! Had the *gotcha* look meant he'd seen her use his shirt for a napkin, as she originally thought, or did he mean...

She sucked in a breath, staring first at him, then Beena, who watched her closely.

"Uh—" Her mind scrambled around for something to say, something plausible. "I—I guess it's not much of a compliment—since I can't remember anything. Huh?" She tried on a smile for size. It didn't fit quite right. "I—I guess we know one thing about me. I'm a cliché freak. I'll probably blurt out I'm 'busy as a beaver' or 'pleased as punch' or 'sharp as a tack' or..."

"'Lie like a rug'?" Beena said, looking delighted with the game.

"Yes, er, I mean, no. I mean—" She shut up. Babbling would only give her more chances to slip up.

When she peeked at the handsome doctor, she wasn't happy to notice that he continued to observe her. After a very uncomfortable moment, he pursed his lips. "Hmm-mm."

She felt even more uncomfortable after that long, drawn out utterance, dripping with doubt. How could she have been so stupid to say that about the dratted hash browns? Now he was suspicious. She could see it in his face. "What does 'hmm-mm' mean?"

"Nothing." He lifted a shoulder in a shrug and sat back. "Not a thing."

Yeah, sure! She went prickly with panic, but tried to remain outwardly calm. *Dana Vanover, don't go off half-cocked,* she admonished herself silently. "Hmm-mm" probably means absolutely nothing. He may say "hmm-mm" all the time—like some kind of stress-reducing mantra. Or he might have a nasal passage blockage, and that's how he clears it.

"I know!" Beena slammed her hands on the table, waking not only the gray cat in Dana's lap, but Gargantua and the orange fur collar. The sparkle of inspiration in the older woman's blue eyes didn't do a thing for Dana's heart rate.

"What do you know?" Sam asked, then winced as Gargantua rearranged her bulk in his lap. "Hell, cat." He looked down. "Watch the claws."

The calico yawned, stretched, and closed her eyes.

"Angel is a Cuban refugee!"

Dana was stunned. Whatever gave the woman such a nutty idea?

"Whatever gave you that idea?" Sam asked, and Dana experienced another prick of discomfort. He couldn't possibly read her mind, but his word choice was eerie. "Why would you think that, Aunt Beena? She hasn't spoken a word in Spanish."

Beena stroked the orange cat's tail and cackled. "Of course not, Sammy, love. She has amnesia. She can't remember how!"

Dana strangled a laugh, turning it into a cough.

"Yeah, well..." Sam passed Dana a look. "I bet Angelfish here would like to clean up and put on something besides my shirt. Wouldn't you?"

Dana nodded, figuring even an amnesia victim would know if she needed to wash her hair or not. "I'd appreciate it."

"Sammy, show her to the room next to yours. It's got a lovely view of the ocean." Beena picked up a silver pot and served herself another cup of coffee. "Do you have any clothes, Angel, dear?"

Dana was taken aback by the question and gave herself a heartbeat to make sure she would answer like a real amnesiac. "Uh, only what I have on."

"That's a lovely shirt, Angel." Beena took a sip from a fine china cup. Gilded figures of cats pranced nose to tail around the brim.

"It's my shirt," Sam said. "But thanks."

Beena smirked at him. "She looks well in your shirts. Why don't you let her have some of the clothes you've left here over the years? I'm too scrawny for her to wear mine, and I don't feel it would be right to impose on the help, do you?"

Sam frowned at his aunt. "So you impose on me?"

She set down her cup. "Certainly, Sammy. That's what relatives are for." She waved a hand. "Now off with you. Madam Rex and I have a full morning of readings." She reached over and poked Gargantua in her rump. "You're first, sweetie. Let's see what's in the stars for my voluptuous girl."

Gargantua peered at Beena and gave her an irritated-sounding meow.

"Sorry, old girl. I've got to go." Sam hefted Gargantua off his thighs and settled her on all fours. Immediately the cat plopped onto the shaded flagstone and began to lick her foreleg as though the move had been her idea.

Dana lifted Gray Ghost from her lap. It's little body was slack in her hands, as though it trusted Dana absolutely. She gingerly placed it on her chair and gave it one more pat before facing the doctor. "I—I don't want to be a bother."

"Not to worry, Angel, dear," Beena said. "Sam is such a clotheshorse, he'll never miss a few pairs of shorts and shirts. Sam?" She touched his hand. "I think that purple shirt with the big yellow flowers would do nicely, and the mauve and coral stripe. Oh, oh—that dazzling rose-colored one with the kittens all over it." She shook her head at him. "Why you left those masterworks here, I'll never know."

He bent to kiss her cheek. "I must be insane."

"Unquestionably, since they were all gifts from me."

He winked in Dana's direction and she felt its affect sizzle in her belly. "Clearly, I have a few bats cluttering up my belfry." He straightened. "Are you still determined to walk on your own, Angelfish?"

She nodded. "I'm much better, thanks." Now was her chance to find out how long he intended to stay. At the last second, she remembered her manners and turned. "Thank you for the wonderful breakfast, Miss McQueen."

"*Beena,* Angel, dear. Nobody calls me Miss McQueen."

Dana nodded and smiled, then felt a hand at her elbow. "This way, Angelfish." He tugged her through the entrance they'd come out earlier. "We'll share a bath, but—"

"Like heck we will!" She jerked from his hold. "This may be a private island, but some social values still apply. I bathe alone, buster."

He glanced at her, his expression skeptical; a hint of mirth played around his lips. "You know..." He cleared his throat, as though he were swallowing a laugh. "The name angelfish suits you."

She frowned. "And since angelfish are pretty, I presume that remark is some kind of weird veterinarian come-on?"

"Angelfish are beautiful. However, I was referring to their attitude." He took her elbow again. "Angelfish can be cranky."

She glared at him. "Well, if I'm so offensive, why would you suggest we bathe togeth—"

"Let me clarify," he cut in. "We'll share a *bathroom*, but I'm clean, so you can have the place to yourself." He leaned toward her, eyes twinkling. "Does that arrangement abuse your social values?"

Dana swallowed hard. Humiliated, she shook her head. With a deep inhale of lavender-scented air, she prayed to be devoured by Gargantua—now!

"After you bathe, feel free to rummage in my closet." He spoke matter-of-factly, and Dana was grateful for small favors. At least he'd resisted the impulse to call *her* a pervert. "I'd appreciate it if you'd pick from the pastels," he said. "No matter how much Beena enjoys buying them for me, I don't look good in pink and lilac."

She chanced a peek at him and his troubling grin. She hated the way that crooked show of teeth made her breath leave her body. *Dana, get your mind on what you're supposed to be doing!* she warned herself. *Don't let a set of straight teeth and a well-*

developed tanned male body, sidetrack you. Focus!
"What are you going to do?" She gritted her teeth,
wishing the question hadn't come out sounding so
desperate. She wanted to seem casual.

He tugged her around a bend in the candlelit hallway. "I'm going to get my medical things off the
boat."

The boat! He had a VHF radio on the boat! Agitated, she chewed the inside of her cheek. "Are
you...are you going to call the coast guard about
me?"

"Why?" He indicated stone steps curving upward
and out of sight. "Is there some reason I shouldn't?"

She swallowed around a lump of panic. "No—I
mean—why should there be?"

He continued to hold her elbow as they started up
the steps. She wondered if he was being gallant or if
he wanted to guarantee she didn't make a break for
it. After seeing Beena's ostentatiously displayed
wealth, Dana could understand why her nephew
would be distrustful of strangers who appeared on the
island—no matter how innocent their arrival might
be.

She stopped abruptly. "No!"

Sam glanced at her. "No? Are you saying you
don't want me to radio the coast guard?"

She manufactured a laugh, as gay as she could
muster. "Not that. I just realized how selfish I've
been. First making you carry me up here, with me
snapping at you all the way. Now you're forced to
turn over your clothes!" She shook her head. "No! I
wouldn't think of bathing and relaxing until I've
helped you carry up your things."

"That won't—"

She threw up a halting hand. "Ah! Not another word." She about-faced so quickly, she almost tumbled down the stairs. Sam's quick reaction saved her when he slipped an arm around her waist.

"Whoa," he said. "There's no big rush."

She warily removed herself from his touch, but some irritating imp in her brain made note of how warm and firm he felt. "Uh...but there's no reason to put it off, either."

"You're not up to carrying stuff up from the boat."

"Pish tosh." She mimicked Beena with another laugh. "Sammy, lead the way!" He could be right. She was awfully wobbly, but she hid her exhaustion. This was important!

Her attempt at levity didn't make him smile. As a matter of fact, it inspired a wrinkling of his brow. He scrutinized her for several ponderous ticks of the clock, and she had the same scary feeling he was trying to get inside her mind.

He looked as though he was about to object once and for all. She knew she'd better show him she was adamant. Now! "I refuse to bathe until you say yes." She crossed her arms in front of her, attempting to look as unmovable as a giant redwood.

His expression grew wry. "There's that charming pit bull quality again."

She experienced a prickle of irritation. "This time I know you're calling me a dog!"

"Not technically." He took a step down. Moving ahead, he startled her when he took her hand. "If nobody's reported you missing," he muttered, "We'll know why."

She eyed him furtively, but made no comment.

When her father passed away the year before—rest

his sweet soul—Dana lost her protector, her champion. She sorely missed the anchor of trust and wisdom he'd been in her life. If she had any chance to shatter Tate's scheme, she had to stay hidden, and had to figure out a way to accomplish that—alone. Therefore, there could be no communicating to the mainland about amnesiac blondes being fished out of the sea.

When she noticed Sam watching her, she gave him her wide-eyed, one-celled-organisms-outscore-me-on-IQ-tests look. *You'll never know if I've been reported, Doc,* she threw out telepathically, daring him to read her mind.

Dana's dad had been handy with tools. Being Ray Vanover's daughter, Dana knew how to repair a VHF radio. It would be a piece of cake to sabotage one.

3

DANA TAGGED A STEP BEHIND her doctor captor, his hand clasping hers as he led her down the gradual sloping landscape. They exited the grounds of the castle and set out across sandy dunes and seagrass toward the cabin cruiser.

Dana didn't know much about boats, though she'd lived in Miami all her life. Her mother hated the water, so even before her father lost his fortune in several ill-timed ventures, they'd never owned a boat. But Dana's father, being the great guy he was, had always been willing to help friends who needed something fixed on theirs—be it the radio, the engine, fog lights. He could fix anything. And so could Dana, since her dad let his adoring daughter tag along.

Her legs quivered as she shuffled over the uneven ground, but she mastered her fatigue and set her mind on the problem at hand. "So, how long did you say you'd be staying on the island?"

He glanced her way. "I don't think I said."

She stumbled over a clump of seagrass and fell to one knee. Thank goodness he didn't release her hand or she wouldn't have had the strength to stand.

"Are you sure you're up to this?" he asked.

She smiled as brightly as she could, but even her

face muscles were pooped. "I'm as tack as a sharp! I mean—*sharp* as a *tack*."

His brows went up in blatant skepticism. "You really are into clichés, aren't you?"

Dana decided it would be better to speak in clichés to keep herself from saying anything too distinctive that might give away the fact she was faking amnesia. She shrugged. "I never promised you a rose garden, Doc."

His lips quirked. "And old song titles."

"Is that a song title?"

He shook his head. "Never mind."

He pulled her along. As she tramped through powdery sand, she grew more and more irritated that he hadn't answered her question. She decided to try another tack. "How long does it take to doctor seventy-nine cats?"

"Depends on their condition and needs."

She made a face at the back of his head. He was being so darned evasive you'd think she was asking for top secret military codes or something. "Okay, then how long, in general? Usually?"

He glanced her way. "In general, usually, it depends on their condition and needs."

She fought the urge to kick him in the shin. "Oh?" She tried to look amused. "That long?"

They reached the dock. The creak of boards under his deck shoes and her bare feet were the only sounds, except for the piercing cry of seagulls and shushing water swirling around the pilings.

Sam let go of her to climb into the boat. She had half a mind to leap into the water and find another island without any veterinarians hanging around all buff and tan and skeptical, wearing nothing but shorts and shoes. Facing the fact that she was being silly, Dana climbed into the boat after him. Even if she had the strength to swim more than fifty yards, this place was perfect—sexy, irksome veterinarian or no sexy-irksome veterinarian.

Once on board, Dana glanced around, guessing the cruiser was about forty or forty-five feet long, not new but in good condition. The doctor clearly was a ship-shape kinda guy. She glanced forward to scan the helm, and spotted the VHF radio.

"I'll go below and get the supplies," he said, drawing her gaze.

Experiencing a surge of relief, she nodded. Good, he wasn't going to call the coast guard immediately. "Wild horses couldn't drag me away. I'll hold the fort and I won't move a muscle."

His brows dipped with her newest plunge into Cliché Bog, but he didn't comment. She smiled innocently. *Just stay below long enough for me to zap your VHF.*

He disappeared down the steps. She tiptoed to the helm, hoping the boat didn't creak and give away her sneakiness. Swiftly, she reached behind the radio and located the screw-on coupler, easily removing it and disconnecting the antenna. The next time Sam keyed the mike to send a message, he would blow the radio into VHF heaven. Since the sabotaged radio would die without a whimper, he would have no idea why it didn't work.

Her heart pounding with guilt, she tiptoed back to where she'd been standing. Not a moment too soon, either. The pesky pet doctor stomped up the steps, hefting an armload of boxes. "Take what you can. I'll carry the rest."

She grabbed the top two. "What's in these?"

"Medical supplies."

"No kidding?" She tried to mask her exasperation. "I was sure you were a gun runner, arming the cats for a revolution."

He'd bent to set the other boxes on deck, but peered at her. "Why don't you take those on up? Eartha will show you the clinic. Wait for me, there, and I'll show you to your room—and the bath."

A blush crept up her neck at the reminder of her bathroom blooper. He emphasized that last part on purpose, the bum! Deciding she needed some breathing space—and enough distance to keep from strangling him—she gave a saucy nod. "Aye, cap'n."

When she reached the ladder, she couldn't figure out how to get down and hold on to the boxes at the same time. After a minute of uncertainty, she felt the containers being lifted from her hands. "Climb down. I'll hand them to you."

"Good idea." She avoided eye contact, unsure what exactly was causing her bashfulness—the zapped-radio guilt thing or the buff-tan-turn-on thing.

Safely on the dock, she had to look up into those troubling blue eyes. She noticed how thick his lashes were. Bedroom eyes! That's what the doc had. The kind of eyes that sucked you in and made you feel all melty, and want to tear off clothes—his first, then yours. It was a good thing he was a dog doctor, since any bedside manner that included those eyes would cause female patients to rip out stitches trying to jump his bones.

"Hey, earth to Angelfish," he said. The appearance of brown cardboard in front of her eyes snatched her back to reality. She grabbed the boxes and angled away. "Catch you later." *And good luck contacting the coast guard, Doc Bedroom Eyes.* She was glad her back was to him. Any suspicions he had about her would only intensify if he saw her smirk.

Now to find the radio in the castle—and *fast.*

EARTHA LED DANA to an interior room very different from the rest of the castle. It had a white tile floor and walls, and looked like a doctor's office, which it clearly was. One area was partitioned off for surgery. Eartha showed Dana where to store the supplies, then left her there to wait for Sam.

As soon as the security chief was gone, Dana scurried into the hallway, checking rooms swiftly, stealthily, hoping to find the communications center in this lavender-scented maze. When Sam found out he couldn't call from his boat, he'd head straight for the castle's radio. She figured she had ten minutes, max.

She chewed the inside of her cheek. "Now, if I were a radio, where would I be?"

She heard a sound and flattened herself against the wall, grateful for the dimness. Eartha appeared in a doorway, then headed down the hall, away from Dana. After Eartha disappeared around a corner, Dana darted to the door, peaking inside.

There it was! The radio. A floor unit, it was an unassuming boxy setup with glowing indicator lamps and a microphone for transmitting. But it wasn't a VHF; it was a satellite system. That made sense, since VHF radios had limited range. But it was okay. She could handle it.

As she tiptoed in, she quickly surveyed the room, noting there was also a console and several monitors, showing various views of the island's coastline. This must the security headquarters as well as the communications center.

Dana didn't know where Eartha had gone, but figured she'd be away for at least five minutes. That's all she needed. Now, if only her luck would hold, and Eartha's brawny twin didn't suddenly appear and kick unattractive dents in her head.

Hurrying to the radio, Dana gave it a quick once-over to find out where the coaxial cable feed line led from the radio. As would be expected, it skirted along the wallboard, then at the corner, snaked up the wall to disappear through the ceiling, no doubt winding its way to a satellite dish positioned someplace on the vast roof.

She slipped off one cubic zirconia earring, grateful they'd survived the trip with her. The earring clutched in her hand, she squeezed her upper torso behind the radio to reach the wallboard.

Thrusting hard, she stabbed the cable with an earring post, then snapped off the fake diamond head. The broken metallic piece, buried inside the cable, would short circuit the signals. Though her sabotage wouldn't damage the transmitter or receiver, the radio was off the air until she—or somebody else—removed the metal post.

No matter how desperate she was, Dana couldn't leave a whole island full of people helpless in case of a life-threatening emergency. She could only hope that Eartha was hired more as a leg-breaker than an electrician. Luckily for Dana, even a good electrician would need pretty advanced technology to detect the tiny metallic fragment imbedded in the cable. From the look of it, Beena's equipment was not cutting-edge technology.

Silently she eased out of the tight space and beat it back to the doc's headquarters.

The scrape of shoes brought her up short as she realized Sam was there ahead of her. *Drat!* What was she going to tell him she'd been doing?

"Doc?" she called.

"I'm over here."

He was behind the partition.

Stealthily, she stuck the cubic zirconia inside her bra to dispose of later, then she arranged her face to look harmless and not quite bright. She didn't want him thinking she had the mental wherewithal to vandalize anything that required the cunning of a two-year-old. "Oh? I was just over there." She forced a giggle. "How did we miss each other?"

He didn't respond. She tried not to let that fact bother her, and strolled around the partition. "So, this is where you fix broken kitties?"

He removed bottles from a box and began to place them in a shelf over a white countertop. She figured the bottles were antiseptics and other specifics needed for surgery, but opted not to ask, since he'd probably just say they were bottles.

When he emptied the box, he turned and shot her a critical squint. Though the look lasted only a fraction of a second, it jarred her. Without a word, he walked to the wall and pressed a button. "This is Sam. I'll need the operating room scrubbed down before tomorrow morning."

"I'll see to it, Doc," came the squawky response. "Glad to have you back."

"Thanks, Mona. It's good to be back."

He released the intercom button and headed toward Dana. When he gripped her elbow she winced, antic-

ipating a harsh grab and a demand to know what
she'd done to his radio. The harsh grab she braced
for turned out to be nothing more than a light, guiding
touch. There was no shouted accusation, either. She
peeked at Sam's face, checking for signs of irritation,
or even an indication that he was aware his radio had
met with foul play.

He smiled benignly. "Now, Angelfish, I'll show
you to your room."

It took her a few steps to get herself together mentally. "Uh...who's Mona?" She hoped she sounded
conversational.

"She's Aunt Beena's personal secretary and animal
psychic."

Dana was more than a little startled that he'd given
her a straight answer. Or was it? "Animal psychic?"

He ran a hand through his hair but didn't glance
her way. "Right."

"Your aunt has a cat astrologist and an animal psychic?"

"Mona prefers Trans-species Clairvoyant Dialogue
Expediter."

Dana couldn't help giggling. "I'll try to remember
that."

"Or you could call her Mona."

She smiled. "You're very indulgent of your aunt
and her eccentricities. That's sweet."

"I owe her a lot." He looked at her, then turned
away. "And I love her."

Dana felt a renewed stab of guilt. He seemed basically nice. But as the old saying went—*the nut
doesn't fall far from the insane family tree.* Besides,
he had his own little quirk of feeling up strange
women who washed up on beaches.

She glanced at his somber profile and had another thought. Maybe he really was trying to be helpful. She didn't want to soften toward him. He was so cute, liking him might be risky. After the Tate debacle, she didn't intend to get involved with any other men until they'd proved themselves six ways to Sunday. She made a face. Was that a cliché? Whatever, she wasn't into "trust" these days, especially with people who might not be rowing with all their oars.

She decided to get her mind back to the subject at hand. "How long has Mona-the-trans-species-clairvoy-ant-dialogue-expediter-personal-secretary been here?"

"The house is ten years old. That long."

Dana glanced around as they entered a large room. The walls were stone, the floorboards polished, and the windows strongly defined. Cats lounged or scurried around in the cool, dimly lit room. Tall wrought iron candle holders, encrusted with melted wax, held flickering beeswax candles that gave the place a mellow glow.

Sam didn't say any more as he pulled her along. At the far end of the hall, he led her up a set of wooden steps into a narrow corridor. A few steps ahead, she recognized the curving staircase they'd only made it halfway up earlier.

"So where did Beena live before ten years ago?"

"Miami." Sam tugged her up the stairs. "My aunt had fifteen cats then, which was over city ordinance maximum. She decided to get a place where she could set her own limits."

Dana laughed. "She certainly did that. Couldn't she have bought property outside the city and been able to keep her cats?"

Sam glanced at her, his lips quirking. "From what you've seen so far, does my aunt impress you as someone who would do what most people would do?"

Dana shrugged. "Now that you mention it…"

His brow creased. "You've lost an earring."

Dana almost reached up, but caught herself. "Earring?" She kept her face blank. "I—I didn't know I had any on."

He touched her naked earlobe. "I was sure you had them both earlier."

She made a show of feeling the ear after he'd lowered his hand. "Really?" She touched the other earring, pretending not to be familiar with it. "What does it look like?"

"A little square diamond."

"A diamond?"

"I'm a vet, not a jeweler. Since you've lost one, I hope it's not real."

"Me, too." She bit her lip, deciding that's what someone with amnesia would do if she thought she'd lost a real diamond. "What a shame."

"Maybe we'll find it."

Not if I have anything to do with it, Doc! She smiled wanly. "I'll hold a good thought."

They reached the top of the stone steps and Sam indicated a long hallway, not surprisingly hung with more tapestries. "Mine is the first room here. Next is the bathroom." He stopped in front of a third door. "This is yours, but you'll have to go into mine to get the clothes." He pressed a wrought-iron handle and the door creaked open.

"Make yourself at home," he said, and she realized he was leaving.

"Where are you going?" she asked, hoping he hadn't detected anxiety in her voice. What difference did it make, now? She didn't need to watch him like a hawk any longer. He couldn't call anybody, and he wasn't going far. She knew he would be here for several days. She smiled lamely. "I mean—what should I do when I'm—I've changed?"

He pressed the door wider so she could see the deep, arched windows. Bright sunshine spilled inside, illuminating a room sparsely furnished with strong, unadorned furniture. "Just look out the window." His offhand wink did weird things to her insides. Before she found wits enough to respond, he was gone.

DANA FELT a thousand times better after her shower. One thing about Beena's medieval castle, was the totally modern luxury of the bath. The spacious chamber held a huge Jacuzzi tub and a separate shower with two shower heads that belted out the nicest, most relaxing spray. She could have stayed there all day.

The only stupid thing she'd done, no doubt due to being extremely tired, was forget to find any clothes before her shower. So now she stood in front of Sam's closet wearing nothing but a towel. It didn't make for a leisurely perusal. She kept worrying that he'd burst through the door. Of course, the towel covered a lot more of her than her underwear had, so she didn't know why she was worried. He'd already seen—and felt—more of her than... She swallowed hard. Well, more of her than any veterinarian had a right to. She gritted her teeth and redoubled her determination to get this over with and get out of his room.

She yanked out several hangers containing pastel-colored shirts. But what about shorts? With a pile of pastels over one arm, she scanned his room, wondering where he kept his pink pants.

His room was much like hers, but his bed was bigger and didn't have heavy woven hangings draped over it. Hers had a canopy of bright pink and purple tapestry that matched the spread. Sam's bedspread was woven with more earthy colors. Darker and more masculine. The floor was covered with the same woven rushes. Around the room and between his tall, arched windows were chests, coffers and straight chairs of simple plank construction. In one corner resided a table consisting of a wide board resting on trestles. As well, there were a few bronze art pieces and hand-thrown pottery jugs and bowls scattered about. Once again, Dana felt as though she'd been swept back in time. Amazing.

Enough gaping! She had *shorts* to find. She couldn't spend two weeks wearing nothing but men's shirts. She decided to check out the tall wardrobe opposite the bed. Inside she found drawers of underwear, socks and *finally* shorts. There were a couple of pairs of yellow linen shorts, several in emasculating shades of violet and rose, and even two pairs of madras walking shorts. She smirked. She hardly knew Sam Taylor, but since most of these pants sported store tags, she sensed he wouldn't mind if she confiscated them.

"Now for underwear," she muttered.

"There are some silk boxer shorts over here."

She spun around, her heart jamming in her throat. Why didn't his door creak like hers did!

He closed the door with a soft click, his expression wry. "Sorry. I figured you'd be finished by now." He ambled to a tall chest and pulled out several silky items. She stood dead still, shirts and shorts crushed to her chest. She only hoped her towel didn't come lose because of her violent wheeling about.

He eyed her speculatively. "Okay, I'll come to you." He held out the short stack of boxers. "This is the best I can do underwear-wise. Sorry."

She managed to free up a finger and stretched it out. He hooked the elastic of all five pairs around it, and she clamped the finger back. "Thanks." Darn, she could feel her towel giving way! With both elbows she held it firmly at her sides, but she knew her backside was out there catching the breeze. Thank goodness the bathroom was on the same wall as the wardrobe. She started edging sideways. "I'll...I'll just go get dressed."

"You do that." He watched her, looking baffled by her sideways withdrawal.

His quizzical expression became too much for her and she halted. "My towel's coming loose!" she said. "That's why I'm walking this way."

He didn't quite grin, but his eyes made a mockery of his serious expression. "Angelfish, I hate to be the one to break this to you, but you're standing in front of a mirror."

She gasped, spun around, then sensed her horrible blunder and whirled to face him again. Mortified and flustered, she half tripped, half stumbled backward into the wall. Pressing her naked derriere against rough, cool plaster, she glared at him. "You think this is *funny?*"

He peered at her from beneath craggy brows. His hand covered his mouth. With a brisk shake of his head, he turned away. "Nope." He cleared his throat.

"Not at all." He coughed. She knew he was trying—
and failing—to hide his laughter.

"Pervert!"

"For owning a mirror?"

"You could have warned me!"

"I thought that's what I did, Angel."

How dare he be logical at a time like this! *"Ooo-
ooh!"* She lunged toward the bathroom door.

"I've decided to shower. Let me know when
you're through in there."

"Listen up, Doc, and you'll know!"

It took two seconds for Dana to reach the other
side of the bath and dash into her room. She slammed
the door with all the strength her humiliation could
produce, then reached for the lock. To her dismay,
there wasn't one. "Oh, fine!" Spinning away, she
inspected the room for something heavy she could
shove in front of the door. Not that she believed Doctor Laughing Hyena would barge in. She just didn't
like knowing that a man who was suspicious of her,
an expert with sharp instruments—and seriously
warped—had the *choice.*

She chose a trunk with rope handles, and dragged
it over, shoving it against the door with a loud thud.

"What the hell are you doing?" he asked from the
other side of the door.

Dana cringed and sank down onto the trunk. She
didn't know what was inside it, but dragging it from
the foot of the bed had used up the last of her energy.
"Nothing," she wheezed. "Don't mind me."

"You're barricading your door?"

She squeezed her eyes tight. He was too perceptive.
"Apparently you've heard the sound before," she

said, too tired to do more than loll her head against the wood.

She didn't hear a sound for a full minute.

"By the way, Angel, the VHF radio on my boat doesn't work."

She sucked in a shuddery breath and counted to ten before she tried her voice. "Oh?"

"Neither does the one in the house."

"Really?" Her heartbeat thundered, but she forced herself to sound confused. "What...what does that mean?"

"Why don't you guess?"

"I'm, uh, not very good at guessing games."

"How do you know that, Angel?"

She covered her face with her hands and cursed herself, wishing she would learn to keep her mouth shut. "I mean—I'm too tired to think straight. I don't understand." She yawned. That was no lie. She was dead on her feet "What are you saying?"

"I'm saying, we can't contact anybody."

"Not even the coast guard?"

"Right," he growled. She heard water and realized he'd turned on the shower. "Not even the coast guard."

4

DANA WOKE and winced with pain. Coming up on one elbow, she realized she was lying on the floor in a position that would indicate she'd slid off the trunk she'd jammed against the bathroom door, and sprawled on her face.

She shook her head to clear her sleep-fuzzy brain. She'd slept like a corpse. "I'm surprised there's no chalk line around me," she muttered.

She could tell from the dim light, it must be nearly nine o'clock in the evening. She'd been asleep for more than twelve hours.

Struggling to her feet, she grasped the towel around her and moved to the window. Long, long ago, Doctor Burst-in-the-Room had told her to look out the window when she finished her bath. He probably hadn't meant fourteen hours after her bath, but it was the path of least resistance and she didn't feel like doing much heavy-duty thinking right now. She was wobbly, woozy, and starving.

Scooting onto the deep window ledge, she clutched the towel to her breast and peered outside. Lanterns burned around the perimeter of the patio and the pool. Reflected firelight sparkled in the fountain and waterfall, but what snagged Dana's immediate attention was the annoyingly robust doctor, swimming in the pool. Apparently he was doing laps, because when he reached one end he executed a quick, racing flip and headed back the other way.

Dana was a strong swimmer, but she was impressed by the doc's seemingly effortless style. Slumping against the wall, she watched him eat up the distance, then flip and reverse direction.

"Enough!" she told herself, hopping down. "Get dressed. Didn't you learn anything from Tate? There's more to determining the worth of a man than great pecs and a tight tush."

Tate was a handsome, smooth devil who'd swept Dana off her feet. On her next dip into the finding-a-man waters, she planned to pick some shy twirp who spent his leisure time in library stacks humming sickly sweet ballads, researching the habitat of the dung beetle, and respectfully referring to her as ma'am.

She walked to the bed where she'd tossed the armload of men's clothes, and was startled to see a cat curled in the middle of them. "Well—" She eyed the creature skeptically. "I don't remember seeing you on any hangers in the doc's closet."

The feline, a rather random concoction of black and white blotches, lifted its head and yawned.

"How did you get in here?"

The cat didn't look interested in responding. It took a leisurely lick of a paw then resumed its nap.

Dana glanced at the closed door. In the fading light she noticed the pet door. Amazed at herself for her lack of alertness, she ran both hands through her hair. She must have been more exhausted than she'd realized. Facing the kitty, she gently extracted a flowered shirt and a pair of yellow shorts from beneath it. "Forgive me, your majesty," she said. "I'll be out of your way in a minute."

The cat stirred, seemed to frown, then began to snore.

Dana slipped on the shorts. They left a bit to be desired in the "perfect fit" department, gaping at the waist. She looked as if she'd been half devoured by a yellow shark.

She dragged the wooden chest away from the bathroom door and went in to retrieve her bra, dry by now. Heat warmed her cheeks when she realized the doc couldn't have missed her flimsy lingerie hanging there on the same rack with the hand towels.

She hurriedly slid it on, then the shirt. Barefoot, she padded into the doc's room to look for a belt. Since he was swimming, she knew he wouldn't burst in on her. Besides, she was dressed, so that doubled the odds he wouldn't show up.

She couldn't find a belt, but spotted a rack of silk ties. Most were pink or magenta or rose, so she had a feeling they weren't at the top of the doctor's I-must-wear-these-immediately list. She picked a coral and chartreuse paisley and ran it through her belt loops. Cinching it, she headed out of his bedroom and down the stairs. With only one or two wrong turns, she finally found the exit to the patio.

"Greetings and salutations!"

Dana recognized Beena's squawky welcome and looked around, spotting her sitting cross-legged on the patio, near the fountain. Two cats sat in her lap. The orange kitty still hung around her neck. Another woman sat beside her. This one—a gaunt cadaverous creature with long black hair—looked up. Or at least Dana had the feeling she did, though she couldn't detect any movement.

Beena's fingers sparkled as firelight reflected in her jewelry. "Come here, Angel, dear. Meet Mona. We were just completing our Trans-species clairvoyant dialogues for the day."

Dana managed a smile, adjusting her features to look minimally bright. Pretending to be a blonde dim-wit in front of the skeptical doctor was her safest route, and would probably go unnoticed by his ec-centric aunt. She waved. "Why, hello, Beena."

"Sit!" Beena motioned toward the flagstone. "Mona, this is the sweet little package I was telling you about. Sam fished her out of the sea." Beena gestured as Dana took a seat on stone still warm from the setting sun.

Dana noticed Beena's knees, knobby and sun-burned, jutting out of baggy denim shorts. Red and yellow argyle socks fought for color palette suprem-acy over turquoise-and-plum beaded moccasins.

On the other hand, Mona's palette contained only one color. Black. From her straight hair to her lipstick to her monklike garb, she resembled a big, dormant bat.

One other element to Mona's attire drew Dana's gaze, unsettling her. Hanging from the breast of her smock were small reptilian-looking brooches. *Yuck!* Dana thought. *Of all the jewelry choices in the world! Tiny Tyrannosauruses!*

"How do you do." Mona-the-bat stuck out an emaciated hand.

Her long, curling nails were shiny and black. With

more trepidation than Dana had ever felt just shaking hands, she reached toward the woman. As their fingers touched, Dana felt a blow, and screamed. An embarrassing second later, she realized she wasn't suffering some horrible bat-woman touch of death. A chubby kitty had pounced into her lap.

She covered her thudding heart with her hands. "Oh—I'm *so* sorry! I—I'm not used to..." She wanted to say, *Shaking hands with the living dead* but opted for "...cats jumping into my lap. It scared me."

"So your memory has returned."

Dana jumped in alarm. The doctor sounded way too close to be swimming laps. She looked around. He stood a couple of feet behind her. His quizzical expression aimed her way, he began toweling off. The dripping swimsuit clung to him in all the right places, hinting at things better left unhinted at. She pulled her glance away. It slid down powerful legs, then, re-thinking, shot above his waist. The muscular contours of his torso caught the flickering firelight just right. Drat! No matter where she looked, there was something to be avoided.

Irked at herself, both for her aroused turn of mind and yet *another* slip of the tongue, she spun away. "How could I possibly be used to having cats jump in my lap. I have amnesia," she rejoined.

So there!

"Stop teasing the poor dear, Sammy, love." Beena beckoned. "Come join us." She turned to Dana. "I imagine you're starving, Angel."

Dana couldn't deny it, and nodded. "I don't mean to be a bother, but I am hungry."

"I'll tell Cook," Mona said in a low-moan-of-cold-wind monotone. For a cadaver, she moved swiftly. Her vacated place was immediately filled with cat. It was almost as though the animal just lay there as the ghost-bat-woman's molecules scattered and reassembled around it.

When Mona turned her back, Dana notice with alarm that one of those ghastly pieces of jewelry was crawling up to perch on her shoulder. She heard a scream and realized it had come from her own throat.

Mona didn't react, but Beena touched her knee. "What's the matter, dear? Did Parsley claw you?"

Dana peeped askance at Beena. "That dinosaur brooch *moved!*"

"Oh, that." Beena tittered. "They're not brooches. They're baby iguanas. Mona has a number of them as pets. She hangs the babies from her clothes. That's how they bond."

Bond? Dana found that vaguely disturbing. "I—I thought they were jewelry."

"Oh, Mona doesn't believe in jewelry," Beena said with a gay cackle. "She's a rabid back-to-the-earth person."

Dana didn't doubt it. Rabid-bat-woman looked as if she'd be perfectly at home *under* six feet of it.

A scraping sound drew Dana's attention. Against her better judgment she turned to see the very-nearly-naked doc pull up a metal chair. He turned it around to face away from them. Straddling the seat, he settled down and rested his forearms on the chair back. "Have a nice nap, Angel?"

She shrugged. "I fell asleep on a trunk, slid off and ended up taking a siesta on the rug."

His grin was crooked and bothersome. "That explains the waffle pattern on your face."

Unable to squelch a blush, she self-consciously touched her cheek, praying it was dark enough so her flush wouldn't be detectable.

"Maybe I should have explained about beds and what they're used for."

She gave him a narrow look. "No, thank you. I'll just struggle along in my ignorance."

"That's a good sign!" Beena clapped her hands.

Confused, Dana turned her way.

"How is that a good sign, Aunt Beena?" Sam asked, once again echoing Dana's thoughts.

"She said *siesta!* Don't you see? Her Spanish is coming back."

"It's a miracle," Sam said.

Dana glanced his way, noting his taunting grin, his eyes glittering with mirrored flame.

"Pretty soon she'll regain her memory and we won't be able to understand a word she says!" Beena went on, clearly not grasping her grand-nephew's sarcasm.

"You haven't asked about the radios."

Dana felt a stab of misgiving, but masked it with wide-eyed dumb innocence. "Radios? What radios?"

"Remember, I told you the VHF on my boat and the satellite system don't work?"

"Oh? Must have slipped my mind." She gave him her most innocent severely-mechanically-challenged look. "I guess we'll just have to watch TV."

Beena giggled. "Not that kind of radio, dear. Our communication radios. We can't call anybody."

Dana screwed up her face to look bewildered. "Don't you have a phone?"

"No, dear," Beena said through a sigh. "We have to use radios from way out here in the boonies." She scratched her orange kitty between the ears. "Isn't it the strangest coincidence that both our radios would go out on the same day?"

"Very strange," Sam said.

Dana forced herself not to look at him, worried that he might see something amiss in her eyes.

"We can't imagine what's wrong." Beena shook her downy head. "Luckily, the mail and supply boat comes in a week. We'll get a message to the mainland about needing repairs."

Dana's heart lurched to her throat. She shifted to face Sam. "A week?" *This was bad news!*

He nodded. "You don't have any urgent plans, do you?"

Yes, and they don't include a boat showing up in one dratted week! "I—how would *I* know?"

He gave her a long, scrutinizing look—head to toe, then toe to head. She grew restive under his inspection. What did he think he was looking for that required so much investigation? "Checking for fleas, Doc?"

His lips quirked. "How do the clothes fit?"

Dana hadn't expected such an abrupt subject change. She wanted to grill him about the supply boat. But she decided she'd better not rush things, or appear too agitated. With a shrug she hoped looked breezy, she said, "Loose, but comfortable."

"You look very whimsical, dear," Beena said, plainly unfazed by the zigs and zags of topics. "Sam is such an unwhimsical dresser. I try to whimsy-up his wardrobe, but he resists.''

Too aware of the doctor's mellow laughter, Dana looked at the furry beast curled on her legs. She noticed with some surprise she was petting it. She also noticed she was too aware that Sam's leg was practically brushing her arm. He must have dried off from his swim, because she could swear she felt radiant heat from his calf. She set her teeth, irritated with herself. She didn't need to be thinking about his heat!

In the silence, she heard a noise and wondered which cat growled, then registered with chagrin that the noise came from her stomach.

"I'll check on that food," Sam said.

As he stood, his leg brushed her shoulder. She gave him a look that was half grudging, half grateful and half fearful. Or was that too may halves? Whatever, she felt all three emotions. She had a feeling he received all three. His wink was impertinent and disabling. He was ambling away before her breathing kicked in. She stared after him, grudgingly inspecting the flex and bunch of muscle—doing exactly what muscle was meant to do in extremely well-toned male bodies.

"He's a nice boy, my Sammy," Beena said, drawing Dana's attention. "Don't you think he's a nice boy, Angel?"

She cleared a rustiness from her throat. "Oh, I— yes, I'm sure he's...nice."

Beena chortled. "For somebody without a speck of whimsy, you mean!"

"Not a speck," she admitted.

Dana ripped her gaze from the doc's brawny back.

He might be short on whimsy, she grumbled inwardly, *...but for a man who didn't trust her as far as he could throw his boat, he sure was obscenely long on whoop-de-do!*

LOGICALLY, SAM KNEW the woman sitting on the patio, playing bingo with Beena, Mona, Madam Rex and Bertha, couldn't possibly have sabotaged the radios. Even from his vantage point above them, from the window of his room, he noticed it had taken several rounds for the blonde to figure out that she was supposed to look *down* the column, beneath the letter that had been called out, to see if the matching number was on her card. She gave every impression that somewhere out there a village was missing its idiot.

On the other hand, his Angelfish might be the shrewdest little vixen he'd ever run across. Just what her game was, he couldn't imagine. But he knew it had something to do with swindling his great aunt out of her money. He'd had experience with innocent-looking types before who'd wangled their way into Beena's off-center world. His aunt was too trusting. She'd been robbed before, and he damn well didn't intend to let it happen again.

Sam had tried to put a stop to it by personally doing all Beena's hiring. The past five years had gone fairly smoothly for his great-aunt and her comical little queendom—*not* one hundred percent, though. And that one mistake rode Sam hard.

There was something about this leggy blonde that troubled him. Something *besides* her long, pale legs and her wide, green eyes. Ever since she'd washed up on the island things had seemed strangely out of kilter.

He planted the flat of his hands on the deep windowsill and examined her with a critical squint. She said something and laughed. The others joined in. She didn't give off treacherous vibes; she just seemed friendly and not quite bright. His emotions warred— was she that innocent, or that shrewd?

He frowned, angry with her. No, damn it! He was angry with himself. He found her annoyingly tempting, and that made him nuts. He had a girlfriend! He'd been content with Liza for four years. And here came this woman, crawling out of the sea....

He bit off a curse. Two radios blowing on the same day, practically at the same time, was so bizarre he had trouble believing it was a fluke. Angel had been alone—in the proximity of both—moments before they were discovered to be malfunctioning. He eyed her narrowly, his gaze drifting without permission to her legs as she recrossed them beneath the glass tabletop. She had the legs of a swimmer, or a runner, well-toned yet feminine. But she was so pale, unusual for Miami residents in mid-June. Of course, if she were a con artist from out of state, a strong swimmer with an electrical engineering degree, that would explain a lot.

Sam was no engineer, so he had no clue how a nearly naked woman, without access to even a screwdriver, could disable the radios, and in only a matter of seconds. In all likelihood she was as innocent and dumb as she looked.

Just in case, though, he planned to keep an eye on her—day and night.

DANA HAD NEVER SPENT such a weird, intensely exhausting day in her life. She'd been awakened at seven o'clock when a breakfast tray was delivered to her. She was told by the maid to report to Doc Sam's "surgery" by seven-thirty, and to change into the hospital scrubs waiting for her in the office.

Dana hadn't been happy about it, but "Doc Sam" turned out to be the kind of man who didn't take no for an answer. He'd been waiting, already dressed in greens. He'd explained that his assistant, who usually came with him, was seven months pregnant and her husband hadn't wanted her to leave. So he needed Dana's help. *Period.*

Without a say in the matter, Dana reluctantly learned what Sam called the "Spock Death Grip" for holding cats immobile while being given shots. She'd unwillingly become accomplished in administering ear mite medication, but hardly adroit at avoiding getting the stuff all over her and in her hair when the cat tried to shake every last molecule out of its ears. She'd learned that cats can and do—without the slightest hint of regret or remorse—spit pills at the unsuspecting pill-giver, and that most cats resist being flea-dipped with every fiber of their being, not to mention claws and teeth.

Dana was positive her skin had absorbed enough dip to keep her protected against flea infestation for the next ten years.

Oh, and one other thing. She'd learned that it's politically incorrect to toss one's cookies directly on the cat—or on the doctor's shoes, no matter how gross the medical procedure.

These were revolting, wearisome lessons Dana

hoped she had no reason to remember, but she had a gut feeling she'd better try.

She looked around the office and spotted the wall clock. Nearly six. She stretched to get the kinks out of her spine. For the past hour she'd been updating medical files while the doc checked his patients, now resting in cages.

Some cats, which had received less intrusive treatments, were released on their own recognizance. Others roamed the office, awaiting the doctor's say-so before they could regain their freedom. A tortoiseshell cat with an angelic face and rotten personality, plopped down in the middle of Dana's paperwork, apparently believing batting at her pen was just the right cure for its head cold.

Dana gave it a severe look. "You're slobbering purple baby aspirin juice on my records, cat."

The feline rubbed Dana's knuckles with the side of its face, leaving a glob of purple slobber.

"Yuck!" Dana wiped her hand on her soiled greens.

"The torti's marking you as her property," Sam said. "Which is generous, considering she hates taking pills, and anybody who dares to try to feed them to her."

"No kidding?" Dana held up her bandaged thumb. "I thought she just enjoyed a hemoglobin chaser after a session of spitting pills in my eye." Her right eye still stung and watered from that fiasco.

Dana could tell when Sam came near. The hair at her nape stood up. She was so provoked with him for what he'd forced on her today, she itched to get her hands on his neck and squeeze until he coughed up a fur ball. Unfortunately, she didn't have the strength.

Besides being drained physically, she was worn out emotionally. She'd never been so frightened or upset in her life as she was this morning when he'd demanded that she assist him in the clinic. After all, there were at least fifty other people he could have shanghaied to help him. But no! He'd ordered *her* to do it.

She had been horrified. She knew nothing about animals! She'd never even had a pet, but she couldn't tell him that and still stick to her amnesia story. So, without argument, she'd kept her irritation and fear to herself and done her best. It had been hard to hold on to the dumb blonde act, too, since she didn't want to kill any kitties by pretending not to understand his instructions. All in all, it had been a rotten day.

Dana avoided looking up at him, though one watery eye was hardly working, anyway. Instead she concentrated on the cat and its single-minded batting of her ballpoint. She couldn't help visualizing the doc in her mind, the way he'd looked today. Even though most of the time he'd worn a surgical cap and mask, she'd had to struggle with the melting effect his azure bedroom eyes had on her. Those thick, dark lashes slanted her way whenever he'd ask for a sponge or suture or swab.

Once, she'd been positive he was laughing behind that mask. Okay, so she probably looked hilarious when she was up-chucking, but he could've had the decency to show the tiniest shred of concern.

"Are you hungry?" he asked.

Startled by his question, she wasn't sure her shrug

visted back and made a face. "Give me a
-astrophe, or whatever your name is!" She
t the goo. "You nearly put out my eye ear-
t that enough abuse for one day?"

nething wrong with your eye?"

was *really* sorry he'd heard that. She'd tried to
he teary side of her face away from him. "No,
ot thing. I'm as healthy as a horse."

"Let me see."

She pushed up from the chair, giving the torti a
darn-you look. "I'll be going now."

She shuffled sideways in her attempt to escape, but
his hand at her elbow dragged her to a halt. "I'd
better check that eye. The cornea might be
scratched."

"It's not. It's fine."

"Don't you want a doctor's opinion?"

"Not especially."

She felt his fingers on her jaw, urging her to face
him. "Don't make me use the grip, Angel."

She was beginning to see that Doc Sam got exactly
what he wanted, exactly when he wanted it. Bully that
he s. Since he outweighed her by at least fifty
she decided she had no choice but to give
way. She didn't have to be happy about it,
She lifted her chin and glared one-eyed at
other eye watered and teared. "Look, I'd be
or your professional opinion if I needed
" she said. "But in case you hadn't noticed,
an eyes!"
d."

one good eye, she met his two very ex-

looked all that casual. "Well

long."

His laughter was r

warm at the sound. "Yo

When he rested a hand

rigid.

"Dinner should be ready in a

Go on up and shower."

The torti batted at Dana's pen, kno

her debilitated fingers. "Uh, what about the

"They'll wait."

"And—the cats?" She couldn't imagine why

voice was so faulty, or why she wasn't dashing pe

mell out of the room.

"The night shift's coming on. I'll stay to leave in-

structions. When you're out of the shower, knock on

my door."

She nodded, clearing her throat, thinking *Get you

hand off my shoulder so my stupid body can move*

nearly shocked her out of her seat when he di

she'd mentally commanded. A shuffling sound

her he'd turned away. "Thanks for the help

fish."

She shifted to frown at him. "T

help?" There was no mistaking

tone. "Are you suggesting I h

He opened the cage door f

to stroke her furry back.

his grin was as annoyin

He turned away an

Dana continued to s

Just then the purple-drib

to rub slobber against Dan

ceptional ones. He squinted slightly. "Hold still." He leaned closer.

She tilted backward until she was bowed over the desk like a reading lamp.

"Darlin', if you lean any farther you'll be lying on that desk and I'll be on top of you. Is that *really* the position you want to be in while I examine your eye?"

Some evil imp in her brain applauded and hooted with glee at the prospect, but Dana's better judgment grabbed hold of the idiot imp and shook the stuffing out of it. She clamped the desk edge with her fingers. "Just hurry."

With a gentle touch, he held her eye wide, dipping closer, closer. A flicker of panic chased through her, and her breathing became shallow. She swallowed, but her throat was dry.

His breath warmed her cheek. She could detect his scent, clean, manly, with a hint of antiseptic. It wasn't a bad smell, just unusual. Like his eyes.

She watched those eyes as he examined her teary one. "It's not scratched," he said at last.

When his gaze met hers, the effect snatched her breath away. She blinked, and lowered her gaze. "Thanks. I—I told you...." *Why didn't he back off?*

"When you take your shower, flood it with warm water."

She nodded. "Right—warm *waaaaaaaaaaaouch!*" Something jabbed her in the backside. She jerked forward, slamming into Sam. Reflexively, she grabbed his neck. "Something stabbed me! Or bit me!"

"What the—"

His arms came around her.

"Am I bleeding?"

"Do you want me to check?"

"No!" she cried, realizing where he'd have to look. "That cat attacked me!"

His chuckle rumbled through her. "Pouncer. Bad girl."

Frowning, Dana peered over her shoulder. The torti's head was down, ears back, butt up and tail swishing from side to side.

"Don't even think about it, Pounce!" Sam's tone was a little too amused for Dana's taste.

She sucked in a shocked breath when his hands slid to cup her bottom. "What do you think you're doing?"

"Covering the target."

"Yeah—well, that's not what it feels like!"

He released one cheek and slid open a desk drawer. Dana watched as he tossed something to the opposite side of the desk. "Okay, Pouncer, get the tuna munchie."

The cat's ears shot up and her butt went down. An instant later she'd pounced on the kitty treat, no longer interested in Dana's posterior.

"Pouncer likes you," Sam said as his hand returned to cup the unprotected cheek.

Dana shifted to meet eyes, which sparkled with unrepentant laughter. "Pouncer needs therapy," she muttered. "Doesn't your aunt have a cat psychologist on the premises?"

"She's vacationing in the south of France at the moment." He scanned her face. "You know what, Angelfish? I've discovered a couple of important facts about you, today."

She experienced a jolt of trepidation. *Drat!* She'd tried so hard to keep her wits about her, even when she was barfing. How had she slipped up? "What— important facts?"

"You're not a doctor."

Relief made her weak and she scowled at him. "Did the upchucking help with that deduction?"

His grin flashed, bright and appealing. "It didn't hurt."

She made herself frown. "And the other thing?"

"You're not a mother."

That insight took her by surprise. She wasn't, of course, but how on earth would he know? "Don't tell me you can detect an episiotomy scar through a woman's clothing?"

His eyebrows lifted a fraction. "I'm good, but not that good," he said. "No, it was when you tried to stick that rectal thermometer in Gray Ghost's mouth."

"A mother would know better than that, huh?"

He nodded, but only faintly. His eyes remained on her. *Those dratted, beautiful, taunting eyes.*

Dana found his closeness and his intimate touch way too stirring. All she needed was to rebound into this good-looking doctor's arms. *No!* She'd learned her lesson where it came to smooth, sexy studs. She would never again be swept off her feet by good pectoral muscles and the whiff of agreeable pheromones. The next man she got involved with would *prove* his worth, *show* he was honorable, trustworthy, and most importantly of all, willingly grovel at her feet. Dana had a feeling the doc didn't grovel well.

Steeling herself, she fought her attraction. "There's

an important fact I've learned about you, too.'' The assertion came out breathy.

His long lashes slid to half mast, a cruelly erotic act. ''Really?''

''Mm-hum.''

''What fact?''

''The fact, that if you don't get your hands off my posterior, you're going to be walking funny.''

His brow furrowed slightly, but an instant later he grinned and stepped away. ''Thanks for the insight.''

''My pleasure, Doc.'' Avoiding further eye contact, she slid from behind the desk and skittered out the door.

5

SAM WATCHED HER LEAVE his office. Sometime after she was gone, he noticed he was still standing there, grinning at the empty door like some infatuated doofus. He glanced at his hands, oddly cupped, as though her tush was still...

He made a disgusted sound and dropped into the seat behind his desk. Pouncer had curled herself in the middle of his records and was watching him intently, purring. He eyed the cat with skepticism. "Did you have any idea what you were doing, young lady?"

She extended a forepaw and lay it atop his hand, then rested her head on the outstretched foreleg. Her purring continued unabated.

Sam grinned wryly and shook his head. "I can see you feel real bad about it."

Pouncer closed her eyes, seemingly content in the knowledge that she held him captive beneath her paw. A dribble of purple slobber escaped from the side of her mouth and oozed onto a hapless medical record.

"She's not as dumb as she pretends."

Pouncer opened one eye.

"There aren't many people who can learn to shave a cat for surgery that quickly. Besides, if she were as dumb as she wants us to believe, she wouldn't know an episiotomy scar from an Iggy Pop video.''

Pouncer leaked another purple globule of drool.

Sam bent down as though confiding a secret. ''She isn't being straight with us, Pounce. That can't be good.''

The feline closed the eye, purring and drooling.

Sam straightened, watching the exit through which his blond enigma had recently departed.

He had no proof she was lying about anything. Just because she'd caught on to what he needed her to do in the clinic didn't mean she was a calculating sleaze hiding behind a mask of big-eyed dumbness. Maybe she simply had a knack for nursing animals—that is, after she got past the puking.

What was her game? Or was she even playing? He'd never felt so torn in his life. He'd watched her closely all day. She'd been distracted and upset and even sick, yet she hadn't said a word that suggested she didn't actually have amnesia. Still, there was something elusive about her that disturbed him. Something he couldn't put his finger on.

He heard a noise and realized two staffers with first aid training were coming to take over the night shift.

Enough woolgathering! He was a doctor, and his work wasn't done. He patted the cat and stood. ''Don't shove her into me again, Pounce,'' he murmured. ''It's a bad idea to get hot for a con artist— no matter how nicely her derriere fits into my hands.''

AFTER A LATE DINNER Beena, along with her quaint sorority of oddballs, shambled off to bed. That was an hour ago. Dana was tired, but too restless to sleep.

It hadn't dawned on her until a short time ago that this was Saturday night.

Her wedding night.

She experienced a twinge of sadness for what might have been—if Tate had been the man she'd believed him to be. In all her twenty-six years, she'd never fallen so hard or so fast for a man. He'd played her like a pro, pressing all the right buttons, and she'd taken his handsomely displayed bait like a starving guppy.

She supposed his yacht had been an echo of the glittery life-style she could only distantly recall, and she'd been sucked in. Dana hated herself for her unforeseen streak of shallowness. But she supposed she couldn't have lived with her mother all those years and not have some of that ache for The Good Life rub off.

Dana slid her hand along the stone banister as she trailed slowly down the steps that led from the upper patio to poolside.

She flicked away a tear. "Don't you dare feel sorry for yourself, nitwit!"

Listless, she leaned against the railing and stared up at the sky. The night was full of stars—millions and millions of them, so radiant, innocently twinkling, giving off all that beauty for free. She felt a pang, unhappy to realize the idea of anything being given away free seemed foreign to her now. Her experience with Tate certainly had taught her a scary lesson about life and people.

She inhaled, the soft scent of tropical flowers filling her lungs. Another benevolent gift. A fresh tear trickled down her cheek as she stared at the stars, wishing she had no reason to be startled by the beauty of nature and how it was so unselfishly and freely bestowed on the world.

The flickering torches cast everything in a russet glow. The pool, with its underwater lighting, seemed blinding compared to its surroundings. She turned away, deciding she needed darkness. She wandered onto the lawn, heading nowhere in particular. Dana never had a wedding night before. She wasn't sure how one was expected to spend it—alone and feeling violated.

The kitties that had romped everywhere only an hour ago were nowhere to be found. Dana had a feeling several of them would be snoozing on her bed when she went inside. Funny, the idea of finding small, furry beings on her bedspread didn't bother her nearly as much as it would have a few days ago. She'd learned a lot about cats today—and more than she cared to know about their doctor. Like the fact that he had long, expressive hands, nimble, gentle fingers, and an endearing tenderness in his voice and his eyes as he soothed and calmed panicky animals.

When he looked at her, that tenderness became shadowed with caution. He *sensed* she was lying. She knew he'd decided to keep an eye on her, no doubt to make sure she wasn't casing the joint for vaults to pilfer. Things would be so much easier if he weren't so darn perceptive. Maybe a veterinarian had to have keen insight, dealing with patients who couldn't communicate by words.

She'd been so careful, trying not to give him any more ammunition for his suspicions. Had something in her posture or her expression added to his misgivings, or was she reading wariness in his gaze simply because her ability to trust had been crippled?

Her wedding night. She inhaled to staunch another surge of self-pity.

Just as she had been duped into falling for Tate's suave line, her mother had been beguiled by his promise of a money-making property that would return her family to the pinnacle of Miami society. Something her mother had craved for the past twenty years. *How perfect,* both she and her mother had thought. Dana did, after all, love Tate Fleck. How marvelous to match his flair for enterprise with their proud family name.

Only by accident had Dana thwarted Tate's plan, overhearing him drunkenly jeer to an accomplice how the money-making property was a dead loss, rife with labor dissent and a harbor for his lowlife buddies.

She had also discovered, to her shock and anguish, that Tate's big business deal was completely bogus. He'd needed a venerable old name—which her family's reputation could provide—to run a scam that would net him a fast fortune before the bottom dropped out, ruining thousands of small investors. By then, however, Tate would have disappeared, leaving Dana and her mother, Magda, to cope with the scandalous aftermath.

Dana wondered what Tate was doing right now. Had he been interviewed by the media, fielding question about where his bride had disappeared to? Had he made up some excuse—that she was ill?—determined to find her before it was too late for him to pull off his fraud?

And what about her mother? Dana knew Magda

Vanover well. Blinded by the need for status and
wealth, Magda would remain staunchly at Tate's side,
parroting anything he told her to say. Mrs. Vanover
would assume Dana had caught a case of cold feet,
and would be retrieved, reassured, and then walk sub-
missively into holy wedlock with Tate.

Holy! That was a laugh. "Unholy" was more the
word for what that lying, cheating slimebag planned.
Tate was a determined, ruthless man with powerful
allies. Dana didn't know who she could trust, didn't
dare confide in anybody. Her only hope was to stay
hidden until the clock ran out on his scheme.

That deadline was still nearly two weeks away. As
long as the deal simmered, Tate would rip apart
heaven and earth to find her. He would make their
wedding a reality, even if he had to use force.

She couldn't let that happen.

"No way!" she vowed grimly.

"There's always a way, Angel," came a disem-
bodied voice. "What is it you want?"

Dana spun, stunned at how close Sam sounded. She
pressed her hands to her thudding heart. "Are you
trying to scare me to death?"

His husky laugh filled the night. "If I'd have
wanted that, I'd have jumped out at you and said
boo."

She caught movement as he stepped out from behind a clump of palmettos.

Though the night was black, the torches touched
him with sufficient light to show off wide shoulders
and a nicely contoured chest. He wore dark, baggy
shorts, yet enough of his long, athletic legs were visible to be bothersome.

"Do you do a lot of creeping around barefoot in the bushes, or have you decided to become my personal stalker?"

"Your personal stalker." His grin was a sexy flash. "If you'd give me a hint about where you're going it would make stalking you at night much easier."

"Why didn't you say so, Doc?" She shot him a sarcastic grin. "I *live* to make your life easier."

His easy chuckle made her suddenly nervous. Not scared nervous. Female nervous. Drat the doctor! He radiated a wily charisma that reached out and nudged her libido. *No!* she told herself. *No more good-looking, sexy-grinning, masterful hunks for me. No more making value judgments with my eyes and my hormones! The next man who turns me on will do it with sparkling conversation and a willingness to ask my permission to kiss my feet!*

Besides, the doc didn't trust her. He was out here spying on her to make sure she wasn't absconding with the family jewels.

She made a point of turning away. "I'm just walking."

"A night person, huh?"

Oh, no, you don't! You won't make me slip up that easily! "I have no idea."

"Why don't I walk with you?"

"That's not necessary."

"I think it is."

She faced him. "Don't you trust me?"

He winked. "Come on." He took her arm and began to steer her across the lawn. "There's a path not far away that leads to the beach."

She didn't pull from his grasp, and that made her

furious with herself. The last thing she needed was to go all tingly about a man who was only there to make sure she didn't commit any Class-A felonies. "I gather you're a night person?" she asked, trying to sound one notch above bored.

"Depends on the night."

She didn't respond. Something about his answer was too suggestive to even go there.

They headed down an easy grade toward the wall that separated the velvety lawn from the sand and dune grass. The stone structure looked to be about five feet high. When she halted, so did he. "How do we get over that?"

"I'll lift you."

She peered at him. "Some great pathway to the beach."

He grinned. "Don't worry. It's there."

He tugged her along. When they reached the stone barrier, he let go of her arm and stepped behind her. "When I lift, you swing up a leg and get a hold."

"Really? I thought I'd go limp and you could toss me over."

He laughed and took hold of her waist. His hands felt warm and strong against her bare skin. Suddenly, Dana regretted tying the tail of his shirt beneath her breast. She didn't need his hands on her at that moment. Heck, she didn't need them on her at all!

"On the count of three."

"What?"

"Jump on three."

"Oh, now I've got to *jump*, too," she scoffed. "What exactly are you good for?"

He released her. "Okay. You jump. I'll watch."

She eyed him with animosity, then braced her hands on top of the wall. She'd show him she didn't need or want his hands on her! With a mighty push, she swung a leg up. Before her trembling arms gave way, she'd levered her upper torso high enough to drop, stomach first, onto the stone surface. She cringed at the slap she got, and feared she'd scraped her belly, but refused to groan.

She took a couple of breaths and used her remaining strength to right herself. Once she'd settled on top of the wall, her feet hanging over the far side, she smirked at him. "Piece of cake."

His grin crooked, he nodded. "Congratulations." He placed the flat of his hands on top of the wall. With a mighty leap, he cleared it, landing with hardly a sound on the sand. The jump across took all of a second. Looking as though hurdling tall barriers was no more exerting than stepping over cracks, he leaned against the wall a hairsbreadth from her leg. "Do you want help down, Tarzan?"

She surveyed the terrain. The slope here was steeper. If she missed her step, she could end up rolling a long distance—possibly spraining and breaking bits and pieces of herself along the way. She faced him without enthusiasm. Tall, with the deliciously fit body of a pro baseball player, he watched her. Dana watched him back, cursing herself for not being able to pull her gaze from the display of corded muscle, flexing and coiling, in the dimness.

After a strained minute he held out a hand in silent invitation. The move shook her out of her daze and she jumped down, determining that broken body parts was a chance she had to take.

She made a perfect two-point landing, then in an alarming turn of events, slammed to the flat of her back. The wind rushed out of her in a painful *whoosh*. She lay there, wide-eyed. Stars darted and tumbled around in the heavens. She squeezed her eyes shut. *Drat!* They were still shooting and zipping and somersaulting! This wasn't a good sign—not to mention the fact that she couldn't breathe. She gasped and winced, gasped and winced. Finally, glorious air began to trickle into her lungs.

"Yes, I can see that was a much better plan."

A fire burned in her chest and he was making jokes! Opening one eye, she glared at him, but she was still too occupied with taking in air to tell him to go to blazes. Even so, she held up a hand and shook a finger at him.

He knelt and grasped her wrist as though he were taking her pulse. "It's a little fast."

She opened her mouth, but could do nothing but gasp for air.

He settled on the sand, facing her. Releasing her wrist, he leaned across her, resting his hand in the sand near her waist. Their hips touched, but any erotic stirrings were overpowered by her desire to live.

He watched her solemnly for a moment. Then his lips began to twitch. *"¿Habla Español?"*

"No—" she wheezed. "I didn't—get my memory back, if that's what you're groping for." She glowered. "I think—my back is broken, in case you're interested."

A dark brow rose. "Oh?" He lifted his hand from the sand and trailed a finger across her bare belly. "Feel that?"

Her mouth opened in shock. She certainly did! To be agonizingly honest, she felt *that* in parts of her body that weren't even close to the skin above her navel, but were, evidently, hot-wired directly to it. This irksome winking-smirking-touching vet knew more about the female anatomy than he could possibly have learned in vet school.

He returned his hand to her side, but this time his arm made contact with her waist. "Well?" He cocked his head in question. "Feel anything?"

"Okay. Okay," she muttered. "I guess it's not broken." She pushed up to sit, and brushed his arm away. "I seriously doubt that your stomach-finger-brushing thing is a recognized test for loss of sensation, though."

"It's real new." He offered her a hand. "I realize this is futile, but..."

She was shaky, and told herself she was tired from clambering over the wall. With great reluctance, she accepted his hand. "Just pull."

He straightened to stand, hefting her up. She felt wobbly and flinched at the stab of pain coming from her tailbone. She was sure to have a bruise tomorrow.

He didn't let go of her hand, tugging her down the slope. "I love the ocean at night."

She peeked at him. He was a step ahead of her, pulling her along the path. The moon was a sliver of weak light off in space, but she could see well enough. The sand was so white it fairly glowed with a strange luminescence.

The night breeze tossed her hair and caressed her scorching face. Her stomach sizzled, and she had a sinking feeling it wasn't due to the scrape, but the remnants of the doc's absurdly erotic touch.

If she were to tell the whole truth, it wasn't pain she felt, it was the stirring of banked fires. This was her wedding night, after all. She'd been preparing for tonight with every fiber of her being—the fulfillment of her love for a man who'd turned out to be a world-class stinker. Dana supposed it wasn't all that odd that she might react strongly to another good-looking man who touched her intimately and gave off sparks of sexuality. She was primed, and he was prime.

She compelled her gaze away from his broad back. She didn't need this! What was she doing out here with him, anyway? How did this hap— Oh, *right*. He was suspicious and didn't plan to let her out of his sight.

She glowered at him. "My spy submarine is a thousand yards out. How am I supposed to signal it if *you're* hanging around?"

He turned and winked, and her stupid knees went mushy. "That's the point, Angelfish."

She yanked from his grasp. "You *really* think I'm up to no good, don't you?"

He gave her a level look, his smile dimming. "It's crossed my mind."

She wished she could tell him the truth. But she didn't know what he might do. He seemed honest enough, but so had Tate. Just because this guy was good to animals didn't mean he couldn't be bought.

She cast her gaze to the sand, staring absently as the ocean pushed a frothy offering almost to her toes, then with a whispering sigh returned to the sea. "Well, I'm not." With a rush of bravado, she looked him straight in the eye. "I'm exactly what you see. Nothing more." Okay, so that was a lie. Two weeks from now, maybe she'd tell him everything. But not now.

He pursed his lips, those bedroom eyes lazily taking her in from her breeze-tossed hair to her flip-flop rubber sandals, compliments of Cook. When his gaze returned to her face, he grinned. "Ever been skinny-dipping, Angelfish?"

"Uh—" Thank heaven she was so stunned by the question it took her a few seconds to respond. She had just enough time to remember she wasn't supposed to know if she'd ever been skinny-dipping or not. "I—I sincerely doubt it!"

"Wanna go?" He reached for his waistband, plainly intent on shoving down his shorts.

"No!" She whirled away. "Don't you dare take off your clothes!"

"Too late." She heard a slap-splashing sound. He was running into the surf. "Are you sure you don't want to join me?"

She gulped in a breath, which wasn't easy for some reason. Her heart thudded a mile a minute. "You're a pervert, you know!"

"The water's great."

"You're twisted!"

He didn't answer.

"Did you hear me?" she called. "You're sick!"

No response.

Finally, she had to turn and look. What if he drowned out there? "Sam!" she called. "Don't be a fool! You're not supposed to swim alone—especially at night!" She bit her lip. Would an amnesia victim know that? Darn the man and his trickery. He did that on purpose to fluster her and make her flub her story. He hadn't been able to do it all day while he'd sliced and stitched and lanced revolting pustules. How crafty of him to get her to blunder just shucking his swim trunks.

"Sam!" she cried, fighting an unwelcome stab of worry. He was nowhere to be seen. *"Sam!"* She jabbed a finger down at his swim trunks, her glance following. "Come back and put on these…" Where were they? She let the command trail off. There were no swim trunks on the beach!

He'd been *teasing* her! "Why you…" Planting her fists on her hips, she shouted, "I hope you *drown!*" Twirling away, she trudged up the sandy beach toward the castle. "It would serve you right!"

When she looked up, she stumbled to a halt. There in front of her, lounging casually on the wall, was Sam, glistening and grinning. He sat up and made a "come on" motion.

With clamped jaws, she marched forward.

"Miss me?" he asked, brushing wet hair off his forehead.

She scowled at him, then shook her head. "What are you, some kind of spook?" His grin was so irresistible and utterly unfair she wanted to smack his knee. "Shouldn't you be checking your patients or something?"

"Just did."

"Maybe you should check them again."

"Your concern is admirable." He jumped down with easy grace and relaxed against the wall. "Does this mean I'll see you bright and early in the clinic?"

He crossed his legs at the ankles, idling there, tall and handsome. *The rat.*

"Do I have a choice?" she asked, startled by the raspy quality of her voice.

"No choice at all, Angelfish." He grinned.

She opened her mouth to protest, but anything she might have been about to say flew out of her head when he took her into his arms and hoisted her to the top of the wall.

She squealed, then gasped as her bottom was settled onto cool stone. Before her head quit reeling, Sam catapulted himself to the other side. Dana felt his hands at her waist, and all too quickly her feet touched grass. He let her go, and she sagged against the wall.

"That wasn't so horrible, was it?" Amusement rode his tone.

She ran a hand through her hair and glared at him. "You had no right to do that!"

"I thought I was helping."

She was angry, both at herself for her ridiculous heart rate, and at him for taking such physical liberties. Was there no escape from dominating men? "Well, you weren't helping. You were *controlling!*" She pushed away from the wall. "I resent your suspicions, Doc. Don't believe for one second I don't know why you're keeping me practically glued to your hip in that clinic! But I'll do it—I'll do it because I owe your aunt for her kindness, and because I know how much she loves her cats. But I want you to be assured, if it weren't for her, I wouldn't set foot in that clinic! I *hate* controlling men, and never again will I allow a man to maneuver me or coerce me into doing anything! Is that clear?''

She stalked by him, aware that his grin was gone. *Good enough!* she thought.

''So, we have a past, do we?''

6

"SO, WE HAVE A PAST, do we?" Sam's question echoed in Dana's brain, firing a shot of terror through her. *Oh, no!* She'd revealed too much! With an apprehensive inhale, she spun on him.

His gaze was speculative under drawn brows.

What was she going to do? Her mind stumbled around for something credible. Anything. Any thread to clutch. She lifted her chin as she stalled and struggled for a believable insight. *"Maybe!"* she blurted, fighting to gather her wits. "Maybe—maybe your man-handling brought something to the surface."

There! That was good! She could go with that! She chose her words carefully. "I don't know what exactly it was. But, yes. Yes, obviously I've known men like you in my past, and it seems the experience was vastly unpleasant!" She regarded him with searching gravity. Was he buying this? "I should thank you for bringing back a sliver of my memory—no matter how distasteful you were going about it!" Dana couldn't imagine why she felt it necessary to make such a cutting remark. Or possibly she knew. She needed to make sure he didn't smile that sexy smile at her again.

He pursed his lips, looking annoyed, then, after a tense moment, he shrugged. "Glad to be of service,

Angelfish.'' Dana was startled when he took her elbow. ''Allow me to *control* you back to your room.''

She glared at him, and tried to pull away, but failed.

His response was a calculating grin. ''Maybe on the way, I can provoke a few more memories.''

''I don't see why not! You're the *most* provoking man I've ever met!''

''To your knowledge, you mean.''

She glowered at him. ''I'm willing to give you the benefit of the doubt.''

His chuckle was hardly more than a grunt, and Dana sensed it held little humor. ''Your dumb act is blown, Angelfish.''

She peered his way. ''Uh—what dumb act?''

''The one where you look at me with those big green eyes and pretend you don't understand the meaning of the word 'salad fork.'''

She harrumphed. ''That's two words.'' They arrived at the patio steps, and Dana felt as if she was being dragged to the gallows. He was right, of course. She'd completely forgotten her naive-blond guise tonight. ''Why would anybody *pretend* to be dumb?'' she asked, hoping she sounded sincere. ''You're as nutty as a fruitcake—as crazy as a loon—bigger than a bread—uh...'' She ran a hand through her hair, thinking fast. She was scraping the bottom of her cliché barrel.

''It's not going to work this time,'' he cut in.

Feeling trapped, she glared at him, but opted not to respond.

He opened the door that led in from the patio, allowing her to precede him. "You're smarter than you want us to believe. What are you hiding?"

Though he'd let her go as she entered, once inside, his hand closed around her wrist. It was quite dim, with a few dwindling candles to light their way. A sleeping cat, here and there, stirred or meowed at the audacious interlopers. Dana clamped her jaws. She had no intention of making any admissions.

"Well?" Sam coaxed.

She didn't face him, though he'd dropped back to be even with her. "You're a suspicious man. I'm sorry for you."

A tense minute passed as they began to climb the stairs. She could feel his stare. "Is that all you have to say?"

"No." She pulled on his grasp. "You're hurting me." She shifted to glare at him.

His jaw muscles clenched. "No, I'm not."

She yanked. "It's my arm and I say you are!"

"Quit yanking and it won't hurt."

She halted, forcing him to come to a stop. Halfway up the curving stairway, candlelight from the top of the landing faintly touched them. Dana leaned against the wall and raised her captured hand in front of her face. His touch wasn't painful. Not physically, but she didn't relish her tingly reaction.

"What are you up to?" he asked. "Don't tell me you're a karate expert, and you're getting me in position to throw me down the stairs."

She shook her head.

"What, then?"

It almost made her smile to realize he not only

doubted her, he was a little intimidated by her. Or at least what he imagined she was capable of.

She grinned in spite of herself. No man on earth had ever been intimidated by Dana Vanover. Though she was capable in a lot of areas—she fixed cars, did her own taxes, even replaced roof shingles—no man on earth had ever been *intimidated* by her.

Because she idolized her father, she'd always held men in some awe. Luckily, she hadn't fallen head-over-heels in love before smooth-talking Tate came along, or she might be a babbling idiot in some home for terminal suckers by now. Well, Dana was a fast study. She wouldn't make *that* mistake, again. Her father had been the exception in men, not the rule.

So here she stood, connected to this big, strong hunk, and he was intimidated by the mystery she presented. No doubt Sam envisioned her as some kind of Emma Peele character or female James Bond of the underworld. How laughably irresistible!

"What are you smiling about?"

She shook her head and stifled the grin. "Nothing. Just—never mind…" Unfortunately she wasn't in a position to share the joke with him. Dropping her arm, she resumed her trek up the stairs. Sam remained a step behind her, and it almost seemed as though she pulled him along.

Maybe Sam was a man she could get to grovel, after all. He was a gorgeous man who believed she was a crook. From time to time, didn't all men fantasize about walking on the wild side? Was she "the wild side" to the kitty doctor?

They reached the top of the staircase in silence. The thick stub of a beeswax candle flickered atop a tall, iron stand. The faint sweet wax fragrance mingled with the lavender permeating every castle byway.

Dana faced him, far from surprised that he observed her grimly. She smiled again, her mystery-maiden flight of fancy providing her with a curious boldness. "Thanks for the escort, Doc." With a tug, she indicated her desire to be released. "I'd invite you in for a drink—" she fluttered her lashes, mischievously "—but, I don't like you."

He watched her closely without releasing her arm. "What's going on, Angel?"

He clearly sensed her change, but didn't know what to make of it. She lifted a shoulder in a subtly flirtatious shrug. In all honesty, she had no idea what she was doing. She only knew it was fun being enigmatic for a change. "Why, whatever do you mean, Sam?" She gave the query a decidedly coy tone.

Sam's lips parted slightly. His puzzlement tickled Dana. She had never toyed with a man. Never even flirted. Her new brazenness was due, in part, to Tate's harsh lesson. But she was also reacting to the fact that this should have been her wedding night, and that this powerful male animal, with the bedroom eyes and silky touch, turned her on unmercifully. To think he might willingly become putty in her walk-on-the-wild-side hands, titillated her.

She was a bubbling cauldron of mixed emotions— angry at him for what he'd put her through in the clinic today, and for his everlasting suspicions. But unhappily for Dana, her body throbbed with a wayward urge to taste his excessively kissable-looking lips.

You are a sick woman, Dana Vanover, she warned

herself. But she was a woman *first*. A woman, who for the first time in her life, deliberately and with malice of forethought, wielded power over a man— even if her only true power was the tired old fantasy of tasting forbidden fruit.

"You want to kiss me, don't you, Sam?" she whispered, astonished to hear such nervy words coming out of her mouth.

His eyes widened slightly and she reveled in her power. Her sly smile fairly screamed, *I am forbidden fruit. Lust after me!*

He hesitated, measuring her quizzically. Dana could tell he was no longer in full command of his world. This moment of indecision was doubtless the first twinge of uncertainty in his adult life. *Good!* Let him be insecure. See how he liked it, for a change!

"Yes," he said, sounding hoarse. "I guess—I do…"

Warming to the experiment, she lifted her chin.

She watched as he swallowed, plainly tossing around the pros and cons. Should he or shouldn't he? She was a stranger who had washed up on his beach, practically naked. Her arrival was mysterious, and very likely a foreboding of treachery afoot. It was a romantic scenario suitable to open any James Bond movie.

She wanted to laugh out loud. Dana Vanover, treacherous librarian of mystery!

Something hot and sizzly touched her lips. Shocked, she lurched away. "What do you think you're *doing?*"

He straightened abruptly, as though struck. "I thought…"

Mortified, she jerked on his hold and he let her go. "You were wrong, Doc! Once again, you misjudged me!" He had, hadn't he? She'd never had any intention of kissing the man. Had she?

It was one thing to engage in a little mental exercise, but quite another to act on it. Dana Vanover was no femme fatale. She was a lonely, frustrated librarian who was obviously not thinking straight. "It's been a long day," she muttered. "I'm going to bed."

"In a minute, Angel," he muttered.

With stunning suddenness, he claimed her lips with his. She didn't know if it was the unexpectedness of the act, or the kiss, that threw her senses into a wild swirl, but she was instantly dizzy. Her arms tingled with the need to snake up and curl around his neck, but she couldn't lift them. They hung at her sides like limp pasta. Her legs were hardly more substantial. If he hadn't crushed her in his arms, she would have been sprawled on the floor in a dead faint.

His mouth moved hungrily, searching, demanding a response. *Oh, Lord! This couldn't be happening.* Desperately she tried to hate his taste, his texture, tried to struggle, but nothing happened. But the kiss. The kiss went on, deliriously and beautifully on....

With a sinking feeling, Dana realized that there was nothing to hate about the experience—and everything to adore. This veterinarian was as talented at kissing as he was at healing—and leaping tall obstacles in a single bound. Was there nothing he couldn't do?

His lips cajoled and beguiled, flooding her limbs with new energy. Unable to help herself, she began to kiss him back. Her arms stole upward to encircle his neck, relishing the hard heat of his flesh. Her lips parted, surrendering to his lusty petition for a deeper, more exhilarating taste.

She moaned against his mouth, her heart soaring even as her brain recoiled. What was she doing? Where did she think this would lead?

With the quickness of a lightning bolt, the kiss ended, and Dana was set away. She found herself swaying unsteadily, staring into Sam's face. She blinked, trying to get him in focus.

"*Now* you may go to bed." He folded his arms across his chest. "I don't know what that little performance was all about, but..." A muscle flexed in his jaw. "Don't come on to me again, unless you're prepared to get what you ask for."

She gaped, appalled. She *had* asked for that kiss— at the very least! In fact, she'd practically said, *Do me, Doc!* Was she deranged?

His jaw shifted from side to side. "I'll see you at seven-thirty in the clinic. Don't be late."

Before she could find her voice, he stepped into his room and soundlessly closed the door.

SAM DIDN'T SLEEP very well. Hell, he didn't sleep at all. What had come over him last night? He *knew* better. With a curse, he threw off the sheet and tugged on a pair of shorts. It was still dark, but he might as well get up. He had a full day ahead of him in the clinic. He took a step toward the door, then stopped, peering over his shoulder.

The woman.

With a burdened exhale, he silently entered the bathroom, then turned the knob that led to her room. He was surprised when he met with no resistance from a barricade. As he cracked the door, he told himself he was merely making sure she was there, asleep.

She was. She lay on her side, facing him, wearing a T-shirt of his. A trace of pale, bare hip was exposed to his view. She looked sweet in repose. Even innocent—in a cruelly sexual way. His gut tightened and he scowled, irritated that his body didn't react to her with even the slightest degree of antagonism.

From his vantage point he counted three cats in bed with her. One that looked surprisingly like Pouncer, rested its head on her ankle. A second, he couldn't see very well, lay behind her on her pillow. The third, snow-white and definitely Mr. Chan, was curled against her breast. She'd draped an arm across it, cuddling the lucky little bastard close.

He winced at the contrary thought and backed out, stealthily closing the door.

Angelfish had made a *big* mistake when she came on to him last night. He had to admit, she was good. Even knowing she was a liar and most likely a career criminal, she'd made him lose focus for a minute. He didn't know what the hell she was planning, but he didn't intend to get sucked into her trap. All she'd accomplished with her female razzle-dazzle was to firm up his suspicions and put him on full alert.

A nagging inner voice taunted, *That's not all she firmed up, Gomer.*

"Oh, shut up!" He flinched as he bounded down the stairs. "Hell," he muttered. "She's got me talking to myself!"

THE NEXT TWO DAYS were pure hell for Dana, forced to spend countless hours in close proximity to Sam.

Practically attached to his hip, she assisted him in doctoring Beena's precious felines. Every minute his scent taunted and the memory of his kiss grew more and more troubling. It seemed as though she'd been required to look into those deceptively sleepy eyes, tens of thousands of times, only to see distrust and hostility flare in their depths.

On the up side, she stopped heaving her cookies by Monday afternoon. The other "up" thing was, today was Beena's birthday, and there would be a party tonight. Dana had become very fond of the eccentric woman, and looked forward to their Bingo games after dinner. One surprising thing Dana discovered about herself was that she enjoyed having a cat curled in her lap and was starting to feel almost naked without one.

She still thought Mona was extremely weird. She looked a little too much like the living dead for Dana's peace of mind. But she did smile every so often. An eerie sight to say the least. Dana almost expected to see Dracula fangs when she bared her teeth.

Madam Rex had been the antithesis of what Dana expected. The woman looked more like a stock broker or a real-estate agent than a cat astrologist, in her linen suits, three-inch heels and perfectly coifed, platinum chignon. Though on the surface Madam Rex looked cool and businesslike, she jabbered like a magpie, and had a guffaw so high and screechy it wrenched birds out of trees and into frenzied flight.

"Shall we go, Angel?"

Dana was jerked from her reverie by Sam's hand

at her elbow. The dratted suspicious doctor escorted her everywhere she went. On the surface, to the staff, he looked like a gentleman. But deep in his eyes she read the true story. He didn't trust her as far as he could fling her.

She glanced his way. "I thought I'd stay in the clinic. With a couple of discarded swabs and suture thread I figured I'd build myself a time bomb."

"Didn't MacGyver do that once?"

"Who's MacGyver?" She didn't know if amnesiacs were supposed to have gaping holes in their memories when it came to TV reruns, but she was taking no chances.

His lips quirked in a cynical smile. "Touché." She felt herself being propelled toward the exit as Sam nodded a friendly goodbye to the night shift. "So, who are you coming to the party as?"

She frowned, confused. "What?"

"The birthday party. We're supposed to come as our favorite singer."

She studied him, her frown intensifying. "You're joking."

A wry brow rose. "Beena's birthday party is no joking matter."

"Who are you coming as?"

"Elvis."

Dana stared.

"No cracks." He steered her toward the stairs. "It's Beena's request. She loves Elvis."

"Even though he's a man?"

"Beena thinks he had more whimsy than most men."

"He had more something, but I wouldn't have

called it whimsy." She gave him a serious once-over. "I suppose you look a little like Elvis, around the kisser, *lips!*" She bit her tongue, wishing she could cut the mutinous thing out. Talk about Freudian slips! That had not only been a slip, it had been the corset, cincher, bustle and pantaloons! Obviously her rigorous attempts over the past forty-eight hours to banish memories of those gifted lips had been an unqualified failure.

Sam made no comment, but his grip at her elbow tightened. No words were necessary for her to understand that the subject was not his favorite, either.

"I don't think I'll go to the party," she said once she got her voice back. "I'm worn out."

"You're going."

She shot him a look of incensed indignation. "You're not my keeper!"

"Dream on, Angelfish." He eyed her levelly. "I am your keeper, your shadow, your worst nightmare." They climbed the stairs side by side, his pace deliberate, as though he intended to sustain his intimidation for as long as possible. "Until you give me a solid, credible reason to trust you, I'm going to hound your every move."

She glared at him. Unfortunately her stupid power experiment the other night had made things worse. "You haven't trusted me since I washed up on the beach!" she said.

"Yes, I did. For about five minutes."

She dropped her gaze, unsettled by the intensity of his stare. "I wouldn't hurt your aunt," she murmured, too tired to fight. "Never in a thousand years."

"I've heard that before." They reached the top of

the staircase and he shifted her to face him. "Look at me."

She had no intention of obeying his barked order, yet she found herself lifting her gaze. She glowered, stiff and unhappy.

His lips crooked in a mocking grin. "Because of me, my aunt lost something very valuable a few years ago. I'd taken over the hiring of her staff, thinking she wasn't business-like enough." He laughed, the sound caustic. "I knew so much. I saw right through to people's souls." His blue eyes flashed fire. "I hired a sweet little thing as a housemaid. Barely eighteen and right off the farm, she looked as naive as Kansas corn. A month later she disappeared with—something Beena treasured." His nostrils flared, and Dana had the feeling he was experiencing a stab of self-recrimination.

"Beena kept me and my dad from starving after the accident. I owe her everything. If it weren't for her I wouldn't be a veterinarian today. I don't know what I'd be—or where."

"Accident?" She heard the word as she spoke it.

He winced. "Hurricane. The shelter wall collapsed. My mother, my little sister..." He gritted his teeth and looked away, as though trying to escape a painful vision.

"They were killed?"

He didn't speak for a moment. "My father was a paraplegic after that. We had no insurance. Beena paid his medical bills for the rest of his life. And how did I repay her? By sending a thief to her on a silver platter." His voice lashed out, but Dana detected the

crack of emotion. "It won't happen again, Angel."
His stare was hard. "Do you understand?"

So they'd both been fooled by a skillful con, huh?
She experienced a pinprick of empathy, and had to
fight the urge to hug him. No wonder he was so suspicious of her and so protective of his aunt. Dana's
anger melted away. She wondered for a quick moment if she could trust him, tell him why she was
here. But as quickly as the thought struck, she batted
it back.

She didn't dare. In a little over a week she would
be free to come clean without fear that Tate could
still pull off his scam. "I—I see," she said softly,
then indicated her door. "This is where I get off."

She moved toward the entrance, noting that his
hand remained on her elbow. He wasn't giving her
an inch. That was fine, for now. She'd already done
all the sabotage that needed doing. Unless the doc
decided to leave before the two weeks were up. In
that case, he'd find his boat suddenly dead in the water. Meanwhile, she opted to work on *not* inciting any
more distrust in the man than she already had.

At her door she arranged her face placidly. "I've
thought of a singer I can come to the birthday party
as, who's even more whimsical than Elvis."

He pressed down on the handle, unlatching her
door and pushing it open. "I'm locking you in. Be
ready at seven."

Dana's animosity flared in spite of her vow not to
aggravate him. She was getting pretty weary of his
dictates. "Flatterer," she cooed, batting her lashes.
"I bet you say that to *all* the hostages." With a sar-

castic smirk, she stepped inside her room and slammed the door.

SAM SAT BESIDE his great-aunt at a long table on the patio. The guests consisted of all staffers not specifically on duty. They laughed and chattered, enjoying Beena's birthday rose petal ice cream. Dinner had consisted of rose petal sandwiches and rose hip tea. Sam ate nine of the little triangular mouthfuls, but felt as if he could still down a couple of burgers. Visiting an island full of women and trying to subsist on finger food had its drawbacks. He took another bite of the pink-tinted ice cream blended with real petals, striving *not* to follow Angel's every move.

She looked cute in her makeshift Carmen Miranda costume. She wore a bright purple-and-yellow-print shirt, tied beneath her breasts. A pair of mauve silk boxers served as modest underwear. A green-and-blue-striped woven table covering, tied at her waist, became a long skirt with a side slit. Sam had no idea how, but she'd managed to attach a bunch of bananas to the top of the jade towel wrapped like a turban around her head. Bunches of grapes hung from the towel for earrings.

Damn it if she hadn't won first prize in the costume contest. Oh, sure, she'd tried not to accept the little ruby and gold drop necklace, but Beena—being Beena—had insisted. He took another bite of his ice cream and eyed the blonde with misgiving. She'd certainly wormed her way into his great-aunt's heart. It didn't hurt that she'd volunteered to cut the tunafish cake. He watched her, placing china plates full of the stuff on the patio surface for the swarming cats.

"Angel's such a dear child," Beena said, drawing Sam from his morose preoccupation with a woman he didn't trust but craved like hell.

Sam glanced at his aunt. "I'm not sure about her. She's not being open with us."

"Sammy, love, she has amnesia." Beena placed a tiny, cool hand on his arm. In a black turtleneck and slacks, and with her hair plastered down around her face and tinted chocolate brown, she looked like a withered, smaller-than-scale Beatle. Sam wasn't sure if she was supposed to be Ringo or Paul, and decided not to incite her exasperation by asking.

"Sammy, love, how can our Angel be open when her mind is closed, even to her?"

Sam frowned. "I don't believe she has amnesia."

Beena looked bewildered for a second, then tittered. "Silly Sammy." She patted his arm lovingly. "Of course she does." She fluttered a beringed hand in the blonde's direction. "Look at that costume! Carmen Miranda was from Cuba! Doesn't that make you realize Angel is subconsciously trying to get her memory back?"

"I don't think Carmen Miranda was from Cuba. I think she was from Brazil."

"Pish tosh." Beena waved off his correction. "Spanish is Spanish."

"Unless it's Portuguese," he murmured.

"What did you say, love?"

"I think Portuguese is spoken in Brazil."

Beena rolled her eyes. "Well, how would Angel know that? She has—"

"Amnesia, I know," Sam said, defeated. He'd never figured out how to fight his aunt's non-logic.

Beena leaned nearer to her grand-nephew. "Speaking of Cuba..." She tittered again, lifting a hand to hide her mouth from the others sitting around the table. "I foiled the border patrol, yesterday."

Sam experienced a twinge of unease, but had no idea why. Her comment made absolutely no sense. He bent down so he could hear her better. "Did you say something about a border collie?" He hoped.

"No, Sammy!" Beena grinned broadly. "The border *patrol.* I foiled them!"

Sam shook his head, still not getting it. "What border are you talking about?"

"The United States, Sammy. Don't be dim!" She pinched his cheek, giving him her why-can't-you-be-more-whimsical look. "Yesterday while I was down on the dock, fishing with Whiskers and Sweetmeat, they swung by in one of those sleek 'Go Fast' boats."

"They?"

"Two border patrol men."

"What made you think they were I.N.S.?"

She looked confused. "I.N.S.? What's I.N.S.?"

"Immigration and Naturalization Service—Border patrol."

Beena nodded and smiled in understanding. "Ah." She took another bite of her ice cream. It seemed like a year before she swallowed. "Well, these patrol officers asked me if we'd seen or heard of anybody strange on the island."

Sam felt peculiarly apprehensive. "Did they specifically mention a woman?"

Beena shook her head. "No, but I knew they were asking about Angel."

Sam remembered the "foiled" remark and a knot tightened in his gut. "What did you tell them?"

She giggled. "Well, naturally I told them this was a very small, private island and with our security system, nobody strange could possibly be on our island."

That was a matter of debate. Everybody on the island was a little strange. He frowned at her. "You told them that?"

"Of course, Sammy." She shook her head at him at though he were a lost cause in the whimsy arena. "I wouldn't think of being a party to sending that sweet child back. Besides, she's not *strange* at all." She giggled at her little witticism.

Sam closed his eyes and counted to ten. What had his aunt done? At the very least Angelfish was truly an amnesiac who's family was desperately searching for her. At worst, those men were cops hunting down a criminal. "Did they show you badges?"

She made a scrunched-up face. "No, silly. They didn't have the time. I suppose if I'd told them Angel was here, they'd have produced the badges so they could drag her away. But why get all official when they think there's nobody to drag off?"

Sam exhaled long and low. *Damn.* "What did they say?" he asked, trying to keep the exasperation out of his voice.

Beena lifted skinny shoulders and let them fall. "Nothing. Just frowned a little, looked at each other, gunned the engine of their boat and phfffff-fffft—" she wagged her fingers toward the sea "—they were gone."

Sam stared, disbelieving. "But, Aunt Beena..."

She patted his cheek. "Not another word, Sammy.

You're getting worry lines and you're way too young for that.'' She stood, then watched him for a moment, her expression going serious. ''You're still eaten up about that maid who stole dear Norman's gift to me.'' Her lips pressed into a thin, melancholy smile.

The sight of that sad, hard-fought smile, the glitter of memory in her eyes, caused Sam more agony than any ranting or raving could ever do. ''Sammy. The ring was merely a symbol of his affection. If he hadn't died on the eve of our wedding...''

She faltered, freshening her smile with obvious difficulty. ''I still can't believe that the darling, sweet man had already made out his will to leave me his entire fortune. Such a sweet thing to do.'' She sighed. ''I'll always have the memory—of the world's most whimsical man. The ring...''

She shook her head and gently stroked his temple. Sam could tell she was making an effort to recover her voice. ''Don't let the theft of that ring make you jaded, Sammy, love. I don't blame you.'' She licked her fingers, then repaired the Elvis lock on his forehead. ''I could never be mad at my darling Elvis. You're human, so you're not perfect. Though I rarely admit it out loud, I'm not quite perfect, myself.''

She glanced at Dana, chatting with Bertha, who was dressed like the head-bustingest Madonna Sam could possibly imagine. ''I suppose our Angel isn't perfect, either.'' She gave Sam a fond slap on the cheek. ''But I'd throw my lucky brooch into the sea before I'd believe that sweet girl is out to bilk me of a thing.'' She stroked the diamond kitty pen on her shirt. Sam knew it was Beena's other most treasured gift from her late, everlastingly lamented fiancé, lost so long ago. "Now stop fretting and have fun. It's my birthday, and I insist!"

He frowned and opened his mouth to speak, but Beena shushed him. "Go over there and get that pile of silk scarves by the door, Sammy."

He started to protest, to insist Beena be on her guard, but she gave him a shove. "Go—*go!* Daylight's wasting."

He passed by Madam Rex, costumed as Dolly Parton, and Mona, a remarkable likeness for a totally wasted Mick Jagger. The two women relaxed on lounge chairs, munching rose petal desserts. Mona's baby iguanas clung to the dirty-white T-shirt that hung loosely over her scrawny chest.

With great reluctance, he peered toward the table that supported the big tuna sheet cake slathered with cream cheese icing. The surface of the table teemed with cats that had decided to forgo the nicety of a plate.

Bertha and Angelfish backed away in self-defense, laughing as the painstakingly decorated kitty dessert became trampled hash. Sam shook his head. He'd be treating more than a few cases of tuna hangover tomorrow.

He heard Angel laugh. The sound seemed unnaturally loud amid the din of thirty-odd party-goers and carousing cats. Irritated that his brain seemed bent on singling her out by sight *and* sound, Sam snatched up the scarves. He had no idea what his aunt had in mind. Knowing her, it could be anything from making silk kites, to using them as blindfolds for a game of pin-the-tail-on-everybody. He returned to Beena's side as she began to tap on a water goblet to get everybody's attention.

"Okay, okay. Dinner's over," Beena shouted. "Let the games begin!"

Sam felt her take his arm and hug it to her. "Since it's my birthday, I make the rules, as usual. And, as usual, I have complete sway over who wins."

She tugged one scarf from Sam's fingers and held it high. "First, we're going to have a three-legged race. Each team will have three scarves with which to tie their legs together—one leg per team member, that is—at the thigh, knee and ankle." She cleared her throat importantly. "After much reflection, I have settled on these two-man teams. There shall be no substitutions! My word is law. I have the list right here." She flipped her hand so a piece of paper snapped open. "Without further ado—team one, Bertha and Eartha. Team two, Madam Rex and Mona..." As Beena read down the list, Sam scanned it. He read the bad news, and peered at Angel, catching her frowning his way.

He sensed she dreaded what he already knew. Angelfish-of-the-wrinkled-brow would be his partner in the three-legged race.

He wasn't any happier about it than she looked. The last thing he needed was to be tied bodily to the woman. Ever since he'd grabbed her and kissed her two nights ago, he'd been furious with himself. He'd known *then* that getting hot and bothered for a con artist was mega *stupid*. So, what had he done? He'd grabbed the woman and kissed the hell out of her. He gritted his teeth, forcing back the notion that it had been the purest sensual experience of his life. Damn it.

Damn her!

"Team eight, Angel and Sammy."

Sam saw her wince, making it obvious she was no more thrilled than he. For some grotesquely absurd reason, that fact pricked his pride. In a surge of annoyance at her for making him crazy, he flashed his most sardonic grin.

She squeezed her eyes shut and mouthed something. He had a hunch it wasn't "Hallelujah!"

7

DANA MANAGED TO MAKE IT through dinner and dessert without saying a word to Sam. She knew it wasn't the best way to make herself seem less dishonest, but she also knew Sam was so suspicious she could probably tell him the truth, and he would only stare at her with that I-wasn't-born-yesterday scowl.

Why Beena paired her with Sam for the three-legged race was anybody's guess. Dana would never have imagined the elderly woman had cupid inclinations, but it was beginning to look that way. How ironic! She and Sam were about as likely to become a compatible pairing as the Miami Dolphins and the Bolshoi Ballet.

She caught movement out of the corner of her eye and shifted, wary. Oh, no! Here he came. Elvis Sherlock Holmes, carrying three scarves in his fist. It was a real shame he looked so…whimsical. Yes, whimsical was a better word for her to use than sexy, since she was about to be bound to him, and she was still trying to forget how he tasted.

He wore a loose white silk shirt, open midway down his chest, silver belt buckle, form-fitting white silk pants and white bucks. He wore his hair the way Elvis had, a heavy lock curled in the middle of his forehead. And just to make her totally nuts, a silver medallion hung from a heavy chain around his neck, flashing as he walked, drawing her attention to his chest, over and over and over.

She stood on the lawn near what had been determined to be the starting area. She shifted from foot to foot, glancing across the golf-green turf to where a couple of servants had been posted. A long strip of crepe paper stretched between them served as the finish line.

Sam came to a stop in front of her, giving her costume a quick once-over. Her heart fluttered maddeningly, but she told herself she didn't give a fig what he thought.

"May I have a banana?" he asked. "I'm starving."

She met his gaze as he plucked a grape from her earring and popped it into his mouth.

"Hey, you're eating my costume!"

"You're lucky you're not wearing steak and potatoes." He relieved her of another grape and popped it into his mouth.

"Didn't you eat dinner?" She knew very well he had. She'd caught herself peeking at him a time or two. Or six hundred. With a little more force than necessary, she yanked at a banana, only managing to slide the turban askew over her eyes. As she straightened the headdress, she succeeded in breaking a banana off the bunch.

Sam took it and began to peel. "Don't tell Beena, but as far as I'm concerned, rose petals are a poor substitute for food."

"I'll leave it out of my report," she wisecracked, looking him up and down. This getting-tied-together thing was a bad idea. She had to figure out a way to get out of it. But how? Maybe if she came up with a good enough argument? "This game is dangerous. You'll stomp all over my bare feet with your big shoes."

He took a bite of the banana, glanced at her, then at his shoes. "I'll take them off."

She grimaced. She'd wanted him to say something like, "Rather than ruin my look, let's forget the whole thing, *chiquita!*"

Scraping the heel of one shoe against the toe of the other, he stepped out of one white buck, then the other. He wagged his brows. "Okay?"

No, it wasn't okay! She thought fast. "You're too big to be my partner." She swept an arm out. "Beena partnered everybody else according to size. You outweigh me by a hundred pounds!"

He finished the banana and tossed the peel beside his shoes. "Yeah? You're the most Junoesque eighty-five-pound anorexic I've ever seen."

Junoesque? Librarian that she was, she knew it meant "stately," "majestic" and "statuesque," but she doubted the naive blonde with amnesia would know. She planted her fists on her hips. "Is that a crack?"

His eyes narrowed as he ambled to her side and butted a hard thigh against her bare leg. "This one okay?"

She backed off. "No."

He nodded and walked around to her other side. "This leg's covered by your skirt. You'll need to take it off?"

"Right after you take off your pants!" she snapped.

"Okay." He grinned and went for the belt buckle.

"No!" She exhaled heavily, then realized she needed to inhale. Her heart thudded stupidly. "Never mind." She touched her bare thigh. "This leg's fine."

He nodded matter-of-factly, and walked back around. "Stick it out."

She glared at him, but did as he ordered.

Once again, he pressed his thigh to hers. "Hold these." He thrust her two of the scarves. "I'll tie."

She clamped her jaws and reluctantly took the scarves. This was *not* happening!

His hand skimmed around her inner thigh and she gasped.

He glanced up. "What?"

She shook her head, swallowing. "Nothing."

He returned to his work, tying the scarf in a double knot.

"We'll never get that off!"

"Sure we will. Hold still." He grabbed another scarf and slid it around her knee. "Our knees don't quite come to the same place."

"No kidding, Sherlock."

He paused, seeming to study the situation. While he considered, he cupped the back of her knee in his palm. The contact was way too warm and bordered on suggestive.

"Would you just tie it, *please!*"

"Don't you want to win?"

"I don't even want to play."

He glanced at her, his gaze speculative. "You look like a player to me."

For some crazy reason, his comment seemed off-color. She crossed her arms in front of her. "I wouldn't know."

He grinned, and a quiver of wayward appreciation raced down her spine. "Right. The amnesia thing. It slipped my mind for a second."

"Just *tie*."

He went back to work, his fingers brushing, stroking and highly unsettling—a torrid counterpoint to the cool, airy silk.

After what seemed like a decade, he finished. They were bound together like a book—a huge, unhappy book from which pages couldn't be torn without bloodshed.

He straightened. "Put an arm around my waist." He slid his arm around her shoulders. "It'll keep us steadier."

She hesitated to unclench her arms from beneath her breasts. For two days he'd looked at her as if she were a rash he couldn't cure. Why was he being so agreeable? "You're awfully helpful."

His brows rose in a resigned shrug of sorts. "She's my aunt."

Dana could accept that. Sam was merely going along to please the woman he owed so much. With a small nod, she slipped an arm behind his back and around his waist.

"Okay, everybody!" Beena shouted from the sidelines. "I want all the partners to walk a little for practice." She looked at her watch. "You have five minutes!"

Dana heard the groan, then realized the sound came from her own throat.

Sam's low laugh rumbled through her, and she peered his way. He squeezed her shoulder. "Let's walk, Angelfish." He watched her for a minute while she glowered at him, then inclined his head. "On the count of three."

On three, Dana stepped out with her left foot as Sam propelled her right foot forward, leaving her upper torso trailing behind. She squealed as she began to fall. Sam's arm tightened around her, saving her toppling bacon.

"I meant, on three step forward with your *tied* leg."

She flicked him a withering glance. "Oh? You think reading your mind is that easy?" She was so irritated! Not because she'd almost fallen, but because being nestled against him ignited ever nerve in her body. Her pulse was behaving like that of an adolescent Elvis groupie lashed to The King himself. Unsettled, she snapped, "*I'll* count this time."

"That's all right, mama," he drawled Elvisly, glancing at her with twinkling bedroom eyes. "Remember, start with the tied—"

"One!" she shouted, dying for the game to be over. "Two! *Three!*"

This time they managed to take three whole steps before Dana reeled and clung to him bodily. "Wait! You're taking too big steps! I'm not six feet tall!"

"Hell, when we run—"

"If you don't shorten your stride, you'll be dragging my lifeless body behind you." She made quick work of righting herself. The last thing she needed to do was cling to the man! "Is that how you envisioned crossing the finish line?"

"I haven't really dwelled on it."

"Well, *dwell* a little."

"Smaller steps. Check." His jaws worked, and Dana could tell he was finding it more and more difficult to hide his irritation at being partnered with her—aunt or no aunt.

"On the count of three," she said.

He nodded, but didn't look her way.

After several more false starts, they got a rhythm going, and Dana finally felt comfortable with the three-legged thing, but not with her close proximity to Sam. He smelled delicious, and beneath the soft silk shirt, his taut flesh tormented her relentlessly.

As they came to a stumbling halt after their tenth practice walk, her turban was skewed over her eyes; she pushed it back. "Hasn't it been five minutes, yet?" Affliction was ripe in her tone. "It seems like five hours."

"If that was supposed to be a compliment, Angel, you need to work on your people skills."

His cheeky grin added fuel to the fires of her distress. She fought an urge to stick out her tongue, but remembered she'd presented that mutinous bit of anatomy to the doc far too liberally in the past twenty-four hours.

"One minute, people!" Beena blew a whistle to make sure she had their attention. "All teams, move to the starting line!"

"Thank heaven," Dana muttered.

"Okay, we start with the tied leg," he said. "All you have to do is hang on."

She shot him a perturbed look. "That's not what we practiced."

"We didn't practice running."

"We don't have to win, you know."

"It's in my nature to try." His lips crooking wryly. "Isn't it in yours?"

She shook her head, aggravated by his everlastingly sneaky interrogations. "Nice try, Doc. But as far as I know, I'm a loser, and lovin' it."

"Not today, you're not." He slid his hand from her shoulder, crooking it under her arm. His fingertips brushed the side of her breast. "When the race starts, grab my waist and hold on."

"Just be careful what *you* grab." She scooted his hand down her rib cage. He now embraced bare flesh, but the erogenous zoning was less consequential.

"On your mark!" Beena shouted. "Get set!"

Dana felt Sam's muscles tense. She knew at that instant she was out of her element if she had any illusions about keeping up with him. Why did she have to suffer this paralyzing insight a millisecond before Beena blew the starting whistle?

"Go!"

After the first jolting stride, Dana reflexively grabbed Sam around the waist and held on for dear life. The contest became a blur. Every so often her left foot connected with solid ground, but most of the time, she hung around Sam's body like a hundred and twenty-five pound sack of kumquats.

All of a sudden, they lumbered past a fluttering crepe paper tape. Dana had the vague sense they didn't break it. However that thought didn't linger long. Sam made a guttural noise, and the next instant she found herself on the ground. Well, not quite. She was, more or less, on Sam.

"Whew!" He sucked in a gulp of air. "How much do you weigh, woman?"

She was sprawled half on his chest, her left leg thrown over his right. Coming up on one elbow she pushed her turban out of her eyes. "I weigh practically nothing. How *rude* of you to ask." Her smirk was smart-alecky. "Out of shape, Doc?" It gratified her that she could breath normally, while his chest heaved with his effort to take in deep drags of oxygen. "Want me to help you up?"

He frowned, lifted his head, then seemed to reconsider, relaxing back down in the grass. "Angelfish, have you ever seen a horse and wagon when the *wagon* was tired?"

She made a face, struggling to hide her amusement. She had no idea why she found this so funny, but she did. "I told you not to take such big steps. It's your fault." His arm was still around her; his fingers splayed over her bare torso. "By the way, did we win?"

"No, we didn't. Bertha and Eartha won. Probably because nobody had to *drag* anybody on their team."

"Maybe nobody took gigantic, dinosaurian strides, either."

"Dinosaurian, huh?" He tugged off her turban and tossed it aside.

"Hey!" She grabbed for it, but wasn't quick enough. "That's my tutti-frutti hat!"

"It's gone to tutti-frutti heaven. It might have helped if you'd actually been able to see."

"I could see! Part of the time…with one eye…" She couldn't hold back her grin any longer. "Okay, okay. I wasn't much help. So, where did we finish?"

"Second." He squinted, scrutinizing her. "Nice hair."

She ran a hand through the mess. "Second?" She mulled that over, stacking her hands on his chest and resting her chin on them. "Second seems good."

"Considering." His grin was teasing, his heavy-lidded gaze lazily erotic.

She took the bait, trying not to dwell on the fact that the hard length of his body was disconcertingly cozy. "*Considering* you took mutant Abominable Snowman steps."

"Considering I had a Volkswagen lashed to my leg."

She laughed, which was bizarre, since he'd just insinuated she weighed as much as a car! "So what do we win?"

"I hope, food." His hand slid from her rib cage to the middle of her back. Dana sensed he was letting go, and caught her breath in dismay. But he didn't quite relinquish his touch. His hand lingered at the small of her back.

She told herself she was stupid to be alarmed that he might take his hand away. She commanded her body to slip off, get away from his scent, his touch, but nothing happened. Some insubordinate imp in her brain had taken control of the cluster of cells regulating arm and leg function. She had no choice but to idle on top of him, grinning, sniffing, cuddling and—

Cuddling! Dana Vanover have you mislaid your mind?

Where had her good intentions gone—the ones where she'd vowed to shun physical male beauty, to look deeper into a man's soul to discover his worth?

With a new sense of urgency, she shoved herself off, thudding onto her back with a *woof!* She closed her eyes and cursed herself for the pain her abrupt plunge caused.

"I can't give you many points for that dismount," Sam said.

By the time Dana steeled herself to peer at him, he'd come up on one elbow, his expression amused and quizzical.

She indicated their bound legs. "Just untie us, please."

He sat up and began to work the knots loose. After another minute she scooted to her elbows and glanced around, trying not to obsess over his warm fingers brushing against her leg. Strangely enough, two teams still hobbled toward the finish line. The rest were already over the finish line. Some sprawled, as she and Sam. The rest standing, hanging on to each other, laughing so hard they were in tears.

Dana shifted to watch the last teams strive for the finish. One of the couples Dana recognized as part of the cleaning staff. The other team was Mona and Madam Rex. Mona virtually dragged her teammate, who kept crumbling to one knee and screeching, "Let me die! Let me die!" But Mona plodded on. Her gaunt features were a study in grim determination, the likes of which could only be found among the living dead, stiff-limbed and blank-eyed as they lurched from the grave to terrorize the living.

Dana couldn't stifle her giggle at the absurd sight.

The other team staggered across the finish line. Two seconds later so did Mona and a caterwauling Dolly Parton.

"There, you're free." Dana felt Sam's hand drop lightly over her knee. She jerked to face him. He lifted the hand and extended it. "Need help getting up?"

She shook her head and pushed up to stand. Rather than look at him, she shifted to watch Madam Rex and Mona. Madam Rex was shrieking something unintelligible as she hauled Mona to the ground and clutched her around the neck. The baby iguanas hopped off Mona's shoulders and scurried to safety.

"Oh, dear!" Dana envisioned murder most foul, and took a step in their direction.

Sam grasped her wrist. "They do this every year. It's tradition."

Dana stared at him. A grin tugged at his lips.

"You *lie!*" she said with a laugh.

His eyes lost their sparkle. "No, Angel. That's your department."

The remark was like a pinprick to a bubble, and the fun went out of the moment. Dana hiked her chin, but couldn't form a reply. Slipping from his grasp, she turned away. "I have a headache. I'm going to bed."

"What about your prize?"

"You eat it for me," she called.

"What if it's not food?"

"Even better!"

He didn't toss back anything caustic, and Dana took a relieved breath. She quickened her pace toward the patio steps.

"Get plenty of rest," he shouted. "The supply boat comes tomorrow."

She faltered, almost tripped. Tomorrow? Already?

Her blood ran cold. There was no way on earth Sam would let that boat leave the island and *not* contact the coast guard.

How was she going to stop him?

8

SAM YANKED OFF HIS SHIRT and dropped down to hunker on the edge of his bed. A cat meowed its objection to being awakened and Sam glanced over his shoulder. "Sorry, Gargantua. Go back to sleep." He exhaled wearily and leaned forward, resting his forearms on his knees. "Damn it! I'm such a fool," he muttered.

It had been an hour since Angel left the party. His body still thrummed with the feel of her, lying on top of him, all curvy and soft. He mouthed a curse. If her plan was to slyly seduce him, make him let down his guard long enough for her to strike and disappear, she wasn't doing half bad.

He groaned and shoved his hands through his hair. What was the matter with him? Why did it seem this woman had taken something from deep inside him the first instant he laid eyes on her—something precious and essential—something he could never get back?

He didn't know much about love. His mother died when he was six, and his aunt had never married. Yet, he was well aware of Beena's abiding devotion to the man who died hours before their wedding was to have taken place. He knew Beena had loved Norman Gaylord so fiercely his death broke her heart. She'd never considered marrying anyone else.

Because of his aunt, Sam knew that a love-at-first-sight-and-forever kind of passion existed. How many times over the years had he heard about the day Norman Gaylord walked up to Beena, a petite nineteen-year old, and asked her out. She'd thought the wealthy entrepreneur was teasing, and she'd made a flip remark that she would be delighted, but she had to sell all the magazines in her stand first.

Norman had bought the stand, lock, stock, and barrel. In Beena's opinion, the romantic act had been exquisitely whimsical. They became engaged a week later.

It was a pleasant little yarn, but Sam had always assumed a man had *some* choice in the matter. Why, then, was he crazy-lost over a lying, conniving...

He shook his head and straightened, trying to get perspective. Hadn't he and Liza been a steady couple for a long time? They'd had their ups and downs, breakups and reconciliations, but they were basically compatible. Though marriage hadn't actually come up. It had been assumed that one day it would happen.

Even so, in these past four years he'd never felt that forever kind of tug in his gut. Lately he'd begun to think that the concept of love, as Beena described it, was romanticized fiction she'd conjured up over the years.

Now he knew differently. He saw the fire and spirit he'd looked for in Liza in a completely unexpected source. In Angel. Now he understood why marriage had never specifically come up, why he hadn't been able to make a permanent commitment to Liza. ''Because it was never love,'' he mumbled. Nothing that even resembled love, or come close to the exhilarating wholeness he felt around a woman who didn't even have a name.

He sank to his back and stared up at the vaulted rafters, a dark realization chilling him.

Doctor Samuel Taylor—straight arrow, and champion of the world's suffering creatures—was in love with a fraud.

THE NEXT MORNING Dana caught a break on her way back to the clinic from the laundry, her arms loaded down with warm-from-the-dryer surgical greens. Bertha whizzed by with the news that the supply boat had docked.

Dana counted herself lucky that Sam kept his own council about his misgivings. Otherwise, Bertha wouldn't have babbled that news flash to *her* of all people. As innocently as she could, she nodded. ''Oh? That's nice.''

The ploy she'd painstakingly worked out would require split-second timing, and had to be pulled off immediately, before anybody called Sam on the intercom with the news. She'd been worrying over the scenario, trying to work it out, since last night when Sam reminded her the supply boat was coming. To pull off her plan, Dana only needed a screwdriver and a narrow window of opportunity. Another lucky break happened when Sam left the clinic for a few minutes to talk to his aunt. *There was her window!*

Now, all she had to do was get Sam to cooperate—just the tiniest bit.

As she reentered the clinic and closed the door,

Sam was pulling off rubber gloves and dumping them in the trash. He dragged off his mask and cap, eyeing her with the same troubled expression he'd aimed at her all morning. The air was so tense Dana could almost feel it pulsating around the room.

She shook herself. She mustn't get sidetracked! It was now or never. She headed into the storage room and stuffed the clean scrubs onto a shelf at the back. Steeling herself for her surprise attack, she screamed. Long and loud.

"What the—"

She heard him, knew he'd be there in a second, so she turned away from the door, positioning herself precisely where she needed to be. She screamed again.

His scuffling footsteps told her when he'd entered the small room, so she flailed her hands, as though in panic.

"What is it?" he shouted.

"Snake!" She pointed vaguely beneath the lowest shelf to her left. "It went under there!"

He moved far enough inside the door for her to initiate Phase One. She stumbled backward, kicking the door with her heels until it clicked shut. All the while she pointed and screamed. "It's poisonous! It tried to bite me!"

Sam's expression was a mix of concern and skepticism. "How could a snake get—"

"There he is!" she cried, jabbing a finger at nothing in particular. "I saw his head for a second!"

Initiate Phase Two!

She leaped to the second shelf of the tall section of wooden shelving on her right and curled her fingers

around the back of an upper shelf. Hanging off the
front the way she was, her weight would topple the
five foot by seven foot framework forward. She only
hoped Sam had fast enough reflexes to jump farther
back in the storeroom to get out of the way.

It began to pitch forward.

"Angel, don't—"

He didn't have time to finish before Dana initiated
Phase Three. She leaped off the collapsing unit onto
the shelving on the left. For good measure, she
shrieked, "It's a coral snake! Save yourself!"

The horrendous crash of the first cabinet almost
drowned out the last of her warning as she got a solid
hold of the now-doomed section of shelving. This one
was filled with paper supplies, rubber gloves, things
that were heavy in bulk, but not breakable. It took
effort to get it tumbling. And worse, Sam stepped in
to try to keep it upright. Reacting quickly, she went
into a hysterical act and swung wildly, knocking him
away in time to keep him from ruining her plan.

The unit lurched forward. Dana sprang away, giving one last panicked scream for good measure, and
did a soft-knee landing on the far side of the storeroom.

The second cabinet fell on top of the first with a
deafening roar, followed by the rumble as supplies
dropped, filtering through the first fallen shelves to
the floor.

As soon as the collapse was a done deal, she clam-
bered onto the top of the pile, reviving her shrieks.

"Damn it, Angel, *shut up!*"

She only had one more phase to complete. Picking
up a clipboard, she wielded it like a weapon. "Climb

up!'' she cried. ''Climb up before it gets you!'' She held the clipboard over her head with both hands. ''Can coral snakes climb? If I see it, I'll *wham* it!'' She swung the board forward, praying she was directly under the light bulb.

She heard a small pop, and the place fell into darkness. She'd hit the bulb on the first try. Glass tinkled onto the ruins, not far in front of her. Though the place was black as tar, from the sound, she didn't think Sam had been close enough to get hit.

''What happened!'' she yelled, adding just the right hint of a moan. *''Sam?''* She shut up. Her job was done.

When there was no sound for a few seconds, she manufactured a sniffle. ''Sam? Are you there?''

''Damn it, where else would I be?''

So far, so good. She pulled her lips between her teeth to keep from grinning. It was very dark, but he might have excellent night vision. ''Are you okay?''

''I'm in better shape than the stock room.''

''You'd better climb up here, so the snake can't—''

''If there ever was a snake, it's a pancake now.''

''What do you mean, *if* there ever was a snake!'' Her indignation echoed around the small room, a wondrous likeness of the real thing.

''We're deep in the castle. A snake couldn't make it all the way in here undetected.''

''I saw it!''

''Okay, okay. We can debate that later. Right now, we have bigger problems.'' He paused. ''Where are you?''

''I'm—I'm standing on the...stuff.''

''Rubble?''

She swallowed a giggle. She was horrible to do this to him. But a lot was at stake. "Uh-huh."

"It's dangerous, especially in the dark. You'd better get off."

"But—what if the snake…"

"Will you give it a rest?" She heard footsteps, then a bang. "*Ouch*. Okay. I'm at the edge. Come to me and I'll help you down."

"Are your arms out?"

"Yes." He sounded as though he was talking with his teeth gritted.

She bent to feel her way with her hands. Then realized she still held the clipboard. She dropped it and it clattered down the four feet of piled shelving to smack against the floor.

"What was that?"

"Just something I was holding. Are you sure your arms are out?"

"I'll check." He sounded exasperated. "Yeah, they're out. Come on."

She felt her way along the back edge of the shelving as though she were crouched on a tightrope. One hand skimmed the edge to her left, for balance. She wagged her right arm in front of her. "I don't feel you."

"Keep coming."

Finally she made contact. "Is that your arm?"

"Does it *feel* like an arm?"

Oh, Lord! She snatched her hand away. "Uh… actually—"

"Hold still," he cut in. "I'll find you."

"No—no. I can do this." She felt higher, and ran

into something. "Is that you?" She prided herself at the dumbness of her question.

"No, it's Laurence Sterne."

Laurence Sterne? He was being sarcastic, but why pick the name of a long-dead British novelist? Dana was crazy about Sterne's *Tristram Shandy,* and wondered if she and Sam had a love for his writing in common, but supposed she would never know. "Sterne?" she asked, manufacturing a puzzled tone. "Is that the shock jock guy?" She forced a giggle as if going along with his joke. "Well, Mr. Sterne, fancy meeting you here."

"It's a small storeroom. Can you find my other hand?"

"I think so." She let go with her balancing hand and waved it around to make contact. When they connected, she vaulted onto him, encircling his waist with her legs. "You don't mind, do you?" she asked. "I'm afraid of snakes."

He stumbled a step backward before his arms came around her. Clearly he hadn't expected her to clobber him with her whole body. "Good Lord, you could warn a guy."

"I'm sorry, Sam." She clung to his neck, her cheek brushing his ear. "I figured you knew what I'd do."

"In the past few minutes I've been pretty clueless about that."

She strangled a laugh. "I can't see a thing. Are there candles in here?"

"On the back shelf, I think."

"Take me back there. What about matches?"

"There should be a box."

"Okay, let's go." She tapped his butt with her feet. "Giddy-up."

"You're in a fine mood for somebody who barely escaped death by snakebite, was nearly crushed by five hundred pounds of shelving, and who has single-handedly destroyed my stock room. Your resilience amazes me."

There was that nasty suspicion in his tone again. Surely he didn't think she could have planned all— well, okay, she *had* planned it. But surely, he couldn't *think* she had! She worked hard at sounding contrite. "I'm sorry, Doc. I guess I'm in shock."

"If this is shock for you, I'm afraid to see what having a good time looks like."

He turned with her toward the back of the store-room. She thought silently, *At least I didn't have to demolish all the shelves. Be happy about that.*

"You know, Angel, either you're the luckiest clumsy woman alive, or you're one of the Flying Wallendas."

She wasn't thrilled with the direction this conversation was taking. Why couldn't the man assume something was an accident with her? Why did he always have to believe she was lying and scheming?

Maybe because you've done nothing but lie and scheme since you met the guy, her mind charged. She told her mind to mind it's own business, then said aloud, "Uh...candles? Which side?"

"I'm backing up to them. Reach out, they should be at shoulder level."

She felt around. "Found them! Now hold me tight." She squeezed her legs more firmly around his waist. "I have to let go with both arms to light these."

"Why don't I let you down?" He sounded as if he was under a strain.

"Am I heavy?" She turned slightly, and felt his breath on her lips. A quiver of longing coursed through her body, but she fought it.

"In a way," he said.

"What about the snake?"

"I'll carry the snake."

She laughed, unable to stop herself. "That's funny, Doc."

"I'm letting you down."

"*No!* I'm lighting a match."

He muttered something, but Dana couldn't make it out. She had a feeling that it was just as well. With the strike of a match they had the miracle of light. Dana blinked, amazed by how bright the flicker of one tiny flame could seem in a pitch- dark room. Hurriedly, she held it to the wick of a chunky beeswax candle, then another. Before she blew out a second match, four candles illuminated the darkness. At least the darkness in the immediate vicinity.

And Sam's eyes—liquid and sensual in candlelight. She had a hard time compelling her gaze to the door, barely visible at the far end of the room.

In the waiting silence, Dana surrendered to the lure of Sam's face. She sensed a hard-fought reserve in his eyes, and sadness. Before she could be positive what she witnessed hadn't been a trick of the light, his lashes slipped to half mast, obscuring his thoughts.

She felt the heavy thud of his heart, and his scent seemed to be all around her. Why hadn't she foreseen that her ploy would require that they be stuck in close proximity for who-knew-how-long? The stillness grew electrified, and a trembling thrill raced through her. The impulse to move that tiny distance toward him, to taste his lips again, was almost a tangible entity, growing larger. Taking over.

She struggled to get herself under control. Faking a laugh, she searched for some way to funnel her thoughts to things that didn't involve kissing him. "Uh—this could be romantic—with the right two people." She cringed. *Yeah, that's funneling your thoughts, idiot!*

He squinted, looking as though he was in pain. "Unclench your legs, Angel. We need to get out of here."

A jolt of regret hit her, and she forced herself to look away before she did anything even more stupid. "Sure, okay." She let go. When her feet were beneath her, he released her and stepped away. It couldn't have been any clearer that he had no desire to linger in her arms—or her legs—if he'd painted the words Go Away! on his forehead.

Turning his back, he rested an arm on the shelf with the candles. After a few seconds he ran a hand through his hair.

"Are you okay?" she asked, wondering at his hesitation. The sport had gone out of her ruse. She was too aware of him, too in need of throwing her arms around his neck and begging for his kisses. How could she be such a selfish, manipulative fool?

She'd done nothing but maneuver this man since she'd met him, and now she wanted to use him to ease her sexual frustrations. What a rat she was! "I—

I didn't strain anything, did I?'' She truly hoped she hadn't caused him physical damage, too.

He cleared his throat and turned toward the shelf. "I'm fine. Just thinking how to get out of here." He picked up a candle and faced her, but his glance went to the door. "Looks like the shelves are blocking the exit. They have to be lifted out of the way."

She scrunched up her face as though trying to grasp that. "You mean, we can't get out?"

"Not without work." He looked at her. "How strong are you?"

"I—I think I wrenched something." She rubbed her shoulder, trying to look pitiful. It wouldn't do to lose everything she'd accomplished by going soft now. "But I'll do what I can."

He didn't look like a happy man. "Hold the candle." He thrust it at her. "And stay out of the way."

She nodded meekly, hoping he couldn't wrestle the shelves back against the wall too quickly. She had no idea how long that supply boat would be docked on the island, and could only pray nobody would come looking for them. In all the time she'd assisted in the clinic, they'd had few visitors. Not even cats. Most associated the antiseptic smell with negative experiences and steered clear.

Sam turned his back on her, planting fists on hips. He studied the situation, his heavy exhale revealing volumes about his mood.

She held the candle a little higher, and backed up a step. "Okay, now what?"

"I'm thinking."

Fifteen minutes later Sam had single-handedly bullied the shelves into place. He'd taken off his scrub shirt; his chest and back glistened from exertion. Dana had a hard time witnessing that gorgeous torso in action. Drat her hide! Why hadn't this possibility crossed her shriveled little mind?

He was well-built as it was, but bulging pecs and quads and—well, *bulging,* those various muscle groups drove her to the brink of promiscuity. She'd never had an urge to physically attack a man before, but if Sam had taken one more minute—*No! Thirty more seconds*—to get those shelves upright, she would have jumped him and had her way with him, right in the middle of two gross of Q-Tip swabs.

"Okay. We're out of here," he said, yanking her from her seriously depraved stupor.

She snapped her shoulders back and gave a hasty nod, avoiding looking at his glistening muscles, hard and distinct and alluring by candlelight. "Right, uh, good."

She could see well enough to step around and over the debris to get to the door. Sam got there first and turned the knob. It dropped off in his hand. "What in the..."

This last bit of business wasn't a particularly satisfying victory for Dana, but necessary. *Thank you, Daddy, for making me self-sufficient!*

She leaned forward, holding out the candle to put more light on Sam's handful of doorknob. She gasped, for show. "Why did you do that, Doc?"

With the speculative lift of a brow, he peered at her.

DANA STOOD IN THE SHOWER under a steady spray of warm water. She felt dirty, and she feared all the water in the world couldn't make her feel clean. She'd been as unscrupulous as Tate in her treatment of Sam and Beena.

She pressed her forehead against the cool tiles. Could she ever forget Sam's expression once he'd managed to get the door open, only to discover the supply boat had been and gone? He'd looked at her with such explosive rage, she was surprised the power of it hadn't blasted her through a wall. During the entire week she'd hid out on the island, she had never had a worse minute than that one, staring back at him, trying to appear the wide-eyed innocent.

She heard a sob, dismayed to discover she was crying. She pressed her hand over trembling lips, choking back the forlorn sound. Sam was on the other side of the bathroom door, hopefully, asleep. It was late. She'd avoided him for as much of the afternoon as she could. Played bingo after dinner with Beena, Eartha and one of the off-duty kitchen maids. She'd even gone so far as to take a circuitous route to her bedroom to dodge him. Looking into Sam's eyes had become a painful experience she didn't care to repeat any more than necessary.

He'd ensconced himself in his office the rest of the day, no doubt clearing up the mess. She should have helped, but it was obvious he didn't want her around. Every glance he shot her flashed his antipathy. It was as though he were saying, *Just because I can't prove it, doesn't mean I don't know what you've done!*

She choked back another sob at the irony of her situation. To escape dire straits in which she'd been lied to and used, she was having to lie to and use these people. Regardless, she had to keep up the pretense. Sam was so angry now, he would probably report her to the coast guard simply because he thought she deserved whatever she got.

Even if she broke down and told him everything, she couldn't prove it. Why should he believe her confession wasn't merely another ploy to get him to pity her, to pull him off his guard? She'd dug herself such a deep hole, she was stuck with digging it a little deeper.

She promised herself, as soon as the two weeks were up, she would tell them the truth. She had a feeling Beena would forgive her. But Sam? Why should he? Dana could never forgive Tate, even if he reformed this very day and came crawling back to her. She would never trust him again. Why should Sam ever feel he could trust her after what she'd put him through?

What difference did it make? After the deadline, she would tell them the facts and go on with her life. Sam and Beena would go on with theirs. End of story.

She turned off the water and grabbed the towel she'd slung over the top of the glass stall. Patting herself dry, she stepped out onto the bathroom rug, squeezing excess water from her hair.

Wrapping the towel around her, she opened her door and stumbled to a dead stop.

A huge green monster stared back at her!

Dana and the scaly reptile stood stock-still for a few seconds, each apparently startled to see the other. At last, the beast opened its mouth and made a threatening noise, snapping her out of her paralysis. Whirling on her heel, she sprinted through the bathroom, slamming into Sam's room.

It was dark, but she hit the bed on the run. A big cat leaped off and squeezed under the bed as she scrambled up next to Sam. Squatting on her knees, she shoved at his shoulder, urgently whispering, "Sam! *Sam!* There's a dragon in my bedroom!" She shoved harder, trying to wedge herself under and behind him.

"What?" He sounded groggy. His eyes fluttered open and he lolled his head in her direction, clearly half asleep. "A what?"

"A Komodo dragon! A man-eater! It tried to bite me!" He squinted, coming up on one elbow. She squirmed further behind him. "Kill it, Sam!" Looking confused, he pushed up to sit, and she scrambled to squat behind his back, pointing over his shoulder. "It may have already eaten the cats!"

He shifted to better see her, his glance sliding down to take in the scrap of terry. When his gaze lifted, something in his eyes, something hot, yet inexplicably poignant, sent a surge of fire along her pulses. She sucked in a quivery breath.

He frowned and ground out a curse. "A Komodo dragon tried to bite you?"

She nodded vigorously. "I—I think that's what it is."

"Not a coral snake, this time?"

She shook her head. "Too big. This is really *big*, with legs! It roared at me and—bared hideous *fangs!*"

"Fangs..." he muttered, running a hand through his hair. He looked frustrated and cuddly. If Dana hadn't been so overwrought, she would have found him unbearably charming. Sadly, this wasn't the time, or the man, to find charming—especially while she was wearing nothing but a towel.

"Aren't you going to do anything?" she pleaded.

"You know what, Angelfish?" Muscles bunched in his jaw and he looked as if he might be counting to ten. "This game has quit being fun for me."

She stared, openmouthed. "Don't you believe me?"

"What's really going on?" he asked. Even dubious and irritated and frustrated, whatever his major emotion was, he was gorgeous. Dana's heart did an appreciative flip-flop, amazing her to discover she could be scared and aroused at the same time. "Why are you *really* here—in a towel?"

She grabbed his shoulders, then thought better of it and let go. "I'm telling the truth!"

He pursed his lips, plainly trying to remain composed. "Okay. You want me to go in there, is that it?"

"Yes! Go. Kill it."

"There'd better be something in there, and I don't mean falling roof beams."

"There is!" She shoved on his back. "Please!"

He glanced toward the bathroom door, then at her. "Just one thing."

"You're stalling!" she accused in a frustrated moan. "You're afraid to face it!"

"Yeah, that's why I became a vet. Four-legged creatures scare me." His expression was pained, as though he'd been injured. "What I was asking, Angel, was, is there anything *you* might be afraid to face—since I'm naked."

9

ALMOST EXACTLY twenty-four hours after coming face-to-face with Godzilla, Dana wedged herself in the pet door of her bedroom. She muttered, "Last night I was jumping into Sam's bed screaming 'man-eating dragon,' and tonight I'm stuck in a hole in a door. Interesting life!"

She twisted and tugged, but remained stuck. *"Drat!"* Too bad she couldn't call Sam to help her, but it was because of his suspicions her door was locked, and she'd decided to try to sneak out through the cat slot.

Her thoughts skittered back to last night, when he returned from doing battle with Dana's fire-breathing monster. Sam wore shorts she'd retrieved for him and around his neck was curled what he'd called "a very affectionate iguana named Agamemnon." Agamemnon was the daddy of the miniatures Mona wore like brooches. Somebody had apparently left a door open somewhere, allowing 'Memo' to get utterly and completely lost.

Sam informed Dana she frightened the poor thing so badly, he'd slithered up to hide on top of her bed's canopy. The green beast that lovingly nuzzled Sam's cheek turned out to be barely three feet long, and embarrassingly fangless. Dana had felt stupid, but vindicated. At least Sam had to admit she hadn't made the whole thing up.

She tugged and joggled her body, but her hips raised painful objections to being forced through the cat door. She began to fear her escape would cost a pound of flesh. Okay, maybe five. "Come on, hips," she mumbled. "Sam's going to the nearest populated island tomorrow to call the coast guard. I can't—" she strained, yanking, and flinched "—let him!"

She had overheard Sam asking Beena if she'd told the supply boat captain about the malfunctioning satellite system. Beena's admission that she forgot rankled Sam. He asked his aunt if she'd really forgotten or if she were protecting Angel from the so-called border patrol. Beena just grinned. So Sam informed her he had to do something.

Not if Dana could help it! The time bomb of Tate's scheme was still ticking. This was Friday night—well, maybe the wee hours of Saturday. Next Wednesday was Tate's deadline. She had no choice but to hold Sam hostage for five more days. She squeezed hard, baring her teeth. *Rats!* She began to wonder morosely if he would find her stuck here in the morning like a size-twelve mouse in a size-ten trap?

Something sharp rammed her in the rear. Thanks to a reflex tensing of her gluteus maximus, her hips shot though the hole, and she sprawled on the hallway matting. She lay there for a minute, stunned. When her wits returned, she panicked. Had she screamed? She listened, afraid to breathe. The place remained dead quiet. After what seemed like a week, she felt positive Sam hadn't stirred, and raised up on an elbow to rub her perforated backside. There was something excruciating familiar about the indignity.

Peering at the pet door, she saw a little black nose and one yellow eye, peeping out over her ankles. "Thanks, Pouncer," she muttered. "Remind me to do something for you one day."

Moments later she'd filched a penlight and screwdriver from Sam's desk, and crept to his boat. Quickly, she slipped through the manhole-sized cover into the rear of the engine room. Five minutes later the twin engines were good for little more than bookends—until Dana opted to make them operational again. Dropping from the boat, she inhaled with relief. What a shame she had to pay for her security with overwhelming guilt.

She couldn't think about that now. She needed to get Sam's flashlight and screwdriver back in his desk, and then squeeze her backside through that dratted cat slot without being caught. She rounded the corner leading to Sam's office.

"Morning, Angelfish."

Dana screamed, nearly jumping out of her T-shirt and boxers. Even caught in the act, Dana wasn't one to give up. She looked around blankly, made a show of blinking, pretending to see Sam for the first time. A candle flickering a few feet away made him easy to spot. He lounged against the clinic door, arms crossed over his chest. Clad in a pair of shorts, he watched her with a "you're toast" expression on his face.

Worse even, Beena stood next to him. She wore a pink robe, her lucky cat pin glittering on the lapel. "I thought my aunt should see you in action,'' he said quietly.

She swallowed and placed a hand over her heart, concealing as well as she could the screwdriver she held. "What—where am I?" It was corny but it was all she had. "What's going on?"

Sam's expression closed further. "I was about to ask you that question."

She stared, using her most befuddled look. "I—I have no idea."

"There, Sammy, love, you see?" Beena touched his arm. "She was sleepwalking!"

"Oh, sure." Sam peeled Dana's fingers back from her chest and plucked the screwdriver from its hiding place behind her hand. "With this?" He flipped it into the air, catching it.

"Why—I never saw that before," Dana said, grateful it was dark so her mortified blush wouldn't be detectable.

"Or this?" He snatched the penlight from her other hand with such a lightning-fast move, she jumped and gasped. Which probably didn't hurt her story, since she looked as startled to see the penlight as Beena. "These were both in my desk earlier today," Sam said.

Dana examined her hands as though seeing them for the first time, then looked up vacantly. "I wonder how I got them?"

Beena moved forward, taking her hand. "Sleepwalkers can do the strangest things." She faced her grand-nephew. "Sammy, love, I sleepwalk all the time. Why, once I woke up with a wire whisk in one hand and a shoe in the other. If Mr. Chan hadn't meowed and wakened me, I would have walked right into the kitchen freezer." She chortled. "I'd have been a wrinkled old puny excuse for a Popsicle." She patted Sam's cheek. "Enough of your naughty doubts. Leave poor Angel alone. She's had a terrible trauma. The poor child can't even remember her native tongue!"

Sam shifted toward Dana, his eyes igniting with exasperation. "I'm not aware that sleepwalking is a characteristic of amnesia."

Beena squeezed Dana's hand, fortifying her confidence. "Maybe not in *dogs!*" Dana said, jutting out her chin with bravado. "But you're not a people doctor, remember?"

"Yes, Sammy, love." Beena pressed a kiss to her fingertips and reached up to plant it on his cheek. "Off to bed with both of you. I'll hear no more of this silliness." She yawned and covered her mouth with her hand. "Especially in the middle of the night. I need my beauty rest." She headed away from them, her bedroom slippers making a muffled skuff-skuff sound along the matting. Neither Sam nor Dana reacted until the whisper of Beena's footsteps disappeared.

Sam moved first and Dana flinched, expecting almost any act of violence. She knew he was furious. But when her glance snapped to him, he merely tucked the penlight and screwdriver into his hip pocket. "I'll put these somewhere safe." He took her arm. "I wouldn't want you sleepwalking with dangerous pointy objects. You could fall and hurt yourself."

She didn't speak, didn't look his way. Just allowed

herself to be tugged along. When they reached her door, Sam glanced at her, then the pet entrance, then back at her. "I'll stay here to see that you get inside—safely."

After a moment when he said nothing else and made no move to unlock her door, Dana looked at him with reluctance. "Well?"

He indicated the cat door with a nod. "Go on."

She gaped. He didn't think she was going to chance getting her whopping huge backside stuck while he watched, did he? "You can't mean that I crawl in!"

"You crawled out."

She was startled he insisted she *crawl* in, so her expression was genuine, though the words were a lie. "I—I did?"

"Or you flew out the window."

"Well—maybe people can do things in their sleep they can't do awake."

"And maybe little green men from Mars beamed you through the roof." His jaw worked.

"Look, Doc, if I try to crawl through that thing, I might as well paint a bull's-eye on my backside."

A brow rose, indicating surprise. "No matter how badly you deserve a spanking, Angel, I don't hit women."

"So you *say!*"

His expression grew stormy. After a moment he dropped his hand into a slash pocket, drawing out a key. "I hope to hell that I'm not stuck here with my boat out of commission."

Her heart lurched. *He knew!* She faked mystification. "You're talking in riddles."

"In the morning my boat had better start."

She swallowed bile, but guarded the lie. Too many livelihoods were at stake to go soft now. "Are you leaving tomorrow?"

"Just a trip to the nearest populated island." His gaze searched her face, and Dana had the feeling he was trying to probe into her mind. "When I leave for good, have no doubts about it, you'll go with me," he warned. "So what about tomorrow? Will my boat start, or not?"

It was heartbreaking to keep silent. Sam's expression was bleak, his eyes glimmering with frustration and strain. The sad beauty clutched at her heart, making her falter. *No, Dana! No weakening!* "How would I know?" she snapped, her choices slim to none. "I—you're a crazy paranoid, you know that?"

For what seemed like an hour their eyes locked in open warfare, fighting a silent battle of wills. Anger and frustration thickened and heated the air, and breathing became painful. The instant Dana could no longer abide the tortuous silence, Sam broke eye contact. A curse on his lips, he unlocked her door.

"Understand this," he muttered. "Hurt my aunt in any way, and I *will* find you."

IT WAS DANA'S TURN to be suspicious. Sam had been down at his boat all morning, trying to get it to run. She stayed away, acting as if she had nothing to do with the fact that it wouldn't work. She'd expected Sam to show up with a big wrench in his hand and bludgeon her to death. But he hadn't.

However, he was doing something she hadn't seen him do before. He was crossing the lawn, heading toward the castle wall. But not in the direction of the beach, toward the interior of the island. Where was he going? Dana reclined on a lounge chair beside the pool, next to Beena and Madam Rex. The older women had fallen asleep and were snoring so loudly they'd caused cats to leap off nearby chairs and retreat to quieter locales.

Dana feigned calm, but she was as jumpy as...as— she couldn't think of a single cliché that fit. But she was plenty jumpy. She watched Sam clandestinely through lowered lashes, so when he turned her way, it looked as though all three women were sleeping. Dana figured the noise was so earsplitting, he'd have to assume all three of them were snorting and wheezing.

After he vaulted over the back wall, Dana was instantly on her feet, running. She didn't know where he was going, but she didn't intend to let him get very far from sight. He had to be furious and desperate. Those two emotions had a way of breeding a single-minded sense of purpose. She should know. Just look what her fury at Tate and her desperation to get away had fostered in her!

What if there were another boat on the far side of Haven Cay? Even with a little outboard, Sam could make it to another island. With a knowledge of the waters and enough anger, she bet he could swim there!

She scurried to the wall and peered over. He strode down the gradual incline toward the woods. Taking a deep breath, she scrambled over the barrier and dropped to the other side, recoiling from the pain to the bottoms of her feet. She started after him in a semi-crouched fast walk, planning to drop below the knee-high grasses if he looked back.

She was afraid she would lose him in the dense wood, but the path was relatively well-defined—a lucky break. She wasn't exactly Daniel Boone when it came to tracking. She crept to the far edge of a clearing in time to see him halt at the edge of a pond, twenty feet off to her left. With a suddenness that took her breath away, he shucked his shorts, and she gasped. He wore nothing underneath.

She covered her mouth, to stifle her outburst. He was magnificent, poised there, all tanned muscle and—and so generously endowed. Any woman worth her X chromosomes would have gasped. Dana's cheeks sizzled and she prayed Sam hadn't heard her.

He stretched his arms above his head and plunged off the bank, executing a sleek dive. Dana sagged against a tree, relieved that she hadn't given herself away. She was afraid she wouldn't make a particularly brilliant spy. Especially if it required watching great-looking naked men.

She shook herself, gawking as he swam the length of the pond, did a flip and began to swim back. Lord, he was a sight to behold. Her legs went mushy and she sank under the cover of tall grass and crawled toward the edge of the pond. She knew she was ogling, and that prying was not only rude but doubtless against the law. Much to her regret, however, she couldn't help herself. "That's probably what all the perverts say," she mumbled.

His route curved away from his starting point, but that didn't bother Dana. In fact it was a titillating stroke of luck, for he had veered in her direction. The water was clean and clear. As he neared, she witnessed the entire drama and beauty of his body in action, every supple component in concert with the others. She cupped her chin in her palms and smiled dreamily.

When he reached the side, she was too lost in the moment to realize he didn't flip and turn. Instead, he planted his forearms on the grassy bank, not two feet from her face, and rose up to eye level. Water dripped from his hair and sparkled on his lashes. He stared at the vegetation as though he suspected the yellow butterfly flitting in the grass wasn't the only creature lurking there. "I don't mean to wake you, but what the hell are you doing?"

Caught off guard, Dana didn't know what to say. For an instant she thought he might be bluffing, but that fool's paradise didn't linger long. She grimaced, noting his blue eyes were wary, melancholy. The spectacle disconcerted her, and she could neither think nor run.

"Do you have other hobbies, Angelfish—*besides* sabotage and voyeurism?" he asked quietly, "or don't you remember?"

She made a pained face. *Drat!* Sam had heard her stupid gasp, after all! Her brain scrambled for any excuse. How was she going to explain—*yeeeeaaooow!*

Something painful goosed her forward. Instinctively, she grabbed for support. An instant later, she and whatever she grabbed hung suspended in cool, clear water.

Confused and disoriented, Dana opened her eyes. Her head smarted, as though she'd hit something.

Sam's face was very near, and not quite in focus. He watched her, unblinking, his features somber, his hair slightly uplifted, wavy, as though in a gauzy, slow-motion dream.

Her arms were wrapped loosely around his neck. His slipped slowly, deliberately, around her waist. Deep silence and cool unreality prevailed in this place where gravity held little sway. She levitated there, drifted, floating her legs up to enfold his middle.

Their eyes locked in this hushed and weightless realm. Suddenly, they were no longer adversaries. Their guards melted away, replaced by an urgency as age-old as the sky, the sea, and the human desire to be joined, held—loved…

She felt herself flowing toward him, into him, pressing her breasts into his solid torso. His body tensed, his eyes widened. Dana intuitively recognized the need in him to cherish rather than conquer, to give rather than take, trust rather than doubt. Her reaction to this thrilling new wisdom was immediate and over-whelming. All the repressed passions within her shot upward and outward; her body ached to be one with his strength, his fire.

Their lips met softly, tenderly, a divine melding. Nestled within the haven of his body, their kiss deep-ened. Languidly, Dana opened her lips in invitation. It was so quiet, and no longer cool. She felt warm and peaceful and safe. Her eyelids fluttered and closed, and she wondered if this is what heaven was like.

Her consciousness began to dim as she yielded to a serene, hazy half sleep.

She experienced a vague sense of renewal and

fought the cobwebs enveloping her brain. At first her
lids were too heavy to do more than flutter. Then,
some small part of her brain began to perceive that
Sam was breathing into her mouth. She opened her
eyes, suddenly aware of his gift, nourishing her body
and soul.

Her next few minutes were an inglorious mix of
coughing and shivering, hunched on shore as Sam
made sure she was alert and recovering.

"You have a bump on your head." His fingers
smoothed her hair away from the stinging injury.
"I'm sorry."

She hugged herself and leaned into his strength.
"It's not your fault." She felt terrible about sneaking
up on him, then ramming him with her head.
"Pouncer and I are totally to blame." She glanced
around for the kamikaze cat, but it was gone. Probably pretty satisfied with an assault well done. Dana
inhaled, thankful her lungs functioned at full capacity,
again. She nestled against Sam's shoulder. "How's
your jaw?"

"Very hard." He nudged her chin, coaxing her to
look at him. His expression held no amusement, but
his lips tipped up slightly. She sensed it was because
she'd stopped wheezing and gasping. "How many of
me do you see?" he murmured.

"Still just the one." She turned into his neck and
closed her eyes, comforted by the steady beat of his
pulse. "I don't know what came over me," she whispered hoarsely. "It's not like me to feel faint..." She
didn't know how to explain her near-blackout. She'd
had worse bumps getting thunked on the head by falling library books. "I'm so embarrassed."

He put an arm around her. "I should have brought you right to the surface, but I..."

When he didn't go on, she looked up. "You— what?" She already knew. She'd felt the same urge, but for some demented reason she needed to hear him say it.

His brow furrowing further, he watched her. "I thought I saw..."

A kiss in my eyes? she finished silently, her smile timid. She knew it was insane, but whatever else happened under that water, one thing had been clear, to both of them. She *had* wanted Sam Taylor to kiss her. She'd wanted that kiss as she'd never wanted anything before. She'd wanted it so badly, she would have lingered over it with her last breath! Which she almost did.

"Sam?" she asked, defying her natural timidity with men and allowing her desire for him to guide her. "I need to ask you something."

His expression was troubled, charmingly so. "Okay."

"Would you..." she faltered, afraid yet determined. This beautiful, naked man held her tenderly in his arms. He had saved her life, but gratitude had little to do with the tangle of emotions, desires and doubts that swirled inside her. She took his wrist. Taking a deep breath, she forbade herself to tremble as she lifted his hand to where his shirt was knotted beneath her breasts. "Undress me, Sam."

His long, dark lashes swept up in surprise.

SAM SAT at his office desk, his head in his hands. He was completely out of his ever-lovin' mind! First their little blonde mermaid had crawled up from the sea, claiming amnesia. Without tools or even clothes, she'd somehow disabled the radios, then managed to get him trapped in his storeroom to keep him from using the supply boat's radio. And finally, she vandalized his boat engines, essentially holding the whole island hostage, though nobody seemed particularly concerned about it but him. And what did he do?

He made love to her!

If that wasn't rockin' and rollin' his unstable butt right into a straitjacket, he didn't know what was. And the final insult? As they lay on a bed made of their clothes, sated and cuddling, she still looked him straight in the eye and lied. "What sabotage?" she'd asked. "What fake amnesia?"

He cursed, raking his fingers through his hair. Then, there was Liza to consider. *Damn!* Even though in his heart, he and Liza were no longer a couple, he still hadn't been able to let his long-time girlfriend in on that fact. No phone and no way off the island, had put a substantial stumbling block in his path. But the most hilarious detail about this whole crazy farce was that the *reason* he had no options in reaching Liza was due to the same designing woman he'd fallen recklessly in love with.

His chuckle was dark and ironic. It would be intensely educational to see just how big a fool he could be. He sat back, hauling in a breath. He had to get his head on straight. So he'd lost his mind for a minute and made love to her. So he'd fantasized for a few deluded moments—okay, more like sixty lusty, extraordinary minutes—that she wasn't *really* a bad person, that she had some plausible, understandable, even noble reason for doing all this.

"Hellfire and damnation, man!" He slapped his hands on his desk, vaulting up. "Get a grip!" He had to face facts—she was a siren. She lured him onto the rocks, and he was damn thrilled about it.

The rage in him billowed into a living, pulsating thing. He was incensed with himself. How dare he fall in love with somebody as deceitful as she? How dare his body betray him with her, knowing as he did, that there was no future for them? Knowing that beneath that beautiful, naive-blonde facade lurked a woman of wit, intelligence and sizzling sensuality— and a greedy, Machiavellian heart! "Your good sense sucks, big time," he muttered.

"Sammy, love, is that any way to speak to the only woman in the world who would put up with such a non-whimsical grand-nephew?"

His head snapped up as his aunt pranced in. Though she was loaded down with rolled up newspapers clamped against her chest, her hands fluttered free. She flapped her fingers, as though drying her nails. Which Sam was sure she was doing, since her nails were so precious to her, the miniature cat art always changing.

"Here." She let the papers fall to his desk. "I don't want to smudge Mr. Chan." She held out her right hand, prominently displaying the index finger. "Look at that masterpiece! The head is tilted perfectly! I swear, Maya Angelou couldn't have done better."

"I think you mean Michelangelo."

She waved her fingers in a gesture that was part

dismissing and part nail-drying. "Well, whoever. Madam Rex has outdone herself this time."

With an elbow, she nudged the pile of newspapers scattered on his desk. "I couldn't remember what part you wanted—cartoons or crosswords or the obituaries—no, that's Mona—anyway, I brought all the papers the supply boat left." She paused, looking confused. "Which part of the newspaper was it you read, again?"

"The news part." He tried to smile at his aunt, but the expression came with effort. Had it only been a few hours ago that he and Angel had been tangled in each other's arms, making crazy love...

He cleared his throat, snapping himself out of it. Dwelling on it would do nobody any good. "Thanks, Aunt Beena."

She blew him a kiss. "Dinner's in an hour," she started to turn away, then halted, scrutinizing him. "You look a little flushed. Are you feeling all right?"

He glanced uneasily around the room, then lowered himself to his chair. "I'm fine," he muttered. "Just—fine."

"Well, don't be late for dinner. I noticed you missed lunch. You and Angel." Her pause was long and meaningful. When he didn't hear her turn and leave, he looked up. She was grinning like the Cheshire cat. He frowned at her. "I'll be there."

She made a face, as though she wanted details and was irked that they weren't forthcoming. "Okay, I'll ask Angel where you two were during lunch."

"Don't!" he snapped, then wished he could cut out his tongue. "I mean, I'd rather you didn't say anything." Yeah, like bringing it up would make it real

and leaving it alone meant it never happened? *Right, Taylor. You look good in denial.*

Beena's chortle filled the room. "There's no reason to be embarrassed, Sammy. I understand about honest passion, and I think she's charming. I couldn't be more delighted if I'd picked her for you myself. She's so much sweeter than that Liza Cold-Cut person."

He winced at the reminder, mumbling, "Colecutt."

Beena wagged her fingers. "If you ask me, that girlfriend of yours is full of *baaaa-low-nee!*" Beena turned away. "See you at dinner, love. And don't be late. You need your strength." She giggled behind her hand as she closed the clinic door.

Beena was more savvy than Sam had ever guessed. *Damn!*

Absently he picked up one of the papers and unfolded it. He glanced at the front page headlines, then flipped through the section. He felt as though he'd been stranded for a month. For all he knew, ten or twelve new political sex scandals had been uncovered in Washington, the stock market had roller-coastered through several more "worst" and "best" days in history, and, with luck, somebody had come up with a better place to store pollutants than our lungs.

He opened the editorial page and tried to pay attention to the words, but they blurred and ran together. With an irritated growl he flipped to the next section and froze.

Before him lay a photograph of Angel. Wearing a black strapless dress, she stood beside a tall, blond man, his arms wrapped possessively around her. Sam felt gut-punched and green-eyed jealous. Hesitantly, he scanned the caption. "Dana Lenore Vanover with her fiancé, Tate Fleck, on the evening before her mysterious disappearance.''

The notion that Angel—rather, Dana Lenore Vanover—was a member of Miami's social elite had never occurred to him. Hope surged that he'd been wrong about her—his opinion having been tainted by the betrayal of the hired girl who turned out to be a thief.

His chest aching with the need to breathe, he scanned the society column. He hardly ever read it, the writer notorious for slinging mud and innuendos. But this was all he had.

He read. '''What's with Miami's wedding of the millennium, where the old name marries the new money? Though the dashing fiancé insists his ladylove is merely ill and incommunicado until her recovery, rumor has it the bride forsook the groom and is trolling for bigger fish—or at least a fish with a bigger wad.'''

Sam stirred uneasily in his chair, rereading the last sentence. After going over it a third time, he slumped back and rubbed his temples. *Lord.* His worst fears seemed to be confirmed. She had the name but no more money, so she'd decided to get back in the fast lane-any way she could.

It was strange that her fiancé, this Fleck person, insisted she was ill, and not missing, since she clearly was. Sam assumed the lie was a pride thing. Maybe Fleck thought he could find her and get her back without adverse publicity. That made sense. The men who came by on the boat were no doubt friends of the groom. Sam had to admit, he'd probably have done the same thing in Fleck's position. Losing a woman like—Dana—wouldn't go down easy.

It looked as though Miss Vanover decided, at the last minute, that marriage was too confining. Why not con a daft old lady out of a few million and still be footloose and fancy free!

Ice spread through his veins. He didn't want to believe it, but… *"Hell!"* He'd known it! He'd felt it all along. So why did his heart feel like winter-kill?

He bowed his head.

Because you love her, stupid.

10

DANA WAS SICK at heart. How could she have asked
him to undress her, of all crazy things! What of her
vow to look into a man's soul? Oh, she'd done a lot
of looking, and feeling, and sighing with Sam—even
some outright moaning—but none of it had had much
to do with searching his soul. She quivered with the
delicious memory of his hands on her, his lips—his
gentleness.

How could she have let herself go like that, in his
arms? It must have been the head injury. Or she'd
been more affected by lack of oxygen than she'd
thought. What was with her? Having sex with Sam
Taylor was about as wise as walking barefoot over a
pile of glass shards. Did she think she would come
through the experience without spilling blood?

She bit back a sob. She was in no position to be
falling for any man. Her heart had been battered and
was in no shape to take chances. She couldn't trust
her own feelings—not after the Tate debacle.

What she and Sam shared had been a rebound
thing, nothing more. She had to recognize it as that
and get herself under control. Besides, practically
every second of their relationship had been based on
lies and tricks. Sam didn't trust her. He might fancy
her a little—the mysterious stranger fantasy—but

nothing meaningful could come from it. He could never be positive of a word that came out of her mouth.

She'd avoided him since that disaster at the pond on Saturday. Or had he avoided her? Did it really matter who avoided whom, as long as it worked? She'd eaten every meal in her room, explaining that she had a terrible migraine. Beena seemed to think this was a good thing, and came by periodically to shout through the door, words like *taco, adiós, olé* and *que sera sera,* which Dana suspected was Italian. However misguided and inexact Beena's efforts, her concern was well-meant and endearing.

Dana adored the elderly sprite, and couldn't bear being the lying hostage-taker she was. She spent Sunday gazing blankly out the window or sprawled on her bed, crying. She came to depend on the cats for company and comfort as they wandered in and out. After an hour or two of being snuggled and slobbered on, they escaped to nap in peace.

Sam knocked several times, insisting he needed to speak with her. She repeatedly pleaded that he go away. Today, he wasn't taking no for an answer.

"Please, Sam!" she cried as evenly as her despondent mood would allow. "I'm not feeling well."

"It's Monday morning. If you still have a headache, you need a doctor. Let me in."

"I'd think you'd be happy I'm staying in my room," she called. "I can't *steal* anything in here!"

He didn't immediately respond, and she held her breath, hoping he would go away. She was afraid to see him. Afraid to see anger in his eyes—eyes that could be tender, could drink her up, make her feel clean and new and special.

So here she sat, a prisoner of her own lies and longings, defeated and miserable.

"Dana," he said grimly, "let me in."

She lay on her back, her mind exhausted, without hope. "No, Sam, there's nothing..." She frowned, her brain insisting that she quit wallowing in guilt and self-pity and *think* for a minute. What had he called her? Dana? She lolled her head from side to side, denying the notion. She was more fuzzy-witted than she'd thought.

She heard the rattle of a key and sat bolt upright, tugging her T-shirt snugly over her hips. "Don't you dare!"

The door cracked open; she could see his face, angular, handsome. Deep shadows darkened the skin below his eyes. He looked as if he'd had less sleep than she. "I know who you are," he said. "Dana Vanover."

She stilled, tried to swallow, but her throat was dry. "What did you say?" *How could he know?*

He stepped inside and closed the door. "It was in the paper."

"What?" She hadn't had much rest, but she didn't know she was so far gone she couldn't handle the meaning of simple words like "paper" and "it" and "was" and "in" and "the." But they confused her, didn't make sense.

"The supply boat brought last week's Miami newspapers." He held out the article with her picture. "Tell me that isn't you."

She stared. Yes, she remembered the news photographer who'd been on the yacht snapping pictures that night.

The jig was up, it seemed. She flicked a glance at his face, so solemn, so dear. "You're right. It's me."

"Admit you never had amnesia." His voice was more afflicted than angry.

She exhaled, not sure she was sorry she'd been found out. It had been a hard, cruel secret to keep. "You're right. I never did." She shifted to sit on her feet, wadding her fingers in her lap. "But—" Her heart turned over with a wayward need to hug him, beg his forgiveness, and for him to make love to her again. But she resisted. "I'm so sorry for all the lies, but I—I can't explain. Not yet."

He frowned at her, blinking with astonishment. *"Why?"* He asked the question with such incredulity, it was as though she'd said she had no choice but to set her hair on fire.

She shook her head. "After Wednesday everything will be all right. After Wednesday, I can go home." She dropped her gaze, unable to look into those tormenting eyes. "And so can you."

He moved to the edge of the bed and knelt, gripping her by the upper arms. "What are you saying, Angel—*Dana?* Why have you pretended to have amnesia? Why did you screw with the radios and my boat? What's going on, damn it?"

She peered at him from beneath her lashes, wanting badly to tell him everything. Wanting to wipe the distrust from his eyes. Wanting him to take her into his arms, kiss her, make tender love to her again. But that was a selfish fantasy. She couldn't trust him. She couldn't trust anybody. Not even herself, it seemed.

It was impossible to fall in love with someone when the whole relationship was based on lies. Wasn't it? And even if it weren't impossible, she'd blindly allowed herself to trust someone she'd loved before, and that had ended badly.

At least she'd thought she loved Tate. Yet what she felt for Sam—out there by the pond—*Lord,* what she experienced in his arms, was so much more profound than anything she'd ever felt for Tate.

"I—please, Sam. Just two more days," she pleaded. "Trust me."

She knew what his reaction would be. A nasty laugh and a cynical retort. When he didn't immediately speak, she grew more and more uneasy. She knew he was watching her. He still held her arms, but his grip wasn't painful.

"*Trust* you?"

Her glance shot to his face, to eyes displaying the rueful luster of skepticism. "Trust *you?*" She watched a gamut of emotions cross his features. "That's very…" He squinted, peering around the room, as though he needed a moment to reorient himself. When he faced her again, his gaze caught hers and held like a vise. He stared, clearly wishing he could reach inside her mind and drag out the truth. "All right, Dana," he finally said, his voice solemn. "I'll trust you."

She stared, tongue-tied. She hadn't expected this. She'd expected outrage and sarcasm. But he didn't sneer, or smirk, or even glower. He just watched her with grave, glorious eyes that seemed to inquire, *Are you going to deceive me?*

She shook her head, a mute vow. She had no

words. A shuddering thrill danced through her and she experienced a lightness in her heart she hadn't known in...in *forever*. After all she'd done to him, he'd promised to trust her. She was so grateful, she wanted to cry, to fall into his arms, but she didn't dare. She was beyond tears, drained of them. And falling into his arms would be a reckless indulgence.

He released her and stood. "I may be the world's biggest fool..." He started to say more, then frowned and shook his head, as though arguing with himself. "I'll be ready to listen when you're ready to tell me."

Dana nodded, bewildered by his manner. It seemed almost as though he...but that wasn't...especially, not after everything....

Mystified, she watched him leave the room.

AFTER LEAVING DANA in her room, Sam was at his wit's end. He'd gone over the article more times than he could count. He couldn't think logically anymore, couldn't sleep. Absently he went into his room and lay down on the bed. He closed his eyes, but his mind churned.

A light knock on his bathroom door startled him. "Yes?"

"It's me." She sounded calm, perhaps resigned. He sat up in surprise. "Dana?"

He heard a click, and shot a glance toward the handle in time to see it move. After only a brief hesitation, the door opened slightly. She stood there, looking tired. She'd changed into a bright mauve-and-yellow-striped shirt and pink shorts. One of Beena's more gaudy tie-gifts threaded through the belt loops, cinched the shorts at her waist. Her hair was slicked back in a ponytail. Sam noticed she wasn't wearing the ruby drop she'd won at Beena's birthday party. As a matter of fact, he'd never seen her wear it since Beena had placed it around her neck at the party.

"Could we walk on the beach?" she asked.

He nodded, and jumped up as she opened the door enough to join him. She didn't speak or look at him, not even when he took her arm. He knew body contact wasn't a great idea, but he needed her touch. He needed to inhale her subtle fragrance. He'd been a starving man for nearly two days. He'd eaten, but wasn't nourished. Hunger gnawed all the time, deep in his belly. It was a hunger that nothing and no one but the taste, touch and scent of Dana Vanover could slake.

In silence, they walked out of the castle, across the manicured lawn, through the stone arch and over the undulating dunes.

The shrill call of gulls winging overhead and the hiss of surf were the only sounds that broke the quiet. Sam waited, trying to let her open up to him in her own way, in her own time. Lord knew, he'd waited for what seemed like an eternity already.

"Sam?" She halted and faced him. "I want you to know, I had no choice in what I did. I couldn't afford to trust anyone." Her brow creased and she looked out to sea. "You see, I trusted Tate with all my heart, and he—" Her voice broke and she shook her head, plainly trying to get her emotions under control. "Anyway, I didn't know you. I didn't dare hand over the power to give me away."

He didn't understand. Give her away? Though he

wanted to believe her, he tried to discipline his mind. He was afraid, because he loved her, he might jump at any explanation she came up with. He needed to know she was telling the truth. Even if it was a truth he didn't want to hear. "Why don't you start from the beginning?"

They walked along the water's edge, away from the dock, as she quietly and sometimes brokenly told Sam the story of the whirlwind romance, of Tate's charm and charisma. These things were hard to hear, but he kept his own council and let the words spill out of her as she chose to release them.

Dana told him about discovering that she and her mother were pawns in a scheme, requiring Tate to marry a respectable old Miami name. Their marriage would legitimize his ploy, sucker unsuspecting investors. Tate would then grab a fast fortune before he disappeared, leaving Magda and Dana to deal with the scandal.

"So you see," she said, tears glistening in her eyes, "I had to get away. I jumped off the yacht and swam and swam for hours—until I washed up here." She swept out her arm. "I thought I was swimming toward Miami. I didn't have any plans. But when I realized how perfect a place this island was to hide..." A tear trickled down her cheek. She paused to get her voice under control. "I was desperate, Sam." It came out in a faulty whisper. "I'm sorry."

He wanted to believe her. Nothing she said conflicted with the newspaper account. But it was so...so Hollywood. His cynical inner voice reminded, *She's lied so much, how do you know this isn't another trick to get your sympathy, to pull you off your guard?*

"Can you prove any of this?" he asked, wishing he could sweep her into his arms and tell her he believed her, tell her he loved her and wanted nothing more than to show her how much.

She blinked, shooting him a startled-fawn expression. "I—no. That's the reason I had to hide. I can't prove any of it. Tate has powerful friends. I..." She shrugged, looking small and helpless. "You don't believe me?"

He experienced a surge of compassion, but it failed to erase his doubts. He didn't know if he could get past all the lies. How crazy was it to love a woman, yet require *proof* that her every move, thought, or act wasn't choreographed to hurt or swindle?

"You don't believe me." She chewed on her lower lip, frowning and pensive. "I deserve that." She took both his hands. "Every word is true, Sam. Honestly."

He frowned, his heart battling with his head. "Dana..."

He heard a sound, and glanced toward the sea. A sleek sport fishing boat headed toward their dock. Someone waved and called out from the flybridge. He couldn't make out the words, but the woman looked familiar. He squinted. "Liza?" The realization hit so quickly he hardly grasped the fact that he'd spoken her name aloud.

"Who's that?" Dana asked.

His gut clenching, he pulled from her grip and waved. "I only recognize one of them."

"They're coming *here?*" Panic edged her words.

"Looks that way." He peered at her. "Should I fear for their equipment?"

"This isn't a joking matter." She anxiously stuck

a stray wisp of hair behind an ear. "Tate has until the end of the workday, Wednesday, to do his sleazy deal. I put my trust in you, Sam. Please don't betray me!"

"I won't," he promised in a whisper.

The boat slowed, pulling up to the dock. The woman was definitely Liza. She no longer waved or shouted, just watched. Sam had a feeling his jealous soon-to-be-ex-girlfriend was weighing the situation, wondering about the pretty blonde. He glanced at Dana. "You'd better go."

"Hey, Sam, *honey!*"

He faced the boat and grinned. "Hi, Liza." Without looking at Dana, he whispered, "*Go.* I'll get rid of them." He waved, loping toward the pier.

He had no clue why he was protecting Dana. *Hell, he knew, all right!* He just didn't like to think about it while being scrutinized by the woman on the boat. To call Liza merely obsessive was like calling Shakespeare merely a man who scribbled words on paper. Sam and Liza had their biggest fights after she'd surprised him at work, accusing him of giving some female pet owner too much attention, which was a crock. But her jealousy was part of her makeup, and he'd learned to deal with it.

He bounded onto the dock, a very unhappy man.

She scrambled down from the flybridge and jumped onto the wharf, running into his arms. "Darling!" She kissed him with all the overcompensated ardor of a women with a "Who's the bimbo?" look in her eyes. "I've missed you, honey! I thought you were coming home Friday. I tried to call, but couldn't get through. What's going on?"

Sam took her by the shoulders, moving her slightly

away. He needed space. His heart was no longer in their relationship, and he saw no reason to try to put it back. But he had to let her down easily, and this wasn't the time nor place. "Nothing's wrong. Just a radio snafu." He glanced at the boat, not recognizing it. "Who are your friends?"

She resisted being held away from him and snaked her arms around his neck. "I was about to ask you the same question," she murmured against his mouth. She indicated the direction of the castle. "Who's the blonde?"

Here it came. Liza's no-nonsense, scratch-her-eyes-out method of handling every situation that included Sam and any female over the age of consent. Unfortunately, in this case, Liza would definitely have a case. "She's a guest of my aunt," he said.

"A young, pretty guest." Liza's suspicions were apparent, even masked beneath a facade of purring and rubbing. "Weren't those a pair of shorts your aunt sent you for your birthday last year?"

Hell! She recognized the clothes. When a woman had on a man's shorts, it was pretty damning, even in a trusting woman's mind. With all the incriminating evidence at hand, he and Dana might as well have been rolling around naked on the beach screaming, "Yes! Yes! Oh, *baaaaaaby!*"

How did he explain the fact that Dana had crawled out of the sea, practically naked. And for days and days she'd worn his clothes completely platonically. Since that was no longer the case, he opted for a lie. "You're mistaken. Those were hers."

"And the tie?"

Good Lord, the woman had the eyes of a spy sat-

ellite. "She forgot her belt?" He didn't like the way that came out.

"Come on, Liza!" a man wearing a backward baseball cap shouted from the flybridge. "Tell him to get a move on."

Sam peered at the boat. "Is he talking about me?"

"One second, Amos!" she called. "Go help Andrea mix the bloody Mary's. The fish aren't going anywhere." She turned back and smooched Sam's jaw. "Honey. The Sawyers invited us to go deep sea fishing, so I said yes." She reached up and twisted a breeze-tossed lock of his air around a finger. "You need a day off."

He had no intention of leaving the island. Not that he didn't believe Dana's story, but he couldn't allow himself to—not completely. Not yet. He didn't intend to set a foot off Haven Cay until Dana went with him. A voice deep in his head whispered, *And you hope like hell when that happens, she'll leave as your fiancée.* "You know I hate deep sea fishing, Liza," he said, trying to sound reasonable. "I keep wanting to patch up the fish and throw them back."

She made a pretty pout. "Not even to be with me?" Liza was a delicate beauty, with willowy Audrey Hepburn looks. Even her black hair was cut short and pixie-like. Though she had lovely eyes, she added fake lashes, and she emphasized her full lips with a thick pencil line, making her mouth appear puffy. He knew balloon-lips were the latest trend. Why that was baffled him. Yet, even with the unnatural additions that annoyed more than aroused, Liza was hard to say no to.

He decided to lie again, realizing with some irony

that lies did have a way of cutting troubling corners. "I have to perform surgery this afternoon." He knew Liza well, and though he needed to get things settled with her, it would be cruel to break off with her abruptly after all they'd been to each other. "I'm shorthanded in the clinic. I could use an assistant during the operation. Why don't you stay?"

She pulled a face. "Gag me, Sam! I can't stand that stuff. Can't you put it off?"

"I'm afraid not. You know how my aunt is about her cats."

The brunette's brows dipped. "Insane?"

He smiled wryly. "Now, now. She's my only family."

"Oh, Sam," she said, looking put out, but doing it prettily. "If you have one *big* flaw, it's your loyalty and duty to that old lady. If you ask me, it's pathological!"

"I owe her a great deal, Liza," he said. "You know that."

"Let's not fight, honey." She smiled, and he could tell she was reloading her arsenal of reasons he should go with her. "I haven't seen you in so long."

"I know." Once again he took her by the shoulders and pressed her slightly away. He had no desire to be unkind, but he didn't feel right about playing a game his heart wasn't in. "Since this isn't a good time for me to leave, you go fishing with your friends. I'll be home Wednesday evening—I'll call you. We need to talk." He winced. That had come out sounding more portentous than he'd intended.

Her eyes narrowed slightly.

"Hey, Liza!" the man shouted. "Get a wiggle on, babe!"

Sam flicked a glance toward the boat. The man waved a glass, sloshing something red.

"One minute!" she shouted, then turned to Sam. Tilting her head back, she peered into his face. "Okay, honey. I'll go." Her smile was a little thin. "But first, I have something to tell you."

Her tone told him she didn't intend to be put off. With a stab of irritation, he manufactured a grin. "Sure, what is it?"

"This is hardly the way I pictured it, but..." Her features brightened with enthusiasm, mixed with a hint of something else. Sam couldn't quite make it out.

He experienced a prick of foreboding.

Foreboding?

The idea was so stupid he shook it off.

Hugging him to the familiarity of her slim, toned body, she whispered, "I'm pregnant, sweetheart!" She kissed his jaw. "It's time we set the date."

DANA PEEKED OUT from the castle's double doors, watching the exchange on the dock. She watched Sam kiss the slender brunette, watched the intimacy of their body language, the significant smiles. A terrible sense of loss assailed her. She felt sick, and clutched the door to keep from slumping to her knees.

She hadn't wanted to face it, but the truth hit her like a cannon shot to the stomach. She was in love with Sam. She even knew when it happened—under the water, in his arms. He may have given back her life with his breath, but he'd stolen something equally precious.

Her heart.

Watching him and his lady, Dana's misery became a biting, physical ache. She loved a man who couldn't trust her. Couldn't believe her, even after she took him into her confidence and revealed a perilous truth. A man who clearly had a very close relationship with this Liza person.

Sam helped Liza onto the dock, and she headed toward the boat, throwing him a kiss. He turned away, toward the castle. Dana wondered if he told her to notify the coast guard. She shuddered, clutching her hands to her chest.

But what if he hadn't? She felt a swell of hope. What if he cared enough for her to trust her, even after all she'd done? What if he loved her? She'd had the strangest feeling when he'd visited her room today. And there had been something in his eyes out there on the beach. She watched him as he approached, a small smile twitching at the corners of her mouth. In her woman's heart she knew he cared for her. He couldn't have made love to her the way he did if it had been nothing more than a conquest.

She looked past him as the fishing boat accelerated and motored off. Maybe Liza *had* been his girlfriend, but that was in the past now. It had to be! Dana felt that so strongly she wouldn't allow herself to believe otherwise. She was so certain she had trusted him with her heart and her secret. Sam was honorable, like her father. He was nothing like Tate. No power on earth could make her believe he was!

When she glanced back at him, he was mounting

the stairs. She opened the door and stepped out, but the smile on her face died. He wore a stony mask of cold dignity, a watchful fixity in his eyes.

"Sam?" Unable to stop herself, she took his hands. "What is it?" She sensed it couldn't be the guilt of betrayal, for she knew in her heart he wouldn't give her away. She knew so much in her heart, now that she'd finally made a clean breast of everything. "What happened?"

He squeezed her fingers, his faint smile haunted with sadness. "Congratulate me, Dana," he said. "I'm getting married."

The shock held her immobile for a moment. Grief overwhelmed her. Perhaps he hadn't betrayed her secret, but...

She had no right, no reason, to feel betrayed. He'd never made her any promises, never even whispered words of love. After all, she'd asked him to make love to her, hadn't she?

Still, in her shattering despair, she did feel betrayed. He cared for her! No—*he loved her!* She knew it as surely as she knew he hadn't informed on her to the coast guard. "This...this is sudden," she said, fighting the need to scream, *Why, Sam? Why her and not me?*

His nostrils flared. "It was time." He pulled from her grasp, but she felt his reluctance to do so. With a distracted gesture, he indicated the door. "I need to get back to Miami, but I'll stay until Wednesday evening. Can you have the boat repaired by then?"

Her fingers tingled with the memory of his touch, and she clutched her hands together. "Uh, it won't take long."

"What about the radios?" He was all business as he opened the door for her to precede him.

"I can fix the satellite, but yours is blown." She faced him, her mind reeling, her body an insubstantial mess. "I'm sorry about that. Please, send me the bill."

His jaws working, he didn't glance her way.

"So...so when is the happy day?" she asked, unable to help herself.

"Soon."

She nodded, but he didn't see, for he was walking away from her.

11

SAM FELT DEAD INSIDE. He went through the motions of working in his office, but he couldn't feel. What had he done, promising to marry Liza? He held his head in his hands. He loved Dana, yet…

So what if he had a strong sense of duty? That wasn't all bad, was it? He owed Liza a great deal, and he cared for her. Even if his sense of duty really was pathological, he'd taken four years of Liza's life, he'd had sex with her. He'd conceived a baby with her. And until Angel—Dana—came along, he'd been content with her as the woman in his life.

When he looked into Liza's eyes out there on the beach, all he could think of was Beena and how she'd been cheated out of her wedding day. So he promised Liza a wedding. Just as soon as she could arrange it. Maybe he'd been rash; maybe he'd been foolish. Nevertheless, he'd promised.

Very likely, once he got back to Miami, this whole episode would seem more like dreamlike lunacy than reality. Some crazy outbreak of summer dementia brought on by a silly obsession with a beautiful, mystery woman who'd crawled out of the sea. Any man might get a little confused under the circumstances.

He didn't know if he believed anything he was telling himself. But for Liza and their baby, he would try.

WEDNESDAY AFTERNOON, Dana ran into Sam in the hallway. She had hardly seen him since Monday, which she considered a blessing. It was difficult to be around him, under the circumstances. No matter what else had happened between them, Dana knew no one on the island would betray her, so she had taken the metal earring piece out of the satellite cable and it was working again. Five minutes in the engine room yesterday repaired Sam's boat.

"Hello," she said, trying to sound placid.

He flicked her a glance, and she stared into his eyes against her will. She was almost physically staggered by the frightful reserve she saw there. It hurt. And it also made it clear that she had built up very little unbreachable resistance to him over the last two days.

"Can you be ready to leave after dinner?" he asked.

She nodded. "Of course, I have no luggage."

He looked away, his jaw muscles working. "Right."

"Around seven?" she asked, her heart crying out to say more, so much more.

He nodded, flicking his glance back. He opened his mouth to speak, but quickly clamped it shut, merely nodding.

"Sammy! Sammy, love!" Beena's anguished cry pierced the air, and they both turned to see her fly around the corner toward them. Even from a distance Dana could see tears stream down her face. "My lucky brooch!" she sobbed. "It's gone!"

Dana was keenly aware of Sam's scrutiny. She faced him, startled to see a flicker of assumed betrayal in his eyes. Betrayal? If anyone had been betrayed, it hadn't been Sam! She stiffened. "You can't believe I took it!"

"Of course we don't believe any such thing, Angel." Beena grabbed her hands. "It's just that the pin is a keepsake from someone very dear to me. I can't bear to lose it." Distraught, she clasped Angel to her, crying against her shoulder.

Dana's glance clashed with Sam's. "You can frisk me if you want."

He kept his expression under stern restraint. "If you insist."

She blanched, stunned.

Beena waved a hand. "Don't be silly, Sammy!" She choked back a wail. "Let's look for it. I'm sure the clasp gave way. I should have allowed a jeweler to check it to make sure it wasn't in need of repair. *It's all my fault.*" The sentence trailed off in a moan.

Sam coaxed his great-aunt away from Dana, and with a protective arm around her, began to lead her toward her room. "You rest, Aunt Beena. I'll get the staff on it right away." He peered at Dana. "I'll see you in your room."

"I can't wait!" She lurched to her room, feeling bereft.

When Sam arrived thirty minutes later, she threw her arms wide. "Let's get it over. Strip search me."

He came inside and closed the door. "I intend to."

A blush crept up her neck and burned her cheeks, but she held her stance. "Go for it! Pervert!" This was so wrong! They'd gone full circle in their rela-

tionship. Once again, he didn't trust her. *Period.* And
she was calling him names. Suddenly it was all too
much to stand. Tears welled in her eyes, and he
blurred in front of her.

She loved him. *Loved him.* He didn't trust her, and
though she felt he cared for her—even if those soft
feelings were against his will—he was marrying another woman. Tilting her head with bravado, she bat-
tled to staunch her weeping, but it was no use. One
traitorous teardrop after another escaped and slid
down her face.

His blasphemy cut through the heavy silence. "Just
be ready to leave at seven."

A moment later Dana was alone.

WITH A GAPING HOLE where her heart used to reside,
she said a tearful goodbye to Beena, and climbed into
Sam's boat for the return trip to Miami.

Though Beena was still distraught about the loss of
her cat pin, she was happy Dana had regained her
memory, but not quite convinced she wasn't a refugee. She made Dana promise to write.

Of course, this was another lie Dana was forced to
tell to appease the older woman. She knew Sam
would never allow an association between them. And,
in truth, Dana didn't want one. She wanted—
needed—to be completely severed from any connection with Sam. For her heart's sake.

The trip back to Miami was made in awkward silence. Dana knew Sam cared for her. Yet, for his own
reasons, he chose to betray them both with his decision to marry Liza—a betrayal more devastating than

anything Dana could have imagined enduring at Tate's hands.

The sea grew rough. Deep in the night, under a sky full of stars, Dana was tossed into Sam's arms. The moment was bittersweet, and she feared the memory would rest uneasily in her heart for a very long time.

At the marina, they parted without words.

12

"OUCH!" Dana wagged her scraped knuckles. One thing she'd never been very good at was changing the water pump in her old clunker. She always, *always* scraped her knuckles.

And her back hurt. Cringing, she bent farther beneath the hood and gave the pump a dirty look. "It's you or me, buddy. And I'm betting on me!" She applied her wrench again, then stilled. Something on the radio caught her attention. "My—goodness," she murmured. The reporter said Tate Fleck, along with several high-ranking city officials, were under indictment for fraud. She inhaled a shuddery breath. Vindication, at last! Perhaps her mother would stop looking at her with that pinched expression, and be grateful she wasn't embroiled in a full-fledged scandal.

And maybe Sam would...

Shut up, Dana! she told herself. *Sam is out of your life.* She hadn't seen any announcement about a wedding in the paper—not that she'd been obsessing or anything. But it had only been three weeks. Planning a wedding took time.

She hoped Beena had found her brooch. It would have been nice of Sam to let her know. She bit her lip. Maybe Beena hadn't found it! Maybe he still believed she was a thief. "So, why haven't you sent the police to search my place?" she muttered. "If you're so sure I—*aaaaaaooooooch!*"

The jab in her backside made her bang her head on the hood. With both her cranium and her rear throbbing, she staggered around to slump against her car. "What was—"

Stars danced and whirled around in her garage. She squinted, trying to make out what else was there that hadn't been a minute ago. Pouncer? And—and... *"Sam?"* Backlit by the late afternoon sunshine, he stood just out of reach. Her heart reacted wildly. Even dressed in slacks and a knit shirt—more clothes than she'd ever seen him wear—she marveled at how he could possibly be more handsome than she remembered.

He walked to her and picked up the cat, holding it toward her. His smile was breathtaking, yet his eyes were watchful. "Pouncer was despondent after you left," he said.

Too stunned to form words, Dana accepted the kitty.

"I was, too," he added softly. "No matter what I told myself."

Pouncer meowed and leaped from Dana's arms onto the roof of her car. Dana hardly noticed. Sam was too what? She opened her mouth, but nothing came. It was hard to remain composed and rational, being so close to him, even when she wasn't suffering from a concussion.

"Dana," he said in a husky whisper. "I was miserable without you." Very slowly and gently he took her into his arms, as though giving her time to break

and run. "I wanted to believe you. In all honesty, I
did. I was just—I had other problems..."

She frowned, confused. He was apologizing, she
could tell. So Beena must have found her brooch. But
that didn't change anything substantially. He was still
marrying another woman. She tried to say it, tried to
tell him to take his hands off her and get out of her
life, but her brain had gone all dopey. She had the
thinking capacity of mush. She had a feeling the blow
to her head didn't have much to do with it.

He scanned her face, his smile disappearing. "I
love you, Dana. I've loved you from the first minute
I saw you." He pressed his cheek against her hair,
his lips brushing her ear. "Let's start over—forget
everything—all the lies and doubts."

He held her close. She could feel his heart. Racing.
Pounding. Hardly the heartbeat of composed indiffer-
ence. She pulled back to stare into his face, dazed and
dizzy. Unspoken hope shimmered in his eyes along
with a breathtaking sadness.

"Dana?" he asked, frowning. "Don't you know
me?"

She swallowed, shaking herself out of her stupor.
"Aren't...aren't you an engaged person I used to
know?"

He shook his head. "Not anymore. Liza told me
she was pregnant. She wasn't. I guess, when she saw
us together on the beach, she sensed how I felt about
you and decided..." He shrugged, the action weary.
"When she faced the fact I was marrying her out of
duty, she broke down and told me the baby was a
lie."

Dana saw the irony and smiled sadly. "It seems you've been beset by several lying women lately."

He kissed her on the forehead. "Please—let's forget all that." His kisses trailed to her cheek. "Marry me, Dana."

She closed her eyes, allowing the precious request to penetrate to the marrow of her bones. Her heart spilled over with joy, so much so that she couldn't hold back a husky laugh.

Sam lifted his head, his expression unsure. Uncertainty in a man as imposing as Sam was endearing. Her heart soared to heights she had never even dreamed possible.

Touching his face lovingly, she teased, "You want me to marry you, even after I scammed Beena out of Pouncer?"

His expression softened as he glanced at the cat, contentedly grooming itself on top of the car. "Beena found her brooch," he said.

"Of course, she did."

Sam's gaze returned to Dana. "It dropped off in a cereal box. She almost ate it."

"You don't have to explain, Sam."

"Yes, I do," he said, contrite. He ran a hand lovingly over her face and through her hair. When he inadvertently touched her bump, she winced.

"Oh—darling," he murmured. "I'm sorry."

Darling! He called her darling! An overwhelming sense of contentment engulfed her. The man she loved, loved her back. What in life could be more perfect than this one, wonderful miracle?

"I'd better examine you," he said, worry glimmering in those heavenly eyes. The sight was so galvanizing it sent a quiver of longing through her. A longing, she realized, she no longer had to deny.

Slipping her arms around his neck, she placed a butterfly-light kiss on his jaw. "I think you're right, Doctor. You should examine me." Her kisses moved gradually to one corner of his mouth. "Very..." She kissed the other corner, detecting a slight upward quirk. "Very..." Her mouth brushed his. "Very thoroughly—darling."

And to her everlasting delight, he did.

COLLEEN
COLLINS

Married After
Breakfast

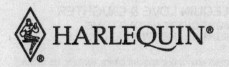

HARLEQUIN®

TORONTO • NEW YORK • LONDON
AMSTERDAM • PARIS • SYDNEY • HAMBURG
STOCKHOLM • ATHENS • TOKYO • MILAN • MADRID
PRAGUE • WARSAW • BUDAPEST • AUCKLAND

At three years old, **Colleen Collins** did Jack Benny impressions (or so her father claims). It must have been prophetic, because she eventually performed stand-up and improv comedy in Los Angeles and Denver. Along the way, she cowrote a joke book *(How To Exercise with Your Computer)*, which landed her on the cover of *National Lampoon* magazine.

The writing bug had bitten. She entered a Harlequin Temptation synopsis-writing contest and placed second.... Several years later she was thrilled to sell her first novel to Harlequin Love & Laughter.

Romantic Times has said: "Colleen Collins' quirky characters and humorous escapades will amuse." *Rendezvous* concurred, writing: "Ms. Collins has a delightful sense of humor and knows how to make her readers laugh while touching their hearts."

Married After Breakfast was inspired by Colleen's love for the old screwball comedy movies, especially road stories. Ten years ago she drove three days cross-country with a drugged cat. She thinks it was three of the loveliest days she and her cat ever spent together, although the conversation was one-sided.

Books by Colleen Collins
HARLEQUIN LOVE & LAUGHTER
26—RIGHT CHEST, WRONG NAME
54—RIGHT CHAPEL, WRONG COUPLE

To Malle

1

"HOLD ON, Lover Boy, for the longest, hottest ride of your life."

A tumbleweed, reminding Belle of the Western song "Tumbling Tumbleweeds," rolled across the highway. Too bad she'd never installed a radio in her fifteen-year-old Jeep. Music would add to the mood. She tapped her glossy peach fingernails against the worn metal of the steering wheel. No problem. She'd hum.

"Any requests?" Belle gave her head a shake, luxuriating in the hot desert breeze that blasted through the driver's window and ruffled her short hair. Good thing she liked fresh air, because she'd gotten a lot of it after sideswiping that drive-through automated teller—an incident that permanently dented the driver's door and forever disabled the window from rolling up.

She might be growing accustomed to the open window, but not to driving through the Nevada desert at high noon in mid-July. She'd have left Las Vegas earlier, but Lover Boy made her run late—so late, she was down to forty-two hours to make it to Cheyenne, Wyoming.

More than forty-two, and she'd miss her chance to start a new life.

Stepping harder on the gas pedal, Belle glanced

toward the passenger seat and warned, "No requests and it'll be hummer's choice." The only response was a chattering rattle from somewhere behind the dashboard. "Okay, Lover Boy, here goes."

She began humming "Fly Me to the Moon" as the Jeep soared up a hill. At the top, the tune caught in her throat as she viewed the expanse of aquamarine sky spread out over the beige sand. *Awe-inspiring.* Why had it always surprised people that she preferred the open country over the city? As though a Vegas showgirl couldn't appreciate beauty unless it was slathered with makeup.

Make that *former* Vegas showgirl. At thirty-seven, she knew her strutting days were numbered, but had no clue what her next career might be. And then, yesterday morning at eight o'clock, a lawyer called to say her Aunt Meg had died—and if Belle signed papers in Cheyenne within seventy-two hours, as stipulated in Meg's will, Belle would be the new owner of Meg's Blue Moon Diner. Despite her shock and grief, Belle had to smile at the seventy-two hour cutoff. While some people used ultimatums, Meg preferred deadlines, claiming they were more "energy efficient" because they fired people into action with a tenth of the words and angst.

And obviously Meg, beyond the grave, wanted to fire Belle into action. Because if she missed her deadline, the diner would be sold to a nationwide chain, the Pancake Palace Corporation. It took Belle twenty-four hours to pack and ready her Jeep. She had planned to make the long-distance drive within forty-eight hours, easy. But thanks to Lover Boy's antics this morning, that number was down to forty-two.

Belle looked down from the skies and her musings

to see the Jeep's front bumper nearly kissing the rear end of a sleek sedan with a California license plate that read COMUNIC8.

She stomped on the brake pedal. A squawking sound mingled with the squeal of brakes. Sand kicked up. As she fought the steering wheel for control, the Jeep lurched off the asphalt and slid down a bank, away from the highway.

"No, no!" She pumped the brake madly. Teasingly, the Jeep turned, then slid sideways toward a prickly limbed cactus.

Thunk!

Squawk!

A whirring sound—punctuated by a series of chirps—ended in a resounding clunk.

Silence.

Dust blew in through the driver's window. Blinking, she peered out the windshield at a mottled and spiky cactus against the Jeep's right fender. She shifted her gaze toward a creaking sound. The passenger door swung ominously open, swaying slightly with a passing gust of wind.

Open?

She struggled to sit up. "Lover Boy?" she croaked.

Squawk! Chirp! Squawk!

She peered over her shoulder into the back seat. A tipped birdcage held one upset parakeet. A bundle of puffed-up green feathers, the bird jumped, flapped, and squawked as though warning of impending doom. Louie the parakeet was okay, but what about...

"Lover Boy?" she tried to yell, but her voice was wispier than the desert breezes. Taking a deep breath, she tried again. "Lover Boy!" she cried, fighting her mounting hysteria.

"Are you…talking to me?" asked a man's deep voice.

Through the driver's window, a pair of steel-gray eyes stared intensely into hers. The man swiped sweat off his brow, panting to catch his breath. He must have seen her run off the road, pulled over, and run down to help.

"It's Lover Boy," she rasped. "I think he—" with her free hand, she gestured toward the passenger door "—is lying out there." A second, horrifying thought chilled her. Looking past the stranger, she eyed the Jeep's sandy path off the highway. "Or…or maybe I…" she swallowed, hard "…rolled over him."

The stranger's eyes widened as he flashed her a quick once-over before glancing into the back seat. "Lover Boy…looks safe to me."

"That's Louie," she snapped. This chitchat was wasting time. She grabbed the door handle. "I have to get out and find—"

The stranger reached through the opened window and touched her gently on her arm. "I can assure you," he said with authority, "nobody's lying on the road. Or off it. Now, are *you* all right?"

She fumbled with the door handle. "Of course I'm all right. Help me open the door."

"The handle…"

She looked up. He was squinting at the outside of the door as though he'd never seen one before. "The handle is missing."

She'd forgotten. It had been dislodged during the automated-teller incident. "Get out of the way, then!" Tugging on the inside handle, she shoved her body against the door. "I need to find Lover Bo—!"

On "oy-y-y!" the door flew open. Gripping the

armrest with one hand, the door jamb with the other, she plummeted downward, then jerked to a stop as though at the end of a short bungee rope. Momentarily stunned, she stared at a pair of unscuffed, tan-and-white loafers.

Squawk! Squawk!

"Don't move," the stranger said.

"Like I could," she said evenly, watching a drop of sweat roll from her nose and splat on the formerly unstained loafers.

Strong hands slipped under her arms. "Step out."

She stumbled out of the Jeep and fell, full-bodied, against him. Her cheek pressed against a firm, smooth jaw. She caught a scent of male cologne—musky—as she pulled back her head. For the first time, she noticed the man wore a blindingly white Polo shirt. Probably some coolheaded corporate type who thought he had all the answers. Like Bernard, fiancé number two. All logic, no instinct.

"I'm standing on your feet," she said.

"That makes two of us."

She frowned. This wasn't the time for humor. She staggered back a step. Damn. And it wasn't the time to be barefoot in the scorching sand, either. She'd kicked off her sandals while driving and now the sand prickled and burned under her bare soles. Hopping from one foot to the other, she shot a look toward the highway. "He must be on the road."

"As I said, no one's up there," the man repeated. "Or down here. I had a clear shot of the thoroughfare—and the terrain behind your vehicle—when I ran down here."

She jumped back into the Jeep and leaned her head against the warm steering wheel, avoiding the stranger's perplexed gaze. Just her luck to be stuck in the middle of the desert with a white-shirted, loafered dude who used words like *thoroughfare* and *terrain*. Where were those cowboy heroes when you needed them? Pressing her feet against the warm rubber matting, which offered little comfort after the hot sand, she said, "I'll put on my shoes. We'll search for him."

Chirp. Chirp.

"Don't worry, Louie, I'll be back."

But as she slipped on the first sandal, her legs started shaking. She gripped her knees, willing them to behave. Physically, she had survived the accident, but not emotionally. And she still didn't know what had happened to Lover Boy, who, besides Louie, was the only living being in her new life. Fright swept through her. *Living.* He had to be living. She closed her eyes. And she *had* to keep it together. If she fell apart now, she'd not only lose Lover, but also lose her last chance to build a future.

A familiar musky scent. She opened her eyes to find White Shirt leaning in the window, his gaze filled with concern. "Let's see if your vehicle will start," he said gently.

"It's a Jeep," she corrected, holding one hand on her knee, clutching the other to her stomach. She hated being weak. Normally, she was the one with the level head, the one taking charge. Whether it was with her six siblings or with her former co-workers, twenty show girls. To add to it all, her head spun, as though trying to catch up with the Jeep's crazy ride.

"You're pale. And this Lover Boy..." Murmuring something about hallucinating, the stranger extracted a cell phone from his pocket. "I'm calling 911," he said. "You need medical attention."

That's exactly what she *didn't* need. Some do-gooder calling an ambulance, which would eat up the little money she had to get to Wyoming. As his fingers punched numbers into the phone's keypad, she grabbed his arm. "Don't call! Or I'll—"

Meow.

She bolted upright. "Lover Boy?"

Meoooow.

Smiling, she squeezed the man's arm. "He's here! He's alive!" Crying with joy, she tossed aside a newspaper. Nothing. Reaching into the back seat, she shoved her large pink purse. Nothing. Turning, she glanced frantically around the front seat.

Me-o-o-o-w.

Underneath a wadded shirt on the passenger floor-board, a black-and-white paw inched forward.

"Lover Boy!" She swiped the shirt away.

Dirk Harriman stared at the large lump of black-and-white fur that magically appeared, as though it had materialized from underneath a magician's cape. A round, furry face with soulful golden-green eyes looked up at the woman, who cooed, "Lover Boy, Lover Boy" as she petted and stroked the animal.

Dirk squinted. It was either the fattest cat he'd ever seen or a fur-upholstered ottoman. It also looked remarkably like the collared peccary he had once encountered in the wilds of Argentina, but he doubted those beasts lived near Las Vegas, Nevada.

Although it wouldn't surprise him if this woman owned one.

"Oh, my precious baby, you were so scared," the woman murmured, gently touching the cat's chubby legs and back. "Your tummy needs rubbing, doesn't it?" After reaching over to shut the passenger door, her long, manicured fingers expertly turned the living ottoman over and stroked its tummy.

Dirk's stomach flinched as ripples of sensation flickered up and down his abdomen. He shifted his weight, surprised at his unexpected reaction. Had to be the heat. Time to refocus his attention. His gaze traveled from the feline, up the woman's slender arm to the back of her short-cropped blond head, which she dipped this way, then that, as she lavished the animal with affectionate phrases and caresses.

Blond hair? No, it was more the color of frothy champagne. He liked how the tendrils curled at the nape of her tanned neck, clinging to her moist skin. A trickle of sweat disappeared behind her collar. Collar? If he wasn't mistaken, she wore an oversize man's shirt.

He observed how the fabric clung to her back.

And if he wasn't mistaken, she wasn't wearing a bra.

"Can you believe he was here all along?" she asked, still administering tummy-rubbing therapy to the fat feline.

"No." And Dirk couldn't believe he was standing in this absurd heat, wondering if this woman wore undergarments. Time to prioritize. Get this situation resolved and get his mind back on business. After all, he had exactly two days to get to New Mexico or the deal was off.

She turned, her eyes moist with emotion. The blue eyes he'd stared into when their bodies had been pressed uncivilly close. Azure blue. Like the Caribbean. He gave himself a mental shake. Blowing out a pent-up breath, he said, "Let's try to start your vehi— Jeep."

"Right." She shifted into position behind the steering wheel, then stopped. "Hey," she said softly, turning to look at him. Her voice was different. Where before it had been edgy, it was now smooth and sweet, like honey. Leaning toward him, she said, "Before I leave, I want to thank you. You were swell to stop and help out."

The way she leaned, her shirt fell open to expose a deep shadow of cleavage. From Dirk's angle, it was difficult to avoid the sight, just as it would be difficult to stand at the top of the Grand Canyon and not look down. He was swell, all right.

"Start the motor," he said thickly. He was beginning to think everything in this whacky Jeep was oversize: the shirt, the feline, the breasts...

"Sure thing." With a wink, she twisted the ignition key.

Nothing.

Chirp. Squawk.

She tried again.

Except for another chirp, the only other sound was the arid wind that whistled past the stranded Jeep.

Dirk reached inside and opened the driver's door. "Plan B. It's too hot for us to remain here and figure out what's wrong with the Jeep. Let's move your... *entourage*...to my car. We'll turn on the air-conditioning and plan our next move."

Maybe they'd been out of sync before, but now they acted efficiently in unison without further discussion. She motioned to an old cloth-covered suitcase in the back seat, which Dirk picked up, along with a quieter Louie in his birdcage. Meanwhile, she slipped on her sandals and gathered Lover Boy into her arms, a single feat that took more effort than Dirk's two-handed load. It crossed his mind that carrying Lover Boy, the living ottoman, in this heat must be like wearing a fur coat in a sauna.

"My precious Lover Boy. You signaled to us that you were under the shirt, didn't you? You smart, darling kitty." She stood outside the Jeep, sweet-talking and cradling her pet as though it were a baby. If she treated a cat that way, how would she treat a man?

Chirp. Chirp.

Dirk looked at Louie. "Just what I was thinking," he said under his breath.

"What?"

"Just, uh, conversing with Louie." He must be losing his mind, talking man to man with a bird.

"Oh—could you get my purse?" Her arms full with Lover Boy, she dipped her head toward the back seat. "It's the pink—"

"I see." He'd have to have been blind to miss it. It was big and bright enough that if he hadn't come along, she could have thrown it outside the Jeep and some passing airplane would have seen it in the middle of nowhere and radioed for help. Shifting the suitcase under the arm that held the top rung of the birdcage, Dirk reached inside with his free hand and grabbed the potentially lifesaving purse.

Slamming shut the door with his foot, his mind tumbled with images: fat cats, pink purses, men's shirts. This woman made the word *eclectic* seem mundane.

"It's hotter than a Turkish steambath," he said. "Let's get going—" He stopped and stared at her feet.

"What?" she repeated.

"Those...shoes."

She looked over her cat at her neon-pink sandals. "Did one of the ties come loose?"

"No, no. The ties are fine." Big pink satin ties that matched the color of the purse. Why such a woman also drove a Jeep was mind-boggling. "You're wearing heels."

Her blue eyes met his. "Most shoes have heels."

"Not *high* heels. It's going to be difficult to navigate in those."

"They're not that high. Besides, my hiking boots are packed." With a toss of her head, muttering something about "navigate," she took the lead as though to prove her point. A lizard, scurrying across the sand, stopped momentarily to cock its head at her.

Dirk had to admit she maneuvered well in those heels. Even in this sand, and holding a cat that could double for furniture, she sashayed ahead, placing one foot directly in front of the other in a smooth, fluid motion. It wasn't a walk, it was a *style*. With grudging respect, he followed.

After a few strides he caught up. Glancing over at Lover Boy, who stared, fixated, into his mistress's face, Dirk said, "Lover Boy seems quite calm."

"He's on drugs."

Dirk paused. "Just don't tell me he buys them on the street."

She flashed him a frown that broke into a smile. "Tranquilizers, silly. Acepromazine. He gets nervous on trips, so I had to pick up the medicine from the vet this morning."

No one ever called Dirk Harriman "silly." As CEO and president of Harriman Enterprises, he was called "sir," "Mr. Harriman," but never "silly." He liked it if people relaxed more in his presence, called him Dirk, but he guessed his reserved manner, honed from years of being in the business limelight, created a wall against such familiarity. Except for his housekeeper Lucy and his best friend and lawyer Ray, no one called him by his first name.

And except for this woman, *no one* ever called him "silly."

He glanced over, pleased that he'd made her smile. It softened her features, exposing a delicacy that was at the opposite spectrum of that punkish hairdo. A delicacy that complemented her pleasing honeyed voice.

Chirp.

She nodded toward the parakeet. "Louie acts as though he needs tranquilizers, but that's just his personality. He demands attention as a matter of course, accident or not." She did that head-dipping thing again. "Poor dear. Your cup tipped over. We need to get you water."

"I have plenty in the car." Dirk craned his neck to check his watch. Twelve-thirty. They'd get to the car within minutes, he'd turn on the air-conditioning, pass around the bottled water, then call his assistant back in L.A. to hunt down local resources. A garage. A towing service. Possibly a hotel or car-rental agency for the woman and her brood.

Despite the heat, the desolation, and the life-and-death crisis of Lover Boy, Dirk smiled to himself. He, who avoided strangers at all costs, had managed to get involved, in the middle of nowhere, with a curious crew. Louie, Lover Boy, and...

"What's your name?" he asked. He liked how her

hair glowed in the sun, as though streams of light had interwoven with the strands.

"Belle," she answered. "Belle O'Leary."

He repeated her name under his breath. "It's melodious."

"My family's melodious. We love to sing together. And you?"

"Dirk Harriman." She didn't seem to recognize his name. Or him. "So you sing?"

"No, I hum." She stopped. "Let me catch my breath before we head up."

They stood at the base of the sandy incline that led to the highway. Thanks to his morning workouts, he knew he could scale it with reasonable ease, even with a suitcase, a gargantuan purse, and a parakeet in tow. He glanced over at the fattest cat in the world, which lolled contentedly, paws up, in its mistress's embrace. It would be a struggle for Belle, in her pink heels, to hike up this hill with that additional furry weight.

"Want to switch? Louie for Lover Boy?"

"No." She cuddled the cat. "He's had quite a scare. He wants to stay close."

Did she always speak for her cat? Dirk avoided looking at how close druggy Lover was to the Grand Canyon. He cleared his throat. "Okay, let's go." He knew better than to comment on her sandals again. He dug in one foot after the other, heading up the incline. Reaching the road, he turned around, expecting to see Belle teetering far behind. Hardly. Within moments, she stepped onto the road next to him.

He blew out a gust of air. "You made it."

"What'd you think?" She breathed in and out several times. Catching her breath, she finished, "That I'd stay at the bottom, waiting for you to rescue me?"

Gone was the honey. Back was the edge.

He squared his shoulders and flashed her an appeasing smile. She might go braless and wear pink shoes, but she grew defensive if she thought someone was treating her as a helpless female. He hitched his head down the road, wishing he could scratch where a drip of sweat tickled his chin. "My car is over there—"

A sound somewhere between a shriek and a gasp cut off the rest of his sentence. At first he thought Lover Boy was coming down from the tranquilizers. Or that Louie was throwing another feather fit. Then he realized it came from Belle, who was staring aghast at his vehicle.

"Communicate!"

"Uh, yes." Amazing that she could read the license plate from this distance.

Those Caribbean eyes turned an Arctic-blue. "Because of you," she said forcefully, "I went off the road."

Momentarily taken back, Dirk rubbed his chin against his shoulder. "Madam, I did nothing to cause your accident." He started walking toward his car, hoping she'd follow suit. From the sound of her honeyless voice close behind, he realized she had.

"Madam?" she repeated. "You make it sound as if I run a brothel."

Chirp. Chirp.

He continued walking, wondering who's side Louie was on. Dirk always treated women with respect, and that included referring to them with terms of courtesy, whether they liked it or not. At least he hadn't called her "silly."

Reaching his Jaguar sedan, he set her purse on the roof and fumbled in his pocket for the keys. From the corner of his eye, he saw Belle approaching, the look on her face hotter than the temperature.

"Your driving technique caused me to run off the road."

At least she was off the "madam" topic. He opened the passenger door and set Louie's cage on the back seat. Straightening, he said calmly, "I suggest we continue this discussion inside, *after* I start the air conditioner."

She hesitated for a moment before marching to the door and getting in. If the situation wasn't tense, Dirk would have complimented Belle on her skill at hiking and cat-carrying in this sweltering heat. Instead, biting his tongue, he crossed to the driver's side and opened the door. Inserting the key into the ignition, he said soothingly, "This will feel good." With barely a hum, cool air filled the car.

Leaving his new companions to enjoy the air-conditioning, Dirk walked to the back of his car and put the suitcase into the trunk. Slamming shut the lid, he eyed the license plate.

"Communicate," he murmured. He prided himself on his communication skills. For years, he'd headed an empire of corporations—magazines, television shows—whose very foundations were built on communication. He couldn't even count the numerous boardrooms in which he'd confronted and wooed adversaries with his communication skills.

But he had a gut feeling that those skills were going to be seriously challenged by Belle O'Leary.

2

DIRK SLID INTO the driver's seat and slammed shut the door. The air-conditioned interior was a balm after the sizzling temperatures outside.

He looked over at Belle.

Unfortunately, not everything was cool on the inside.

After flashing Dirk a miffed look, she turned, shifted onto her knees, and leaned over the ivory leather passenger seat toward Louie's birdcage on the back seat. Belle had inserted a neatly folded newspaper underneath the cage, Dirk noted. She might be irked, but that didn't stop her from being considerate of his possessions. He could deal with anger—and typically had to, most days, as CEO of Harriman Enterprises. But not so often did he deal with someone's thoughtfulness at the same time. Belle's contradictory character was more complex than her pink sandals led one to believe.

As she reached to fill Louie's water cup from a bottle of Evian, her shirt hiked up over her jean-clad rear end. As Louie chirped and Belle poured, Dirk's gaze dropped. Another contradiction. She wore oversize men's shirts and undersize women's jeans.

I'm a cad for admiring her upright character one moment and her backside character the next.

He eased in a slow breath. But a member of the

male species would have to be seriously farsighted—
or dead—to not admire the nicely rounded attributes
of Belle O'Leary. Her gluteus maximus made him
wish he'd studied Latin longer. His gaze slid to her
molded thighs. What did she do to get such thighs?
His ex-fiancée, Janine, had worked out with a personal trainer every day, but her thighs couldn't hold
a muscle to Belle's. Those shapely contours had to
be from some special exercise—maybe something she
did for a living?

"I took squatter's rights," Belle said.

Dirk shifted his gaze to her face, which peered at
him over her shoulder. "What are you doing?" she
asked, narrowing her eyes.

"I was..." Thigh gazing? "I was...wondering
what you did for a living." He flashed her his most
charming smile.

Belle, still leaning over the seat, pressed her eyebrows together in a frown. She started to speak,
stopped, then lifted the bottle of Evian. "Louie was
thirsty, so I took squatter's rights and stole your bottle
of fancy water." She swiveled and slid back down
into the passenger seat. "Why were you wondering
what I did for a living?"

He didn't like how Lover Boy, lolling on the floor
of the passenger seat, stared up at him. He swore the
feline's deadpan stare had an accusatory glint.

Dirk fiddled with some buttons on the instrument
panel. "Doesn't that cat of yours ever blink?" Felt
warmer in here. He punched a button several times,
decreasing the temperature.

"Of course he blinks." Belle peered into her pet's
face for a moment. "He's just...meditating. It's been
a rough day."

Meditating? There she went again, translating her cat's moods. Did she have some kind of pet-and-owner psychic connection? Inwardly, he shuddered at the thought of having a mind meld with the living ottoman. One probably received random images of oversize kibbles cavorting with cans of tuna.

"I have an idea what *you* do for a living," Belle said emphatically, interrupting Dirk's thoughts. "You *communicate*."

Worse than the kibble-tuna fantasia was how she pronounced *communicate,* infusing it with indictment. Somehow his license plate was responsible for her accident. Rather than attempt *that* leap in logic, he decided to defuse the stressful conversation. "That's my favorite word," he said agreeably, pulling the mobile phone out of his pocket.

"And the last word I saw before I went off the road."

She had a death grip on that bottle of water, Dirk noted. He decided *non*communication at this point was the better approach. For all he knew, she was a professional wrestler. If he irritated her further, he might find himself saying "uncle" in a thigh hold.

No she'd probably make him say "communicate."

He punched in the phone number harder than he meant to. His breaths were labored despite the computerized, air-conditioned environment.

"Are you okay?" Belle asked.

Dirk hesitated before punching in the last number. "Battery on the phone looks low," he mumbled. "Needs charging soon." Which is what his overcharged libido *didn't* need. Damn, he was losing it. Fixating on a strange woman's thighs when he needed to focus on the emergency at hand. His place was behind his desk, haggling with people for whom multinational corporations were named. Instead, he was behind the wheel of his car, haggling with the woman for whom the Thigh Master could easily have been named.

"Obviously," he said, adopting his professional persona, "you were driving behind me and saw my license plate. But mada—uh, Belle, I did not cause your accident. If you'll recall, I was the Good Samaritan who stopped to help you." He tapped in the last number with just the right amount of pressure. Good. He was in control of his physical functions again.

"What is it with you California drivers?" Belle rolled back her shoulders, a move that made Dirk glad he didn't have to test his manual dexterity again. "You think cruise control is the answer to life. But they're two completely different things. To *cruise* is to let loose, experience the road. *Control* is uptight, possessive—"

"Merci?" He was grateful to hear his assistant's familiar voice. Merci—down-to-earth, antithighbuilding Merci—would bring some sense of sanity to this out-of-cruise-control conversation. "I picked up a stranded traveler in Nevada and she needs assistance…"

As he itemized the tasks for Merci to accomplish—starting with finding a local towing service—he watched Belle's champagne-blond hair flutter slightly in the air-conditioned air. And how her face, flushed from the heat and her anger, had the hue of a woman aroused. As the cool air swirled through the car's interior, it picked up traces of her flowery perfume. Just as her tight jeans didn't match her oversize shirt, her flowery scent didn't match her spark. Most people he summed up quickly, but Belle kept him off balance. She reminded him of the Jack-in-the-box toy he had as a child—you cranked and cranked the handle, never knowing when it would pop up.

"And her Jeep will need to be towed..." As he discussed the particulars with Merci, Dirk's gaze slipped to Belle's manicured hands. On her fourth finger, left hand, she wore a sparkling pear-cut diamond, at least two carats. He tried to focus on his conversation with Merci. But the notion that Belle was engaged, maybe married, trigged a reaction. Surprise? Disappointment?

"Cha-Cha's Garage? Are you certain that's the name?" He paused. It *was* disappointment. "All right, give me directions." He'd been alone too long, that's all. No grown man experienced disappointment that some woman—a stranger, really—was spoken for. Extracting a pen from his console, he said, "Ready," and jotted down the information Merci gave him.

A few minutes later, he hung up. "My assistant is calling a local towing service, which will retrieve your Jeep. We'll rendezvous at Cha-Cha's Garage, which is a few more miles down Highway 15, off Doyle Road."

He swore Belle's manicured toes danced a little when he said "Cha-Cha." *Get off the toes before you return to more thigh thoughts.* "Did you know," he said, hearing the strain in his voice, "that we're near the Valley of Fire and the Lost City Museum?" Safe topics. Local landmarks. Thank God they were no where near the Grand Canyon. Or some national monument that had the word *thigh* on it.

"Did you look those up on a map?"

"Why would thighs be on a map?"

They both looked at each other in surprise.

"Thighs?" Belle repeated.

Dirk busied himself with pressing another button or two on the instrument panel. He inadvertently turned on a small pin light in the back. Louie began chirping incessantly.

"He thinks he's onstage," murmured Belle.

Dirk turned off the light. Louie stopped. Deciding not to ponder that too long, Dirk attempted to smooth over his faux pas. "My assistant mentioned some exercise class she's taking while referring to some of the local sights."

Belle stared at him oddly. "Is your assistant from around here?"

"No. Los Angeles."

Belle's odd look intensified. "You called *California* for a *Nevada* towing service?"

"I needed Merci to check on a few other things as well."

"Merci?"

"Short for Mercedes."

Belle paused. "You drive a..." She looked at the ornament on the hood. "A leopard—"

"Jaguar."

"Whatever. You have an assistant named Mercedes. Next, you'll tell me you have a dog named Rolls-Royce." Before he could answer, she added, "I suggest you try driving normally instead of going cruise control."

If he had to hear how his Jag forced her Jeep off the road one more time, he'd ask Cha-Cha's Garage to offer him asylum. "Let's cut to the chase," he said calmly. "What's bothering you?"

Belle pulled back her shoulders. "If you'd been driving the speed limit, my front bumper wouldn't have been on top of 'Communicate.'"

He thought briefly about baseball before responding. "I'll drive normally," he promised.

"All right," she said softly, avoiding his eyes. She stroked Lover Boy's head. "Let's go to Cha-Cha's Garage." She stretched the seat belt across her chest. "Too bad we don't have time to sightsee the Valley of Fire and Lost City Museum. Did you know we're also near the Virgin River?"

Dirk stepped on the gas pedal a little harder than he meant to, fully aware he wasn't on cruise control.

AS THE JAGUAR SPED along the highway, Belle cuddled Lover Boy and stared out the tinted window. From her Jeep, thanks to its incessant gyrations, the world had a slightly jarred look. From this Jaguar, the world sped by, cooly serene through windows tinted blue.

Serene. The opposite of how she felt inside, which was anxious. And if she slapped a color on it, flaming red.

She glanced at her wristwatch, a Swatch she'd picked up at a flea market. She was down to forty hours. If the Jeep got fixed soon, she could still haul A on the interstate and make it to Cheyenne by 8:00 a.m. Wednesday.

But her Jeep had made an ominous clunk right before it parked on that cactus. What if it required more than a few hours labor to get fixed? Plus there was the repair bill. Years ago, because of her tendency to charge too many trinkets for nieces and nephews, she'd stopped carrying credit cards. Not that it stopped her from spending all her spare cash on them, which she justified was her prerogative as a doting aunt with no children of her own to spoil. Unfortunately, years of such generosity meant she now had only enough cash to buy gas and feed three mouths— make that two mouths and one beak—until she started making a living at the Blue Moon Diner.

So how would she pay the repair bill? She ran her thumb over the chiseled surface of her diamond ring. Cha-Cha's Garage…Belle offered a silent prayer that Cha-Cha was the Carmen Miranda of the Desert, a fruit-capped female mechanic who loved jewels.

As Belle gazed at the sparkling diamond, a pang of nostalgia shot through her. Engagement ring number four—which she'd tried to return as she had the others—was from Louie, her parakeet's namesake. Louie Capraro. Funny. Chivalrous. Their only quarrel was that he didn't believe a wife should have a career—which brought back memories of Belle's mom stuck in the home, raising six kids, never fulfilling her own personal goals. Although her mother hadn't complained, sometimes she'd reminisced—with a faraway look in her eyes—about her girlhood dreams of running a beauty salon.

It was that faraway look that had always haunted Belle, as though her mother's dreams were distant images, never to be reality. At a young age, Belle swore she'd never have that same look in her own eyes. In retrospect, maybe she wished too hard because she always ended relationships before she had a chance to have children, something she had yearned for. *Funny how life tosses you Catch-22s.*

And funny how Louie, who didn't believe in

women running businesses, might inadvertently—
through the engagement ring he insisted she keep—
provide the financing to help her get her own business.

She stroked the silky fur behind Lover Boy's ear.
Too much to think about. She slipped a look at Dirk's
hands. No wedding ring there. And no telltale tan line
around a white strip where a wedding band should be.
Not that she cared.

Her gaze slid over the corded muscles of his forearm—no real tan—probably didn't go outside much.
But if the muscles in his arms were any indication,
he worked out. She scanned the length of his arm, up
the white Polo shirtsleeve, to his face.

The guy wasn't hard on the eyes. He had that
nicely aged clean-cut look, a preppy boy who'd ma-
tured into a distinguished-looking man. Under a tou-
sle of chestnut hair, with a touch of gray at the temples, he had a broad forehead. Not too many lines,
either. She liked that in a guy—showed he didn't
worry. And those steel-gray eyes. In the short time
she'd known him, she'd caught looks of concern and
care. And, when she accidentally stood on his feet,
she swore she caught a twinkle in his eyes.

An expressive man. She liked that, too.

Well, if she liked him so much, why had she fumed
out loud about his cruise-controlling? Worse, he
hadn't barked back, the way Louie might have done.
No, Dirk Harriman had been gallant by offering to
help her.

"I'm sorry," she murmured.

He shot her a confused look. "For what?"

"For blaming the accident on your cruise control."

"I have to admit it's a first. I've been accused of

controlling, but not *cruise*-controlling." When he smiled at her, one side of his mouth crooked a little, making him look boyish. And sexy.

Sexy.

She squirmed a little. Lover Boy opened one eye and checked her out as though to say, "Hey, I'm sleeping, keep still."

"Sorry to you, too," she whispered to her cat. And sorry her libido had been resurrected. She hadn't thought about hot stuff in weeks. Maybe months. But stuck next to a preppy guy with a sexy smile, her libido announced itself loud and clear. Not that anything could ever happen between the two of them. He probably had a string of debutantes—or whatever these guys fell for—in his wake. She sighed heavily.

"What's wrong?" Dirk asked, his gray eyes darkening with concern.

"I'm..." *Recovering from a hormone surge.* "I'm on a serious deadline."

"You and me both."

You and me? Belle and Dirk, the showgirl and the prince, actually had something in common? "Tell me about yours," she said.

"I'm finalizing a deal to buy a magazine."

"You finalize decisions like that? I just plunk down three bucks and call it done."

"I meant a company that publishes a magazine."

"Ohhh." As Belle tapped her fingernail against the upholstered armrest, she scanned the interior. This car had more polished wood, blinking lights, and leather upholstery than a posh restaurant at Christmas time. "Afraid I can't offer any advice. The biggest thing I ever bought was my Jeep."

"I thought it was your cat."

She gave Dirk a double take. "Watch what you say," she teased. "He's sensitive about his weight." Dirk Harriman was not only preppy and sexy, but funny, too. Forget the diner business. She could bottle this guy and make herself a fortune. "So, tell me more about your deadline. Where you headed?"

His fingers played along the steering wheel. "Taos." He paused. "Taos, New Mexico."

"Heard of it." Actually, she hadn't. But it felt so good to be talking about something they had in common, she figured a little white lie wouldn't hurt.

He gazed out the window as he drove. "Thought this would be an education, taking a road trip by myself across the country. I rarely get out into the world."

So she'd been right about his not getting outside often. Although with such a to-die-for car, it was surprising. Belle waited for him to say more, but he let his last comment hang in the air.

After several moments of silence, he said, "You don't know who I am, do you?" His voice sounded strangely somber, unlike the measured tones she'd grown accustomed to. She had to admit *something* about him looked familiar, but then, being a showgirl, she'd seen a lot of faces in a lot of audiences. "Should I?"

He gave her the strangest look, as though analyzing her response. But rather than answer, he picked up a remote control and pointed it at the dashboard. "Music?" But it wasn't a question. He touched a button. Soothing classical music filled the car.

Since he obviously wanted to end their conversation, she decided not to mention she preferred cowboy tunes.

CHA-CHA'S GARAGE looked like a small-scale Woodstock reunion. Instead of thousands of hippies on a remote farm, there were twenty or so tie-dyed characters at a middle-of-nowhere automobile garage. On the periphery were several rainbow-decorated vans, a vintage VW painted with a portrait of the Beatles, and several motorcycles. Various men and women, all sporting ponytails and bandannas, watched Dirk's Jaguar pull into the lot.

He parked next to a phone booth and contemplated its missing glass and phone book, wondering if these hippie types still nursed antiestablishment grudges. And if so, would they attack his Jaguar as a symbol of the bourgeoisie? He looked at the sea of faces staring back at him. He, who typically commuted with a chauffeur and private secretary, who never entered a restaurant without being immediately ushered to a private table, was going to walk into a throng of retro hippies who probably despised overt signs of conspicuous consumption. He might as well hang a sign around his neck, Beat Me Up Now.

"Why are we sitting here?" Belle shifted the drugged Lover Boy in her arms.

"All those people." He decided to skip the paranoid particulars.

"Not that many," Belle said. "I've danced in front of ten times that number."

Dance? Is that what the Thigh Master did for a living?

"Does it…bother you to face that many people at once?" Belle asked.

Chirp.

Dirk was getting the sense that Louie always liked to have the last word. Or last chirp.

"Sit tight," he said, more to Louie than anyone else.

Stepping out of the car, Dirk inhaled dust and incense. The door slammed shut with a sharp click that reverberated through the air. "Communicate," he said under his breath.

Approaching a group of ponytails, he asked, "Is one of you Cha-Cha?" hoping it was the frail girl in the Indian print dress who sat cross-legged under an umbrella.

From behind her stepped a burly guy with a beard that could double for a table runner. A black, fringed leather vest barely covered his protruding belly. "I'm Cha-Cha," he said gruffly.

At first, Dirk wasn't sure what had spoken—the stomach or the head. He extended his hand, wondering if Cha-Cha's parents had been dance instructors.

"Nice car, man," Cha-Cha said, as he grabbed Dirk's hand with a crushing grip.

Dirk tried not to wince as Cha-Cha pumped his hand in a male-bonding shake. "Thank you." Breaking loose, he motioned with crimped fingers toward the desert.

"The woman I'm traveling with had a car accident. Her Jeep is being towed here for repair."

Minus the help of any handkerchief, Cha-Cha snorted and blew his nose. Dirk was glad they'd done the male-bonding handshake first.

"*Her* Jeep's being towed?"

"Yes. My assistant arranged for a towing service to deliver the vehicle here."

Cha-Cha, stroking his runner-beard, squinted at Dirk. "She's your assistant?"

Dirk breathed in deeply. In his mind, he heard his

father say, "It's not who you are, but who people *think* you are." He didn't know who this Cha-Cha character was—or the twenty-plus people who camped out here. Maybe they didn't care about conspicuous consumption, but Cha-Cha, leader of this tie-dye tribe, seemed overly interested in Belle.

Dirk cleared his throat. "She's my woman," he said, infusing his tone with macho possessiveness. He'd never made such a statement in his entire life. But saying, "She's my traveling companion" lacked punch.

Cha-Cha scratched his belly. "What're you doin' in that fancy car while your woman's driving a Jeep?"

Borrowing Cha-Cha's gesture, Dirk scratched his chin. "She's a four-wheel type."

"That's right," said a honeyed voice with a distinct edge. "I dig the outdoors."

Dirk turned. Belle stood next to him. With those tight jeans and neon-pink sandals, she hardly looked like a nature girl, but her no-nonsense tone was hard to argue with.

The sound of an engine broke the silence. Along a side road, a dilapidated tow truck dragged Belle's Jeep. As the truck turned onto the dirt road that led to Cha-Cha's garage, dust mushroomed behind the minicaravan.

This seemed to be the event they all lived for. Cha-Cha and several hippies migrated toward where the truck slammed to a stop. As the people moved away, Belle stepped closer to Dirk. "I'm *your woman?*"

Her perfume swirled through the warm air, that flowery scent that hinted of the sweetness always beneath the surface. "I was communicating with them."

"Communicating?" She gave her head a disbelieving shake. "By calling me 'your woman?'"

He looked into her Caribbean-blue eyes. "Biker talk."

"You know biker talk the way I know debutante talk."

Debutante talk? He cocked one eyebrow, wondering what in the hell that was supposed to mean. Rather than ask, he confided, "I was protecting you."

She looked at him as though he'd gone crazy. "From what? The urge to tie-dye?" She paused. "For a preppy kind of guy, you sure have an overactive imagination."

Around Belle he certainly did. In the past hour, her body had driven him from images of the Grand Canyon to fantasies of the Thigh Master. Even if he left her body out of it—which was difficult—he was also starting to imagine her pets had psychic insights into his brain.

He should never have left L.A.

Cha-Cha's rumbling voice broke into his thoughts.

"Bad news, man." Cha-Cha slowly shook his head. "The Jeep's mortally wounded."

3

"MORTALLY WOUNDED?" Belle repeated. "It's a *Jeep,* not a human."

Dirk swore Cha-Cha's beard bristled. After staring at Belle with a look of utter incredulity, Cha-Cha solemnly placed his hand over his heart. "Man," he said, elongating the word until it sounded like a mantra. "All things have molecules. Like Einstein said, 'Life is more energy than matter.' We're preparing to say last rites."

"Einstein? Last—?" Belle shook her head and checked her Swatch. "I don't have time for a religious Jeep ceremony—I have less than forty hours to get to Cheyenne." She rolled back her shoulders in what Dirk recognized as your-cruise-control-pushed-me-off-the-road gesture. "If you don't get my Jeep fixed pronto, somebody else will be having last rites—"

"Two rites don't make a wrong," Dirk said exuberantly, smiling at a confused looking Cha-Cha while pulling Belle aside. "You're not communicating," he whispered between frozen-smile teeth, "you're threatening." When she started to disagree, he tightened his hold. "And to worsen matters, *threatening* a tie-dye tribe who, considering their expertise in death ceremonies, might mangle more than Einstein quotes."

Belle yanked loose of his grip. "My entire future depends on that Jeep—and they're sprinkling it with holy water!"

On "holy water," Cha-Cha, his hand still over his heart, pivoted and walked away.

"Hey!" Belle yelled at him. "No last rites!"

Obviously smart enough not to tangle in fender-melting heat with a furious woman, Cha-Cha nodded slowly. "It's cool," he said over his shoulder. "No rites."

Belle, seemingly mollified by his response, turned back to Dirk. "No rites. There's hope."

Dirk pulled at his shirt, wishing he was back in his air-conditioned car. "Considering we're in the middle of nowhere, I'll take the mechanic's expert opinion that the Jeep is dead. Plan B. We inquire if there's a local airport, and I drive you there—"

"Whoa." Belle raised her hand. "Who said I have the bucks to buy a plane ticket?"

A fly buzzed past. Dirk eyed it, envious that it was moving toward *its* destination. "I'll pay for your ticket."

"I have two other passengers."

He had no problem visualizing Louie as a passenger. The brash parakeet would probably insist on his own seat, demand special attention from the flight attendants, then for the entire trip, loudly compare his flying techniques to the plane's. "I'll pay for them, too."

"Don't you get it?" Belle made an exasperated noise. "I don't take handouts. I make this trip on my own, not on a stranger's generosity."

The logic was about as flawed as when she'd blamed his license plate for causing her accident. But beyond her harsh independence, Dirk heard something else in her tone. She was accustomed to being on her own. No handouts. It saddened him that Belle O'Leary had never let someone pamper her. But he'd be a fool to try to change a lifetime's worth of behavior in one conversation.

And he'd be an idiot to attempt further discussion in this inferno.

"Look," Dirk said, brushing a drip of sweat off his chin. "I'll *loan* you the money. The sooner we get back on the road, the better the chances we both meet our deadlines."

"A loan?" Belle frowned. "You'll never see me again—how do you know I'll repay you?"

In his gut, Dirk knew he had her pegged. No handouts. No pampering. He had negotiated with people like her before—their handshake was as binding as a written contract. Yet they'd insist you make them play by the rules. He knew how to close this deal.

Sauntering back to the car, he said nonchalantly, "We'll sign an agreement. I'll call my lawyer and have him draw up terms, including strict penalties if you miss a payment."

After a beat, he heard her pink-sandaled footsteps behind him. "A signed agreement?" Her voice was dipping into its honey range again. "Sounds fair. I'll accept the loan."

Belle O'Leary might ridicule his license plate, but he was figuring out how to communicate with her.

BELLE TAPPED HER FOOT against the carpeting on the Jaguar's floor. It was almost 5:00 p.m. They'd been on the road four hours—and no airport. It didn't help that they'd made that wrong turn over an hour ago and had to backtrack to the main highway. Unfortunately, the detour had been her idea.

"Can we turn off the highbrow music?" she asked, tapping her foot faster. "It's making me anxious."

Dirk flashed her a surprised look. "I thought it might be soothing."

"All those violins jangle my nerves. Plus, I jump every time they hit those drums."

"That rowdy Mozart can do that to people," Dirk said dryly, punching a button.

Except for Lover Boy's snoring, there was silence. That made her anxious, too. "Any cowboy tunes?"

"Cowboy tunes?" Dirk repeated, as though speaking a foreign language. He gestured toward the radio embedded in wood paneling. "Power button is on the left. Hit Scan for local stations."

Belle did as instructed until she located a song. "Garth," she said on a release of breath. "He can compete with Mozart any day."

Dirk cast her a sidelong glance. "This Garth fellow has violins and drums in his song—doesn't that bother you?"

Belle carefully placed her feet over Lover Boy, who lay in a furry heap under her legs. "No. He knows how to mix 'em up just right." She smoothed her shirt over her lap. "How long before we get to the airport?" She could have bitten her tongue as soon as she asked.

"If we hadn't taken that last detour, we'd already be there."

"Sorry," she murmured, "I misread the sign."

"I'll never understand how you misinterpreted Harry's Hot Dog Stand Ahead to read 'Airport.'"

"We already discussed this," she answered peevishly. "I thought it said 'Something-Something Airport Straight Ahead.'"

Chirp. Chirp.

"Why does Louie always take your side?"

"Because he's a smart bird." Staring out the window to avoid Dirk's look, she spied an approaching sign. "Look!" She tapped her window's glass in case Dirk wasn't sure which way to look. "It says 'Airport Next Exit'!"

"Are you certain? I don't want to detour to a hamburger stand this time." He slowed the car to a near stop as they approached the sign. "Airport Next Exit." He glanced into the back seat. "What's wrong, Louie? No chirp to second your mistress?" With a light chuckle, Dirk reached over and patted Belle on the arm, a gesture that took her by surprise. Most guys meant something else when they copped a pat, but Dirk Harriman's touch was sweet. Reassuring.

Actually, except for that moment at Cha-Cha's garage when he'd accused her of threatening the last-rites mechanic and his tribe, Dirk had been mostly sweet to her. In a few miles, they'd be at the airport and this part of her trip would end. An unexpected gloom washed over her as she thought of never seeing him again.

"You've been swell," she said softly, surprised at the catch in her voice.

Dirk shot her a look that confused the heck out of her. Maybe the guy didn't like compliments? Most men ate them up. Perhaps it was her use of words—after all, Dirk Harriman had a thing for "communicating." "You know, swell," she explained. "Great. You've been a real pal."

"I know what you mean. It's been my pleasure."

Pleasure. Now *that* word communicated loud and clear—she felt it all the way from the tip of her toes to the top of her head. Maybe it was a good thing she'd be on a plane soon, flying far away from Dirk. She had a life to kick start—the last thing she needed was her libido getting in the way.

Half an hour later, they walked into a small terminal that looked like a remake of the *Wings* TV show. Belle carried a blissed-out Lover Boy and her purse. Dirk carried an agitated Louie and her suitcase. After weaving their way around several clusters of people, Dirk located three adjacent seats where he deposited Belle and her possessions.

"You stay here. I'll get your ticket." He looked at Lover Boy sprawled across one seat, then at Louie's cage, which filled another. The bird hopped back and forth on his perch, eyeing Dirk. "I mean tickets." After squinting at the parakeet's frenetic jumping, Dirk asked, "Do you think Louie's jealous of me?"

"Louie's jealous of Lover Boy, not you. If you were an animal, it'd be different."

Dirk arched one eyebrow. "Guess you'll never know." He checked out the room. "Time to face another crowd," he murmured, heading toward the ticket counter.

But Belle was still stuck at "Guess you'll never know." Rarely at a loss for words, she was momentarily speechless that preppy Dirk Harriman had flashed her an overtly saucy side. That was *her* technique. Despite the craziness of this trip, and the stress of losing her Jeep, she smiled and watched his exiting form.

What else had he said? *Time to face another crowd.* If he felt any qualms, he didn't show it. His walk had a lean assuredness, like Pierce Brosnan in one of those James Bond films. But there was a distinct difference. Whereas Pierce might charge into the world, Dirk seemed happier to observe it from a distance.

No wonder his car has tinted windows. It's like a curtain against people. Which tied into his not liking to face crowds. *Who was Dirk Harriman?*

Just as the question hit her, he disappeared behind a group of people. Belle jumped up from her seat, paced a few steps, then stopped when she spied him across the room. Relief filled her.

Now what was that all about?

Crossing her arms under her breasts, she paced back to her seat, but didn't sit. "I've never needed a guy, yet here I am feeling all insecure when he gets out of sight for a moment," she said under her breath. Must be the car. Being cooped up, driving through unknown territory, must create some kind of unnatural connection. Like what happens to kidnapped people when they bond with their abductors. Not that Dirk Harriman had abducted her. He was hardly the kind of man to take a woman against her will. Even a woman with a very strong will.

Belle leaned her head back and stared up at the tiled ceiling. The beige squares blurred into a creamy haze, within which she saw a sleek Jaguar. In the passenger seat, she envisioned herself getting a manicure, in the throes of being abducted by Dirk "Animal" Harriman, who was forcing her to accompany him to Taos or Laos or wherever that landlocked magazine was.

She breathed in and out deeply. From the car radio, she could almost hear the twang of Garth's guitar,

Dirk's new music of choice since kidnapping the fair maiden Belle O'Leary.

Belle O'Leary of Taos.

The beige tiles zoomed sharply back into focus, their jagged edges puncturing her kidnapped-in-a-Jaguar-and-forced-to-have-a-manicure fantasy.

Taos? What would she do there?

She lowered her gaze back to the room and its unfamiliar faces and buzz of conversations. In Taos, she'd be alone, just as she was now, except she wouldn't have a future. *Her* future. She'd be nothing more than an accessory to Dirk Harriman's life. Exactly what would have happened with her former fiancé, Louie.

She looked at her parakeet, who cocked its head and blinked at her.

"We're on our way to *our* diner," she said forcefully. Nothing was standing in the way of her future. She checked her Swatch. *Five-thirty.* While driving, Dirk had phoned the airlines and made reservations for a 7:00 p.m. flight. Soon, she'd be in Cheyenne, heading straight to the Blue Moon Diner where she'd stay in one of the back rooms that her Aunt Meg had used for living quarters. She'd have a full day to recuperate before signing papers Wednesday morning.

The signature that meant she'd be a businesswoman. And, since she'd given away all her money, her signature also meant the chance to start a new life.

Sitting down between her two pets, Belle leaned toward Louie on her right. "Your cage will be close to the cash register, where you can keep an eye on the money. I know you'll like that."

Chirp.

She turned to her left. "And Lover Boy..." Although he was in the ozone, one paw stuck up in the air, as though to say, "Here I am." She ran her finger along the soft, furry paw, then held it gently. "Your station will be in the kitchen, your favorite room. In a corner, you'll have your never-empty food bowl, under a sign that reads, Lover Boy's Domain. And you'll never again be on drugs because you'll never have to be in the car. Well, except for an occasional trip to the vet's, but you'll *never* have to drive cross-country again."

Her eyes stung with tears. "But you did it for me, didn't you," she whispered hoarsely. "Traveled hundreds of miles to my new life. Our new life." All the emotions of the day caught up with her. Sniffling, she dabbed at the corner of her eye with the tail of her shirt. "You're my special Lover Boy."

A deep voice spoke. "I'm beginning to worry about you and that feline."

She turned to find Dirk looking at her with an amused expression on his face. "Don't you think Lover Boy should be the name of your amore, not your cat?"

Maybe it was Dirk who was jealous of Lover Boy? She cleared her throat. "He's a cuddler—that's how he got his name." Cuddling. Manicuring. Abducting. Suddenly, all the words in her fantasy seemed to end in "ing." A rush of heat filled her cheeks, which were probably pinker than her shoes.

But Dirk didn't seem to notice. In fact, his amused look had turned serious. "I have bad news."

"The plane is mortally wounded?"

"I couldn't get tickets."

"You…you made reservations on the phone while we drove here. I heard you."

"It's your traveling companions. Airlines don't fly animals unless they have health certificates, signed within the past thirty days by a veterinarian."

"Lover Boy just saw his veterinarian this morning!"

"Did you get a health certificate?"

She paused. "No. Acepromazine." Her mind reeled with images of distant diners—was that how it was for her mother? Always in the corner of her mind, a faraway image of a dream…

"There's a bus terminal in a nearby town—we'll try there next." Dirk picked up Louie's cage and Belle's suitcase.

"How nearby?"

"If we don't detour at any hot-dog stands, not long."

"How long?" Hysteria threatened to break through her pieced-together composure.

"Gentleman at the counter wasn't sure—he's a recent transplant from New York." He glanced at Belle, then Lover Boy. "I know he's a cuddler, but you can't stand there holding hands all night."

She'd forgotten she was holding Lover Boy's paw. She released it, but the furry appendage remained poised in the air.

"Belle, you coming?"

Dirk looked questioningly at her. So did Louie. If Lover Boy wasn't blitzed, he'd be doing the same. Here she had three supportive men in her life—great odds for any woman—and she was toying with hysteria. *Buck up, Belle*. This journey isn't about three men and a baby—it's about three men and a strong-willed lady.

Pulling back her shoulders, she forced a smile. "Coming."

FOR THE PAST FORTY MILES, Dirk's right eye had developed a mild twitch. At work this sometimes happened after an arduous deal-making session. In this car, it had happened after two-plus hours of nonstop country music.

"If I hear one more cowboy croon about his woman doing him wrong," he said, competing with some yodeling, "I'll either lose my mind or develop multiple personalities with the names Garth, Gill, and George."

Belle briskly tapped the power button on the radio. Silence engulfed the car.

His eye stopped twitching. Finally, he could check out southern Utah's red-rocked scenery without it jumping every other second.

"You could have asked an hour or two ago," she said matter-of-factly. "It's not healthy letting your resentment build like that."

"If you ask me, it's not healthy listening to grown men who dress like Wyatt Earp and sing about relationship-challenged women."

Belle waited a beat. In an oh-so-cool voice, she said, "You're mad because we've been driving over two hours and haven't found the bus station."

Chirp.

Dirk bit his tongue. When he and Louie were alone, they'd have a talk about why the bird always took *her* side.

Clusters of buildings appeared on the horizon. Dirk pressed on the gas. "This *has* to be the town."

"You've been saying that every town for the past four towns."

"Turn the cowboy music back on."

"Now, now…" Belle patted his leg. She let her hand rest there, its heat penetrating his khaki pants down to his skin. He caught a trace of her perfume, its flowery scent winding around him like tendrils. Belle O'Leary, hard-boiled one moment, could turn pliant and sweet the next. Her contradictory character did more than keep him off balance—it stimulated him.

Suddenly, he didn't care if they were lost, didn't care if singing cowboy aliens took over the planet. All that mattered was to sit next to Belle, her hand on his leg, her fragrance teasing his senses.

"Soon I'll be a diner owner," said Belle, looking outside at a passing fruit stand that advertised the Biggest Strawberries in the West. "My own place. My own business."

He'd heard her edgy voice and her honeyed voice, but this was the first time he'd heard her sound wistful, almost childlike. She was close to accomplishing a personal milestone. An old remorse edged into his mood. Despite his numerous professional successes, personal victories had been elusive.

"I'm happy for you, Belle."

"I think my Aunt Meg would be happy for me, too. This is exactly what she wanted, to surprise me with this…dream. She used to do that all the time when I'd visit her."

It was difficult to imagine Belle with her champagne-blond hair, killer thighs, and manicured nails trekking to Wyoming for visits. On the other hand, Belle was addicted to country music. Had even said, "I dig the outdoors."

"Once Meg told me I had two days—another of her deadlines—to get the old barn into shape," Belle continued. "I was thirteen, spending the summer with her, and I much preferred hanging out in the diner and flirting with boys than sweeping and scrubbing an old barn. But I cleaned it up anyway."

It got so quiet, Dirk wondered if Belle realized she'd left the story hanging without an ending. "And?" he prompted.

She cleared her throat. "And," she started, her voice breaking slightly. "She surprised me with a horse. My very own horse."

He placed his hand on hers. "Whose home was the newly cleaned barn." He glanced over. Belle was blinking, fighting tears. It hit him how strong she was, continuing this journey with no Jeep and little money; moving forward even though she'd only learned of her aunt's death a day ago.

He hadn't suffered a close family member's death, although his mother's near-fatal car accident when he was in college had shaken up his world. Irrevocably.

"You loved her very much," he said solemnly.

"Like a second mom. My 'other mother' I'd call her. She'd scoff at me, but secretly, I think she liked someone calling her 'Mother.' But—" Belle swiped at the corner of her eye "—as much as I loved her, I never wanted to live her life." Belle eased her hand from Dirk's.

"What does that mean?" he asked, watching her retreating fingers.

But Belle was oblivious to the subtle meanings

Dirk was trying to read from her actions. Staring out the window, she answered, "Like me, Aunt Meg never got married, never had children. Instead, her family consisted of her regular customers at the Blue Moon and a community of pets that could fill a small zoo. My dad said she'd been engaged once, during World War II, but her fiancé died in battle right before the war ended. Maybe she never found another man to love. Maybe she didn't care to. But I remember thinking, even as a young girl, that I never wanted to end up like Meg, alone, surrounded by a few animals for companionship."

He was thinking how to respond, when Belle squealed, "Look! It *is* the right town!"

After surviving the rush of adrenaline—he wasn't accustomed to exuberant women—he focused on where Belle was pointing. Ahead, on a square green sign, the town's name—in bold white letters—reflected the dwindling sunlight. Below, in smaller print, it stated the population as eleven thousand and something.

"Good." Dirk fumbled in his pocket for the cell phone, which he handed to Belle. "Dial information. Get the number of the bus terminal and we'll call for directions."

Twenty minutes later, they pulled into the terminal lot. As he eased into a parking space, two faded white lines on buckled asphalt, he said, "Let's figure out how to bypass that no health certificate, no ticket rule."

"Those rules apply to buses, too?"

He cut the engine. "Have no idea, but to be on the safe side, let's assume." Outside a bird soared from one tree to another, twirping energetically. "I suggest you sit in the back of the bus so Louie's chirps won't be overheard.''

Chirp.

''Sitting in the back of the bus is one thing, but how am I going to disguise these guys?'' she asked.

Dirk looked at the snoring ottoman, now nestled in Belle's lap, then at Louie in the back seat. ''Your purse is big enough to stash the birdcage.''

Belle made a defensive noise, which was swallowed by the chugging roar of a Greyhound bus pulling out of the lot. When the sound subsided, Dirk continued, ''And your shirt is big enough—''

''No!'' she said, inferring the rest of his sentence. ''I'll not stuff Lover Boy under my shirt. I'll look nine months pregnant!''

Dirk checked out the pile of fur. ''More like eleven.''

They both burst out laughing, a welcome relief after the stressful day. He liked how she rolled back her head and laughed heartily. Unlike his former fiancée, Janine, who seemed afraid it would give her lips stretch marks if she emitted more than a conservative giggle. He much preferred Belle's let-it-rip laughter—it revealed a woman with a lust for life.

''Eleven,'' she repeated. ''I guess that's a small sacrifice to meet my diner deadline.''

''Well then, let's get you packed—you have a dream to catch.''

Just as they'd fallen into unison unpacking her stranded Jeep, they fell into a quiet rhythm unloading items from Belle's oversize pink purse into her suitcase. As he covered the birdcage with the now-emptied purse, Belle made a pouch with her shirt, into which she slipped the comatose Lover Boy. After ensuring he had a breathing hole between two buttons, she slipped on a light cardigan sweater to cover any telltale kitty-cat shapes.

Waddling toward the bus terminal, she quipped, "Hope they don't require near-birth women to have health certificates."

A few minutes later, while eleven-month-pregnant Belle sat on a bench with her strangely shaped purse, Dirk went to the counter and bought a one-way ticket to Cheyenne. It was several hours until the bus boarded, but it would get her into town by early the following afternoon, plenty of time to beat her deadline.

After purchasing the ticket, Dirk bought several sandwiches for Belle's bus trip. He rechecked Louie, who seemed fascinated by the pink hue surrounding his cage. He almost patted Lover Boy on the head, but didn't want to mistake the head for a breast and end this quirky relationship on an awkward note.

He compromised with a verbal goodbye. "Tell Lover Boy bon voyage for me. Not that he'll remember who I am…"

Belle grinned. "I'll remind him. You're the stranger who asked if I was talking to you when I called for Lover Boy."

It had only happened a few hours ago, but it seemed as though he'd known Belle and her brood forever. He was going to miss them. "You should call a lover Lover Boy, you know," Dirk said, trying to sound easygoing. "*Real* cats have names like Whiskers or Tuna Breath."

She arched one eyebrow. "Good thing Lover Boy is knocked out. He'd be incensed at your last suggestion."

"And naming a parakeet Louie? He sounds like a shrimp salad."

"Actually, he's named after my last fiancé, who among other things was an amateur chef. He wanted us to be married after a ten-course meal."

"*If* you could walk down the aisle. Last being—?"

"My fourth fiancé."

"Fourth?" Dirk emitted a low whistle. "Once was enough for me." His gaze slipped to Belle's rounded middle. He recalled how Janine had made it painfully clear that she refused to get pregnant, but might consider adopting. At first, he chalked it up to her hectic work schedule and high-profile career. Similar to him, she was constantly in the limelight as the fashion market director for the successful magazine *Style*. He figured with time, she'd adjust her schedule so it could accommodate a career and a family. Not so. With the passing months, she not only dropped the idea of adoption, but seemed to cringe at the thought of creating a child that was part her, part him. Being rejected at such a fundamental level had numbed Dirk to ever proposing marriage again.

"You're staring at me funny," Belle said, shifting in her seat. "Is there a paw sticking out of my stomach?"

"No, no, your secret's safe." He heaved a breath and looked around—not that he was searching for anything. It was tough to look at the trio who'd soon be leaving his life. "Time to go," he said crisply. "I need to head toward my own destination or I'll lose my deal."

"Thanks for everything. You're a wonderful guy."

He looked into her eyes, remembering how, earlier

in the day, they had sparkled like sun-drenched ocean water. "Got enough food?"

"Seven sandwiches is plenty. Thanks."

"If you need me, I'll have my cell on."

"Your what?"

"My cell phone."

"Oh. Yes, I have the number."

Dirk rubbed his chin. "Need any money—?"

"We already discussed this," she said, cutting him off. "I'm sending you money for the bus ticket... otherwise, I'm fine."

Ridiculous for him to offer financial aid to Belle "Can Do" O'Leary. "Take care."

"Same to you."

He had to stop dragging this out. In business, he liked to end meetings quickly and efficiently, which is what he'd do now. With a small smile, he turned and walked quickly away—not stopping until he reached his car. Getting inside was one of the loneliest things he'd ever done. It was as though the world had moved farther away again...everything, everyone was at an arm's distance, just as he'd lived for a long, long time.

He sat in the car for ten, twenty minutes. Every time he started the engine, he turned it off. As evening encroached, the sky turned a deeper shade of blue, which matched his mood.

I need to know she's all right—just one more look.

Despite the heat, he jogged back to the terminal. Reaching the glass doors, he pressed his hand against the smooth, cool pane and peered inside. This was exactly the opposite of how he had lived his life, always being on the inside looking out. Yet here he was standing outside, looking in.

Belle sat alone, just as he'd left her, one hand on her oversize tummy, the other arm draped around a strange-looking purse. She was staring, transfixed, at the ceiling. He craned his neck, but saw nothing unusual overhead. He looked back down at Belle and her pets.

I never want to end up like Meg, alone, surrounded by a few animals for companionship.

That did it. He tore open the door and ran inside, nearly skidding to a stop in front of a surprised Belle. Her stomach visibly lurched.

"What's wrong?" she asked, a look of alarm on her face.

"I can't leave you here like this. What if you accidentally let the cat out of the bag—I mean, shirt— and lose your seat? You'd be stuck here for hours. Besides, you look too much like your aunt Meg."

"You never met her—"

"Hold on to your stomach," he warned, picking up her suitcase and birdcage-purse. "The three of you are coming with me."

4

"I DON'T SHARE my looks with Aunt Meg, but we did share one very important thing," said Belle, settling back into the passenger seat, one hand cradling her cat-filled stomach. "We both missed out on having kids." She smiled down at her bulging middle. "I like being pregnant. People look at my body differently." She smiled up at Dirk, who held open her door with one hand while holding the pink-encased birdcage with the other.

"Differently?" A warm, evening breeze sifted through the parking lot, carrying with it the scent of roses and sage. A mixture, Dirk thought, as contradictory as the Dime Store Venus with the oversize tummy.

"I'm used to guys checking out my assets, if you get my drift. But not looking at me as though I were part Madonna." She winked. "And I don't mean the singer."

Madonna. Glowing. Terms, he admitted to himself, that aptly communicated her appeal in that pseudo-pregnant garb. Belle O'Leary, Madonna Thigh Master? He smiled to himself, realizing her contradictory nature had teased him again.

"Now *you're* looking at me that way." She grinned.

"I am?" At board meetings, he was known as the

maestro of the poker face. But a few hours with Belle O'Leary, and his face was showing its hand. "I like how you look pregnant," he admitted.

The words spilled out before he'd had the chance to think them through. Not that what he'd said was bad; it was just too honest. And too painful. Memories of Janine scoffing at pregnancy—at the notion of carrying his child—resurfaced. He breathed in deeply. *Reality check, Harriman. Belle's not pregnant. She's not your woman. She's just a stranger you're helping out.*

Belle missed his internal turmoil because she was busy unbuttoning her shirt. A paw, followed by a furry head emerged. Belle scooped up the comatose cat and gently deposited him on the floor underneath her feet.

So much for needing a reality check. She just gave birth to a cat. Now get Louie into the car and this caravan on the road or you'll miss your deadline.

Holding the birdcage steady with one hand, Dirk shut her door. He headed around the Jaguar, opened the driver's door, and eased the cage over the seat into the back. A simple enough task...if one's attention weren't diverted by a pair of exposed breasts.

Clunk.

Squawk!

The birdcage lay at an angle on the back-seat floor. The pink casing vibrated with an irate parakeet's furious fluttering.

Belle jumped.

"What happened?"

Dirk busied himself with resetting the cage on the back seat. "Slight accident," he murmured, knowing that Louie probably knew—through some perverse psychic-pet thing—*why* Dirk had dropped the cage.

Wondering how to politely mention Belle's double exposure, Dirk pulled the purse off the cage...and stared down at one pissed parakeet whose feathers stood on end like a miniature porcupine.

Squawk, squawk!

"Really, sir, there's a lady present." Dirk cocked his head to smile apologetically at Belle. It strained his character—and manhood—to maintain eye contact. "I missed the back seat," he said as though the admission were a surprise.

Belle stared aghast at Louie. "How could you *miss* the back seat? It's large enough to hold a small family."

Squawk!

Tattletale. Dirk cleared his throat. He, who prided himself on his communication skills, was fumbling with how to tell a woman that she was flashing him. "The cage slipped because my attention was diverted by...by..." He stared at the overhead light and gestured inanely as though hand movements might suffice for words.

"By what?" Belle flashed an irritated glance at Dirk. "Poor Louie has crash-landed. Again. Plus his water cup—"

"Allow me." Anything to avoid the *other* conversation. Dirk grabbed the bottle of Evian, leaned over his seat, and sloshed the liquid into the cup. Despite Dirk's peace offering, he swore that Louie, stalking his perch, glared at him.

"Poor baby," cooed Belle. "You've had it rough."

"You don't know how rough," Dirk murmured.

"I was talking to Louie."

Then let him tell you your shirt's open. Dirk dropped the Evian bottle back into the cup holder, shut his car door, and twisted the ignition key. Shaking, he began randomly punching buttons, hoping one of them was the air conditioner. The overhead light remained on for exactly sixty seconds—one solid minute—in these models. Right now that single minute felt like a sixty-second eternity.

"Are you okay?" Belle asked.

"Are you talking to Louie or me?"

"You, of course."

"Yes," he lied.

Squawk!

Dirk slid a peeved glance at Louie, who stared back with beady eyes that saw all. Belle's pint-size parakeet was more protective than a beefy bodyguard. Time to tell Belle that her "assets" were—

"Ooo!" Belle exclaimed. "It's cold in here." A slight gasp. "Why didn't you tell me my shirt was open?"

Fighting the image of frozen assets, Dirk stammered, "I...I..."

"Not like you to stutter." Pause. "It's okay now. I'm decent again."

The light turned off, dimming the interior.

"You wait until I'm decent to turn off the light?"

"I didn't know you were decent. I mean, you're decent, I just hoped otherwise. I mean—"

Squawk!

Dirk stared into the back seat. In the building shadows, Louie resembled a furry lump of coal in his cage. A furry lump of coal with an attitude.

Dirk looked back at Belle. Silvery blue moonlight

played with her hair and features, casting her in an ethereal glow. His breath caught in his throat. It was as though the evening's starry radiance had magically transformed the Dime Store Venus into a real, live Aphrodite.

"I mean..." He forgot what he'd been trying to say. Hell, if someone asked him his name right now, he'd be stumped for an answer.

"I think I know what you mean," Aphrodite said, her voice soothing. Seductive.

A wave of heat that had nothing to do with the temperature swept over him. How could she possibly have known what he meant? Maybe she was more than pet-psychic—maybe she was also people-psychic. Psychic or not, he wanted to explain exactly why he hadn't told her about her unbuttoned shirt. He might be having a typical male reaction to a not-so-typical female, but he wasn't a self-serving cad who ogled naked women. Especially women who were unknowingly naked.

Naked. He shouldn't have thought the word. It was like pouring gasoline on hot thoughts. He breathed in a lungful of cool air, hardly the panacea for the burning images in his mind. "I wanted to tell you your shirt was open," he began slowly, infusing each word with sincerity, "but I...I didn't know how to say it."

"And your favorite word is *communicate?*"

"I was...momentarily taken aback."

"Taken aback?" Belle frowned. "I'm not sure if I feel flattered or insulted." Moving forward, she said in a husky tone, "I'm accustomed to performing with nothing on but a G-string, so if you copped a look at my breasts, I'm not upset."

As though he needed that G-string visual.

Leaning back, Belle ruffled her hand through her hair. "So what's next?"

Your thighs? For a chilling moment, Dirk wondered if he'd thought the words or spoken them.

Belle hummed a piece of a melody before speaking. "What's next? Are you driving me to Cheyenne or do we see if some rancher needs another hand for a cattle run to Wyoming?"

Belle on a cattle run? Lucky cowboys. "Yes," he said, relieved his thigh-thought had remained unspoken. Summoning his best CEO manner, he continued, "Let me make a few calls. Find you a rental vehic—car." It would be much easier for him to drive to Taos knowing she was safely in an automobile headed toward her destination than for her to be stuck—and if the bus were late, possibly stranded—in that desolate bus station. "We can then go our separate ways and meet our deadlines with time to spare."

Separate ways. He was accustomed to being alone, but he wasn't accustomed to being *lonely*—which is how he felt at the thought of Belle not being in his life.

He pulled out his cell phone and punched in the number for information, glad to be doing something to distract himself from such thoughts. A gregarious operator, whose constant giggling made Dirk wonder if she was sucking laughing gas on the side, informed him there was one local automobile rental agency. She then plugged him into Giddy Up Auto, where a recording of a male voice with a slight drawl announced that the business was closed for the evening and to please call back the next morning. The end of the recording culminated in a twanging-guitar-and-mooing-cow duo.

"Well?" asked Belle as he slipped the phone back into his pocket.

"People in this part of the country need to get out more. In my will, after suggesting the sale of laughing gas be banned to telephone companies, I plan to bequeath my entire classical music CD collection to the Southwestern United States."

"Are you all right?"

He rubbed his forehead. "I have bad news."

"You don't have a will?"

He paused, wondering briefly whether to laugh or cry, then remembered he rarely did either. "Ready to join a cattle run?" he finally asked, resisting the urge to ask Louie instead of Belle.

"Didn't pack my chaps," Belle quipped. But the bravado was followed with a weighty sigh. "No rent-a-car, right?" she asked quietly.

"Right. Giddy Up is closed until the morning."

"But there must be other—"

"And there are no other local car rental agencies, according to the abnormally friendly woman who rules directory assistance."

It was silent except for Lover Boy's snores, which Dirk at first thought was another bus pulling out of the station. After several long moments, Belle turned to face Dirk. At this angle, the tips of her blond hair caught the defused light from outside, giving her a halo effect.

"Let's go to a motel."

"Motel?" Forget the halo. The woman was on fire. "What does that accomplish?" he asked in a choked voice, all the while fighting feverish images of all the things it could delightfully accomplish.

Belle shook her head. The tone of his voice was a

dead giveaway to what the guy was really thinking. She had a keen inner sense of people—especially *male* people. And right now, Dirk Harriman had not only misinterpreted her statement, his imagination was sizzling with possibilities. Time to put a stopper on her miscommunication with Mr. Communicate.

"I suggest we go to a motel to *sleep.*" When he didn't respond, she added, "Figured we could catch a few winks, then get up early and head over to Giddy Up."

"Right. Sleep. Excellent suggestion." Dirk grappled with his seat belt.

Belle neatly adjusted her belt and snapped it closed. Dirk fumbled with his for several more moments before it clicked shut. He then twisted the ignition key. The motor growled.

"It's already on," Belle said calmly.

"Thank you," he said evenly. "Forgot I'd already started the engine."

His or the car's? Belle wondered. She waited until he had successfully selected a gear—which took more fumbling—and they were driving through the parking lot before she attempted further conversation. "Lots of guys think showgirls are always ready for a roll," she began. "One of the megamisconceptions of the biz. Believe it or not, lots of us lead very sane, normal lives. Visitors imagine showgirls dining in expensive restaurants with moneyed beaus, when in reality, we bake meat loaf at home for our hubbies and kids." We? That was a slip. She went home alone to her two pets. They were the best pets in the world, but they had never filled the void of a husband and children. She looked out the window, not wanting Dirk to catch any hurt on her face.

After a pause, Dirk said quietly, "Sorry."

"Not your fault," she whispered.

"Yes, it is. I thought you meant something else, and I feel rather foolish for the misunderstanding."

It kicked in that he was on another subject—the motel subject. Belle was at once touched and amused. Touched by the genuine regret in his apology. And amused because, despite Dirk's outward appearance, he seemed shy in the real world. Had he been raised that way...or had his money made him that way?

She lightly touched his arm. "Didn't mean to beat the motel topic to death. Just wanted to get it straight between us."

The car lurched over a speed bump. After easing up on the gas, Dirk said crisply, "Got it."

She decided not to attempt further conversation until they reached a motel. He seemed to be having trouble controlling himself—with or without cruise control.

TEN MINUTES LATER, on the outskirts of town, they pulled up to the Doc Holliday Inn.

Dirk eased the Jaguar into the lone parking space outside the motel registration office, in whose window sat a stiff mannequin dressed in cowboy garb with a stogie in his mouth and holding a deck of cards. After turning off the engine, Dirk sat and stared at the mannequin for a moment. "Looks like the stuffed mother in *Psycho*—with a Western twist," he murmured. "I suggest we forgo showers until tomorrow."

She recalled his anxiousness at facing strangers before, once at Cha-Cha's Garage and then again at the airport terminal. Was he stalling by talking about the mannequin to cover his reluctance to face people again? She didn't understand what was behind his uneasiness, but rather than question him, she offered a face-saving solution. "I'll go in," she said, undoing her seat belt. "It's my turn."

Dirk grabbed her hand as she reached for the door handle. "Gentleman's prerogative," he said in a low tone. "I take care of my—the lady traveling with me." He released his hold. "Besides, that's one reason I took on this road trip. I want to be part of the world again."

He'd started to say "my lady." And what was this "part of the world" statement? Both lines were so full of meaning, she didn't have the wits to respond. In stunned silence, she watched him exit the car, square his shoulders, then head toward the glass door marked Check In Here.

As she watched him go through the door, it looked as though a piece of night shadow followed Dirk into the motel lobby. Under the glare of light, she discovered the shadow was actually a young man dressed in a black shirt and jeans, wearing a black cowboy hat. At first she thought the guy in black was another guest checking in. When he pulled something out of his pocket, she assumed he was the owner. But when she realized that object was a *gun*, she froze. In numbed silence, she watched him wave the weapon at Dirk, who calmly reached into his pocket and handed over something.

Time slowed to a painful crawl as she watched the stranger stuff the object into his shirt pocket, then run out the door into the night. His footsteps pounded past, matching her heightened heartbeat.

When the steps blended into the night, she finally breathed again. With the danger past, some internal heater shot to high, thawing her mind, then her body. In a rush of movement, she jumped out of the car and tore inside.

Dirk stood in front of the registration desk, a scarred wooden counter littered with some brochures for local sights and a cup filled with ballpoint pens. Belle noted how his face looked whiter than the paper the brochures were printed on. He stood ramrod straight, a glazed expression in his eyes.

"Are you all right?" she asked. Instinctively, just as she'd done hundreds of times with her younger siblings, she wrapped her arms around him, both for comfort and support.

"I was robbed…at gunpoint," Dirk said in disbelief.

She hadn't heard gunfire, but then she'd been frozen in her own time warp back in the car. "You weren't shot, were you?" she asked, searching his body for signs of blood.

"Let me think." A glimmer of life returned to Dirk's eyes. He cocked one eyebrow. "No. Although he threatened to. Said something like, 'Your money or your life.' I was more in shock at the cliché than the fact he held a weapon."

Here they'd weathered a blood-chilling scare, and Dirk was making jokes. Despite the circumstances, she smiled. "We have to call the police," she said, fighting the urge to laugh and cry at the same time. "You can entertain them with the quotes by the cowboy in black."

"Police?" Dirk stiffened. "That's exactly what I need—my face plastered on the evening news. 'Tycoon Dirk Harriman robbed at gunpoint at the Doc Holliday Inn by a cowboy dressed in black.' That media bite alone will cost me more than the few credit cards and bills that Paladin made off with.'' Meeting her gaze dead-on, Dirk said solemnly, ''I started out listening to cowboy music…then I got robbed by 'the bad cowboy'…next I'll discover my name is really Bart and I make my living selling gaudy belt buckles that double for paper weights.'' He shuddered.

Belle hugged him harder. ''Get a grip. Your name's Dirk, not Bart.'' The word *tycoon* lodged in a corner of her brain—who *was* Dirk Harriman, anyway? Later, when things calmed down, she'd ask more questions. But for now, she needed to get him comfortable, and then call the authorities.

She peeked around his shoulder and spied a chair made of wood and cowhide. ''I'm going to help you over to that seat. Then I'll call the police.''

''I said, *no* police.'' He glanced over at the chair. ''And I refuse to sit in that. As soon as my behind hits the hide, some Western tune probably starts playing.''

At least the color was returning to his face. And his antagonism at anything ''country'' assured her Dirk was almost back to normal. ''Stop being a baby and sit down,'' she insisted, becoming overly aware that this was the second time today that they'd been pressed together, full body. She had the fleeting worry that if he did move suddenly, she'd topple over.

Fortunately, Dirk remained stubbornly rooted to his spot. ''I'll stop being a baby when you stop being a drill sergeant.''

''Drill ser—?'' Jutting out her chin, which dug into his soft white Polo shirt, she flashed him her best no-

nonsense stare. "If you don't behave, I'll just have to be one, then. You want strict, you got strict."

A weary male voice interrupted them. "Could you two save your games until *after* you check in? You're going to scare off other customers."

Still holding onto Dirk, Belle looked over at the registration desk where a scrawny older man, leaning against the counter, squinted one eye at them.

"Are you the owner?" she asked.

"Yep." His squinted eye opened slightly on the single syllable.

"Where were you while this man was being held up?" she asked.

The owner looked at her arms around Dirk. "Looks as though he's still being held up. Now, you want a room or not?"

Belle stepped away from Dirk, patting down her oversize shirt to ensure she wasn't inadvertently exposing herself again. "We need to call the po—"

Dirk clamped his hand across her mouth. "We need a room," he said edgily, shooting her a warning look.

The owner scratched behind his ear. "I won't mention what *I* think you two need." He began flipping through the registration book. "Let's see here...we got the Calamity Jane room...Butch Cassidy room...no, here's the room for you two. The Wild Bill Hickcock room. King-size bed. Saddle decor." He glanced up. "Don't mind if you kids wanna play police or drill sergeant or whatever tweaks your tooky. But you gotta abide by the house rules. No guns. No liquor. And we charge for spur marks left in the wood paneling."

"Spur marks—?" Dirk sputtered something unintelligible before continuing. "Yes, yes, we'll abide by the house rules. Give us—" he flicked another look at Belle "—the Calamity Jane room." He leaned down and whispered in her ear, "We'll discuss the police thing—and my reasoning why they're not to be called—after we've checked in. Deal?"

She paused, then nodded. He removed his hand.

Dirk stepped toward the registration desk, then stopped. "Forgot," he said with an apologetic shrug. "I don't have any money on me." He smiled appealingly to Belle. "Darling?"

Belle smiled back. "Unfortunately, *darling,* I only have twenty dollars left."

He blinked. "Twenty? For a three-day trip?"

She blew out an exasperated breath. "I hadn't anticipated my Jeep being mortally wounded. Or the airlines demanding I have a certificate from my vet. Or being pregnant in a bus station and suddenly whisked away by Bart the Buckle Maker."

After a long moment's silence, the motel owner said, "Sounds as though you kids have a few issues to iron out. But, no money, no room. I'll kindly ask that you two leave the premises."

Dirk turned abruptly to the older man. "Leave the premises? We need a room!"

"Yep, I can see you need a room, but you got no money. And I don't argue with bums. If you're not outta here in two minutes, I'm calling the police." As he exited through a door behind the counter, he murmured, "'Course, you two'd probably like that."

Belle and Dirk stood in surprise as the door clicked shut, followed by the grating sound of a bolt.

"He called me a bum," Dirk said in disbelief.

"Don't feel too special. He called both of us bums."

"But I've never been called one."

Belle fisted her hands on her hips. "And you think I have?" Hadn't anyone ever called him a name? That was one of the rites of childhood—learning how to dodge rocks and words. But she stopped herself. Time to cut this guy some slack. After all, he'd almost dodged *bullets* tonight.

She dropped her hands to her sides. He'd had the scare of a lifetime. Maybe he wasn't accustomed to mingling with people, but how many people had ever faced a loaded gun? *And* had the wits to do what was necessary to save his life? If Dirk had taunted the gunman—something she'd have been foolhardy enough to do—or refused to hand over his money, not only would Dirk be lying on the ground bleeding, Belle would probably be lying across the front seat of that Jag with her own bullet wound. Dirk Harriman had saved both their lives. So what if he'd never been called a bum—he was a grade-A hero.

"Let's go," she said quietly.

"No police," Dirk warned, crossing to the motel's door.

"No police," she promised, following him.

When they got back into the car, Dirk retrieved his cell phone. While punching in numbers, he explained, "Need to have my cards canceled. Also need to call Ray Romero, my lawyer, and have him wire me money from our business account to a local bank. I'd go to Western Union right now, but I doubt they'd transfer funds with no identification." He laughed ruefully. "Ray needs to negotiate with the Taos people to get an extension on that contract."

She nodded, glad they were both safely back in the car. As he called the credit card companies, she thought to herself that if Dirk were her man, she'd reach over and tell him to take a breather, that those phone calls could wait a minute. And then she'd hold him, murmur her thanks for his bravery, and whisper all the ways she'd take care of him later.

"What's wrong?" Dirk asked, holding the phone to his ear, flashing her a worried look.

"I was...thinking."

"About?"

Dirk had just gotten his color back. If she told him some of the things she'd been thinking, he'd lose it again. So rather than answer, she smiled. Dirk's worry turned to confusion as he returned a baffled half smile.

"Ray!" Dirk exclaimed, obviously responding to his lawyer's voice over the phone. He gave Belle a double take before commencing into a discussion of funds and contracts. At one point, after Louie offered a squawk of advice, she heard Dirk say, "That noise? Oh, just some animals I'm traveling with." She wondered why he didn't mention her—which made her wonder if there was another woman in his life. Which was none of her business. After all, she was simply a stranded woman he was helping out. Moving away from home and restarting her life was probably making her a bit insecure—something she had always prided herself on not being.

But she'd never been lumped with "some animals." She fussed with her shirt. She'd been called many things. A lady. A doll. And, Louie-the-fiancé's favorite, "a dame deluxe." But never an *animal*.

After a few minutes, a more relaxed Dirk signed

off his conversation with a "Thanks, Ray," punched a button on the phone and dropped it back into his pocket. Dipping his head, he rubbed his neck muscles. "He's working getting me money tomorrow a.m. Ray also thinks he knows how to extend my Taos contract, so all we have to resolve is what to do with you tonight." He stopped rubbing. "I mean," he said, clearing his throat, "what we should plan, considering we can't rent a car until the morning."

A plan for the animals? she felt tempted to ask. But she was more taken with his use of the word *we*. It had a nice ring to it. She hadn't heard a man refer to them—with or without animals—as "we" since her last fiancé. It felt good. Good enough to play with the word herself. "*We* could put gas in the tank and see how far we get until morning."

Dirk laughed. "With our luck, we'll end up in the middle of nowhere, just the way we met."

She joined in his laughter. "And we'll end up towing your Leopard all the way back to Cha-Cha's Garage."

"Jaguar."

"Whatever."

Dirk started the engine, still chuckling. "If they sprinkle holy water on my Jag, it better be Evian."

Belle adjusted her seat belt. "Let me guess. Instead of engine oil, your car uses olive oil."

Dirk winked. "Extra virgin."

The roots of Belle's hair grew so hot, she thought she'd become an instantaneous redhead with his last remark. He'd done it again. Outsassed her. Her libido was so shaken up, she wasn't sure which end of the seat belt fit in where. Fortunately, soon after Dirk drove away from the motel lights and toward the road, the inside of the car was once again dark and he didn't see her flustered reaction.

"Let's find a side road and catch a few winks," she suggested, trying to keep her voice even.

"Sleep in the *car?*"

She'd forgotten. Dirk had probably never slept on anything other than the finest beds. What did rich people sleep on, anyway? Feather mattresses and satin sheets?

"Oops."

"What happened—?" Dirk slowed down the car.

"Nothing." Caught up in her feverish fantasies of beds, she'd misguided the metal tab of the belt, which suddenly seemed overly phallic.

"Trouble with the seat belt?"

"No," she said weakly. "Just a little problem sticking—I mean shoving—I mean…" She licked the sweat from her top lip. "No problem. Keep driving." With shaking fingers, she managed to insert Part A into Part B. Hoping to quell Dirk's overearnest concern, she leaned back against her seat and feigned keen interest in the white lines that dotted the center of the road ahead.

"You okay?" Dirk asked.

"Fine. Fine." Her voice had regressed to some kind of pubescent croak. She never behaved like this…even when she *was* pubescent. If she didn't get back onto the subject—any subject—she'd probably repeat the word *fine* for the next hour. "As I said, let's catch a few winks."

"On a side road?"

Good. He was oblivious to her seat belt antics. "It's only for a few hours," she said, happy to be having a sane, platonic discussion. "This car is big enough. Trust me. I can't tell you how many times I pulled over and took a nap in the front seat of my Jeep.''

In the following quiet, Belle knew Dirk was mulling over her idea. "We don't have money or credit cards," he finally said. "It's late. We need to rest." He slapped the steering wheel. "Your idea is the best approach possible. Let's do it." He looked around the car. "The back seat is bigger. You can take that."

"Probably better if I stay in the front seat. That way, I don't disturb Lover Boy…he can stay on the floor and continue snoozing."

"It's going to be crowded with you, Lover Cat, and Louie all in the front seat."

He seemed to have a mental block against the animal's real name, *Lover Boy*. More importantly, Dirk, without saying it, had communicated clearly he wasn't sharing any seat with Louie. And from Louie's silence, she sensed the feeling was mutual. Putting Louie the Parakeet and Dirk the Communicator together was like mixing bird seed and caviar. But rather than admit it, she said sweetly, "You and Louie will be fine in the back."

Squawk.

"No way," murmured Dirk at the same time.

Belle shifted in her seat and shot Dirk a look. Which, smart man, he ignored. "Louie is only a parakeet. You've had to negotiate with far bigger birds in your job, I'm sure. And Louie," she said raising her voice, "I want you to leave Mr. Harriman alone. No taunting. No unnecessary fluttering. And forget that trick with your water cup or you'll find yourself in a traveling aviary show."

There was a soft tapping sound from Louie's cage.

Belle knew he was pacing his perch, knowing better than to fight the situation.

Dirk pulled into the parking lot of a two-story wooden structure which looked like a school closed for summer. Thanks to the moon and a few strategically placed lights, it was easy to discern the rows of yellow lines indicating parking places in the oversize asphalt lot. Dirk drove up to a fence that partitioned off a playground. Before turning off the engine, he said to Belle, "I suggest you lower your passenger seat so you can sleep comfortably. It'll probably get cold later, so I'll grab a blanket I have in the trunk."

She maneuvered her seat to a reclining position. "Better than the Jeep," she murmured, settling into her makeshift bed for the night.

Dirk switched off the motor and opened his door. Light infused the car's interior. She heard him walk back to the trunk. A moment later, he leaned in the driver's door with what looked to be a fur coat. "If you get cold in the middle of the night, throw this on," he said matter-of-factly.

"You're kidding," Belle said, looking at the plush white fur.

Dirk cocked one eyebrow. "Something wrong?"

"Is that what the rich do? Sleep in mink?"

"Mink?" Dirk looked at what he was holding. "It's faux fur. If it were the real thing, it'd be arctic fox." He folded it over and laid it on the front seat. "I bought it for Janine, my former fiancée, when we drove up to San Francisco one winter. She got cold easily."

From the tone of his voice, Belle guessed Janine's coldness couldn't be cured with any faux furs.

"If you don't mind, I'll also move your suitcase up front so I can lie on the back seat," Dirk said.

Belle fought a surge of guilt. The guy not only rearranged his life for her, now he was rearranging her things so he could nap next to her possessive, uptight parakeet. "Hey, don't bother," she said lightly. "Why not stay up front? You can lower the driver's seat and sleep next to me."

After a short pause, Dirk said, "Uh, better if I sleep back here."

Belle realized that Dirk had virtually confessed that she was more than a road-trip buddy. A zing of happiness shot through her...followed by a wave of sadness. Fate was unfair. A one-in-a-million guy walks— well, drives—into her life and bang...they have to go their separate ways within twenty-four hours. Belle looked up at the heavens. As a kid, she often discussed things with God, but she hadn't done that in a long time. She couldn't even remember the words she used to use. Rather than fumble for the right tone, she simply prayed it like she thought it. *You know, God, having to forfeit a great guy has to rate right up there with Ingrid Bergman's dilemma in* Casablanca.

After Dirk moved her suitcase into the front, he slipped into the back seat and shut the door. After some rustling and a perturbed squawk, she heard Dirk whisper, "Louie, this is the beginning of a beautiful friendship."

Belle smiled to herself. So what if she had Ingrid's dilemma? She also had Bogie for the night.

5

DIRK HAD SLEPT in the finest five-star hotels all over the world. Slumbered on satin-cased king-size beds. Inhaled the fragrance of roses in the Riviera night air. Listened to the distant crooning of a balladeer or, after an evening of dancing, dining and lovemaking, the purr of a satisfied woman.

But tonight he couldn't sleep because he was cramped on half of the back seat of his car. Rather than the sweet fragrance of roses, he smelled the tangy scent of Louie's salt block. And instead of the crooning of a distant balladeer, there was the drugged snoring of a not-so-distant cat.

How preferable would be the purr of a satisfied woman. He glanced at Belle's head on the reclined front seat. In the muted darkness, he could make out the curved line of her profile. It reminded him of the Rubens portrait of a woman, a maid of honor in a royal court, whose beauty was at once striking, yet elegant. His gaze drifted down. Through the gap between the front seats, he scanned Belle's torso. Was it his imagination or did those voluptuous breasts rise ever so slightly with each breath? He wondered if they rose higher when she purred.

Leave it alone, Dirk. Don't lie in the back seat fantasizing—no, torturing—yourself about the luscious lady in the car. The luscious lady with the lus-

cious body who's lusciously curled up in your front
seat…

I think I've just discovered the word luscious. *Years
of honing my communication skills go swiftly down
the tubes as I fixate on a single* l *word in my vocabulary.* His traitorous mind filled rapidly with other
l's…lovely, luminous, lustful…

The words receded, replaced by images. Belle
sleeping, her naked body swaddled in satin sheets, her
eyes sleepy with satisfaction. Belle, kittenlike, arching
her back slightly and purring and purring and pur—

"What are you thinking about?" Belle asked, peering at him over her seat.

"Purring." Damn. If he kept this up, he'd have to
change his license plate to "Over-Communicate."

"Purring?"

"Touring." Well, it almost rhymed with purring.
"I was thinking that *touring* the country has been
enjoyable." He rubbed his eyes, wondering when
he'd lost his focus. Had to be the very moment he'd
heard that soft, forlorn voice call for Lover Boy.

"You call these past nine hours 'touring?' And 'enjoyable?'"

Yes. Despite the craziness of the day, he'd enjoyed
her company more than he'd enjoyed any woman's
in a long, long time. Forget being cooped up in a car
together—he could be stuck in a stalled elevator with
no food or water…but if Belle were there, the experience would be delightfully memorable. Forget hunger or dehydration, the worst he'd suffer would be an
overactive libido.

Another *l* word. He was having one *l* of a day.

Belle rested her chin on the seat and fixed him with
a look. "I think you're suffering from post-traumatic

stress disorder after staring down that robber-cowboy's gun barrel. Let's get you out of this car and take a walk. Stretch your legs. Some fresh air will do you good.'' Without listening for a response—did she ever when she'd decided on a game plan?—Belle opened her car door and stepped outside.

Rubbing a crick in his neck, Dirk murmured, ''Probably orders her cat around, too, when he's not on drugs.''

Chirp.

''Okay, cat and bird,'' he whispered toward the cage as he opened his car door.

Once outside, Dirk stretched his hands over his head and breathed deeply. A scent of honeysuckle traced the air. A few wispy clouds streaked the inky sky. He stared at the silvery crescent moon, unable to pinpoint when he'd last been outdoors, unencumbered by walls and security, and simply savored the beauty of nature.

Belle playfully touched his arm. ''Tag. You're it.''

Before he could disconnect from the nature moment to the Belle moment, she was running across the parking lot toward the fence. Looking over her shoulder, she laughed, an invitation to join in the fun.

He took off after her, impressed at her maneuvering skills in those pink-laced sandals. If the Olympics had a fifty-meter race for people who wore unusual shoes, Belle would win the Gold. Both in the race *and* for the shoes.

As they reached a four-foot-high chain-link fence, he slowed down.

Belle didn't.

Digging one sandal-footed toe into an opening in

the fence, she propelled herself over it effortlessly, landing with a soft plop on a dirt playground.

Dirk stopped and eyed her over the crisscross mesh of the fence. Between breaths, he said, "I knew show-girls kicked...but I didn't know...they also hur-tled..."

She placed her fists on her hips. "I'm the oldest of six kids, four of them boys. Had to be good at every-thing, including climbing fences." Leaning forward, she placed her hands on the rail. "Bet you can't catch me," she taunted.

She might be an alluring woman, but he was also getting a glimpse of the mischievous kid. He didn't head Harriman Enterprises by holding back—Dirk loved a challenge. Grasping the cool metal rail with his fingers, he vaulted over, grabbing a surprised Belle as he landed on the other side.

Holding her close, he said, "Bet I can."

They looked into each other's eyes for a long mo-ment. Belle's flowery perfume wound around them like an invisible lasso. "Didn't know you were a bet-ting man," she said huskily.

Betting? This close to Belle, her scent intoxicating him, eyeing the silver threads of moonlight in her hair, he was more than betting. He was gambling. Gambling his heart, and an important business deal, all because of a woman who undermined his common sense and ignited his fantasies.

He needed a handle on the situation. Fast. She had a deadline...and so did he. He might be all male, but he could also be all business. If he let this predica-ment with Belle and her brood get out of hand, he'd find himself with no Taos contract. And that contract wasn't just a business coup. It would be his first per-

sonal success in too many years. If he lost this opportunity, he might as well flush his self-worth down
the toilet.

He stepped back and dropped his hands. "I'm not
a betting man," he said simply. And coldly. He
wasn't proud of himself, hearing that edge in his
voice. But business was business.

Even in the faint moonlight, he caught the look of
surprise and hurt on her face. "I get the picture," was
all she said before turning away and walking to a
swing set on the small playground.

He followed her, hating himself for cutting off the
moment they'd shared, yet knowing he had no choice.

As she sat on one of the swings, he stopped nearby.
Grasping one of the steel bars that supported the
swing set, he observed her. Had his words hurt? Or
had she turned as cold as the metal under his palm?
Where before she had seemed direct, blunt even, now
she was difficult to read. He listened to the creak of
her swing as she slowly swung back and forth. He
wanted to apologize, tell her he'd just let things go
too far, but he couldn't figure out what words to use.

Finally, she stopped swinging. Sitting quietly, she
dug one heel into the sand. "I got too close to you,
didn't I." It was more a statement than a question.

Rather than dodge the issue, he met her directness
head-on. "Yes."

"You're not so difficult to figure out," Belle continued, tilting her head to look at him. "You might
be a tough negotiator with others in business, but my
inner sense tells me you're a little…anxious when it
comes to getting to know a person, one-on-one."

Overhead, wings flapped—a nocturnal bird on a
solitary journey. That's how he felt in life. Purposeful,

but very alone. He'd been this way for so long, he didn't know how to behave otherwise. Or if he even could.

"That's a bull's-eye, Belle. I'm good in my business, but a failure in my personal life." He'd never admitted that to anyone, not even to his best friend and lawyer, Ray Romero.

"I'd say you're pretty damn fantastic in both," she countered. "You just don't realize it, that's all."

Despite the somber mood, he smiled to himself. He should have hired Belle to head his marketing division—she had a go-get-'em, positive attitude that others spent a bundle learning at business school. "Thanks for the vote of confidence. But the truth is, I'm not…" What was the word Belle had used? Anxious? He sidestepped that one. "I'm not particularly *adept* at interpersonal relationships."

"Particularly adept?" She made a bemused sound. "That sounds like the kind of indirect and bland comment you'd toss out to some boring business associate at a cocktail party. I hope you were more direct with Francine or Janine or whatever her name was."

"Ouch." Dirk mocked being shot. "You certain you're not a sharpshooter? That's another bull's-eye." Dirk eased in a lungful of the cool night air. With a self-deprecating chuckle, he confided, "I'm afraid I was even more indirect when it came to Janine." A pang of old remorse shot through him. Maybe, instead of buying into Janine's no-children stance, he should have pursued the subject, tried to understand—or even persuade her to rethink the issue.

"Hmmm." Belle swished her feet in the sand. "Maybe you chose her because it was easy to keep up your guard."

Forget the head of marketing. He could hire her to be a corporate psychologist. "I believe you win a prize after three bull's-eyes."

"Didn't know this was a game."

He knew better than to comment again. Belle was savvy, and sharp. For several moments, they sat in silence. The only sound was the whisper of sand being swirled in circles by Belle's toes.

"Sorry," she finally said. "In my family, my nickname was Insert Foot."

"I thought it was Can Do. As in can do anything if she puts her mind to it."

Even in the darkness, Dirk sensed her smile of appreciation. "Thanks. That means a lot." She leaned toward him. "Well, as you well know, I'm not indirect. So tell me...why are you afraid of people?"

Typically, his automatic reaction to such personal inquiries was to tactfully change the topic of conversation. No one ever asked him such point-blank questions, not even Ray. But he didn't feel put off. Or uncomfortable. Maybe it was the security of being removed from his everyday life. Or that his and Belle's conversation felt even more private because of the surrounding night and its own secrets. For the first time, he wanted to respond about himself—to let down his guard and be the man, not the icon.

Leaning back, he looked up at the stars. "I grew up privileged. Only child in a wealthy family. Although I had access to many things that other children didn't...culture, travel, private schools...I didn't have their freedom to be whatever they wanted when they grew up because I was locked into my future—I was being groomed to one day manage the family's business. The expectations were high. And unavoidable.

"Knowing what lay ahead, I learned to savor simple pleasures at a very young age. Visits with our housekeeper, Lucy, who'd surprise me with cookies and pastries. Annual fishing trips with my dad and his friends. But especially, I relished the long morning walks to school in the Palisades...the California sun hot on my face, the tangy, sweet scent of a nearby orange tree..."

He looked down from the stars into Belle's face. "Those walks ended when a group of boys beat me up for my leather backpack. I didn't mind the broken nose...or losing the backpack...the worst aftereffect was that I permanently lost my freedom."

Belle gave her head a quizzical shake. "Freedom?"

Dirk shrugged. "I was never allowed to walk alone again. Whether it be to school or to the park or to a friend's house...from then on, I was chauffeured everywhere. One small incident changed my entire life. I no longer touched the world, I viewed it from behind a car window. I remember thinking that I'd been sealed in a bubble."

After a moment, Belle said softly, "For a kid, that's a tragedy."

"For the adult, too. Immediately after I graduated from Harvard, my mother was in a serious accident. My father, wanting to stay by her side as she recovered, stepped down as CEO and I replaced him. At the age of twenty-two, I headed a multimillion dollar empire, managing thousands of people, but in my personal life, I was still in a bubble."

Belle stood. She had the urge to touch him, console him, just as she'd instinctively done back at the motel.

But her inner sense told her Dirk's bubble, although invisible, was up. Maybe he'd confided his secret, but that didn't mean he had lowered his guard.

Instead, she walked several steps across the sand, then turned to face him. "I can't relate to the only child because I grew up with six siblings. And I haven't the vaguest what it'd be like to grow up rich because my dad, a factory foreman, supported eight of us. But I love people, love mingling with them, and it hurts to think you were denied that." She smiled. "Forget what you were denied. It's a crime that others were denied the opportunity to get to know *you* better because you're a very decent, caring guy." She could have added a few more compliments, but stopped herself. Besides embarrassing him, it would have made her feelings too obvious—and Dirk had already made his clear when he'd pulled away. She might be gutsy, but she wasn't a fool.

"You're a sweet lady," Dirk answered.

"Yeah, I know." She heard his chuckle, which is exactly the response she wanted. It had been a long day, with the past few minutes being somewhat tense, but at least they were ending it on a lighter note. "We have to get up early—let's hit the sack. I mean car." She paused. "And when I say 'hit the sack,' I mean sleep, not—"

"I know what you mean," Dirk said gently.

She turned her head away so Dirk wouldn't see the grin on her face. He might be in a bubble, but she could still get to him. Walking toward the car, she said over her shoulder, "Last one in turns off the light."

BELLE FUMBLED with the overhead light, trying to find the On switch. "Lover Boy! Lover Boy!" she cried softly.

"You talking to me?" said a sleepy voice.

She glanced into the back seat. Next to the wiry silhouette of the birdcage was a larger lump, Dirk. "I'm serious. It's Lover Boy," she said, grappling with the dome light. "I need the light on to see him. He's having trouble breathing."

"Let me," Dirk said, reaching up. After a soft click, light flooded the car.

Chirp.

"Lover Boy," crooned Belle, leaning over the pile of black-and-white fur on the floor. She put her face close to his. "He's not breathing," she whispered in a broken voice. Blinking, she straightened and looked at Dirk, who stared, bleary-eyed, at her. "Help him, please."

Dirk reached into his pocket. "I'll call information—find a vet hospital." He began punching in numbers.

"Do you know CPR?"

"CPR, yes." A look crossed his face as the reality hit him. "On a *cat?*"

Reaching over the seat, she said, "Give me the phone." Dirk, still semicoherent, barely lifted it before she'd snatched it. "Come up front—you work on Lover," she commanded. No sooner did she bring the phone to her ear, than directory assistance answered. Opening her passenger door, she said hurriedly, "This is an emergency. We need to be connected to an animal hospital." In the background, Dirk's door opened, followed by his footsteps heading around the back of the car.

By the time he reached her, she had stepped away

from her door, giving him plenty of room to get into the front seat and administer to Lover Boy, who lay in a heap on the floor.

She heard Dirk's heavy sigh, followed by, "I've never attempted CPR on a feline—"

"Hi Ho Animal Hospital? One moment." She looked at Dirk. "Do you need them to coach you on CPR?"

He cocked one eyebrow. "No," he said in a low tone. "I'll...do it. Just get directions." He gently picked up Lover Boy, who lay like a fat, limp fur piece in Dirk's arms. When he shifted the cat, its head lolled back. A little pink tongue protruded from between its lips.

"Oh, Lover Boy," Belle said in a choked voice. "Quick, put your mouth to his!"

"I need to move his tongue," Dirk said evenly, as he carefully pushed the pink object aside, "and clear his throat."

"Then do it! Move the tongue, clear the throat!" She stiffened. Into the receiver, she said tersely, "No, this is not an obscene call. My cat has stopped breathing and my...friend is administering CPR."

Tears blurred her vision as she watched Dirk lean over Lover Boy's head. Haltingly, she said to the voice on the other end, "Please give us directions..."

Minutes later, she cradled a breathing Lover Boy as they careened back through town, past the Doc Holliday Inn, to a twenty-four-hour animal hospital. Later, Belle barely remembered running toward the admitting desk with her cat in her arms, or the blur of questions asked by the overpermed girl behind the desk. Her last clear memory was the girl taking Lover

Boy and disappearing with him behind a slate-gray door with a small rectangular window above the words No Admittance.

At that point, just as her body had reacted earlier in the Jeep when she'd thought she lost her cat, her knees wobbled uncontrollably. As she began slipping toward the linoleum floor, strong arms caught her. The world spun into blackness.

When she awoke, an oversize dog and cat were staring back at her, frozen smiles on their whiskered, furry faces. Words swam underneath them: *If you love me, fix me.* "What—?" she said groggily.

Dirk's head loomed into her peripheral vision. He looked pinched, worried. "You passed out. How do you feel?"

Belle blinked. "Just tell me I didn't get fixed while I was out."

One side of his mouth crooked a little in a smile she'd grown to recognize. "I can tell you're feeling better. That wicked wit is back." He followed the line of her gaze. "Oh. That's one of several animal posters scattered around the Hi Ho Animal Hospital waiting room. Subtle reminders on how to love your pet."

Your pet. Her memory kicked in. "Lover Boy...?" She couldn't finish. She couldn't ask. A cold foreboding filled her.

Dirk's hand covered hers. "He's okay," he said gently. "Doctor couldn't find anything wrong—thinks it was just an anxiety attack."

"But he's on drugs!"

Dirk winked. "Perhaps he has an exceptional imagination. Whatever happened, he's fine now and can resume traveling in a few hours."

Belle closed her eyes, welcoming the warmth of

relief that started with Dirk's touch and inched over the rest of her. *Lover Boy is alive.* She eased in a calming breath. *Alive.* "Where's Louie?" she asked.

"Safely nestled in his cage, which I set in a quiet corner of the waiting room. He has a view of palm fronds and aqua-blue linoleum...probably thinks he's in the Bahamas."

"And using his salt block for margaritas," she quipped, pleased at Dirk's return smile. She liked seeing that twinkle back in his eyes. Everything felt normal again. Dirk's sexy, preppy smile was back. Lover Boy was healthy. Louie was starring in another of his parakeet fantasies. Her body temperature was back to normal....

Well, almost. Her forehead, for some reason, felt icy cold. "The front of my head is frozen," she murmured.

"You're so tough-minded, they tried to revive you by sticking your head in a freezer."

She bolted upward, but Dirk's hand gently pushed her back down. "Sorry," he said. "My retribution to you for making me give CPR to a drugged cat." He removed a cloth from her forehead and held it for her to see. "They brought you a washcloth wrapped around some ice. However, I doubt that, or anything else, could freeze your overactive mind." His masculine features were etched with playful tenderness.

"Thank you," she said.

"For giving CPR to your cat?"

"That, too," she whispered, not wanting to elaborate on the numerous kindnesses he'd shown her. Because if she started to discuss them, she was afraid she might cry. And she, "Can Do" Belle, was rarely one to cry, yet this man had brought her to tears more in a few hours than most did in years. Just thinking of all the things Dirk had done—from picking up her stranded brood to divulging his true self—turned her heart inside out. She bit her bottom lip, which did little to stop her chin from quivering.

"Is she all right?" said a young girl.

Belle looked over Dirk's shoulder at the girl with the overpermed hair. "I'm fine," she said in a quaking voice.

The girl pushed up her wire-rimmed glasses. "Your cat's resting. The doctor wanted to tell you herself, but she's dealing with another emergency. A bird swallowed a dime."

Belle glanced at Dirk.

"Couldn't be Louie," he said with a wink. "If you gave him a dime, he'd invest it, not swallow it."

"My shift is over," the girl continued, stacking some papers. "If you need anything, ring the bell on the counter." She pointed to a domed silver bell in front of a typeset sign that read Ring For Assistance in black letters.

"May we stay in the waiting room until Lover Boy is ready to go?" Belle asked.

The girl shifted her gaze to Dirk. "Uh, sure."

"I meant my cat," Belle clarified.

The girl's eyebrows shot up. "Oh. I thought you meant…" Avoiding looking at Dirk again, she cleared her throat. "You can stay here until your cat's released, which should be in a few hours. I'd offer you a blanket, but our last one is in use by a sow."

After a beat, Dirk waved his hand in a that's-all-right-no-need-to-explain-further gesture. "You've been wonderful. Go on home, we'll manage."

The girl nodded at Dirk, a flush filling her cheeks.

Belle had no doubt the teenager was still thinking of the words Lover Boy in conjunction with Dirk. "Thanks," she said, her voice rising several notches on the single word. With a jerky wave, she turned abruptly and left.

Watching the girl close the door behind her, Belle said, "You have a way with women, Mr. Harriman."

"She thought you called me Lover Boy, that's all."

"Okay, maybe. But you're also a throwback to another era when men were gentlemen, and that charms women whether they're eight or eighty."

"Too bad Janine didn't think the same," he said under his breath. He shrugged as though to ward off the memory. "We'll be back on the road soon—time to catch some shut-eye." He smiled. "With Louie in the corner and your cat in his own hospital bed, at least the three of you won't be snoring in unison. Shall I go to the Jag and get the blanket?"

"No, it's plenty warm in here. And for the record, I don't snore."

Dirk crooked his mouth as though debating how to answer. "Let's just say the three of you could do a mean rendition of 'Snore, Snore, Snore Your Boat.'"

"We do *not* snore—"

"Except when you're sleeping in cars."

Ring ring.

Holding up one hand in a halting gesture, Dirk pointed with the other to the lump in his shirt pocket. "Love to continue this conversation, but I have to answer my phone." After retrieving it and punching a button, he lifted the apparatus to his ear. "Harriman," he answered.

She didn't like that *Harriman* got the last word. Being CEO, he must be accustomed to that. Plus, without taking a breath, he'd changed his tone from teasing to businesslike. CEOs not only wore many hats, but voices, too, it seemed.

"Ray, good morning! What are you doing up so late? I mean early."

He did that sexy, boyish Harrison Ford grin again. That man could tease her about snoring any time. Whoever Janine had been, she'd really blown it. Was he serious with any other woman? Belle thought back. To her best recollection, he hadn't mentioned anyone else. She wasn't sure if she felt sad or glad that all his masculine charms were going to waste.

She watched him as he paced a step, stopped, commented into the phone, then paced another step. She liked how he dipped his head slightly as he concentrated on the conversation. Liked even more the day-old beard that shadowed his jaw. Yet despite being unshaven, and wearing a rumpled shirt, he still looked distinguished.

But something about his demeanor also filled her with melancholy. Maybe it was that no matter how many people he dealt with, she now knew he was a solitary creature. The kid in the bubble. Belle wondered how often Dirk was on the phone in the wee hours of the morning, discussing international business or talking to his lawyer about a last-minute crisis. And when he hung up the phone, did he go back to his bed alone? If she were his woman, she'd be lying there, keeping it warm, ready to listen if he needed it…

His woman?

Belle raked her fingers through her hair, hoping Dirk didn't glance her way because she had no doubt she was blushing worse than the teenage girl who'd just left. Turning away, Belle stared at the If-you-love-me-fix-me poster.

I should be temporarily fixed—it would stop me from fantasizing about Dirk Harriman over the next few hours.

From somewhere beyond the slate-gray door, a dog yapped several times.

"I'm in an all-night animal hospital," Dirk explained into the receiver. "Yes, it has something to do with the animals I've been traveling with."

Belle shifted her gaze to a flickering fluorescent light on the ceiling. The "animals" he'd been traveling with. That was the second time she'd overheard him make such a reference to Ray. What did that make her? An albatross?

Dirk paced a few steps, his head bent as he listened intently into the phone. "Right. Sounds good. Check the fine print—should be something in there to help us negotiate an extension. Just get me an extra twenty-four hours to make it to Taos…"

Belle sighed. Must be nice to have an on-call lawyer who renegotiates deadlines. Belle had no such resources—although if Louie could talk, he'd outnegotiate the toughest lawyer in the country. Belle smiled. Louie would get her a twenty-four-hour extension *and* a shiny new Jeep.

"Thanks, Ray. Call back as soon as you get word." Dirk laughed. "Don't worry, I won't open a zoo. Goodbye." He punched a button and dropped the phone into his pocket.

"Wrong number?" Belle asked.

He gave her a slow, appreciative grin. "Ray Romero. My lawyer.'' Rubbing his eyes, Dirk yawned, then glanced at his watch. ''Almost four. Time to nap or we'll be zombies driving across country.'' He crossed to a vinyl-backed chair at the foot of her bench. ''I'll curl up here. Wake you up in a few hours.''

She snuggled back into a fetal position. ''Last one up makes coffee,'' she whispered.

''And feeds Louie and the feline.''

Feline. ''You don't like to call him Lover Boy, do you?''

He yawned again. ''That's the name for a paramour, not a cat.''

Belle closed her eyes before she said something she regretted, such as she'd consider changing her cat's name if Dirk Harriman was her man.

Minutes later, she drifted into a fuzzy dream where a somber voice asked, ''Do you, Lover Boy Harriman take Can Do Belle to be your wife…?'' Looking down, she saw herself draped in a satiny gown, holding a bouquet of fragrant roses. But instead of a church, she was standing inside a bubble with Dirk.

6

"WAKE UP, SLEEPYHEAD. Lover Boy's ready to go."

Belle's eyelids felt as though they had weights attached. She blinked, once, catching a blur of black-and-white fur floating in front of her. Her big, sweet Lover Boy.

Then who said, "Lover boy's ready to go?" Had her cat learned to speak while interned at Hi Ho Animal Hospital? And levitate? She forced open her eyes.

Lover Boy looked sleepily at her, his pink tongue protruding slightly through his white-whiskered mouth. Two strong, and obviously male, hands held the cat firmly around his ample tummy. She followed one of the masculine arms up to a familiar, and now wrinkled, Polo shirt and over that to a familiar, but tired-looking, face.

"Are you playing ventriloquist?" she asked, shifting onto one elbow. Without waiting for an answer, she looked lovingly into her kitty's face. "How are you, my special Lover Boy?"

"I'm fine," Dirk answered. "I think your cat's okay, too."

She looked back into Dirk's gray eyes, which crinkled at the edges as he grinned. "Oh, so *you're* the Lover Boy who's ready to go."

Dirk shot her a sexy look that was steamier than her usual first cup of hot java in the morning. Before she could remember how to breathe, much less form words to respond, Dirk's sexy look disappeared. In an all-business tone he said, "It's ten o'clock, which is the official Hi Ho opening time. If I'd known that last night—or early this morning, I should say—I would have requested they release your Mr. Boy earlier. As it is, we're late, but ready to go. I've already put Louie in the back seat."

Where'd the saucy look go? Just as he'd switched gears on the playground from seductive to serious, he'd done the same within the past few moments. Gone were the steamy coffee images…she now felt as though she'd been splashed with cold water.

Dirk carefully shifted the cat so it lay across his shoulder like a fat squirrel wrap. "I paid the bill. I was also going to purchase a Kitty Carry—or whatever those contraptions are called—but none were big enough for the living ottoman."

"Paid the bill?" She straightened and looked around. "Where's my purse?" She paused. "Wait a minute." Frowning, she pondered this scenario. "You were robbed. How'd you pay?"

"The veterinarian, a lovely Dr. Hildebrand, recognized me. Seems she still has last year's *People* magazine in which I'm nominated as one of the hundred most eligible bachelors. Anyway, Carole—Dr. Hildebrand—asked for my autograph. I, in turn, asked if I could sign that to an IOU." He shrugged as though nothing else needed explanation.

"You sure Dr. Hildebrand didn't mix you up with one of those most-wanted pictures in the post office?"

Dirk cocked one eyebrow. "At least she didn't mix me up with one of these love-me-fix-me posters."

"Good thing for you," Belle said under her breath. She had to admit that in the beginning, she'd thought

Dirk had looked familiar—but had written it off as someone she'd once seen in a Vegas audience. After telling her his story of growing up privileged, however, she now believed that others recognized him. Especially others who coveted magazines displaying America's Most Wanted Bachelors.

There was still the issue of money to discuss, however. "Even though your IOU is as good as gold, these hospital expenses are my responsibility, not yours."

"Technically, they're your cat's," Dirk said, heading toward the door with Lover Boy lying over his shoulder. "Anyway, it was a tad more then twenty dollars, so I took care of it."

Before Belle could suck in enough breath to argue, Dirk continued, never breaking his pace. "I know what you're about to say, so let me put your mind to rest. The vet's bill will be added to your car-rental bill. And there will be strict penalty fees for late payments, Ms. O'Leary. And if you miss a payment, there will be even stricter penalties, yada yada..." He pushed open the glass door with the backward gold-stenciled words Hi Ho Animal Hospital. A sun-warmed morning breeze drifted into the room, carrying with it the scent of jasmine. The door shut behind him, creaking to a close.

"Yada yada?" Belle repeated slowly, watching Dirk and Lover Boy as they headed toward the parked Jaguar. What kind of CEO said, "yada yada?" The kind who now claimed psychic abilities—*I know what you're about to say*—which was his way of teasing her about her financial obligations, which she took seriously. Okay, they didn't have to be financial—she took *all* her obligations seriously. Wanted to. It was her hold on independence. Paying her own way had sometimes irritated Louie and her other fiancés, but it was as essential as breathing to Belle. Besides, it made her stronger than her mother, who'd sublimated her own dreams for others'.

Miffed, Belle stuck one foot into a sandal. "Just because he has round-the-clock lawyers *and* can pay with IOUs doesn't give him the right to make fun of others' money sensibilities," she muttered, feeling more justified in her anger every moment. She looped the pink satin ribbon in a bow. "He resuscitated my cat, so he thinks he can make fun of my twenty-dollar bill." She tugged tightly on the pink satin bow. "Ow!"

Too tightly. She hadn't simply tied her shoe, she'd bound her foot.

"Are you all right?" asked a girl's voice.

Loosening the offending bow, Belle glanced up. Behind the reception desk was a different girl from the one present the night before. This one had shoulder-length braids and a smile that revealed a mouthful of braces.

Thinking she had been alone during her minitirade, Belle attempted to smile back. "Little problem with my shoe," she murmured. *And a man.*

"I heard you passed out last night, but your husband says you're fine now."

"My hus—?" Belle finished tying the second bow without cutting off her circulation. "I'm surprised he didn't call me a traveling animal." She paused. In a back corner of her mind, Belle wondered if that's what was really bothering her. Forget the money and the yada yada—Dirk Harriman, unlike other men on the planet Earth, had never noticed her breasts or her legs. Not that she depended on them to connect with the opposite sex, but they *were* obvious assets. And behind those assets, she had her hidden assets—her interests and hobbies. Didn't he see that she was a woman with a body *and* soul?

Or was she simply one of three stranded animals he'd picked up on a lonely highway?

Plus he'd kissed her cat and never kissed her. *Upstaged by my own cat, who didn't even attempt to charm the man—but just lolled about, zoned out on drugs.* She sighed heavily.

The girl frowned. "Are you sure you're all right?"

Belle stood. "Yada yada," she said forlornly, heading toward the door.

A FEW MINUTES LATER, she opened the passenger door of the Jaguar and did a double take. "Aren't you in the wrong seat?"

Dirk wiped a hand across his face. "I'm exhausted," he said in a gravelly voice. He leaned back in the leather seat, his long legs forming a bridge over Lover Boy who lay in a furry pile on the floor. "Didn't sleep a wink last night. Figured I'd let you drive to Custer's Last Stand Auto Rental—or whatever Western name it's adopted—help you rent a car, then after you're safely on your way, I'll crash in their parking lot for a few hours before I head for Taos."

She leaned against the open door. The sun hovered behind her, its golden rays highlighting Dirk's features. The long night showed in the dark circles under his eyes and the lines creasing his forehead. Maybe he looked a little rough around the edges, but he still exuded the confidence of a man accustomed to being in charge. The sight made her heart thump madly, like a teenage girl's. Damn the man, anyway. Around Dirk, she didn't know what she was: a grown woman, an animal, or an infatuated teenager.

"On one condition," she said, trying her best to sound grown-up.

Chirp.

Dirk arched one eyebrow toward the back seat before returning Belle's gaze. "Name it."

"No more 'yada yada.'"

Dirk's forehead wrinkled as he frowned slightly, obviously mulling over her strange request. Then, suppressing a grin, he said, "I ran out of words—"

"Then use other ones. I take my obligations seriously, and I don't appreciate 'yada yada.'" She stopped, realizing how she sounded. She wasn't talking *to* him, she was barking *at* him. She had skidded past the grown-up and become the animal.

His gray eyes had a teasing glint. "Did someone get up on the wrong side of the bench?"

"Someone tied her shoe too tightly," she said quietly. No. That wouldn't do. She had to explain more. Gesturing vaguely toward a tree at the edge of the parking lot as though it enhanced her explanation, she continued, "It's very important to me that I handle my finances without relying on others. Not saying 'yada yada' makes me feel that you respect my independence. Deal?"

He looked momentarily taken aback. "I'm not sure if you should be in marketing, the legal profession, or psychology. Yes, deal. No more 'yada yada.'"

Chirp.

He sighed dramatically while jabbing a thumb toward the backseat. "I'd hate to be in negotiations with Louie. He'd always have the last chirp." Dirk lifted a set of jangling keys and singled out one. "Ignition. Be gentle. This baby will roar if you let her."

"So will this one," Belle said, shutting the door on Dirk's surprised look. As she sauntered around the back of the car, she decided being part animal wasn't such a bad thing, after all.

IF SHE WERE an animal, Belle wished it had been a homing pigeon. Two wrong turns and fifty minutes later, she finally pulled up to the front doors of Giddy Up Auto and eased on the brake. She'd been accustomed to driving her old Jeep for miles in the desert without ever getting lost. But plunk her in a fancy car in a small town and she had the navigation instincts of—she looked down at the pile of black-and-white fur on the floor—a comatose cat who needed a booster seat to see over the dashboard. If he could fit into the booster seat.

Cutting the ignition, she scanned the square brick building and its red-and-white Closed, Back In Ten Minutes sign on the wooden front door. She checked her Swatch. Ten-fifty. Worst case, Giddy Up would be open by eleven. Before waking Dirk, she needed to think through her options, gather her thoughts. An old trick her Dad had taught her. "Don't move too fast, Belle," she heard him say. "Take your hands off the wheel—" or the hammer or whatever they were working with "—and think through your options."

Not that she knew what her options were if this place didn't accept IOUs. She pulled a vial from her purse and squirted some of the almond-scented lotion on her hands. Rubbing them together, she aimlessly checked out the building. A wooden beam protruded from the front. Dangling from this beam was a square, brass-colored cowbell on a rope. "Why a cowbell?" she thought. Looking up, she had the answer. On the roof, secured with several ropes, sat a plastic, oversize

black-and-white cow. If Belle wasn't mistaken, its
nose appeared to be a red lightbulb.

"Surely it doesn't light up," she said under her
breath. Rudolph, the Red-Nosed Bovine?

She looked down from the fake cow on the exterior
of the building to the real-wood paneling on the interior of the Jaguar. Talk about two conflicting images. Tacky to plush. If she hadn't been preoccupied
with trying to find this Giddy Up place, she might
have savored the time she'd spent driving the most
exotic car she'd ever set foot in. Rubbing some of the
lotion on her elbow, she reflected on her brief ride in
luxury. Yes, she'd driven a Jaguar, but it had been
like driving a hearse because the passengers had been
dead asleep. Plus, *one* of them had been snoring. Focused on road signs, she hadn't detected if that low,
staccato droning was Lover Boy or...

The other Lover Boy.

She looked over at Dirk, who was still fast asleep.
His chestnut hair looked wild, disorganized—traits,
she guessed, that were in direct contrast to Chairman
of the Board Dirk Harriman. Plus, a lock of his hair
fell across his brow, giving him a bad-boy edge. If
she were his woman, she'd encourage that edge. Oh,
he could keep the button-down CEO look Monday
through Friday. But come the weekends, she'd make
that man loosen up. He'd wear opened shirts, jeans,
leather jackets...and that lock of hair would never be
combed back. It'd always fall rakishly across his forehead.

Here I go again. Fantasizing the impossible. Belle
inhaled slowly, as though a steady stream of oxygen
might calm her thoughts. Hardly. If anything, it
seemed to fuel them.

She rubbed her fingers together, imagining the

coarseness of his stubbled jaw. *And I wouldn't let you shave on the weekends, either. I'd want you rugged and disheveled, the way you'd look after tumbling out of bed.* She followed the line of his jaw to his chin. Funny, she'd never noticed the small shadow of a cleft underneath his mouth.

She ran a tongue along her bottom lip, imagining that mouth against hers. She liked how his lips protruded slightly. Even in sleep, they looked sensual. She closed her eyes, envisioning what'd it be like to wake up next to Dirk and give him a wake-up kiss. No peck on the cheek for this man. No, he'd get the full Belle treatment. A long, lingering, let's-stay-in-bed kiss.

She opened her eyes and checked him out again. She didn't want to invade his space, but considering they were down to their last minutes together, she did want to experience *less* space between them. She shifted forward slightly. This close, she could see the small spiky shadows of his eyelashes on his cheek.

She edged forward a bit more. *This* close, she smelled his musky cologne.

Any closer, she could kiss him.

She'd never stolen anything in her life, but at this moment, she'd risk a jail sentence to steal one kiss from the sleeping, rugged prince in the next seat. *What would Dirk think, waking up to a kiss from a woman he views as "one of the animals?"* He'd probably think he was giving CPR, *again,* to another creature.

Hardly the impression she wanted to leave. With resignation, she let her fantasies sink back into the recesses of her mind. Her only option at this point was to wake up Prince Dirk.

"Wake up, sleepyhead," she whispered, stealing his earlier line. "Lover Boy's ready to go."

Dirk blinked open his eyes and gazed at her. Between his half-closed lids, she caught a glimmer of longing that sent a warming shiver through her. She was rarely one to break eye contact, but she had to look away if she wanted to retain any sense of decorum.

After a moment, she transferred her gaze back to him. His eyes were closed again. *Damn. He's asleep. Mere minutes left together and I've lost my chance to double-check how he might feel about me.*

She crinkled her nose. What had happened to her? She, Belle O'Leary, had *never* bothered second-guessing a guy's intentions. Her intuition had always nailed two things: if the guy had the hots for her, and if he had integrity. And she'd be lying to herself if she said a lot of guys hadn't revealed the first trait. But it was the second trait that meant she said "yes" to a date, and it was, more often than not, absent.

With Dirk Harriman, things were turned around. He oozed integrity. But she couldn't put her finger on what, exactly, he felt for her. Referring to her as "one of the animals" didn't help.

Her thoughts were cut off by a low growl. At first she thought Lover Boy was having a bad dream. But when Dirk shifted in his seat, yawned, and uttered another low growl, she had to curl her toes to keep from growling back.

Maybe they were *both* animals. A girl could only hope. And a girl could gather her wits and start acting as though she didn't have the worst crush this side of thirteen years old.

"Time to get up," she said. Dirk would never

know the supreme self-control it took for her to say that with a normal, adult voice.

Dragging his hand through his hair, Dirk yawned again and looked around. "Where are we?" he asked groggily. Then he froze, staring through the windshield. "Good God. A flying bull."

She joined him in looking at Rudolph the Red-Nosed Bovine. "You're obviously a city boy. It's a cow."

Straightening, he rubbed his eyes. "Tell me it's not alive."

"It's plastic. Except for its nose, which appears to be a lightbulb."

Dirk squinted, then shook his head slowly. "Can you imagine what it's like around here at Christmas? Santa Claus probably wears a Stetson and drives a sleigh named Trigger." He made a disapproving sound. "This part of the country is stuck in a cowboy time warp."

Belle decided this wasn't the moment to admit she adored Max Brand and L'Amour novels, or that she could line dance with the best of them. He'd probably look at her as if she had a lightbulb for a nose, too. Not the last image of her she wanted Dirk Harriman to have.

Unbuckling her seat belt, she changed the subject. "A sign on the rental place—" she avoided saying "Giddy Up" "—says it's closed for a few more minutes. When it does open, however, we need to discuss how we're going to rent a car, considering neither of us has any credit cards."

Dirk massaged the back of his neck. "Damn crick. Happens whenever I sleep funny." After retrieving a comb from the glove compartment, he flipped down the visor and, looking into the mirror, began combing his hair.

"Maybe you can write one of your infamous IOUs," Belle added, barely suppressing the sarcastic edge in her tone. It prickled her that the female Dr. Hildebrand had accepted one...probably after a fair share of cooing over Dirk, Most Eligible Male.

Dirk stopped combing. Flashing her an approving look, he nodded. "Worked once. Let's give it a shot."

Belle flashed him one of her I'm-not-really-smiling smiles.

Which he didn't notice as he tossed the comb back into the compartment. "Here I hadn't wanted people to recognize me, and now our best chance of reaching our destinations is if Mr. or Mrs. Giddy Up does." Looking down, Dirk checked out his shirt. "If I wear this one more day, no one will *want* to get close enough to recognize me. I'm going to pull a fresh shirt out of my suitcase. Be right back." He swung open the door and stepped out.

As he crossed to the back of the car, she relished the fresh air that blew in through the open passenger door. At the same time, she fought a wave of nostalgia, remembering how just yesterday, she'd been in her Jeep, looking at its opened passenger door, near tears because she'd thought her Lover Boy had fallen through it.

And then another Lover Boy had entered her life.

She glanced through the back window and watched Dirk. Over the open trunk, she saw him from the chest up as he pulled off his Polo shirt. His shoulders had definition. Nicely molded...the kind you ran your fingers over, outlining the taut muscles. Maybe he lifted weights before work—or maybe he had a private workout room next to his office. Probably took breaks to work out and deal with the stress. Her gaze shifted down. From what she could see, he had more chest hair than she'd imagined. It spread, thick and black, across his pecs. Like the rebel cowboy in one of her favorite L'Amour novels.

She laughed to herself. Dirk would have a conniption if he knew she had compared him to a cowboy.

He pulled on a fitted gray T-shirt. Recalling the steel-gray of his eyes, she knew it had to be a perfect match. Had Janine bought him that shirt? Or another admirer?

Chirp.

Belle looked at Louie through his cage bars. He tilted his green-feathered head and chirped again.

"You're right, Louie. The guy belongs to another world, another life-style. And probably another woman. I'll turn off my simmering thoughts."

"Hey, I think Giddy Up is opening up."

Belle looked over at Dirk, who leaned in the opened passenger door. She'd been right. That gray shirt matched his eyes. *Sorry, Louie. Until he's out of my sight, I'll turn* down *my simmering thoughts because there's no way I can turn them off.*

"Great," Belle responded, trying to sound happy about this part of the trip ending. "Let's go test your IOU skills." She opened her door and stepped out.

They walked together to the front door. As Dirk gripped the knob, Belle spontaneously touched his arm. "Just one moment."

Those gray eyes flickered with surprise. "Yes?"

She swallowed, hard. "I have to ask you something before we go inside because I'll probably never have the chance to ask you again."

He paused. "Go ahead."

"Do you view me as an animal or a woman?"

Dirk wasn't sure if the doorknob was warm from the late morning temperatures or from the thoughts racing through his mind. At least he had something to hold on to as he contemplated why in the hell one of the sexiest women who ever graced the planet Earth was asking him such a bizarre question. If he knew women at all, he also knew the question was loaded. If he answered "woman," she might be disappointed because she wanted to be something more exotic than simply a member of the female species. If he answered "animal," she might be hurt because he saw only the primal creature within her and not the lady.

He was doomed.

He rolled his tongue in his mouth, as though the right answer might pop into his head if he stalled. It didn't. "Both?"

He didn't have a chance to see her reaction because the door swung open, pulling Dirk and his death grip with it. He half stumbled into Giddy Up Auto Rental and nearly fell into an oversize man who looked like Paul Bunyon's twin. Dirk managed to catch his balance before landing on Twin Paul's snakeskin boot.

"Hello and howdy! I'm Big Todd Billy." The giant grasped Dirk's hand and pumped it as though he might get water.

"Hello-y. I mean, hello." Dirk extracted his hand. Fighting the urge to massage it, he continued, "We'd like to rent a vehicle."

Big Todd's tiny eyes disappeared into folds of flesh as he smiled and frowned at the same time.

"Vehicle?" Dirk repeated, wondering if he hadn't been heard correctly.

The eyes didn't emerge.

"Car."

Big Todd's eyes reappeared as he slapped Dirk on the back. "Hell, boy, I know what a ve-hi-cal is. Wasn't sure if you meant a monster four-wheeler or a runabout V-8." Not removing his hand from Dirk's back, Big Todd steered Dirk toward a desk and motioned him to sit down in one of two metal folding chairs that faced an oversize wooden desk.

Sitting, Dirk glanced around the room. Everything in it was oversize. A wide-screen TV sat in the corner. In the other, a humongous globe of the world that Dirk guessed held bottles of liquor in its hull. But the most impressively large items in the room were the three mounted cows' heads on the wall.

"I see you collect cows," Dirk said, breaking the ice.

"Steers," said Belle and Todd in unison. In the following awkward silence, Belle sat in the chair next to Dirk as Todd lumbered around the desk and planted his seat in a leather-and-wood banker's chair that creaked loudly with the big man's weight.

Todd leaned back. Another elongated creak that sounded as though the leather was squealing from the weighty load. Steepling his fingers, he peered over them at Dirk. "What kind of ve-hi-cal you lookin' for?" His tiny eyes shifted to the window, obviously checking out the Jaguar parked in front.

Even if Dirk had had a cold, he could have smelled this deal a mile away. Todd was a wheeler-dealer par excellence. He'd summed up the fancy car outside and was debating whether to double or triple Dirk's fees. Quadruple if he thought he could get away with it. If there was another car rental business in this town, Dirk wouldn't maybe have hesitated to get up and leave. He'd done that plenty of times at the negotiating table. Unfortunately, Giddy Up was the only "ve-hi-cal" agency in town.

Dirk put on his best poker face. "It's for the lady. Air-conditioning. Four-door preferable. She's headed for Cheyenne and will return the car there tomorrow morning."

Todd unsteepled his fingers. Without looking at Belle, he asked Dirk, "Does she want economy or luxury?"

"She wants to be spoken directly to, for starters," said a honeyed voice minus its sweetness. "*She* knows how to speak English."

Dirk shot her a look. If her hair were green, she'd pass for a Louie-look-alike with that angry glint in her eyes. "It's all right, dear. We're talking business."

She turned her blazing blue eyes on Dirk. "I suppose you think," she said crisply, "that the word *business* isn't part of a woman's vocabulary. What do you think I'm going to be running when I get to Cheyenne?"

"Hopefully, a car," Dirk said edgily. He could tell from the abashed look on her face that she got his drift. The last thing they needed to do was rile Mr. Billy. Get on his bad side, and they'd have an easier time negotiating with birdseed than an IOU.

Blinking, she nodded. "Right." She smiled demurely at Todd. "Sorry." She fluttered her eyelids at Dirk. "Economy is fine, dear. After all, it's only for a day."

Dirk had to bite the inside of his cheek not to laugh. Belle O'Leary acting contrite and passive could earn an Academy Award in Hollywood. It was like watching Sharon Stone play a nun. He *knew* Belle was fully aware that he respected women and viewed them as equals. But obviously Todd didn't believe that. Best to work within his Neanderthal views, no matter how narrow they were.

"I got just the car for her," said Todd, standing. "A black Dodge Neon. If the little lady prefers a prettier color, I also got red."

Dirk knew it was taking all of Belle's self-control not to respond to that little-lady line. Avoiding her eyes, he said, "Either color sounds fine. Now, as to cost—"

Todd slid his hands into his pockets and jingled some change. "Reasonable." *Chink chink chink.* "Just need a credit card, her driver's license info, and she's on her way."

Dirk stood. Always best to negotiate eye to eye. "I had a slight mishap yesterday evening. Got held up. Thief took my wallet."

Todd did the smile-frown thing again. Dirk attempted to maintain eye contact even though he was now staring at two creases of flesh where eyes used to be. Obviously, his comments had been overly vague or there'd be more chinking. Todd was zapping power from every brain cell to figure out what the hell Dirk was talking about.

"I don't have any credit cards," Dirk elaborated. "They were stolen last night. By the thief."

Todd's eyes reemerged. "That's too bad," he drawled.

"So, I was thinking," Dirk continued, taking a few steps as though the most marvelous idea of the universe had just occurred to him, "because my name is as good as cash, I'll write you an IOU."

Todd reared back, the color of his face matching one of the stuffed steers. "An IOU?"

"Yes," Dirk said calmly. "An IOU. You can take

it to your bank and I assure you, they'll cash it. I'll have my lawyer call ahead to verify the transaction."

Todd sputtered something before responding. "You must think I look like a damn fool."

Dirk stepped behind his metal chair, just in case he needed to grab it quickly and use it as a shield. "Hardly. You are a businessman. And I'm offering you a business deal. Because this is an unusual arrangement, I'll even pay extra."

Todd snorted. "An IOU," he said to one of the steers. "Fellow thinks he can scribble somethin' on a piece of paper and drive off with one of my cars."

Dirk wondered if Todd often had discussions with one of the stuffed steers.

Belle stood. Dirk offered a small prayer that she'd stick to the little-lady role. Things were bad enough without her going feminist in front of a gargantuan redneck and his best steer pal.

"Don't you know who he is?" she asked in a bewildered tone. "This is Dirk Harriman, *the tycoon*. Last year, *People* magazine cited him as one of the country's most eligible bachelors."

Dirk winced. He'd never had such an outlandish introduction before. This should go over *real* big with Mr. Billy.

Todd folded his massive arms, straining tight the material of his shirt. "And I'm Todd Billy, the most eligible raccoon in the state of Utah. I don't give a—" he glanced at Belle "—hoot who he is or who you are. Get the hell out of my business before I call the cops."

Belle and Dirk exchanged a here-we-go-again look. Somebody else threatening to call the police.

Dirk gave Todd one more look-over. He stood squarely on the floor, tapping one of his snakeskin boots. The scowl on his face uglier than a *very* bummed steer. It was clear he wasn't budging from his position.

Dirk offered his most gracious smile. "Sorry to have bothered you. Have a nice day." Gesturing to Belle, he motioned her toward the door. "Let's go, dear."

Just as they walked in together, they now walked out together, although Belle let the door slam behind them with a resounding smack.

Standing outside, they both looked up at the cloudless blue summer sky. It reminded Belle of the many times as a kid when she'd look upward, thinking God would write an answer to her dilemma across the sky. She hadn't remembered that in years.

"He didn't recognize you," Belle finally said, looking back at Dirk. "Guess he doesn't read *People* magazine."

"So it appears," answered Dirk drolly, rubbing his neck. "You don't have an aspirin, do you? My neck's killing me."

She watched Dirk grimace as he tried to stretch his neck one way, then the other. "You're really hurting, aren't you?"

"Happens when I've sat too long...the stressful negotiation didn't help. Pain goes down my neck and along my back to my sciatic nerve. If I was in L.A., I'd call my chiropractor *after* I called my doctor and begged for a painkiller." He stretched again and winced. "By the time I get to Taos, I'll be lucky if I can crawl into my meeting."

Belle remembered what she'd done a year ago to remedy a backache during a long road trip. "As a matter of fact, I do have something in my purse. Let's pop you a few, then figure out our next step."

As they headed to the car, she added, "I have an idea. How about you take it easy while I drive to a bank? Once there you can talk to Ray and get your cash, then we'll drive to the next town and I can get a car. One hour, tops, and we'll be going our separate ways."

"Makes sense," Dirk agreed. "You'll be closer to your destination. And I'm counting on Ray's renegotiating the agreement so I have an extra day to get to Taos."

He got into the passenger side, careful not to step on the living ottoman. He swigged water along with the several aspirin Belle offered, then lowered the seat a bit so he could rest until they reached a bank.

Five minutes later, as they hit the main town thoroughfare, Dirk felt the pain decreasing. In fact, he felt pretty damn good, despite what they'd gone through in the past few hours. Smiling, he stared up at the blue sky, imagining it to be the waters of the Caribbean. Lush, warm waters...

"What kind of aspirin are these?" he asked. His voice sounded faraway, like breezes over the ocean.

The last words he heard before falling asleep were Belle's.

"Cat tranquilizers."

7

BELLE HAD A LONG, lonely hour to think over her cat-tranquilizer stunt. Driving along Highway 15, listening to the duet snoring of Dirk and Lover Boy—or Lover Boy and Lover Boy—interspersed with the chirping of Louie that sounded suspiciously like chortling, she felt guilty, an emotion she rarely felt.

And not just your oops-I-messed-up guilty. She felt a-trillion-Hail-Marys guilty because she'd never done anything as stupid as slipping someone a cat tranquilizer.

An old memory flickered to life. Okay, once in high school on the worst date of her life, she'd slipped the guy—Perry Johnson—some Ex-Lax, but he'd deserved it. During the entire date, a dark-haired waif-like girl followed them everywhere, tears streaming down her cheeks. Even at fifteen, Belle had right-on internal radar when it came to men. And her radar told her the waif, whom Perry dismissed as a "pal from Milwaukee," was really a brokenhearted girlfriend who was letting two-timing Perry walk all over her.

While Perry played a pinball game at a local arcade, Belle slipped next door to a pharmacy and bought a box of Ex-Lax. When she'd sauntered back outside, Perry was leaning against a lamppost, smoking a cigarette James Dean style. Although on Perry, it looked more like Jimmy-Dean style. Knowing he feigned class, she offered him a slab of this expensive, exotic chocolate from Belgium. Before you could say "two-timing bum," he'd gobbled the entire chunk.

Belle had smiled sweetly and wished him a good-night. As she'd walked away, she noted the surprised look on his face and wondered if he'd still look surprised hours later on his zillionth trip to the bathroom. Even his friends thought he deserved it, joking that Perry should move to Flushing, New York.

But Dirk hadn't deserved the cat tranquilizer. Her only excuse was that once—on a two-day road trip to Mojave—she'd taken one of Lover Boy's pills for a sore back and it had worked wonders. That's why she thought a few cat tranquilizers wouldn't hurt Dirk. Unfortunately, she misjudged the dosage and knocked the guy out. Considering his body weight, she'd thought three tranquilizers would equal the one she took. Because he occasionally snored and talked a little in his sleep, she knew he was okay.

But at noon, a little over an hour of driving the Jaguar-hearse with a comatose cat and man, she felt the need to *do* something other than feel guilty. Ahead, she saw a road sign that advertised Dot's Diner, with "biscuits so big and fluffy, you can sleep on 'em."

Sleep on 'em. As though she needed another dose of guilt. She glanced at Dirk. "No biscuits for you. But I'll get us a cup of coffee. Maybe the fumes will encourage you to wake up." Because he needed to be awake so she could take him to a bank so he could talk with his lawyer so they could finalize the money transfer so she could get her rental auto... She was getting a headache thinking of the mess she'd gotten them into. Maybe she should pop a cat tranquilizer to calm down a little.

Pulling into the gravel-strewn parking lot, she eased into a small space next to a red pickup truck with a sticker on its fender that read If You Don't Like the Way I Drive, Kiss My Bumper. Belle made a mental note to not leave at the same time as her neighbor.

After killing the engine, she looked over at Dirk and watched his chest rise and fall underneath that soft gray T-shirt. For a fleeting moment, she wondered if he was dreaming about kibbles and mice.

Belle heard a chirping sound, but realized it sounded too electronic to be Louie.

Ring. Ring.

Dirk's phone!

In his other shirt, Dirk had carried it in his front pocket. She scanned his chest. No such pocket on this T-shirt. Belle glanced at his pants and noticed a bulge in his pocket. She should go inside, get her coffee, and ignore whoever was calling.

Ring. Ring.

But maybe it was his lawyer.

If she answered, she might be able to help with the bank proceedings. Dirk would wake up and view her as a heroine, not a cat-pill dealer.

Ring. Ring.

She eased her hand into the pocket of his beige khaki pants. Inching her fingers inside, she touched the edge of the phone. With great care so as to not wake him, she curved her fingers around it and gently pulled.

Dirk groaned.

Belle froze. That was no phone. *That* was Dirk's...Dirk's...

Stunned by the realization of what she was gripping, she froze. What if he woke up, saw the look on her face, felt the hold on his...and thought she'd knocked him out so she could take advantage of him? He'd not only sue her for drugging and kidnapping, but illegally copping a feel—

Ring. Ring.

"Get a grip," she whispered to herself. *But not that kind of grip.*

She released her hold and inched over to the "other lump," a hard rectangular object, and carefully extracted it from the pocket. Lifting it, she checked out the keypad. Not an easy stunt considering her hands were still shaking from the copping incident. Trying to focus on the slightly quivering buttons, she punched one labeled Talk, then held the receiver to her ear.

"He-Hello?" Not only did her hands shake, so did her voice. Cool, calm, always-collected Belle was seriously out of control.

"Hello?" responded a deep male voice. "I'm trying to reach Dirk Harriman."

She fought the urge to say, "Don't reach too far."

"He's...sleeping." *Because I drugged him with cat tranquilizers.*

"Oh."

In the following silence, Belle squeezed shut her eyes, fighting images of FBI helicopters racing out to Dot's Diner, Utah, to arrest her. Television crews would broadcast pictures of her, titled Showgirl Turned Pet-Pill Girl, as she was shackled and stuffed into the back of a police unit. Mr. Kiss My Bumper would be interviewed, claiming she looked suspicious the moment she parked next to his ve-hi-cal, while in the background Dot would be showing off a platter of her "sleep-on-'em" biscuits.

And who would care that her dream of owning her Cheyenne diner had gone down the tubes? Bye-bye diner, hello jail cell.

"Who are you?" the male voice asked.

Like she'd confess after that too real fantasy. "One of the animals?" She didn't dare give her name. Or social security number. Dirk knew powerful people who probably didn't need to call the FBI because they had their *own* helicopters.

"One of the what?"

Don't act suspicious. Stay calm. Talk to the man. "My name's Belle. I'm one of Mr. Harriman's traveling companions." *Mr. Harriman?* She didn't know what compelled her to refer to him so formally. Maybe it made her seem less like a cat-pill dealer who copped feels.

"I thought he was traveling with some—"

"Animals. Yes, I heard him tell you that earlier—that he was traveling with 'some animals'—which is why I said I was 'one of the animals.'" She giggled nervously, something she'd never done in her entire life. But then her entire life had never been at stake before.

"Oh." Beat. "And he's asleep."

"Yes." Her voice cracked on the single word.

"I'm his lawyer, Ray Romero."

"Hello," she said, trying to sound upbeat and failing miserably. "I've heard about you."

"Oh?"

"Mr. Harriman said you're renegotiating the Laos deal."

"Taos."

"Right. Taos."

"Right." Pause. "I had wanted to give him some news, but I hate to wake him. Although it's very important he have this information as soon as possible…"

She cleared her throat. "He's, uh, really conked out. Was up all night. He has a long drive ahead—needs all the sleep he can get." *And brother, he's going to get it because he's out cold.*

"Oh." Pause. "Please ask him to call me when he wakes up."

If what Ray needed to tell Dirk had anything to do with his getting cash, she wanted to make sure he had that information the *instant* he awoke from his stupor. Cash meant a rental car, which meant she'd be on her way to Cheyenne. She didn't want to take the chance that when Dirk finally called, Ray was out of the office. Therefore, she needed to get the information *now*.

"Uh, the battery on the phone is low." She stole that line from Dirk, although she didn't have the vaguest where this thing stored a battery, much less what shape the battery was in. "Perhaps you'd better give me the news so I can tell him the moment he wakes up." Or maybe the following moment. Who knew what the aftereffects of the kitty tranquilizers would be?

"Makes sense." Over the phone, Belle heard paper-shuffling sounds. "Tell him he can go to any bank, have a bank officer call my office, and either I—or if I'm out, my assistant, Paula—can set up the financial arrangements. As to Taos, I have some advantageous news. The Taos property is subject to a trust, which puts a cloud on the title…''

As Ray rattled on, Belle frantically looked around for something to write with. This Jaguar might have more buttons and knobs than a space shuttle, but it lacked a simple piece of paper and a pen. ''I'm not getting any of this down,'' she confessed. ''I'm afraid I'll forget which cloud goes where.''

Ray chuckled. ''No problem. Dirk and I can discuss the details later. What's important is to tell him I'm ninety-nine percent certain we can get that twenty-four-hour extension.''

''I can remember that.''

''And remember to tell him he can get credit at any bank.''

Cheyenne, here I come! ''I can remember that, too.''

''Great. Take care. And, uh, what did you say your last name was?''

She hadn't. But it didn't appear that Ray Romero was going to call the FBI or anybody else with helicopters. ''O'Leary.''

''Nice Italian name.''

Ray had a sense of humor—like his pal Dirk. ''Very northern Italian. Ireland, actually.''

Another chuckle. ''Tell Caliente to drive safely.''

Caliente? ''Okay.''

''Bye.''

She heard a soft click on the receiver. Scanning the phone's keypad, she punched a red button labeled End. The small screen that had shown the incoming number blipped, then turned gray.

Looking at Dirk's sleeping form, she debated whether to return the phone to his pants pocket.

Chirp.

Belle eyed Louie in the backseat. "I'm only thinking that I should return the phone to its rightful place," she whispered defensively.

She quickly looked away from the bird's beady eyes, wondering if she'd been telling the whole truth.

As they danced, Dirk held her tiny hand, which was encased in a soft glove. Luxurious, silky hair pressed against his cheek. The kind of hair a man could nuzzle, lose himself in. Soft music played in the background, a male voice crooning—along with a woman humming—a song of lost love. Across the ballroom floor, someone must have opened the French windows because a cool breeze sifted past, carrying the sweet scent of...Dirk inhaled deeply...almonds?

Pulling back his head, he stared into his dancing partner's eyes...eyes with elongated slits for pupils.

He glanced up to her ears...ears with pointed, furry tips.

A cat? He was dancing with a cat?

Dirk blinked fiercely. The furry ears disappeared. Through the front windshield, Dirk stared blearily at a blacktopped highway that narrowed to a point on the horizon. He blinked again, reassuring himself he was truly awake. After deciding he definitely was, he wondered what in the hell was he doing in the passenger seat of his own car—which was moving at breakneck speed down a strange highway.

Groggily, he looked to his left. The driver, humming along to the music, stared straight ahead at the road, one polished nail tapping the steering wheel in time with the song.

Belle. Driving. Reality was starting to come back. He listened to the country-and-western music playing on the radio—the same music he'd heard in his dream when he'd been dancing with…a cat.

He winced.

Waltzing with a cat. To country music. This trip was taking its toll on his body *and* mind. Next he'd be dreaming he was a belt-buckle-making, relationship-challenged singing cowboy named Bart, riding a horse named Hi Ho.

He rubbed his eyes, thwarting any attempts by his subconscious to materialize *that* fantasy. *Think reality.* Pieces of the recent past assembled in his mind, forming the complete picture. He and Belle had been unable to get a rental car, so she'd volunteered to drive them to a bank. And obviously he'd crashed right after that. Which made sense considering he hadn't slept a wink during the all-nighter in the animal hospital.

And it also made sense he'd dream of dancing with a cat…for God's sake, he'd kissed one the night before.

He looked over at Belle. He'd never kissed a woman's pet before kissing the woman. Not that he'd ever kissed a pet before—but this whole trip was turning backward from driving in the wrong direction to kissing the wrong species.

Species. Belle was one delectable one. Last night, when he'd viewed her in the moonlight, she'd awed him with her ethereal beauty, like an Aphrodite come to life. But today, in the daylight, her beauty bordered on fierce. Maybe it was the way she wore her confidence like armor. He liked how she differed from some of the intense women corporate types he knew—women who walked with their chins jutting forward, looking for a battle. Although he respected women and supported their causes, he had trouble with out-of-the-can feminists who viewed the genders as two opposing camps. Belle could teach those women a thing or two because she had the guts to be her own person.

The air conditioner whipped cool breezes around the inside of the car, blowing wisps of Belle's short hair. In contrast to its champagne blond were her lightly tanned features. A showgirl who loved the outdoors. Whereas before he viewed Belle as embodying contradictory traits, he now saw them as part of her uniqueness.

And even though over the years he'd stared into his share of blue eyes, Belle's were unique, too. Caribbean-blue, full of depth and currents and secrets...

As though responding to his thoughts, Belle glanced over. Her blue eyes widened slightly. "You're awake," she said in a surprised voice.

"Yes," he answered, his voice barely more than a croak. He cleared his throat. "I was more tired than I'd realized." Man, his mouth felt dry. He took a swig from the bottle of Evian, relishing the cool liquid.

Belle sat stiffly, staring straight ahead at the road with a slightly stunned expression.

"Something wrong?" he asked, returning the bottle to the cup holder.

"No," she answered, her voice rising as if she weren't sure.

He looked at her a long moment before scanning the scenery outside the windows. Ahead, the landscape was expansive, raw, wild. Miles and miles of rolling hills and sagebrush. He checked the rearview mirror. Behind them rose the Rockies, cutting a jagged edge along the horizon. Majestic scenery that made one ponder the mysteries of life.

However, right now a certain Belle O'Leary made him ponder other mysteries...such as why was she acting so oddly.

"Want me to drive?"

"No!"

Her response was so sharp, he nearly jumped. If he could. His body felt abnormally sleepy, so it was just as well Belle remained behind the wheel. "Are you all right?"

"Yes-s-s," she answered, elongating the word until it blended in with the air conditioning.

"I could use a cup of strong coffee." Dirk yawned. "I'm not usually this groggy when I first wake up."

Chirp.

Dirk arched one eyebrow toward the back seat. Through his cage bars, Louie cocked his head in response. "Guess Louie's been keeping you company while the rest of us—" he checked out the pile of fur underneath his feet "—were sacked out."

"Yes."

He glanced at Belle, wondering when she'd resorted to single-word responses. Not like her at all. But then, she'd only had Louie's single-chirp comments for company the past hour or so...maybe she'd fallen into the same monosyllabic pattern. At least she wasn't chirping.

They drove past a green highway sign. In white block letters were the words Evanston Five Miles.

"Evanston," Dirk said, mulling it over. "Don't remember seeing Evanston on the map.'' He conjured up the state of Utah in his mind and all the *E* towns he could recall. Enoch. Echo. But no Evanston. ''Must be one of those small, out-of-the-way Utah towns.''

No response.

He looked over at Belle. She didn't look so fierce anymore. In fact, the way her eyebrows were raised a notch, she looked nervous. A little sheepish, even. And when did she start chewing on her bottom lip like that?

''Are you all right?'' he asked again.

She hesitated before nodding. ''I'm okay,'' she answered, sounding anything but. She shot him a look. ''Are *you?*''

He thought a moment, then flipped down the visor. Staring into the mirror, he checked out his appearance. Besides having slept on his cowlick wrong—he looked as though part of his hair had seceded from the rest—he *appeared* to look the same. And the numbness he felt had to be the aftereffect of crashing, hard, after going without sleep for over twenty-four hours. He pushed the visor back up. ''We've never woken up together—is that the problem?''

When she darted him a questioning glance, he realized what he'd said. If his tongue didn't feel like an alien in his mouth, he would have corrected his ''woken up together'' comment more swiftly.

''I assume,'' he said, forcing his tongue and lips to work in tandem, ''that you're asking me if I'm okay because you've never seen me when I first wake up. I have to admit, I'm feeling a little ragged around the edges, but I'm okay.'' He checked the clock on the dashboard. ''Three-thirty,'' he read, enunciating the numbers as though they were a foreign language. He flipped his wrist to confirm the time. "Three-thirty?" he repeated with emphasis.

Hadn't he drifted off around...eleven?

He looked over at Belle. "It's *after three* in the *afternoon?*"

"Yes?" She stared straight ahead as though the road was the most mesmerizing sight she'd ever witnessed.

"Are you unsure of the time?"

"No." She shrugged apologetically. "It's really three-thirty."

Chirp.

Dirk ignored the back seat driver. "You mean I slept—" he mentally calculated the hours "—nearly *five* hours?" Under his feet, the furry pile shifted. He flashed back on his dream where he'd been dancing with a cat.

Then he recalled the last words he heard before falling asleep.

Cat tranquilizers.

Impossible!

Yet nearly five hours has passed since he'd last been in the real world. He rubbed his temples as though he could erase the offending thought. "Did you...give me...*cat tranquilizers?*"

Belle nervously played her fingers along the steering wheel. "Yes."

Yes? "*Cat* tranquilizers?" he repeated through clenched teeth.

As though his synapses were finally kicking in, memories raced through his mind. Like the time some loony had threatened to kidnap Dirk and hold him for ransom. The police had stepped in and offered around-the-clock security—but Dirk had beaten them to the punch and hired his own security firm. For the next three days, until the culprit was finally arrested, Dirk had people monitoring his every move, including every bite of food and drink he ingested, to ensure his safety.

And after all those precautions, he hadn't learned a damn thing. In the middle of his cross-country self-journey, he had trusted a woman who had slipped him *cat tranquilizers.* "Do you realize it's a criminal offense to slip people drugs? Plus, this five-hour detour doesn't exactly get me to Taos!"

"I've already figured it all out," Belle said, her voice oozing sweetness and hope. "While I got gas— my last twenty came in handy—I checked the map. It's a straight shoot from Highway 80 to Cheyenne… From there, you can zip down Highway 25 to New Mexico."

"Zip." Dirk made a disgruntled noise. "Sounds as though I'm putting on a pair of pants." He blew out a gust of air. "When actually, I'm heading toward Cheyenne, the cowboy center of the universe, while recovering from a cat-pill overdose." He glared at the radio. "Could we please turn off that yodeling cowboy tune? If I have to listen to any more, I'll be begging for the rest of those animal tranquilizers."

Belle tapped a button. The music stopped. In the following silence, she said softly, "I'm sorry. I—I saw you were in pain and I wanted to help. I once took one for a horrific backache and it worked wonders."

"One what?"

"One cat tranquilizer."

"You gave me four."

She darted him a surprised look. "Four? You sure?"

"If I meowed, would you believe me?"

Her mouth opened, then shut again as though she couldn't trust herself to speak, much less count. "I thought it was three, honest," she said weakly. She bit her bottom lip, which he noticed didn't stop it from quivering. "Not that I should have given you three instead of four, but the reason I gave you more than one is that you're bigger than me—" she gestured to his body as though he might not be certain what she meant "—and I figured a few would do the trick." She glanced at him, tears welling in her eyes. "I'm so sorry...I only meant to knock out your neck pain..."

"And succeeded in knocking out *me*," Dirk said edgily. "You should have told me first—given me the option of whether I wanted to consume...what was it called?"

"Acepromazine."

"Sounds serious. They probably give it to cats in mental wards as well."

"I was wrong. Worse than wrong." She blinked rapidly. "I'm not sure what's worse than wrong. Depraved?"

A drop-dead gorgeous woman confessing she was depraved was any red-blooded male's fantasy. Her use of the word, plus the fact she sounded so damn sad, so repentant, took the steam out of his anger. When a tear spilled down her cheek, she clumsily swiped at it and missed. He reached over and gently brushed the moisture from her face. For such a strong lady, she sometimes seemed more fragile than a young girl.

"I knew you were okay because you were snoring so loudly," she said, her voice quaking.

"I don't snore—"

"I'm so very sorry," she interrupted, obviously too caught up in her confession to hear anything else. "What a stupid thing for me to do. And to someone like you—even though I still don't know exactly *who* you are except that *People* magazine thinks you're one of the world's most legible bachelors—"

"Eligible—"

"The *worst* part is, I know you feel unsafe in the real world." Sniffing loudly, she lifted the tail of her shirt and patted another tear that trickled down her cheek.

Dirk tried to stay focused on her face, but she'd lifted her shirt a little too high, which meant he caught a second peek at breasts that could put the Rockies to shame.

"And you're probably feeling even *more* unsafe right now," Belle continued, "because a strange, depraved woman slipped you cat tranquilizers." She dropped the shirt.

Dirk raised his gaze. Actually, he now felt more unsafe because his libido was, once again, overriding his intellect. And if she was depraved, he was a low-down, no-good cad for checking out the scenery *inside* the car...especially when the woman behind the scenery was so sad and regretful.

"You can drop me off in the next town," she continued. "I'm sure you never want to see my face again."

He looked at her sweet face, pink and puckered as she fought more tears, and felt far sorrier for her remorse than his foray into veterinary science. He'd dealt with enough people to recognize Belle as the type who punished herself more severely than anyone else could. Besides, he'd been so exhausted, he probably would have slept that long with or without the help of cat tranquilizers.

He reached over and reassuringly touched her arm. "What's done is done. I'm a little groggy, but alive and well. You made a mistake, but you thought you were helping me."

She choked back another sob. "I did! I really thought I was helping you! When I slipped Perry the Ex-Lax, he deserved it, but you didn't."

Dirk paused. "You...you didn't also slip me Ex—"

"No!" She shot him a teary-eyed look. "I was just referring to the only other time when I gave someone something and he didn't know it."

"Perry. Ex-Lax."

"Yes."

"But I'm Dirk, cat tranquilizers."

She half laughed, the sound dissolving into a small cry. "You make me sound like some kind of Black Widow Pharmaceutical Nut. I don't stalk men so I can slip them illegal dosages."

He doubted she'd ever had to stalk any man in her entire life. "No, I don't think that. I'm sorry. You're a strong, kind woman who tried to ease my pain."

She gave him the most grateful look he'd ever seen. "Thank you," she whispered.

"Although I'm not sure you eased Perry's." He gave her a playful pat before removing his hand from her arm.

She smiled, a bit on the mischievous side. He liked the twinkle that returned to her eyes. "That was a one-time deal for a two-timing toad. Besides, you and I are friends.'' Her gaze clung to his as though analyzing his reaction. "Right?"

"Absolutely. If this road trip extended to Iowa—which I'm not suggesting it does—we'd probably end up *best* friends."

"What if it extended to New York?"

"I'd probably have to marry you."

In the following silence, Dirk felt more stunned than if he'd consumed a hundred pet pills. He'd meant to be a little silly, maybe make her laugh...but say the forbidden word *marry?* Had he lost his mind? Ever since Janine, he'd sworn off *ever* saying, "I do."

"Well, let's make sure we go no farther than Iowa," Belle said lightly.

But Dirk didn't laugh. Instead he pondered why he'd so blithely referred to wedlock. In business, he always listened carefully to his opponent, especially if the person said something unusual—because it was the odd comment that typically told the most truth.

And he'd said the word *marry*.

What did he feel for Belle? They'd weathered crises, which strengthened their camaraderie. They'd shared laughter and secrets, which bonded their friendship. And if his carnal urges were correct, they'd shared more chemistry than two nuclear physicists in a lab. Saying the forbidden *word* to Belle hadn't felt like a possible jail sentence. Rather, it had felt like a potential haven. A place, a life, he might like. Could the truth be he liked the idea of commitment with Belle?

On this trip, he'd worried that he was starting to *over*communicate, but maybe it was simply that he was *truly* communicating for the first time in his life. Communicating what was in his heart, not his head. And if that were the case, maybe he felt more for Belle than he realized.

He crossed his arms over his chest, in awe that he was contemplating marriage in New York over best friends in Iowa. But for the time being, he'd keep that insight to himself. "Now that we've agreed we're interstate friends," he said, veering the subject in a different direction, "did you slip me your cat's medication because you view *me* as one of your animals?"

Her mouth dropped open. Glancing quickly at him, she said indignantly, "You're one to talk. I overheard you tell your lawyer I'm one of the animals."

That one stopped him colder than a cat tranquilizer. "I didn't mean it about you. I was simply explaining the chirps in the background." Then it hit him. "So *that's* why you asked if I view you as an animal or a woman."

She cast him a sideways glance. "Why'd you say 'both?'"

Dirk rearranged his legs over the sleeping feline at his feet, buying some time. Finally he said, "Because the best women in the world are a little of both." He caught her smile; she was obviously pleased at his assessment.

"And I have no doubt you've known the best, being a man who's traveled the world over...trains to London...boats through Venice..."

He nodded, adding to Belle's imaginings. "Balloons over Holland, the Concord to France, a road trip through Wyoming." Yes, he'd traveled the world over. And yes, he'd met a number of wonderful women in different cities, each as individual as their culture. But what Belle didn't fully realize was that the world was really a very small place. And what made women unique and memorable wasn't their accents or clothes or manners, but the simple gift of a good heart.

"And which of the best was the best?" Belle asked.

"A unique woman—part animal, part Aphrodite— who traveled by my side during an incredible journey. I thought I knew everything about communication until I met her, but she taught me to listen not only with my head, but with my heart, too."

He tapped the radio button to On. A male voice crooned a gut-wrenching song about the woman who stole his heart.

"Thought you didn't like country-and-western—"

"Sh-h-h." Dirk dipped his head in time to the music. "I'm listening."

8

LOOKING IN the rearview mirror, Dirk checked his appearance. "The next time I take a five-hour nap, remind me to sleep *on* my cowlick, not *against* it." After tugging at a bump of hair with the comb, he tossed it back into the glove compartment. "Well, well!" he enthused, peering inside the niche. "A twenty-dollar bill!" He lifted it for her inspection. "I must have tossed it in here and forgotten about it." He gave his head a shake. "Never thought I'd be so happy to find a single bill. Considering I haven't heard from Ray, and most banks are almost closed for the day, we're lucky to find this cash."

Ray, Dirk's lawyer! The phone call!

Belle had been so caught up in her guilt, then her reprieve—plus the "marry" comment hadn't helped get her thoughts back on track—she'd almost forgotten to tell Dirk about the conversation with his lawyer. "I have some great news—Ray's ready to transfer money to any bank *and* you have a twenty-four-hour extension on your deadline!"

Dirk paused. "How do you know all this?"

"Ray called while you were…out."

"And when you say 'out,' you mean '*out*,'" he teased. "I'll call him right now." He slid the twenty into his pants pocket. Fumbling, he murmured, "Where's my phone?"

She dipped her head toward the leather console between them. "It's between your seat and the leather island."

"How'd it get there?" he asked, frowning.

"It rang, so I...answered it." She played with a strand of her hair, omitting what occurred between the ringing and the answering. "Afterward, I, uh, couldn't return it to your pocket because I was driving."

Chirp.

Tinglings of heat prickled the base of her neck as she remembered groping for the phone and accidentally groping something else. From her peripheral vision, she saw that Dirk was busy punching in a number, oblivious to her response. He'd never know that they'd shared an accidental intimate moment.

Too bad it had been accidental because something about him was more right than anything she'd ever experienced with a man. Although she and Dirk had only known each other a little over one day, her inner radar hummed at a frequency that told her he was "it."

However, when she glanced over, "it"—holding the receiver to his ear—was looking at her with a wicked gleam in his eye. "I need to ask," Dirk said in an undertone, holding the phone receiver against his shoulder. "Why a laxative?"

It took her a moment to realize Dirk was asking about Perry, her high school date. "Because the guy was full of..."

"Hello, Ray!" said Dirk into the receiver, being pulled into the other conversation. Even though he was listening to his lawyer, Dirk maintained eye contact with her. From the playful glint in those gray eyes, she could tell he enjoyed her joke. She liked that in a man…liked someone who didn't take himself too seriously. Plus, she had to admit that she liked poking a little fun at him, keeping him on edge. Someone like Dirk Harriman probably had few—if any—people who nudged him off balance.

"Sorry I called back so late," Dirk continued, looking away. "I…overslept. We're nearing Evanston, Wyoming. I figure I'll…yes, Wyoming. That's right, the state above Colorado. We…took a detour…Belle said there's a twenty-four-hour extension, so it shouldn't be a problem…yes, Belle. She's…"

Belle held her breath. *She's what?* What might Dirk "Tycoon" Harriman say to his all-powerful possibly helicopter-flying lawyer?

"She's my…traveling companion," Dirk finished.

She heard the warmth in his tone when he said "traveling companion." Maybe some of the excitement he'd experienced had happened accidentally—picking them up in the desert, spending the night in an animal hospital, digesting a few cat pills—but she had a sense Dirk hadn't done this much living in a long time. Heck, the guy was now listening to country-and-western music! Maybe Belle had burst his bubble a little. In a good way.

After all they'd been through, all they'd shared, it was a shame that it soon had to end.

Looking up at the blue Wyoming sky, she murmured a small prayer, "There's this special guy who's fallen…okay, driven…into my life. Name's Dirk. We're on our way to two different places…too bad one of them isn't right for both of us…"

One place? That last bit just popped out. But, too

late, it was part of her prayer now. Just as she'd done as a kid, she imagined it floating up, up beyond the wisps of clouds, to heaven. It'd been a long time since she'd talked to God, yet she'd done just that several times in the past twenty-four hours. Maybe Dirk was helping her do more than reach Cheyenne. Maybe he was helping her regain some sense of self she'd thought long lost.

A few minutes later, Dirk ended his call. Belle watched him slip the phone back into his pants pocket, remembering when she'd slipped her hand into the same pocket. That one touch titillated and unnerved her more than anything she recalled with any of her four fiancés.

"What are you thinking about?" Dirk asked.

If he knew, he'd keep that phone safely on the dash. "My four fiancés." Not quite the whole story, but close enough.

"Four?" Dirk gave her a double take. "Think the dose you gave me was symbolic?" Not waiting for a response, he added, "And I thought one was enough." He lowered her a meaningful look. "One fiancée, not one pill."

Dirk shifted in his seat, turning his body so it faced her at an angle. She liked how he slouched so casually, his body at ease in her presence. She flashed on when he had been sleeping and how she'd leaned close and inhaled his musky scent. Her knees weakened at the memory.

"Going a little slow, aren't you?" Dirk asked, checking the speedometer.

"My legs feel—" *weak* "—tired." She forced herself to press harder on the gas. "Maybe cruise control is the way to go."

Dirk laughed. A deep, rumbling laugh filled with mirth and sexiness. "Never thought I'd hear Ms. Anti-Cruise Control make such a confession."

Oh brother, could she make a few more.

"Sorry, you have to drive," he continued, growing serious. "When I feel a bit less groggy, I'll take over."

"No problem," she said, hearing the breathiness in her voice. Forget the car—she should put her *libido* in cruise control.

"By the way, as we're no longer renting a car, I'll stop at a bank in the morning to get money for gas and supplies." He carefully stretched his legs over Lover Boy. "Now that that business is out of the way, tell me why you didn't marry any of your fiancés."

It was more her style to ask the blunt questions, but she liked that Dirk took an interest in her life. Besides, talking about her past fiancés would get her mind off the present man.

"What stopped me every time," she answered slowly, "was that I wasn't certain I would have my own identity—my own career—within the marriage. After watching my mom forsake her dreams for her family, I swore I'd never do the same. If I married, my husband had to understand that I had goals and aspirations, too."

"And none of your four fiancés understood that?"

She raised her peach-tipped index finger. "Number one, Tony, was a pit boss in Vegas. Strong-willed, funny. But he wanted more kids than I could count. I saw myself raising six kids, just as my mom had done, and I got cold feet. No, worse than cold. Freezing. Tony and I went our separate ways, but we remain friends." She raised two fingers. "Number two,

Bernard, was a corporate type, software companies. Somewhat eccentric, but drop-dead smart. Unfortunately, he wanted me to move to Silicon Valley, away from my life and friends. Besides, I had no dreams to pursue there—what in the heck would I have done in Silicon Valley? The only chips I know are potato.''

"You might have taken a few computer science courses.''

She fixed him a look. "And Bernard might have gone to showgirl school.''

"I'll add computer science to the yada-yada list.''

She smiled. Raising three fingers, she continued, "Number three, O.T., drove a bus—''

"O.T.?''

"Overtime. That was the problem. He was always working, half the time in another state. Just as it's impossible to change a tire on a moving car, it's also impossible to maintain a relationship with a moving man. Instead of pursuing my dream, I would have been pursuing him! We shook hands, agreed to always be friends, and he drove off into the sunset. Then along came number four, Louie.''

Dirk noticed that she didn't lift four fingers this time. Instead, she curled her hand around the steering wheel, her gaze fixed on the road ahead. This last one seemed to affect her more than the others.

"You said before that you named Louie the parakeet after Louie the fiancé,'' he said gently, trying to keep the conversation on a lighter note. "Don't tell me your fourth fiancé had green hair.''

She laughed, but he heard a trace of sadness in it. "No green hair, but the same brash personality. Louie, number four, was brazen when it came to the outside world, but a real gentleman when it came to me. European roots, but thoroughly Americanized. He loved me more deeply than I thought possible."

"Sounds like he did all the cooking, too."

"Not all, but most. He'd also figured out all the details of the wedding, from the look of the pew decorations to each dish of the ten-course meal. Seemed kind of excessive to me…"

"Married after breakfast is much simpler."

"I have to say, that seems way too spontaneous for you."

He raised an eyebrow. "In fact, it's carefully planned. You see, if you get married in the morning, it leaves the rest of the day for…"

A blush tinged her cheeks. "*Anyway,* when it came down to it, he didn't want me to work. In fact, insisted I didn't. Easy to understand because none of the women in his family had ever worked. It was a sweet gesture, but not my style. The images of my mother were just too strong. When we ended the engagement, he insisted I keep the ring."

Dirk looked at the diamond ring on her left hand. It was beautifully cut, at least two carats. Louie must have had money, but Belle's integrity had a higher price. For the first time in his life, he'd met a woman who wasn't blinded by the glint of gold. From what he'd just heard, she didn't care if a man was a bus driver or a businessman, as long as he respected her dreams.

If Dirk were to make a qualified guess, after four almost-trips to the altar, Belle had given up hope that she'd fall in love and raise a family. He knew that feeling. After Janine, he'd given up on love, too, and thrown himself into his work. He kept busy, too busy, but it didn't fill the emptiness inside.

Maybe Belle struggled with the same emptiness.

Two people so alike, yet soon to be apart. The thought of her being gone from his life saddened him. "How long before we get to Cheyenne?" he asked.

"Around five hours."

He checked the clock on the dashboard. "It's nearly four. We have those sandwiches and a few hours of Wyoming sunshine left. Let's steal one of those hours and have a picnic. It'll do us good to get out of this car, relax, enjoy some food and fresh air." He had a selfish desire, too. He wanted a chance to talk comfortably with Belle, to look into those Caribbean-blue eyes and watch her moods flit across her face as she told him more stories of her life. And he wanted to hear it all—how she became a showgirl, her favorite books, movies. He wanted to cram a lifetime into an hour.

Otherwise, he'd spend their last few hours together staring at her profile as they drove across Wyoming. And as lovely as her profile was, he wanted more to remember because it would have to last him a long, long time.

"A picnic!" she enthused. "Great idea. I used to do that all the time on my road trips. Let's find a place to pull over."

A mile later, they pulled off the highway and down a dirt road. To the left were a few distant trees. To the right, an old wind-scoured building, its wooden frame splintered with time.

"Must have been someone's house a long time ago," murmured Belle. "Just imagine all of its stories, all the people who once called it home." She pulled off the road into a small dirt clearing and stopped. "I like the view here. Lots of nature and a little bit of history. Perfect picnic spot."

Stepping outside, Dirk inhaled the pungent scent of sage in the air. The sun's heat baked his skin. Closing his eyes, he murmured, "I've been outside, enjoying nature, more in the past twenty-four hours than I have in the past twenty-four years."

A passing breeze pushed the sweet scent of Belle's perfume toward him. When he opened his eyes, she stood next to him, admiring the view. "And I've spent less time outside in the past twenty-four hours than I can remember when," she said. Opening her arms wide, she seemed to embrace the whole of nature around her. "This is the life. Simple, but richer than anything money can buy."

Dirk thought of all the women he'd dated who expected him to spend big bucks on elegant dinners and expensive theater tickets. Yet here was Belle, savoring the moment they were sharing, and not one instant of her pleasure was derived from Dirk spending money. "When I first saw you stranded by the side of the road," he began, "I couldn't put you and that Jeep together. It was like mixing chiffon and rawhide. But now that I've gotten to know you..."

Belle dropped her arms and cast him a questioning look. "This better be good, Mr. Communicate."

"Now that I've gotten to know you," he repeated, "your contradictions make you unique. One in a million. You're a goddess on the outside, a tomboy on the inside. An independent woman with more soul and spark than is legal. A lady who appreciates life's quality, not quantity." He didn't regret speaking from his heart. All these years he'd prided himself on his communication skills, carefully weighing how he phrased things. It was like being on a damn word diet. Maybe it was time to be a new Dirk. He made a pact with himself. From now on, he was going to be a man who spoke the truth and lived his own life.

Belle's blue eyes widened. "When you communicate, Dirk Harriman, you *communicate*."

"That's nothing." He gave her a jaunty wink. "You should hear the stuff I don't say."

He liked the pink flush that filled Belle's cheeks, as though she were a schoolgirl being flattered by an admiring beau. He had the irrational wish that he'd been her first and only man; that they'd met in school, and he'd carried her books and given her her first kiss. Escorted her to her first dance. Been her first lover.

She turned away, motioning toward the Jaguar. Dirk noticed her hand shook slightly. "Let's...get the sandwiches and find ourselves a picnic spot."

Dirk watched her saunter back to the car, her body saying more with its movements than most people said in a speech. He caught up as she reached the car and leaned in the back seat, rummaging about for the food. Dirk tried to avoid looking at the molded shape of her thighs, which were delightfully exposed as her shirt lifted with her movements. He imagined Belle in one of her showgirl outfits. Indecently long legs encased in mesh stockings. And above those, some type of G-string number. And above that...

Chirp.

Dirk shifted his gaze to the cage in the back seat. He swore Louie stared at him accusingly.

"I think you and Louie are becoming fast friends," said Belle over her shoulder. She straightened, the sandwiches in her hands. "Too bad we don't have a blanket."

"We have the one from last night—I returned it to the trunk." Breaking eye contact with his "fast friend," Dirk crossed to the back of the car.

"A picnic on fur," Belle mused. "Is this how tycoons rough it in the wilderness?"

Dirk opened the trunk. "It's velour, not fur. And even if it were fur, it seems the wilderness would be its natural habitat." He retrieved the spread and shut the trunk with a click.

Belle stood with her weight on one foot, causing one luscious hip to push against the loosely hanging shirt. "Sandwiches on a fur blanket is hardly road-trip dining. Stick with me, Dirk Harriman, and I'll show you how to rough it."

The sunlight shone through the sides of her shirt, outlining the round curve of full breasts. That and the jutting hip were enough to rough it all right...rough his senses raw. He stopped in his tracks. "I can't think of anything better than to stick with you, Belle."

She stared at him, her mouth slightly open. He'd caught her off guard for the first time. A feat he'd have thought impossible with the sassy, glib Belle O'Leary. Chalk one up for the new-and-improved Mr. Communicate.

And then she surprised him again. Her blue eyes moistened. At first he thought he'd offended her, but the tenderness in her gaze told him otherwise. Telling her he'd stick with her, stand by her, had obviously touched some secret part of Belle. He'd wager it was because they'd each resigned themselves to being alone for the rest of their lives.

Blinking, Belle turned away. "Would you mind

bringing Louie? He's been cooped up in the car all these miles...a little fresh air would do him good.''

Dirk sensed that Belle was really asking to be given a little time to gather her emotions. ''Will do,'' he said, turning around.

After retrieving the birdcage and a package of seeds that lay nearby on the seat—Dirk wasn't sure when Belle had last fed the parakeet, but it seemed a nice gesture to include Louie in the picnic festivities—he headed back down the dirt road toward where Belle stood, waiting for him. The sunlight caught in her hair, igniting it with gold. And even though he wasn't close enough to see, he knew those blue eyes watched him intently, warmly. He imagined what it would be like to come home to such a vision every day. What it would be like not to walk into an empty house, but to a full life shared with Belle.

The thought tugged so hard at his heart, he ached.

Chirp.

''You said it, brother. I don't want to lose this lady.''

''Were you and Louie chatting again?'' she asked as Dirk approached.

''Guy talk.'' He set the cage down on the ground and laid out the faux-fur blanket, then helped Belle peel the cellophane off the sandwiches. They carried on these activities in silence, the only other sounds the whisper of an occasional passing breeze and a chirp or two from Louie.

After another of these chirps, Belle said, ''I think he's hinting for a snack.'' Belle indicated the bag of seeds that Dirk had brought. ''Care to feed him? This will be the last chance for you two to break bread.''

''Sure,'' he said, trying not to dwell on how they'd

soon be apart. He slid open the little wire door and sprinkled some seeds into the white plastic container that hung on the side of the cage. "Here, pal. Knock yourself out."

After closing the door, he laid the bag aside and leaned back on his elbows. Staring up at the pale blue summer sky, he watched a distant hawk weave lazy circles in the air. It reminded Dirk of how he'd spent too many years going in circles, looking for life's meaning and never finding it.

Until now.

"Penny for your thoughts."

Dirk turned to look at Belle, who was propped on one elbow. Her oversize shirt had fallen open, exposing a creamy shoulder. He imagined what the rest of her body, naked, might look like. Skin vibrant, luminous the way Rubens would have painted it. What had one critic said about his models? *Their skin glows like milk and blood.*

That was Belle. Rich, glowing flesh, with curves that a man could grasp and knead. Not the kind of woman a man hesitantly stroked, silently asking permission to do more. No, Belle would be a true partner in every sense of the word, a woman with passions and desires that demanded—and expected—release.

"Okay," Belle said, a note of playful peevishness in her tone, "I'll up the stakes. A dollar for your thoughts."

"I'd give a million for a single kiss from you."

Her mouth dropped slightly open. He'd caught her off guard, *again.* Probably the only man in the history of civilization who'd been twice able to throw the inimitable Belle O'Leary for a loop. Not that his goal was to shock or surprise her. He was simply being the new Dirk Harriman who spoke his mind. The man who wanted to express his true self. And at this moment, nothing was truer than his desire to taste her lips.

"A million—?"

"I'll up the stakes," he said huskily. "Two million dreams, three million fantasies, four million tomorrows...for a single kiss from you."

Belle drew a breath, her breasts heaving slightly. He would have to be blind not to see she wanted it as much as he did. "Come to me, Belle," he coaxed. He needed to know she wanted him. Desired him. He'd already put himself on the line, now he wanted her to cross it.

She hesitated, then leaned toward him. "Meet me halfway."

He smiled. Just like Belle to be a competent negotiator. "Deal." He edged forward, closing the space.

Their lips touched. Hers were like velvet, soft and pliant. The first kiss was slow, thoughtful, arousing. When a small moan escaped her lips, he sank his mouth fully against hers. She responded with equal passion, hungrily pressing the length of her body against his.

Heat seared through him as he tasted and caressed her. Stroking the back of her shirt, he remembered yesterday when he'd first seen she didn't wear anything underneath. He needed more...needed to touch her skin, feel her more completely...

He slipped his hand underneath her shirt. As his fingers made contact with the taut planes of her back, he shuddered a release of breath. She felt good. Satin skin over firm muscles. The goddess and the tomboy.

Although he'd never been one to rush things, it took every ounce of willpower to take it slowly. He wanted to savor every moment, to savor her. Holding her with one arm, he pulled back slightly.

"Let me look at you, Belle."

Her blue eyes met his as she smiled her assent.

He brushed a blond strand out of her eye, letting his fingers linger in the silky softness of her hair. "Where did I find you?" he whispered.

She smiled mischievously. "On the side of the road."

He grinned. "Just goes to show, I should have taken my self-journey earlier."

She reached up and tugged at a lock of his hair. "I like it when you're a little unkempt, Caliente," she said seductively. Before he had the wherewithal to respond, she explained, "Ray called you that. And for good reason, I'd say."

"Actually, he gave me the nickname a few years ago after I had a run-in with some serious jalapeños...long story."

Belle's eyes twinkled, then turned thoughtful. "And this self-journey you keep referring to...is that also a long story?"

He paused before answering. "This trip is the first time in years that I've faced the world alone."

"And been outside your bubble."

He nodded. "Bull's-eye."

"And Taos is part of this?"

He ran his finger down the slope of her cheek, stopping on the cushion of her lip. "I haven't shared this with anyone except Ray. I'm not buying the literary magazine in Taos because I want to own a new business, but because of the land it sits on. The magazine's offices are in an old hacienda, a ranch, on thirty acres. I want to move my groundskeeper and his family from L.A. to Taos so they can be closer to their relatives, their roots. It's my way of doing something for a family since I'll most likely never have my own."

"Never's a long time," she whispered, her eyes searching his. "This has been a very special journey for you...into the outside world, but also into your heart."

"In more ways than one—"

A rattling distracted him, following by a light swishing sound.

"Oh, no!" Belle clutched Dirk's shoulder.

He straightened, following Belle's line of vision. Through the air, a small green bird flew a zagged line toward the old wooden home.

Belle struggled to her feet. "Louie!"

9

"I CAN'T LEAVE HIM here," Belle said for the umpteenth time. "He can't survive in the wilderness with no food, no one to watch over him..."

Dirk's steel-gray eyes darkened as a sadness crossed his face. "It's my fault you're going through this. If only I'd closed the cage door properly...."

He'd said it many times over the past few hours. She touched his arm in a gesture of comfort. "Neither of us knows exactly what happened."

She and Dirk were sitting on the faux-fur blanket that lay spread on the ground outside the old wooden home. Wind whistled eerily through its broken, splintered slats and empty window frames. Louie had flown inside hours ago, and despite walking through several times and calling to Louie repeatedly, they hadn't found the parakeet. In between, Dirk had coaxed Belle into eating parts of a sandwich and resting a little. As the hours grew, he'd also gently broached the subject of their leaving so Belle could meet her deadline.

Which he was doing again.

Dirk touched her hand. "It's been nearly five hours since Louie flew away—it's almost nine at night. You need to be in Cheyenne by eight tomorrow morning or you lose your diner..."

She sucked in a ragged breath, not wanting to succumb to the emotions that raged within her. The summer sun was hovering on the horizon, threatening to slip behind the mountains. Soon it would be dark. If she couldn't lure Louie from his hiding place in the daylight, she knew the chances were next to nil in the night.

With Dirk's help, she stood. "I need to try one more time...just one last time," she whispered. "Remember, when this happened before, Louie returned." She'd told the story over and over to Dirk. After she'd first got Louie, he'd flown out the opened front door of her Vegas apartment and lodged himself in a palm tree. She'd waited for him all day, the front door open. Just as the sun was setting, he returned.

Dirk stood. "I'll go with you—"

"No." She smiled apologetically. "You've gone with me the past two times. This time, I need to be alone in case..." her insides caved in at the thought "...in case I don't find him." She quickly walked away before Dirk saw the tears forming in her eyes.

As she headed toward the entrance, she breathed deeply, willing herself to keep it together. Her parakeet was more than a sassy, brash bird with the attitude of animals ten times his size. Louie was also her soul-pet. Her confidante.

And over the past few hours, she'd realized he was also her spirit.

When she hadn't thought she could make it through a situation, she'd sat next to his cage and discussed the pros and cons. Louie would chirp, fluff and strut. At some point, his cheeky spirit would infuse her and she'd feel strong enough to tackle anything.

But something she couldn't admit to Dirk, despite the bravado she'd shown him, was her fear that she wasn't strong enough to tackle the upcoming change in her life. Running a new business in a strange town with no network of friends—and add to that, no Jeep for transportation—was just plain frightening. As silly as it might seem, she needed her cocky parakeet's spirit to bolster her.

As much as she had always feared growing old with only her pets for companionship—like her Aunt Meg had done—she now realized how vital it was to build a community with other living beings, be they animals or humans.

She stepped into the gloom of the empty house. Shafts of light speared the shadows. The large room, probably the former living room, smelled musty despite the gusts of wind that seeped through cracks in the walls.

"Louie?" Her voice reverberated throughout the barren room. "You can't leave me now. How do I start my new life without you?"

The only response was a prolonged whistle of wind. Something creaked in a far corner.

Looking around, Belle made a few soft kissing noises. "Here, boy. I'm waiting for you...." Searching the dark recesses of the room, she held up her hand, inviting the errant Louie to return.

But only silence greeted her as her hand remained suspended in the air.

She lowered it. "I can't leave you here," she said, her voice breaking. "How will you survive? Who will laugh at your antics, you shameless parakeet?" The thought of Louie with no audience, no one to witness his strutting and primping, filled her with more sadness, more grief than she thought she could bear. She wrapped her arms around herself, more for comfort than warmth. "You flew away once, after I first got you, but returned and we started our new life. Don't you want to start our new life again?"

She glanced behind her. Through one of the window frames, she watched Dirk pace outside, looking at the house. She'd never seen him pace. It was probably taking all his willpower to give her the space to do what she needed rather than take charge. And if she told him she couldn't leave without Louie, she had no doubt he'd lay out the fact of her deadline, but in the end, if she insisted on staying, she knew Dirk would remain by her side.

But staying meant losing everything she'd ever dreamed of....

Turning back to the room, she ran her fingers through her hair, realizing she had to make a choice. "You're making it tough on me, aren't you? Making me choose between you and my future is unfair, Louie."

The light in the room shifted, telling her the sun was starting to set. It was time to make a decision.

"Okay, Louie," she said to the growing darkness. "I can do it. I can start my new life without you." A pain, like a hand squeezing her heart, racked her insides as she turned to go.

Something fluttered.

Wings?

She stopped and looked around. A flash of green broke through a fading slant of light before disappearing again into layers of shadow. Instinctively, Belle held up her hand. Tiny feet gripped her finger. She pulled her hand close, covering the small bundle of feathers with her other hand.

"Louie," she whispered, fighting the tears. "You grandstander, holding out to the very last moment. You're no bird, but a showman at heart." She began walking toward the door as the light in the room dimmed.

As she stepped outside, Louie held protectively against her chest, she watched Dirk across the expanse of dirt and grass that had once been the front yard. She smiled broadly, although she knew he couldn't see her joy.

"WAKE UP, SLEEPYHEAD," coaxed Dirk. "We'll be in Cheyenne soon."

Belle blinked, then winced as bright lights assaulted her eyes. "Where are we—?" she said, her voice barely a rasp.

"All-night truck stop somewhere outside Elk Mountain." Dirk glanced around the car. "This Jag is like a hearse when everyone's asleep. Even Louie was fast asleep, not a chirp, which must be a first for the *Guinness Book of World Records*."

Belle smiled to herself, remembering the old house and how Louie had flown down to join her at the very last minute. "After his antics, I'd claim I grounded him, but we all know who really calls the shots."

"Louie." Dirk unsnapped his seat belt. "You should change the name of your diner from Blue Moon to Green Bird. Speaking of which, you're a little over an hour from it."

"A little over an hour," she repeated, her voice oozing happiness. Turning toward him, she added, "Thank you, Dirk, for making my dream possible."

She saw him stiffen slightly, and wondered if it was because he was moved by her gratitude. The man in the bubble was probably unaccustomed to receiving personal thank yous. As CEO, his position of power was a built-in bubble. If someone wanted to thank him, they most likely sent it remotely by a memo, voice message, E-mail. Which meant he never saw the joy in someone's face, the personal reaction to something wonderful he'd done.

In a mock serious tone, she added, "By the way, if I named my diner Green Bird, I'd never hear the end of it from you-know-who. I'd probably turn on the TV one day and see him in a commercial, advertising *his* diner."

Amusement flickered in Dirk's eyes. "I'm going to miss..." he let his thought trail off. "I'm going to fill the tank. Be right back."

"Would you get me a cup of coffee?"

Dirk looked at the clock on the dashboard. "It's one in the morning. You sure you want caffeine?"

She straightened, fluffing her hair with one hand. "I plan on taking the wheel this last hour-plus... I want to remember the first time I drove triumphant into Cheyenne."

Dirk grinned, that sexy, preppy grin she'd grown to adore. "You got it. I'll stretch our last twenty-dollar bill to fill the car with gas *and* get a cup of coffee for the lady."

Fifteen minutes later, Belle settled behind the driver's seat and adjusted the belt. "Buckle up, Mr. Communicate, for the ride of your life."

"I think I've already had the ride of my life, Belle. I don't think much else can top the past day or so." Dirk's seat belt snapped closed. "Too bad Louie and Mr. Boy are missing this."

She eased onto the gas. "Too bad Lover Boy missed the entire trip, actually."

"Even my kiss he slept through."

Pulling onto the highway, Belle decided not to respond to Dirk's last comment because it brought back memories of their own kiss. If she dwelled on that passionate moment, her body would again feel the burn of his caresses. A dangerous reverie because she had an immediate reality to deal with. In a little over an hour, she'd be in Cheyenne. With the key Aunt Meg always hid under the third flower pot outside the front door, Belle would let herself inside the diner. After unloading her suitcase and pets, she'd say good-bye to Dirk Harriman, wish him well, and they'd each continue the lives they were meant to lead.

Lives that didn't include each other.

She followed a split in the road, trying not to dwell on its symbolism. "It sure gets dark out here in the country," she commented.

"Locals probably know these roads blindfolded," Dirk surmised. "Maybe that's why they skimped on the streetlights."

She drove in silence for the next twenty minutes, mulling over her new life, trying to feel excited about the new adventure. But something would be missing...and she was afraid that something was Dirk.

"Penny for your thoughts," he asked. When she didn't respond, he upped the ante. "Dollar?"

"Not even a million." What good would it do to say he was more right than the rightest guy she'd ever met, but that they were too independent, too different to make it work for the long haul. Dirk was a CEO with thousands of people who depended on him. Belle was an almost-diner-owner with two pets who depended on her. Dirk belonged in the splashy neon lights of L.A. Belle belonged in the simple sunlight of Cheyenne. But rather than go into all that, she simply kept her eyes on the road, her heart off her sleeve.

This stretch of highway was long, dark. The headlights reflected off a rough-hewn wooden fence that bordered the road. Ahead, two lights, with two more close behind, rose over a crest in the road.

"What are those?" Dirk asked, leaning forward. "I'd swear they're headlights—"

"Heading right toward us—"

"Damn!" Dirk grabbed the wheel with his left hand. "We're on a one-way road—"

"Let go!" Belle yelled. "I have to steer this mother—"

Grappling with the wheel while pushing Dirk's hand away, Belle glanced to her right at the fence— if she swerved off the road and directly into it, the car would become an instant accordion. She jerked her gaze forward. One of the trucks blasted its horn, the sound booming through the night, its headlights like two fiery suns...

She swerved the wheel to the left.

The Jag's tires squealed as she cut in front of the truck, its lights slashing across her vision. For a moment, she was blinded.

Ho-o-n-n-k!

The truck careened past like a giant monster, furious at the pest in its path.

Bump, bump, bump. The car was off the road, kicking dust along the left shoulder. God knew what she'd hit if she stayed here. Twisting the wheel, she forced the Jag back onto the asphalt.

"Belle!" Dirk yelled. "Stay off the road—!"

She faced the second set of headlights. Another truck! Screaming—or was it Dirk?—she cut the wheel sharply, propelling them back across the highway.

Ho-o-n-n-k!

The car lurched off the road and spun as it hit the soft shoulder. Belle pumped the brake pedal, praying the car would spin *away* from the giant truck and not *toward* it. Brakes screeched. For a moment, it seemed they were in a snowstorm as dust and smoke swirled thickly.

The car gyrated for interminable seconds before shuddering to a stop. In the following moments of silence, the only sound was a prolonged hissing from the engine interspersed with several irritated squawks.

She glanced in the back seat. The cage had moved from one side of the seat to the other, but it was still erect. Despite Louie's mood, he was okay. She looked over at the shadowy form next to her "Dirk? Lover Boy?"

"Make up your mind," answered a familiar male voice.

"Are you okay?"

"I've been better. You?"

She ran her fingers along her face, her arms, her legs. No blood. She wiggled her toes and fingers. Nothing broken. "Okay." She leaned over and squinted into the shadows on the floor. "Lover Boy?"

"If you're checking on your cat, he's fine, too," Dirk said dryly. "In fact, he's snoring on my foot. I guess your driving skills don't impress him."

"I'm sorry," she whispered, feeling sorrier than any other time she'd been sorry on this trip. Sorrier than any time she'd been in her *life*. She never felt sorry for herself—she took pride in owning up to her mistakes—but she felt grievously sorry for the havoc, the chaos she'd brought into Dirk's life. She looked out the window. The moonlight played along the rough-hewn wooden fence, now looking rougher than she remembered. Against one of its broken posts rested the Jaguar's front bumper. "I think we...ran into the fence."

She heard Dirk breathe in and out, deeply, several

times. "Into and *along* the fence for a good, oh, twenty, thirty feet." He stared out the window at the mangled wooden structure. "While watching my side of the car kiss that length of fence, I realized there was something missing from my life."

She bit her lip, waiting for him to finish. He didn't. "And that is—?"

"More cat tranquilizers."

"You're kidding."

"Yes, I'm kidding. Although it would have been nice to have slept through that spectacular driving exhibition, as Mr. Boy had the good fortune to. My fingers are still embedded in the leather console from their death grip."

"You're kidding."

He paused. "Yes, Belle, I'm really kidding. Which I'll stop doing as soon as my adrenaline levels are down from highly horrified to mildly terrorized."

She started to laugh, but choked on the effort as her body finally reacted to the near crash. Clasping her hands together to stop them from shaking, she whispered, "I'm so sorry. I didn't realize it was a one-way road. Your poor car—vehicle," she corrected herself. "Your poor, magnificent vehicle which I—" she gulped back a sob "—I *mangled*. I'm so depraved." She covered her mouth with her hands to keep herself from breaking down completely.

Reaching over, he patted her arm. "Belle, as much as any breathing male would love for you to be depraved, you aren't. Second, I have insurance. Third, *neither* of us realized it was a one-way road. Anyway, I shouldn't have grabbed the wheel. Any intelligent man knows when to let a woman run things."

Stunned by his sweetness and sincerity, Belle

reined in her tears. "I'm not going to cry again," she said in a quaking voice. "Really, I'm not that weak."

Dirk chuckled. "Playing chicken with two hefty semis is hardly *weak.* Not only am I impressed with that, but you're actually saying the word *vehicle* instead of scoffing at it." He pulled on the door handle. "I'll get out and inspect the damage, then we'll brainstorm Plan B." The opening door hit the broken fence post with a solid thud. "Wonderful. There's not enough room for even a fat cat to squeeze through." He pressed a button on the dashboard. "Let's see if the sunroof works." He stared at the ceiling as nothing happened. "Guess not. Open your door, Belle. I'll get out on your side."

"Sure." She opened the door.

Leaning toward her, he said thickly, "As much as I'd love to crawl over you, I'll have to ask you to get out first."

Chirp.

"Of course. I wasn't thinking." Belle stepped onto the soft dirt. The night air was cool, laced with scents of sage. She wrapped her arms around her middle and stared at Dirk as he slid out of the car. "Got a flashlight?"

"Yes. Unfortunately, it's in the glove compartment, which is also jammed."

"I had a flashlight in my Jeep—should have remembered to take it with me."

"Well, Cha-Cha probably needed it for his last rites ceremony." Dirk slowly circled the car, itemizing the damage. "One flat. One broken headlight. One seriously dented and depraved car door. Make that two. More hissing than a vat of vipers—probably a punctured radiator. I don't think we should attempt to drive to a station. I'll call 911 and get emergency road service." He fumbled in his pants pocket. "Phone's missing. Did you—"

"No!" She shook her head vigorously. Catching herself—after all, Dirk had no idea what had transpired in his pocket—she lowered her voice. "I mean, no. I haven't, uh, answered your phone again."

"Odd. Wonder where it is..." Dirk leaned back into the car. With the dome light on, he checked out the interior. "No phone," he said incredulously, straightening. "Maybe I dropped it at the truck stop...or the picnic spot." Dragging his hand through his hair, he scanned the vast expanse of land unbroken by any signs of civilization. "Unless another semi comes barreling past, we're really stranded. Even if one does drive by, they might not notice us over here, nestled against this fence." He stared at it, then turned to Belle and said wryly, "I think this calls for a good, mournful country-and-western song. How about 'Don't Fence Me In'?"

She smiled. Not one of her four fiancés would have tried to defuse such a stressful situation. Tony would have vented. Bernard would have overanalyzed. O.T. would have sulked. Louie would have paced. Or baked.

But Dirk, who had more savvy and class than all four of them rolled into one, had the common sense to make light of it. Like her dad might say, "Making lemonade from lemons."

She dipped her head to the side, enjoying how a light breeze ruffled her hair. "Maybe we could make up one called 'Sittin' on a Fence, Thinking How My Cow Done Me Wrong.'"

Dirk chuckled. "We'll have to write the rest of the lyrics and send it to Mr. Todd Billy."

Belle joined in the laughter. "That would be a suitable fate for you, Dirk Harriman, to become a best-selling country-and-western song writer.''

"Speaking of fate, isn't this how we met? Stranded by the side of the road?''

She waited a beat before responding. "Yes, this is how we met," she said softly.

"Hey, it's not that sad," Dirk said, walking up to Belle and placing his hands on her shoulders. "I propose we get back into the car and wait for help—I'd volunteer to walk back to the truck stop, but I think it's rather far, and besides, I don't want to leave you alone.''

She was strong and could take care of herself, but it felt good to let someone else take charge. "We've come this far together, might as well stick it out for the last few hours.''

"Right." He squeezed her shoulders. "Worse comes to worse, I'll jog back to the truck stop when the sun comes up. Figure that will be around five…I'll have help within the hour, by six, which still gives you two hours to reach the Blue Moon. You'll meet your deadline, Belle, if I have to carry you there myself.''

She had the urge to sink against his strength and nestle in his body warmth, but knew better. If they crossed that line again, they might lose the edge they needed to push forward, meet their goals. Maybe in another time, another place, they could have been lovers…

As though Dirk knew, too, he suddenly turned and headed toward the car. "Last one in turns out the lights.…''

THE RISING SUN tickled the skyline with gold, tinting the clouds with vibrant pinks and oranges. Dirk groggily wondered what he was doing in the passenger seat of his car, facing the sunrise with a snoring animal on his foot, a twittering bird behind him, and a blonde on his shoulder.

Reality hit just as the sun, a drop of molten fire, fully emerged over the horizon. Sitting on the side of a nameless one-way road in the middle of Wyoming, Dirk was surrounded by his road-trip family—Mr. Boy, Louie and Belle. The circumstances were whacky—as most had been this journey—but the companionship was real. So real, that deep within, Dirk felt a satisfaction that had eluded him most of his life. Despite his riches, his properties, his experiences, nothing had fulfilled him more than simply waking up with his woman by his side.

My woman?

Reality check, Harriman. You need to get this woman—not *your* woman—to Cheyenne by eight. Then you need to rent a car and hightail it to Taos to make your own deadline, which will be tomorrow morning thanks to Ray's extension. Don't let an overabundance of hormones hinder your opportunity to purchase that land.

He started to gently tap Belle awake, but stopped just as he touched a strand of her hair, remembering when he'd tunneled his fingers into the silky blondness. He still smelled her signature perfume...a little fainter, but unmistakable. Flowery, like a spring bouquet. Closing his eyes, he inhaled slowly, wanting to remember more....

Chirp.

Dirk popped open one eye and darted a look at the back seat. Louie, his green feathers slightly puffed, stared back.

You're no bird. You're a damn chaperon.

Dirk smiled to himself. And good thing, too, because business beckoned. "Wake up sleepyhead," he whispered into Belle's ear. "Lover Boy's ready to go."

Belle blinked, her long lashes fluttering open slowly. When she looked at him with those Caribbean-blue eyes, he had the crazy thought that if he fell into them and drowned, he'd die a happy man. "Where are you going?" she asked sleepily.

Finally, she'd identified him as Lover Boy rather than the cat. One small victory for mankind; one major ego boost for Dirk Harriman.

He glanced at the dashboard clock. "It's a few minutes after five. I'm going to jog—" Down the road he spied what looked to be an oversize box, except that it sparkled silver where the sun's rays hit it. Not too many king-size boxes were made of metal. "...to jog down the road," he finished. "I think I see help ahead."

It took some maneuvering to get a sleepy Belle to exit the car so he could crawl out the driver's side. Louie chirped through their progress while the living ottoman lay like a sack of fur on the floor. Outside, the air was crisp, but already warming. Perched on the fence, a meadowlark twittered its flutelike refrain before winging away.

"Get a load of that sunrise," said Belle, staring in awe at the horizon.

"You're going to see a lot of those," said Dirk, joining her for a moment. "Welcome to your new life."

It was the way she grinned so appreciably at him— a little sleepy, no makeup, her hair mussed—that tugged harder at his heart than any other time over the past day or so. Belle was more beautiful without the trappings of makeup than most women were with it. And he'd wondered how a Vegas showgirl loved the outdoors—he finally realized that it was the other way around. An outdoors girl had somehow stumbled into showbiz, but her heart remained as wild and free as nature itself.

"You belong here, Belle," he said, gently pushing a stray hair out of her face. He turned and left, not wanting to linger. Because if he did, he'd say or do something that might change his life irrevocably.

His loafers were well-crafted, pliable. Best Italian leather available. As he started a slow jog, he remembered the salesman's sleek line, "astonishingly versatile, suitable attire for both business or pleasure." He should write the man and say they're astonishingly versatile, all right; suitable for running along Wyoming highways as well.

Dirk had lost a few pounds over the past several days, but the loose fit of his pants was perfect for the impromptu jog. He passed a sage grouse, which emitted a surprised *kuk-kuk-kuk* before taking flight. He didn't blame the bird. Considering Dirk hadn't shaved—or slept well—in several days, he just hoped he didn't frighten the people in the rectangular-shaped vehicle as well.

Twenty minutes later, he discovered it was a horse trailer.

Dirk slowed to a walk as he passed the trailer to the dented blue pickup truck in front of it. Behind the wheel sat an older man, a well-worn cowboy hat that was either once beige or white, pushed back on his forehead. The man was staring at the sunrise while sipping from a thermos. Through the open window, the scent of coffee curled teasingly through the morning air.

"Hello," called out Dirk.

The man turned, a look of mild surprise on his weathered face. "Well, hello to you, too. You the runner I seen in the mirror?"

Dirk looked at the long side mirror attached to the driver's side. The man recognized him as "the runner," not as Dirk Harriman. This trip had given him many things, including a healthy dose of humility. "The same."

The man looked down at Dirk's loafers. "Fancy running shoes."

"I'm from L.A." He wiped the sweat from his brow, figuring that would explain anything and everything. "We ran off the road and hit a fence last night. Can't drive. Think we could get a lift into Cheyenne?"

The man screwed the lid back onto the thermos. "Sorry to hear that. 'Fraid I have a similar story. Was headed up from Centennial when a gasket blew. I'm waitin' for my son-in-law."

"You have a phone?"

The man frowned at Dirk as though he were crazy. "In my *truck?*"

Dirk opted for another approach. "Think your son-in-law might give us a lift?"

Sucking on his mustache, the man gave his head a shake. "He's on a scooter…heads down this road every mornin' on his way to work. He's gonna be surprised when he sees his wife's old man sitting here by the side of the road—even more surprised if I say you want to pile your L.A. family on top of his scooter." He smiled apologetically. "Doesn't look as though either of us can help you."

Dirk nodded, unable to form words. His insides ached at the thought of Belle missing her deadline.

He looked back down the road, wondering how long it would take him to jog to that truck stop, wherever it was...

"You look pretty down, son."

Dirk nodded again. Meeting the older man's gaze, he explained, "The lady with whom I'm traveling needs to be in Cheyenne by eight this morning or she loses her dream. It's a diner and it's her whole future. You see, she's one of those special people in the world who's given a lot to others and never asked for anything in return. And now she has this one chance, this one opportunity to build a future, and she'll lose it if I don't find a way to get her to Cheyenne."

The older man's eyes glistened. "You ever ridden a horse?"

"I've played polo."

"Polo?"

Dirk paused. "Yes, I've ridden a horse."

The man opened his pickup door, whose hinges creaked mercilessly. "Let's get you saddled up, son. You have a lady who needs to catch her dream."

10

AT FIRST BELLE thought it was a mirage…a cowboy on a white horse, riding toward her. It was every L'Amour fantasy come to life—the good guy on horseback, galloping to her rescue.

A stranger to her rescue? She must be more stressed than she realized. Now she was making up fanciful stories to bail herself out of her crisis. For the nth time, she glanced at the dashboard clock. Almost six. As had become her nervous habit ever since Dirk jogged into the sunrise, she double-checked the time against her Swatch. Almost six. She again felt a nauseating feeling of despair, which increased in intensity as the minutes ticked past.

Two hours to meet my deadline.

"I'm not going to make it," she said out loud. She hadn't thought that, much less voiced it, up until this very moment. As the reality hit, she didn't have the urge to cry—doubted if she could cry. It was as though her insides had been gutted. Maybe that's how one felt when dreams crumbled…

She squinted through the windshield into the sun, which hung like a fiery ball right above the horizon. The man on a horse, silhouetted against the golden rays, loomed larger.

This was no stressed-out mental concoction. This was really a person. Heading toward her. On a horse.

"It's my last chance," she said to Louie as she opened the car door. "I'm going to flag down that cowboy, put my pride on hold, and beg and plead for a ride."

Clop, clop, clop.

She stood outside the door and waved, flagging them down. It hit her that the rider was headed in exactly the opposite direction she needed to go in. She had to convince him to turn around and head back to Cheyenne...but who in their right mind would do that for a total stranger? As she continued waving, the movement caught the light in her diamond ring, which sparkled with small, twinkling fires. Louie-the-fiancé had once hinted that the engagement ring had cost him twice the amount of her Jeep, which fifteen years ago had been eight grand. She held up her hand and stared at the dazzling diamond.

"Sixteen grand for a ride into town." She laughed to herself. "If you get me to my dream, it'll be worth every penny."

The horse and rider had halted several feet away. Backlighted by the sun, she couldn't distinguish his features as she walked toward them.

"This will sound bold," she said, raising her voice so the man could hear. "But it's crucial I get to Cheyenne by eight o'clock this morning. If you'll give me a lift on your horse, I'll make it well worth your while..." She raised her hand to show the ring, but before she could continue speaking, the man cut her off.

"A voluptuous woman like you, Belle, shouldn't offer herself to strangers. Some black-hearted cowboy might sweep you off your feet and gallop into the sunrise." She recognized the deep, rumbling laughter as Dirk's.

She dropped her hand. "I was going to offer my diamond ring. I had no idea you'd show up on a horse."

"You just thought I was your everyday run-of-the-mill CEO? Didn't think I had some cowboy blood in me?" He dismounted and headed toward her. "Let's grab your purse—you'll probably need identification with those Pancake attorneys. Don't worry about Louie and Mr. Boy. Frank will pick them up after he and his son-in-law Gil get the truck fixed. He'll pick up Babe from the Blue Moon Diner when he returns your pets."

Belle followed Dirk as he retrieved her oversize pink bag from the back seat. "Frank? Gil? Babe?"

Dirk turned and winked. "Babe's the horse. I'll explain the rest on the ride into Cheyenne." He placed the strap of Belle's purse over her shoulder, then steered her toward the horse. When they reached it, he put his foot in the stirrup. "I'd normally say 'Ladies first,' but it's easier if I mount before you." He swung his left leg over and sat.

Straightening in the saddle, he removed his foot from the stirrup. "Place your foot in there," he instructed, "and take my hand."

"This whole horse thing," she murmured. "You're kidding, right?"

"I'm dead serious."

"We can make it to Cheyenne by eight?"

"If you stop stalling. Give me your hand."

The authority in his voice didn't allow no for an answer. Obligingly, she put her hand in his. He gripped, hard, and drew her to him. Next thing she knew, her rump landed squarely on the Navajo blanket behind the saddle.

He flipped his wrist. "It's six." Tugging gently on

the reins, he turned the horse east. "Frank says to follow this road until it intersects with Highway 80, then follow that to Cheyenne. We'll have a bit of an upgrade at the Summit, but otherwise it will be a fairly easy ride. Put your arms around me."

She did as told. "What do you know about horses?" she asked, leaning close. Pressed against him, she felt his sinewy back muscles through the thin T-shirt.

"I played polo."

"Polo?"

"You sound like Frank." Dirk turned his head, his breath warm against her face. "Hold on, Belle, for the ride of your life." He kicked the horse's sides. Her heart lurched as the massive beast galloped down the highway.

Wind played havoc with her hair, whipping it about her face. She wound her arms tightly around Dirk's waist, pleased when he reassuringly patted her hand. As her body grew accustomed to the horse's muscular, rolling movements, she relaxed, letting herself sway with the animal's rhythms. She replayed Dirk's words in her mind. *You'll meet your deadline, Belle, if I have to carry you there myself.* In a sense, that's exactly what he was doing. Carrying her, ensuring she made it to her dream. She closed her eyes and rested against him, grateful for his perseverance.

During the more strenuous parts of the ride, she felt Dirk's broad shoulders heave labored breaths. At those times, she silently nestled closer, willing him her strength, her heart keeping pace with the horse's thundering hooves.

When they passed a few scattered ranches and homes that she recognized as being on the western fringes of Cheyenne, she checked her Swatch. Ten to eight. Her insides churned. No use telling Dirk to hurry. She'd seen him check his own watch a few minutes back; he well knew they were down to the wire. She pressed herself against him and prayed fervently they reached the diner in time.

Suddenly, she recognized an old, gnarled cottonwood tree that signaled the diner was around the corner. Leaning forward, she yelled, "It's coming up soon. On the left."

Sure enough, the Blue Moon Diner appeared as though her words had invoked it. Meg had asphalted the small parking lot; otherwise, the diner looked the same as when Belle was a kid. Flat and rectangular, like a shoebox, freshly painted in broad, horizontal blue-and-white stripes. Square glass windows. And on the roof, a smiling blue moon, circled by the neon words Blue Moon Diner.

The churning in her stomach escalated to large, sloshing waves of anxiety. Belle couldn't contain herself any longer. "Hurry!" she pleaded. "Hurry, hurry!"

They galloped almost all the way to the front door. Belle might have needed help getting onto the horse, but she had no problem sliding down by herself. As soon as her feet hit the ground, she ran, pumping her legs as she crossed the asphalt. When she reached the glass front door, she stopped and pushed. It creaked open. Bursting inside, she halted, panting for breath.

The place was empty.

She looked across the tile-checkered floor, past the vinyl-covered booths, to the round stools nestled underneath the L-shaped Formica counter, the same off-white with gold flecks that she remembered. On the back wall, next to the list of sandwiches, drinks, and pies was the familiar round chrome clock.

Two minutes after eight.

"Are you Belle?"

She looked down. A boy, who she guessed to be around ten, stood at the end of the counter, behind the cash register. A mop of chestnut-colored hair fringed his big brown eyes.

"Yes."

A young girl, maybe thirteen, stepped through the swinging kitchen doors located directly behind the register. "Hi," she said shyly. She had the same chestnut hair, which fell in soft curls to her shoulders. "I'm Tiffany. That's my brother, Cory."

"Where are the Pancake Palace lawyers?" Dirk, who had entered behind Belle, was looking around the room.

"They left!" Cory piped up.

Tiffany put her hand on his shoulder. "They were here from seven until eight—"

"And then they *left?* I can't believe it!" Belle spun around to face Dirk. "They didn't even give me ten extra seconds!" She turned back to Tiffany. "Where'd they go?"

"Back to their motel." The girl brushed a hair from her eyes. "They said something about returning to The Silver Spur so they could pack up and leave."

"Pack up?" Belle stomped back to the door. "That does it! They're not screwing me out of my inheritance that easily!"

Dirk followed the determined Belle as she strode back out the door, down the steps, and across the parking lot. "Belle, what in the hell do you think you're doing?" he yelled after her.

"I've come too far, been through too much, to let those slimy corporate types cackle gleefully at their good fortune just because I was *two* fricking minutes late—'' She reached the horse. Without pausing, she lifted one pink-sandaled foot into the stirrup and hoisted herself onto the saddle.

Dirk stopped in his tracks. "What are you doing on that horse?"

"I know a shortcut to The Silver Spur!" With a brisk kick and a "Yee-haw!" she and the horse galloped out of the parking lot.

As they disappeared down the road, Dirk heard the young girl say in amazement, "Wow! Didn't know she could ride like that!"

He glanced behind him. The two kids stood closely together, their eyes wide with amazement as they watched the departing horse and its free-spirited rider.

"I didn't know she could, either," he said under his breath. "Must be where she learned 'yee-haw.'" Raising his voice, he asked, "Where is this Silver Spur motel?"

Tiffany pointed primly down the highway toward Cheyenne. "A couple of miles in that direction. You can see it from the road."

He scanned the lot. "Who's car is that?" he asked, pointing at an old Chevy parked under a lone tree.

"That's Mr. Shaver's, the old far—" The rest of Cory's sentence was muffled behind his sister's hand.

Not removing her hold on her brother's mouth, Tiffany blinked rapidly. "That's Mr. Shaver's, the... grouchy man who lives next to the diner."

Dirk jogged toward the Chevy and opened the driver's door. Keys dangled from the ignition. Smiling, he jumped inside, slammed shut the door, and started the engine. As he cruised past the kids, he yelled out the window, "Tell the old fart I'll bring it right back!"

As DIRK STEERED THE Chevy into the parking lot of the motel, he wondered if a little piece of Las Vegas had fallen into Cheyenne. The Silver Spur parking lot, nestled along a quiet stretch of country road, had more twirling lights, moving people, and animals than a Circus Circus nightclub act.

And in the center of it, handcuffed, was Belle.

She was being led by a disgruntled-looking police officer to a parked unit, ablaze with flashing lights. Belle, looking more displeased than Louie on a bad day, was talking emphatically to the officer, who appeared to be ignoring her. Another policeman was jotting down notes while talking to two smug-looking men in dark business suits. Babe stood serenely to the side, observing the humans and their strange behavior while munching an artistic arrangement of small green plants that spelled Silver Spur.

Or, at this point, Silver Spu.

Dirk parked between two white lines in front of the motel, cut the engine, and stepped out. Pondering how best to communicate and get Belle out of this mess, he approached the officer who was steering her toward a police unit.

"Officer," said Dirk politely. "Perhaps I can help explain."

The policeman stopped and looked questioningly at Dirk. "Is that your Chevy?"

The question threw him off. Glancing back at it, he said, "Well, uh—"

"You drove it in here, correct?" the officer asked.

Dirk paused, then nodded. "Correct."

The officer called to the other policeman, "It's the car thief. Give 'im a set of bracelets, compliments of Old Man Shaver and the police department." As he led Belle away, she said over her shoulder, "Dirk, those Pancake guys called the cops on me! Disorderly conduct, can you believe it?"

"I can't believe I'm getting bracelets," he responded in a stunned monotone. He would have said something else, communicated something intelligent and reassuring, but the second officer, a no-nonsense type with zero facial animation, appeared at his side, holding up a pair of cuffs.

"Turn around, buddy. Your hands behind your neck."

"WHO'D HAVE THOUGHT this was such a popular spot?" said Belle, staring through the bars of the holding cell as a handcuffed delinquent, reeking of alcohol and attitude, was forcibly escorted down the police station hallway.

Seated next to her on the wooden bench, Dirk stretched his legs in front of him. "Lucky for us it's so busy, otherwise we'd have ended up in separate cells."

"You know," Belle said thoughtfully, "at one point on this trip, you didn't want the police to be called—"

"Afraid I'd be recognized, put on the news..."

"But none of the cops here seemed all that interested in who you are."

"What can I say? Obviously, none of them read *People* magazine."

"Very funny," Belle said with a grin. "How do you do that?"

"What?"

"Defuse stressful situations with such ease. Here we are, stuck in a holding cell—me for disorderly conduct, you for car theft—yet you're making me smile."

Dirk leaned his head back against the stone wall. "Probably from years of chairing board meetings. A little humor goes a long way, especially in a roomful of overstuffed egos." As he paused, something in his gaze grew remote.

"Penny?" asked Belle softly.

His mouth tightened as though he wasn't sure whether to continue. When he finally spoke, his voice was low, distant. "I'm not sure that's the life I want to lead anymore. Business meetings, traveling, high-powered negotiations. It's difficult, if not damn near impossible, to have any kind of private life. At one time I thought I could be successful both personally and professionally—that's when I was engaged to Janine—but those dreams crashed hard when I realized—" He clamped shut his mouth as though he'd said too much.

After a long silence, Belle said quietly, "I didn't want to pry…"

"What the hell. I might as well say it." He sighed heavily. "Janine didn't want to have children…at least, she didn't want to get pregnant. I figured it was a phase, but her disgust at the idea of my fathering children with her kept growing stronger. It reached a point where I wasn't sure if it was loving me or having children that bothered her more." He shook his head. "I can't blame her entirely, though. You once suggested I'm sometimes indirect. Perhaps if I had been more direct with Janine, I would have understood the real issues…"

"I find it impossible to believe a woman would be bothered by the notion of loving you," Belle said firmly. Warming her tone, she added, "As for children, not having them is my greatest regret.…"

Dirk squeezed her hand. "Guess that makes two of us."

They sat in silence, holding hands, not speaking further. It was as though it had taken hundreds of miles and a number of crises to reach the point of opening up and confessing what lay at the bottom of each of their hearts.

Several minutes later, the zero-animation cop stopped outside their cell and unlocked the door. "Get up," he said brusquely. "Your lawyer posted bail." He headed back down the hall, his feet slapping against the concrete floor.

As she and Dirk stood, Belle said dryly, "If that guy gets any more emotional, I'll have to slip him a cat pill."

"I thought you were over that."

She met Dirk's gaze, wanting to keep the tone light after their serious talk, but she couldn't. He'd be leaving soon, and she needed to say something before they parted. "I'm over that, but...but I don't know if I'll ever get over you."

Dirk's gray eyes deepened. Something glittered within them, like faraway lights in the darkness. "You took the words right out of my mouth."

"That's quite a compliment from Mr. Communicate."

Dirk moved closer. He kissed the tip of her nose, then feather-touched her lips. "I have to leave right after this. I know you probably want to stay in Cheyenne for a few days, maybe look through your aunt Meg's belongings, but what about joining me in Taos after that?"

"Joining?"

"Oh, hell. I'm going to take the risk and step outside of my bubble. Marry me, Belle. You and I are good for each other.''

Speechless, she sank against him, her arms wrapped around his waist. Underneath his T-shirt, she heard the beating of his heart. A life with Dirk would be good. No, better than good—great—but...

"Where would we live?" she asked. She hadn't meant to blurt out such an unromantic response to the most wonderful question ever asked, but where and how she lived would color the rest of her days...

Obviously, she'd taken Dirk by surprise as he hesitated before responding. "L.A.? New York? What's your pleasure?"

"Cheyenne," she said softly. "It's where I am now. Where I spent summers growing up. Might as well start over here."

She felt a ripple of tension in his body. Pulling back, he looked her squarely in the eyes. "But, honey, there's no future for you here. If it's another business you'd like to run, I'll buy one for you." He searched her face, looking for her response.

She had no doubt any other woman would have jumped at the chance to marry him. Live in a large metropolis as Mrs. Harriman. Run a dress shop or chic restaurant or whatever women with money liked to do for a hobby. But it wouldn't be *her* dream, it would be *Dirk's* dream for her. Something he gave her, not something she earned. Growing up, she'd worked at the Blue Moon, sweated and toiled to fix and build pieces of it, so even if it was willed to her, she had still earned the right to own it. But if Dirk bought her some stuffy business in a strange city, it'd be like living in his shadow.

And she'd be no better off than her mother.

"I can't marry you," she whispered.

STANDING BEHIND the register at the Blue Moon, Dirk covered the phone receiver with his hand. "The diner is yours, free and clear," he said to Belle. As she went from stunned to yelping her glee, he removed his hand and spoke into the phone. "I'll explain it all to her, Ray, when she comes off cloud nine, a good 'cloud' in this case."

After hanging up, he told Belle everything Ray had said over the phone—how Aunt Meg had set up a trust for Tiffany and Cory, the two kids who lived in a nearby orphanage, but loved to spend their free time at the diner. "She bequeathed the diner to you," Dirk explained, "but any other transference of property was subject to the trust for the benefit of the kids."

Belle, flushed from her dancing and yelping, asked, "How did the Pancake lawyers not know this?"

Dirk shrugged. "They wanted the property for their chain. Had probably read the will, knew you had your seventy-two-hour deadline, but neglected to take into account the strings attached to the property."

Remembering the term Ray had once used, she said, "They didn't want a 'cloud' on the title."

"Exactly right."

Belle sat on one of the stools. Louie, in his cage that sat at the end of the counter, chirped and hopped as though celebrating the success. Next to him, Lover Boy, awakening from his long beauty sleep, yawned and peered at her lazily, as though to say, "Hey, what's new?"

Leaning back, her elbows propped against the counter, Belle mused, "But why would Meg set up that trust? If I hadn't shown up, Tiffany and Cory are too young to run this business..." She frowned, obviously mulling this over.

"I'll take an educated guess." Dirk sauntered to the window and looked out at the waiting taxi which would take him to a local car rental agency. "Meg was ninety-nine point nine percent certain you'd show up, but she set up the trust just in case you missed the deadline—or for some reason, you no longer wanted the diner—knowing the trust would ensure financial security for you, Tiffany and Cory. Without you, of course, the kids couldn't *run* the business, but they would have legal rights. There's also another thought..."

Belle raised her eyebrows.

"Did Meg know you wanted children?"

Belle nodded slowly. "It came up every now and then in our phone calls. I tried to act as though it didn't matter, but Meg knew me too well."

"Maybe that's what's really behind all of this. She wanted the three of you to be a family. Although you'd probably never said it to her, she may have guessed you didn't want to end up like her, living alone with a few animals for companionship. Her thoughts might have turned to Tiffany and Cory, two good kids in need of some mothering. And when Meg fell ill, I bet she devised her will to bring all of you together."

Belle choked back a laugh, but Dirk saw the emotion in her eyes. "Another of her surprises! Giving me an instant family."

"Maybe she hoped that might happen. But there's nothing in the will that forces all of you to remain together. In fact, you could sell this place tomorrow, and the trust would take care of all of you. You could each go your separate ways."

Dirk felt a stab of sadness. Separate ways, just like he and Belle. It'd been a surprise when Ray had called, saying the diner was Belle's. But even if that phone call had never happened, Dirk had still lost her.

In business, he cut his losses quickly and moved on. Just as he was going to do now.

"Take good care of yourself, Belle." He flashed her a smile, not trusting himself to hug her. Feeling her body near, smelling her familiar scents, would only torture him. After looking one last time into those Caribbean-blue eyes, he turned and walked away.

DIRK DROVE DOWN Highway 25, enjoying blasts of warm summer air through the open driver's window. He'd rented an economy car, no frills, *especially* no cruise control. As Belle had once said, "To *cruise* is to let loose, experience the road," and that's exactly what he wanted to do from now on, not only with roads but with life.

He had found a local country-and-western station on the radio. He tapped his fingers against the wheel in time to the music, wondering if Belle was listening to the same song as she fixed something in the diner or roamed around Cheyenne. Or maybe the music was playing in the background as she and Tiffany and Cory got to know each other better.

And maybe he'd spend the rest of his life wondering about her, how she was doing, what she and her family were planning, celebrating. Maybe Dirk would be alone, but in his heart he'd always be with Belle, the woman who'd reached through the bubble and touched his soul.

He braked to avoid a tumbleweed that rolled lazily across the highway. As he again eased on the gas, he caught sight of a car, parked at an awkward angle off the road. A stranded driver?

He quickly glanced at his watch. Noon. He could easily make it to Taos by tomorrow morning, his new deadline, but did he want to chance being detoured again? Approaching the stranded vehicle, he realized it was the Chevy he'd "stolen" earlier. Yes, Dirk definitely needed to pull over and help the guy...and work in an apology while he was at it.

Pulling up behind the Chevy, Dirk noticed the man hunkered down in the front seat, a cap on his head. *Poor old codger,* thought Dirk. He recalled how Tiffany had called the man "grouchy." Well, maybe that would be Dirk someday, a lonely, grouchy old fart who needed a helping hand.

As he approached the driver's window, Dirk swore he caught the scent of flowers. But when he saw the face underneath the cap, all sweet and pink with Caribbean-blue eyes, he stopped in his tracks.

Belle pulled off the cap and ruffled her fingers through her hair. "I'm looking for Lover Boy," she said, acting as though they'd never met. "Have you seen him?"

Emotion clogged Dirk's throat. He thought he'd spend the rest of his life dreaming about her, but here she was again, alive and real, his Aphrodite come to life. No doubt she'd sweet-talked her grouchy neighbor, who would probably become the Blue Moon's best customer, into loaning her his car, knowing Dirk would recognize it and pull over.

"Lover Boy?" Dirk repeated, playing along. "Is that your animal?"

She observed him through lowered lashes. "No, it's my man," she answered, her voice so deep and sensual, it sent a shiver of excitement through Dirk. "The best man in the whole, wide world."

He paused before speaking. "You seem like a determined lady. Surely you can go on without him."

"I thought I could. But I was wrong. You see, I have three-fourths of a family in the making, but I need him to complete the picture."

She opened the car door and stepped outside, those pink-sandaled feet taking several stylish steps toward him. "He's a very important man. Runs big businesses. But I figure he can do all that from a diner in Wyoming." She shrugged with one shoulder. "Well, from an office we'll add on. I figure the world is really a very small place—with the aid of technology, he can do his business from Cheyenne instead of New York or Los Angeles." She lowered her voice. "Confidentially, he says he's tired of all those board meetings. This way he won't have to be in the same room with a bunch of overstuffed egos anymore."

Dirk nodded in agreement. "Technology. That would definitely work. After all, he loves communication."

"Me, too." Moving closer, she placed her palms against his chest. "I thought I knew everything about communication until I met him, but he taught me to listen not only with my head, but with my heart, too."

Recalling his own words, Dirk wound his arms around Belle and pulled her close. "Will you marry him?"

"In a heartbeat."

Dirk paused. "Will you have his baby?"

"That'll take longer than a heartbeat, but yes...joyfully. Maybe even more than one baby, if we're lucky."

"I'll need to finalize my business in Taos tomorrow morning, but what about tying the knot right after that?''

"Married after breakfast? Sounds like our kind of wedding, with plenty of time afterward for..."

They looked lovingly into each other's eyes for a long moment. He broke their stare with a saucy wink. "Looks as though you found your Lover Boy, but the cat has to get another name."

"Deal." With a sexy laugh, she clasped her body tightly to his. "Hold on, Lover Boy, for the longest, hottest ride of your life."

"And the happiest," Dirk added, kissing her.

Do the Harlequin Duets™ Dating Quiz!

1) My ideal date would be:
a) a candlelight dinner at the most exclusive restaurant in town
b) dinner made by him even if it is burnt macaroni and cheese
c) a dinner made lovingly by me—to which he brings his mother and two ex-wives

2) If a woman came on to my ideal man, he would:
a) flirt back a little, but make it clear he's already taken
b) tell her to go away
c) bail me out of jail

3) The ideal setting for the perfect date would be:
a) a luxurious ocean resort with white sand, palm trees, picture-perfect sunsets
b) a desert island with just him and a few million mosquitoes
c) a stateroom on the *Titanic*

4) In his free time, my ideal man would most often choose to:
a) Watch sports on TV
b) Watch sports on TV
c) Watch sports on TV *(let's not kid ourselves, even ideal men will be men!)*

If you chose A most often: You are wonderful, talented and sexy. A near goddess, in fact, who will make beautiful music with just about any man you want. The only thing that could make you more perfect is reading Harlequin Duets™.

If you chose B most often: Others are jealous of your charm, wit, intelligence, good fashion sense and ability to eat whatever you want without gaining a pound. The only workout you need is a good evening with Harlequin Duets™.

If you chose C most often: Don't worry. Harlequin Duets™ to the rescue!

Experience the lighter side of love with Harlequin Duets™!

HARLEQUIN®
Makes any time special.™

Look us up on-line at: http://www.romance.net   HDQUIZ

HARLEQUIN®

Makes any time special™

WIN A DREAM

In celebration of Harlequin®'s golden anniversary

Enter to win a *dream!* You could win:

- A luxurious trip for two to
  The Renaissance Cottonwoods Resort
  in Scottsdale, Arizona, or

- A bouquet of flowers once a week for a year
  from **FTD**, or

- A $500 shopping spree, or

- A fabulous bath & body gift basket, including
  K-tel's *Candlelight and Romance* 5-CD set.

Look for **WIN A DREAM** flash on
specially marked Harlequin® titles by
Penny Jordan, Dallas Schulze,
Anne Stuart and Kristine Rolofson
in October 1999*.

FTD

RENAISSANCE.
COTTONWOODS RESORT
SCOTTSDALE, ARIZONA

K·TEL

COMING NEXT MONTH

HARLEQUIN

Duets™

#11

HOW SWEET IT IS by Kimberly Raye

Delilah James had everything—friends, family, a career. Once she'd wanted Zach Tanner...before she found out he was a reckless, macho, sexy-as-sin bad boy. Little did she guess that Zach, owner of Wild Man's Ribs, wanted Delilah, too. Even more than he wanted exclusive rights on her cheesecakes. So when he discovered she needed a fake fiancé, he decided to demonstrate just how sweet a joint venture could be....

SECOND-CHANCE GROOM by Eugenia Riley

Bride-to-be Cassie Brandon had a funny thing happen on the way to the altar—she fell in love with the best man. And now handsome Brian Drake must prove he's the *wrong man* for her. But when his plan for making her fall out of love backfired, footloose-and-fancy-free Brian must face his biggest challenge of all—love!

#12

HEAD OVER HEELS by Sandra Paul

Nicholas Ware had come back to Cauldron to banish tempting Prudence McClure from his system—not to become engaged to her! But when Halloween's magic filled the air, Prudence's tempting spell was nearly impossible to resist!

PUPPY LOVE by Cheryl Anne Porter

David Sullivan's life was going to the dogs. He was amazed to learn about his inheritance—and appalled to discover it was a mangy, *very pregnant* little mutt. Then he was almost arrested for dognapping! Luckily, he managed to convince gorgeous veterinarian Emily Wright of his innocence. Now all he had to do was convince her that he's more cuddly than his dog....

HARLEQUIN WIN A NEW BEETLE® CONTEST
OFFICIAL RULES
NO PURCHASE NECESSARY TO ENTER

1. To enter, access the Harlequin romance web site (http://www.romance.net) and follow the on-screen instructions: Enter your name, address (including zip code), e-mail address (optional), and in 200 words or fewer your own original story concept—which has not won a previous prize/award nor has previously been reproduced/published—for a Harlequin Duets romantic comedy novel that features a Volkswagon® New Beetle®. OR hand-print or type the same requested information for on-line entry on an Official Entry Form or 8 1/2" x 11" plain piece of paper and mail it (limit: one entry per person per outer mailing envelope) via first-class mail to: Harlequin Win A New Beetle® Contest. In the U.S.: P.O. Box 9069, Buffalo, NY 14269-9069. In Canada: P.O. Box 637, Fort Erie, Ontario, Canada L2A 5X3.

    For eligibility, entries must be submitted through a completed Internet transmission—or if mailed, postmarked—no later than November 30, 1999. Mail-in entries must be received by December 7, 1999.

2. Story concepts will be judged by a panel of members of the Harlequin editorial and marketing staff based on the following criteria:

    - Originality and Creativity—40%
    - Appropriateness to Subject Matter—35%
    - Romantic Comedy/Humor—25%

    Decision of the judges is final.

3. All entries become the property of Torstar Corp., will not be returned, and may be published. No responsibility is assumed for incomplete, lost, late, damaged, illegible or misdirected e-mail, for technical, hardware or software failures of any kind, lost or unavailable network connections, or failed, incomplete, garbled or delayed computer transmission which may limit user's ability to participate in the contest, or for non- or illegibly postmarked, lost, late nondelivered or misdirected mail. Rules are subject to any requirements/limitations imposed by the FCC. Winners will be determined no later than January 31, 2000, and will be notified by mail. Winners will be required to sign and return an Affidavit of Eligibility, and a Release of Royalty/Ownership of submitted story concept within 15 days after receipt of same certifying his/her eligibility, that entry is his/her own original work, has not won a previous prize/award nor previously been reproduced/published. Noncompliance within that time period may result in disqualification and an alternate winner may be selected. All federal, state and local laws and regulations apply. Contest open only to residents of the U.S. and Canada who are 18 years of age or older, and is void wherever prohibited by law. Any litigation within the Province of Quebec respecting the conduct and awarding of a prize may be submitted to the Régie des alcools, des courses et des jeux. Employees of Torstar Corp., their affiliates, agents and members of their immediate families are not eligible. Taxes on prizes are the sole responsibility of winners. Entry and acceptance of any prize offered constitutes permission to use winner's name, photograph or other likeness for the purposes of advertising, trade and promotion on behalf of Torstar Corp. without further compensation to the winner, unless prohibited by law.

4. Prizes: Grand Prize—a brand-new Volkswagon yellow New Beetle® (approx. value: $17,000 U.S.) and a Harlequin Duets novel (approx. value: $6 U.S.). Taxes, licensing and registration fees are the sole responsibility of the winner; 2 Runner-Up Prizes—a Harlequin Duets novel (approx. value: $6 U.S. each).

5. For a list of winners (available after March 31, 2000), send a self-addressed, stamped envelope to Harlequin Win A Beetle® Contest 8219 Winners, P.O. Box 4200 Blair, NE 68009-4200.

Sweepstakes sponsored by Torstar Corp., P.O. Box 9042, Buffalo, NY 14269-9042

Volkswagon and New Beetle registered trademarks are used with permission of Volkswagon of America, Inc.

♦HARLEQUIN
Duets™ *Win a New Beetle®*
Contest!

Starting September 1999, Harlequin Duets is offering you the chance to drive away in a Volkswagen® New Beetle®!

In addition to our grand prize winner, two more lucky entrants will also have their winning stories published in Harlequin Duets™ series and on our web site!

To enter our "WIN A NEW BEETLE®" contest, fill out this entry form and in 200 words or less write a romantic comedy short story for Harlequin Duets that features a New Beetle®.

See previous page for contest rules.
Contest ends November 30, 1999.

Be witty, be romantic, have fun!

Name
_____

Address
_____

City _____ State/Province _____

Zip/Postal Code
Mail to Harlequin Books: In the U.S.: P.O. Box 9069, Buffalo, NY
14269-9069; **In Canada,** P.O. Box 637, Fort Erie, Ontario, L4A 5X3

♦ HARLEQUIN®
Makes any time special™

HDBUG-EF